D0089185

Praise for the

Home Repair Is Homicide

mysteries of

Sarah Graves

"Just the right prescription for a post-repair rest."
—Orlando Sentinel

"Everything's Jake—until she starts snooping."
—New York Daily News

"With an intricate plot, amusing characters and a wry sense of humor, Sarah Graves spins a fun, charming mystery that is sure to make you smile and keep you guessing right up until the end."
—Booknews from The Poisoned Pen

"Charming." *—New Orleans Times-Picayune*

"A winning addition . . . A sleuth as tough as the nails she drives into the walls of her 1823 Federal home enhances a clever plot. . . . Many will relish the vividly described Down East setting, but for anyone who's ever enjoyed making a home repair it's the accurate details of the restoration of Jake's old house that will appeal the most."
—Publishers Weekly

"Graves gives us a lively look at small-town life in charming down-east Maine. **Her characters, as always, are captivating examples of Americana and their relationships with each other are inspired."**
—The Old Book Barn Gazette

"Author Graves has **a tart wit and an eagle-eyed perspective** . . . producing a handy-dandy mystery with a handsome cast of local color."
—*The State* (Columbia, S.C.)

"Atmospheric appeal . . . [Graves] captures the charming eccentricity and outdoorsy flavor of life in a town full of seagulls and bed-and-breakfasts . . . with **zingy dialogue and a brisk pace.**"
—*The Santa Fe New Mexican*

"The ride is fun and Sarah Graves seems to be **having a blast.**"
—*Maine Sunday Telegram*

"A reading pleasure." —*The Snooper*

"Working around the house can definitely be murder. Sarah Graves's *Home Repair Is Homicide* series is a much more pleasant way to kill time!"
—*Bangor Daily News*

"What distinguishes the novel are its likable, no-nonsense protagonist-narrator, her references to home repair that the author cleverly fits tongue-and-groove into the story and, especially, the detailed descriptions of the town."
—*Los Angeles Times*

"Eloquently depicts the beauties and hardships of life on an island in Maine. . . . Filled with believable and engaging characters, exquisite scenery and extravagant action."
—*News and Record* (Greensboro, N.C.)

"One cool caper." —*MLB 2001 Gift Guide*

"The town of Eastport and its warmly wondrous citizens continue to enchant!"
—*Booknews* from The Poisoned Pen

"The prose is brisk and the jokes are funny."
—*The Wall Street Journal*

"Appealing." —*USA Today*

"Ms. Graves has created **a bright and personable new detective who has been welcomed into the Eastport community with warmth and affection."**
—*Dallas Morning News*

"Graves affectionately creates believable characters . . . who lend depth and warm humor to the story. . . .The **cozy details of small-town life and home repair make for an enjoyable read."** —*Publishers Weekly*

"No cozy this, it's amusing, cynical, yet warm, populated with nice and nasty characters and some dirty secrets. . . . **All the ingredients fit the dish of delicious crime chowder.** . . . I am already drooling for [Jake's] return."
—*Booknews* from The Poisoned Pen

"Jacobia has a witty and ironic voice, and **the book resonates with good humor, quirky characters, and a keen sense of place."** —*Down East* magazine

"Sarah Graves's novel is **a laudable whodunnit, but it's also a love letter to Eastport,** celebrating the cultural contrasts between the town and some misguided souls from the Big Apple. . . . The funky, low-key fishing community wins every time."
—*Kennebec Valley Tribune and Morning Sentinel*

ALSO BY SARAH GRAVES

The Dead Cat Bounce
Triple Witch
Repair to Her Grave
Wreck the Halls
Unhinged
Mallets Aforethought
Tool & Die

Available in hardcover
from Bantam Books:
Nail Biter

WICKED FIX

SARAH GRAVES

CRIME LINE™

BANTAM BOOKS
New York Toronto London
Sydney Auckland

WICKED FIX
A Bantam Book

PUBLISHING HISTORY
Bantam mass market edition / April 2000
Bantam reissue / March 2004

Published by
Bantam Dell
A Division of Random House, Inc.
New York, New York

This is a work of fiction. Names, characters, places, and incidents either are the product of the author's imagination or are used fictitiously. Any resemblance to actual persons, living or dead, events, or locales is entirely coincidental.

All rights reserved
Copyright © 2000 by Sarah Graves
Cover art by Robin Moline

No part of this book may be reproduced or transmitted in any form or by any means, electronic or mechanical, including photocopying, recording, or by any information storage and retrieval system, without the written permission of the publisher, except where permitted by law. For information address: Bantam Books, New York, New York.

If you purchased this book without a cover, you should be aware that this book is stolen property. It was reported as "unsold and destroyed" to the publisher, and neither the author nor the publisher has received any payment for this "stripped book."

Bantam Books and the rooster colophon are registered trademarks of Random House, Inc.

ISBN-13: 978-0-553-57859-1
ISBN-10: 0-553-57859-6

Manufactured in the United States of America
Published simultaneously in Canada

OPM 17 16 15 14 13 12 11 10

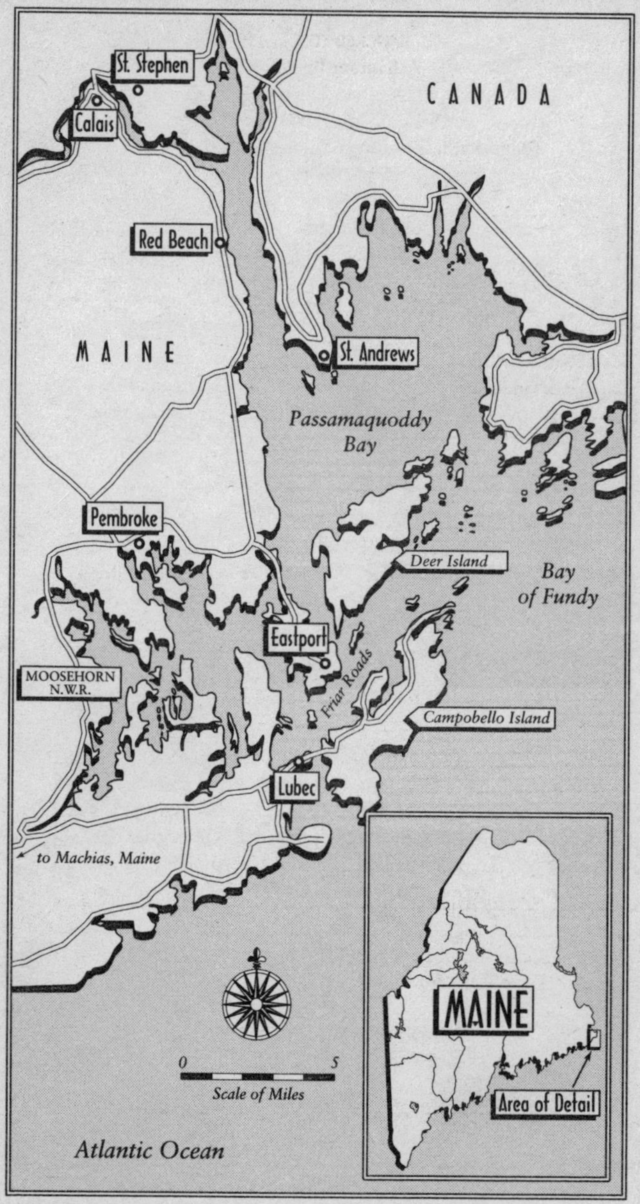
St. Stephen
Calais
CANADA
Red Beach
MAINE
St. Andrews
Passamaquoddy Bay
Pembroke
Deer Island
Bay of Fundy
Eastport
Friar Roads
MOOSEHORN N.W.R.
Campobello Island
Lubec
to Machias, Maine
0
5
Scale of Miles
Atlantic Ocean
MAINE
Area of Detail

1

"I don't see why Reuben Tate had to come back to town at all," Ellie White complained, digging into her lobster tortilla.

We were at La Sardina, Eastport's Mexican restaurant. The menu was south-of-the-border with a downeast Maine twist—thus the lobster—but the atmosphere was all laid-back Key West:

Strings of tiny, twinkling colored lights framed the tall front windows. White gauze beach umbrellas slanted over the old wooden tables. And potted plants grown to enormous sizes lent a tropical flavor: palm, spathiphyllum, a flowering bougainvillea like a tree full of purple butterflies.

With her tortilla, Ellie was having a tomato and mesclun salad with blue cheese dressing, and a Dos Equis. "And I *don't* see," she added, "why he had to come *now*."

Beside me, my son, Sam, went on attacking his combination plate. "You could strip varnish with this hot sauce," he remarked appreciatively; at seventeen,

Sam thought flaming coals weren't quite hot enough unless you doused them in Tabasco.

"Reuben's like a bad rash," Ellie's husband, George Valentine, said. "He comes back."

He cut a slice off his well-done ribeye steak; to George, the French fry is about as foreign as food needs to get, with the possible exception of the English muffin.

"The trick," he added, "is getting rid of him again. But this time I hear he means to stay."

At which my friends all sighed sorrowfully. Reuben Tate was the sly, grinning worm in the apple of their happiness that autumn, and it seemed unfair just when everything else in town was looking up:

Summer had come and gone but we still had the taste of it in our mouths, tart and sweet as a drop of lemonade. Dahlias with bright shaggy heads big as dinner plates bloomed in the perennial beds; ripe tomatoes loaded the vines in our back gardens, and the rosebushes massed along the seawall bowed low under their heavy burden of rose hips, huge and juicy as Bing cherries.

Also, for once the town had cash. Sea urchins and sardines had been freakishly plentiful that season, the boats coming back half-capsized by the unaccustomed weight of their catches, and scallop harvest promised to be as bountiful. Until then, foreign freighters—their names, unpronounceable, stenciled in white, rust-mottled Cyrillic letters on their towering sterns—loomed at dockside, loading paper pulp and particle board from the mills up in Woodland, making overtime for the stevedores and truckers.

Finally, at September's end came the annual Eastport Salmon Festival, the last outdoor bash of the year on our little island in Maine, which meant that cash registers in the cafés and shops on Water Street would soon be jingling with tourist money.

So we were content. Only the thought of Reuben

with his quick, twitchy ways, his pale, wandering eye and odd laugh—a harsh, painful-sounding bark like a strangled cough; when he uttered it, he meant to hurt someone—kept putting a damper on people.

"Could be this time Reuben's luck will run out," said my main squeeze, Wade Sorenson.

Just off the water after guiding a cargo vessel into port—it's what he does, as Eastport's official harbor pilot—Wade wore a navy turtleneck, jeans, and a cableknit sweater the color of vanilla ice cream. His gray eyes reflected the light of the candle stuck in the neck of a wine jug on the table.

"Not soon enough," my ex-husband, Victor Tiptree, said sourly, and I glanced at him in surprise.

"Reuben Tate's luck," he emphasized, "can't end soon enough for me."

"How do you know Reuben?" I asked, and the others around the table looked inquisitively at him, too.

Six months earlier, Victor had moved here to Eastport from the Upper East Side of Manhattan, and in remote, thinly populated downeast Maine his arrival had of course been newsworthy. But I hadn't thought any of the local people were newsworthy to Victor, and especially not a ne'er-do-well like Reuben.

Tonight, Victor's dinner had consisted of the olives from his martinis. "It's not important," he muttered, and gulped the melted ice from his glass.

Annoyed but determined not to argue—the rule, when dealing with Victor, is *never wrestle with a pig; you both get dirty and the pig likes it*—I turned away, as a voice from the next table rose in worried complaint.

"Did Reuben really say that?" Paddy Farrell, who ran a textile design studio out of an old canning-factory building he'd rehabilitated down on the waterfront, had clearly been listening in on our conversation.

Sitting with Paddy was his longtime companion, Terence Oscard.

"Did he?" Paddy demanded, his close-clipped salt-and-pepper head coming up pugnaciously as he caught my eye. "He's staying?"

Paddy wore a navy blazer and a tailored button-down shirt, a maroon silk scarf at his throat. "George?" he persisted as George stolidly went on chewing. "Did you actually hear him say that?"

"What I said," George confirmed after a sip of Miller Lite. "Stayin' in his mom's old place out in Quoddy Village, got the little trust fund she left him to live on. It ain't much, but I guess that's nothing new to Reuben. He's never had any job at all, that I've known of."

Terence Oscard, a big-boned, pale-haired man with a beaky nose and a big, pointy Adam's apple, wore a light blue chambray shirt, khaki slacks, and Topsiders. Good-looking in the way some very ugly men can be, his jutting features regularized by intelligence and kindness, he sat listening with his usual thoughtful attention.

But Paddy seemed agitated. "Reuben can't do that. Why, the town won't be worth living in. It'll be the bad old days all over again."

Terence leaned over to me. "I've got a new Red Cross first-aid book," he confided. "I'll be glad to lend it to you when I've finished it."

He was a martyr to numerous imaginary ailments and, perhaps on account of these, a self-taught first-aid expert. I liked him a great deal; everyone did.

"Thanks, Terence, I'll look forward to it," I said, and he sat back, pleased.

"Doesn't anybody," Paddy demanded, "remember?" He glared at us, fists clenched as if he might punch someone just to refresh people's recollections.

"Don't see as there's much we can do about Reuben sticking around if he wants to," George said, his tone unperturbed as he went on eating his steak and potatoes. "Still a free country."

I noticed, though, that George didn't raise his eyes, a sign that he wasn't enjoying Paddy's conversation. Paddy was intense, quick to anger, and inclined to pound the table, while George was the opposite: the quieter he became, the more tactfully and carefully you'd better go, or eventually he would lower the boom on you.

"Unless," George added to Paddy, "you've got some brilliant new idea."

At this, the air around us seemed to grow darkly electric, charged with some knowledge I didn't share. Silence lengthened as the three Eastport natives at our table—Ellie, Wade, and George—went on eating their dinners, concentrating on their plates. Sam and I looked puzzledly at them, while Victor continued drumming his fingers on the table, wanting the drinks waitress.

"No," Paddy said at last. "No new ideas. Finished, Terence?" Shoving back his chair, he flung down his napkin furiously.

Nodding agreeably, the big man got to his feet. Then he staggered, briefly but unmistakably, placing his hand on the table to steady himself. But he recovered smoothly, dropping some money by his plate and smiling his farewell to the rest of us.

He hadn't been drinking. Terence never did; the faint muzzy feeling induced by even a single glass of wine always made him think he had some rare neurological condition. And as they left together, he seemed fine again: bending as always to hear whatever Paddy was saying, Paddy accompanying his words with his usual energetic gestures.

Watching them go, I sensed an ongoing liveliness of interest undimmed by the comfort of habit; they were by all accounts a devoted couple. I thought they were lucky, and that Terence had somehow simply missed his footing.

But Paddy's comments had dropped a pall over our table, with George, Ellie, and Wade looking suddenly even more dismal.

"Come on," I said. "How bad can it be? I'm sure a few of the boys from the dock can take care of Reuben Tate, if he gets to be too much trouble."

Ellie's lips pursed. "You only know him by reputation," she began, and was about to say more.

But just then a harsh bark of laughter was followed by the warning rasp of barstools being shoved back. Next came the voice of Ted Armstrong, La Sardina's formidable bartender and bouncer.

"Okay, now, that's enough. We don't want to be breaking any expensive glassware, make the price of a beer go up another half-buck just to pay for it all."

The scuffling quieted as the sound system began playing a cut of Bela Fleck's new jazz-bluegrass fusion CD, "Throwdown at the Hoedown." La Sardina's owners had eclectic tastes in music, and so as a result did the guys who tended to occupy their barstools.

Or most of them did. "Throwdown" cut off in the middle of a banjo lick so breakneck, it had to be heard to be believed, and the music switched to something about how lonesome somebody was going to be tonight.

"He's in there," Ellie said quietly. "One thing he hates is decent music. You wait, before the night's over, Teddy'll have to toss him out of the place, and then won't there be hell to pay?"

"Is there anything," I asked, "that Reuben doesn't hate?"

"Money and misery," George replied, forking up the last of his baked potato.

With his dark hair, milky-pale skin, and a bluish black five-o'clock shadow darkening his small, neat jawline, George looks as if he stepped out of the hills of

Appalachia about five minutes ago. His black gimme cap, with GUPTILL'S EXCAVATING embroidered in orange script on the front, sat on the table beside his plate.

"The one he tries getting from you and the other he tries giving you, when he can. Which," George added, "is pretty often."

"Well, what's the matter with him?" Sam asked. "Is he sick? I mean, you know, disturbed?"

Sam's own disposition is so sunny that he has managed to stay on good terms with both his father and me, which as a feat is a little like being Switzerland during WWII, only for longer and with more bombs. In fact, it was mostly due to Sam's ongoing diplomatic efforts that his father was with us that evening.

But as I watched Victor fidget, I thought he had some other motive for coming, too, like maybe he hadn't wanted to be alone for some reason.

Not that I cared much. Victor and I weren't having a truce, exactly. More like a cease-fire.

George looked at Sam. "Reuben Tate's not sick. He's broken. Like a dog you can't cure of being vicious. Stay away from him, Sam. He's got more ways to clean a guy's clock than you'll ever learn. And," he emphasized seriously, "you don't want to."

Sam blinked. "Wow. Okay." For George to utter so many words in a row was unusual. In the tone he'd taken, it was stunning.

"Someone," Victor piped up from behind his fresh martini—the drinks waitress had taken pity on him—"ought to get rid of Reuben Tate once and for all."

As always, he resembled an ad out of *Gentleman's Quarterly:* blue striped silk tie, charcoal slacks, tasteful gold cufflinks. Even the hairs on the backs of his wrists looked groomed. Only the look on his face conveyed a sense of rumpled dishevelment, in part I supposed on account of those martinis. But I remember thinking again that something else was going on with him.

Wade put down his glass of O'Doul's. "Think so,

do you?" he commented mildly to Victor. "Someone should get rid of him? Just take him out?"

"Yeah." Victor glowered. "As a matter of fact, I do."

When Victor first moved here, I was concerned that he would become a serious fly in my ointment, in the romance department especially. Having your crazy ex-husband living down the street from you might just tend, as a for-instance, to discourage your boyfriend from parking his pickup truck overnight right out in your driveway where everybody can see it.

Lately, though, Victor hadn't bothered me quite so much. It wasn't that he had gotten saner; maybe the opposite. His personal idiosyncrasies—his obsession over physical cleanliness, for example—seemed to have gotten stronger. But here in Eastport everyone's a skinful of quirks, so in a way Victor was just like the rest of us. Also, Wade parked his pickup where he pleased, as he always had.

None of this, however, made Victor a congenial dining companion. Now his immaculate, close-clipped fingernails tapped the table again, impatiently, as if he couldn't just get up and leave on his own whenever he wanted to.

"So, are you people finished or what?" he asked.

"Stop it," I hissed at him, and for a wonder he subsided, though his gaze still strayed anxiously to the bar area and then to the door, as if calculating some daring exit strategy.

But I still didn't put two and two together.

Instead I turned back to Wade; the O'Doul's interested me. Ordinarily, he enjoys breweries so micro that they measure their ingredients out by the thimbleful.

But in reply to my silent inquiry he just lifted his glass, and the suggestion his amused gray eyes conveyed to me then was so personal—and so fully detailed, right down to my keeping the dog not only off the bed but actually out of the whole bedroom—that I was struck speechless for a moment.

Wade is not the most verbal guy you will ever meet. Once on a boat in a storm he lost, in short order, his mast, his engine, and a sizable chunk of his left arm, which later required twenty stitches, and I have it on good authority that his only comment was "darn." But when he wants to, he gets his message across.

And not only to me, I realized as Sam got up and announced that he would be bunking at his dad's this evening, so I should please not leave the back porch light on for him or the neighbors would think he had stayed out all night without permission.

"But me and Tom Daigle and some other guys are watching the playoffs," he added, "so I might not get in till past midnight."

The World Series, he meant; Sam and his young buddies were slaves to the guy-stuff scene lately. But that wasn't all of it. Victor peeked at me, figuring how to play this: be-cool dad, or tough, stick-to-the-curfew father?

The deciding factor being which might most irritate me. Like I said, it was only a cease-fire.

But Sam picked up on that, too, cuffing his father on the shoulder affectionately. "Chill out, Dad. It's Friday, remember? See you later."

Wistfully I watched him pass by outside La Sardina's window, its dark condensation blurring him to a neon-lit smear. Once upon a time, I had been that boy's whole world; now, he plotted so that Wade could be alone with me.

And I wasn't at all sure I liked it.

Suddenly a shriek like a bird being torn wing from wishbone came from the bar area. "My ear! That little bastard bit my ear!"

Moments later a boy-sized man strutted from the bar. In his forties, he wore tight black Levi's, a T-shirt with rolled sleeves to show off his small, hard arm muscles, and black leather boots with metal cleats on the heels. He had blond eyelashes and hair so blond it was almost white, combed in a ducktail, and a purple birthmark shaped like a teardrop under his left eye.

It was Reuben Tate himself, and he was obviously out of his skull: tequila, or some other high-proof engine of destruction. His eyes were as bright as highway flares. But he held it well in terms of motor skills; rumor had it that Reuben could walk, talk, and perform an astonishing variety of bad deeds while laboring under a blood-alcohol level that would pickle a lab rat.

The cleats clicked purposefully across the floor and stopped right beside my ex-husband, and all of a sudden I knew why Victor had not wanted to leave without us.

"Well, well," Reuben said smirkingly. "What have we here?"

"Shut up, Reuben," Ellie said, startling me. "Leave him alone or I'll knock your block off."

In a pink cashmere sweater, cream slacks, and a sheen of pink-tinted lip gloss, with her red hair falling in waves and her freckles like a sprinkling of gold dust, Ellie looked just about as dangerous as your standard lace-trimmed valentine.

Reuben ignored her. "My ear!" somebody moaned from the bar. There was a smudge of blood on Reuben's T-shirt.

"Why, it's the *doctor,*" Reuben drawled, his bright eyes surveying Victor's perfect grooming mockingly. He kicked the leg of Victor's chair with the toe of his black leather boot.

"Hey, *doctor*."

Here I suppose I should explain that Victor was, or anyway had been until recently, an accomplished brain surgeon. Back in the city, he was the guy you went to after the other surgeons refused you, because if they took you into surgery you would very likely die on the table, ruining their operating-room statistics.

That, by the way, is why when a surgeon does agree to operate, you will probably survive; surgeons love their win/loss numbers more than they love their own mothers. But I digress:

"Hey, Reuben. Cut it out." George ate the last bite of his steak, washing it down with a final swallow of Miller Lite.

Reuben kicked the leg of Victor's chair again, harder. "Aww, what's the matter? Big-shot doctor, too good to talk to me?"

"Reuben, do you remember that time in the playground?" Ellie inquired sternly. "When I beat you up?"

She sat up straight and gazed at at him without fear. "Well, I'm about to do it again. I'm not scared to get into it with you, Reuben. You know that. You know that I am not."

"Ellie," I said quietly. I couldn't understand why Wade and George weren't shushing her, too. She was half out of her chair.

"Ellie," I repeated insistently. But she didn't look at me.

"Reuben? Are you listening to me?"

There was a moment, then, when anything could have happened. But at the end of it Reuben backed down.

Sort of. "You'll talk to me," he told Victor, stepping away. "Like before. Or you know," he added menacingly, "what I'll do."

"Damn it, Reuben, I told you to get out of here," Ted Armstrong bellowed, charging from the bar hamfisted and ready to thump someone. "I'll drop-kick your butt off the fish pier."

Reuben turned on his cleated heel, hands raised placatingly. "I'm going, I'm going. See you, *doctor*," he promised with an evil wink. "Oh, and . . . thanks for that other thing."

Then he was gone, leaving us sitting there like the

stunned victims of some sudden, cataclysmic natural disaster.

"What brought that on?" I asked Victor, but he only waved an exhausted hand and wouldn't answer.

Ted Armstrong brought us each another drink without anybody asking and motioned Wade's money away. "On the house," he said. "Sorry about that. Jeez, I knew I shouldn'a let him in here. But later, you know, that Reuben makes you pay for it, if you don't. Jeez, does he ever make you pay."

He wiped his hands on his apron, apologetically. "Listen, doc, you probably don't feel like it, and a bite wound's probably not up your alley anyway, you bein' a big brain man an' all."

Victor's prowess as a head doctor was already town legend; in Eastport it was almost as good as being able to fix a crapped-out carburetor with a hairpin and a twist of coat-hanger wire.

"But I got a guy in there," Ted went on plaintively, "he's bleedin' like nobody's business. Friday night, clinic's closed up at this hour, and I'm gonna run outta bar towels."

Victor tucked his beautiful blue striped silk tie into his shirtfront, out of the way of the action.

"Sure," he said. "Tell your guy he's in luck. The doctor"—he downed his fourth martini in a gulp—"is *in*."

"So much for a quiet Friday night in Eastport," Wade said as Victor strode off.

George snorted wryly. "Folks in the big city hear about it, they'll all be up here. Mecca of excitement."

Somebody dropped another coin in the jukebox: Tony Bennett.

"Ellie," I asked, "are you out of your damned mind?"

"I can take Reuben," she replied, "with one hand tied behind me. And wouldn't I love to?"

Resting there in front of her, Ellie's fists looked

slender but businesslike, pale pink nail polish notwithstanding.

"Guys," I said, turning in appeal, but Wade and George just grinned at me.

"Ellie beat the you-know-what out of Reuben, once, out in the schoolyard. Course," George added judiciously, "back then we were all a little wilder."

"Man, that day she took Reuben on, he ran home to his mother, crying," Ted Armstrong agreed admiringly. He had come back to our table and was standing there, listening and nodding.

"That girl," he enthused, "could *punch*. Reuben was a big kid, too, remember. For his age, then. Big and stupid."

"No, Ted. You're misremembering," Ellie corrected gravely.

George and Wade suddenly looked sober again, also, and as I watched I began realizing that in their view, Reuben Tate was far more than a disruptive annoyance. To them he was serious trouble.

But I still didn't know why.

Meanwhile, dinner hour was over, a younger crowd drifting in as the local band Double Shot began setting up on the small stage near the door. Wade paid the check as Ellie and I began gathering our things.

Passing the bar, I glanced in to where Victor was stitching a guy's ear up, using a needle and thread that he always carried with him since God forbid he should lose a button. Also in his walking-around kit were dental floss, a nail brush, some antiseptic hand wipes, and throat spray.

The guy sat motionless, his shirt drenched crimson, his gaze fixed tranquilly on some far horizon no one else could see. I didn't know if the guy was so drunk that he was anesthetized, or if Victor had hypnotized him; Victor is like a snake charmer with patients. One look and they trust him utterly.

Wade put his arm reassuringly around me. "He'll

be okay," he said, meaning Victor. Not for the first time, I went mentally down on my knees and thanked my stars. Wade was so serenely unthreatened by Victor, he actually wished him well.

Meanwhile the fellows at the bar watched Victor over their beers, their rapt eyes following the needle's progress intently and their expressions admiring.

"He can do something useful. And he's willing to. That's the key to it, in Eastport," Wade said sensibly.

"Yeah," I said. "I guess. You've got to wonder, though. A little town like this, light-years from anywhere. You can't tell how it'll affect a person."

And especially Victor, who until six months ago thought a passport was required for venturing out of Manhattan; that and a guide for negotiating the wild, outer reaches of Westchester.

"Kill you or cure you," Wade agreed.

George and Ellie were waiting for us on the sidewalk. "You okay?" I asked Ellie. She was an Eastport girl right down to the marrow, and she had been my friend since my first day in town, a couple of years earlier. Now, though, her expression looked queer to me: distracted. Oddly distant.

"Fine." She forced a smile, while Wade and George conferred privately about something. "I was just thinking again about what Ted Armstrong said."

Her gaze probed uneasily into the shadows along the dock, away from the harbor where the deck lamps of the freighter *Star Hoisin* lit the cargo platform like a movie set. Beyond the ship, the night was so clear and dead calm that you couldn't tell where the stars ended and their reflections on the flat water began.

But the stillness felt ominous and the sunrise that morning had been red, promising weather; maybe not soon, but sometime in the next week or so. All the boats from the fishing fleet were snug at their moorings inside the boat basin.

"What?" I said, wondering again what Victor had

gotten himself into. "About Reuben Tate being so big and mean? Because he isn't. Not big, anyway."

My voice sounded uncertain. I'd never seen him up close before, and his size had surprised me, even reassured me. But now an unwelcome mental picture of him rose up: those arm muscles, and the boots. His small, neatly modeled features radiated malice like the face of an evil, flaxen-haired doll, the more malevolent for being in miniature.

As if summoned by my thought, footsteps came out of the darkness where Ellie was staring. Somebody back there on the seawall, I realized, was walking.

Listening, maybe, too.

"No," Ellie said. "I mean about him not being smart. It's a mistake, underestimating Reuben. He's sharp as a tack." She shook her head, her red hair moving like water under the neons.

Water with something in it. My imagination was getting the better of me, courtesy I supposed of an extra margarita and that guy with the bloody shirt.

"That's what makes him so different. So dangerous. He's *too* smart. I wish," Ellie said earnestly, "he hadn't come back."

Then she thought of something else. "Are you," she frowned, "still involved in that deal with Victor?"

"Yes," I admitted, knowing she disapproved.

I did, too, actually; involvement in anything that included my ex-husband was a prescription for trouble. But now that he was here, for Sam's sake I'd thought I needed to do something about Victor. And the something had involved money: my investment in a new trauma-care center that Victor was starting in Eastport.

"It's a very good plan," I said to Ellie. "All he needs to do is the medical part. I can handle the rest. And once it's all going, it'll keep him out of my hair."

As usual when I tried to explain this, she looked skeptical. Her apparent interest in big money ranged somewhere between zilch and *nada*, and her idea of keeping Victor out of my hair involved wrapping an anchor chain around his legs, then taking him on a boat ride.

"One more week and the financing'll be wrapped," I said. "I'm just the seed money. He's got to meet the people I've lined up for him. The other investors. Afterwards, it's a done deal."

There was, actually, a little more to it than that, and Ellie knew it. Under the neons, she gave me what Sam would have called the hairy eyeball: *Yeah, sure.* But before she could say any more, George came over and took her hand.

Out on the water, a foghorn honked in the distance. Across the bay, the lights on Campobello were like a string of rhinestones. The four of us parted in front of the old Eastport Bank building, a tall brick Victorian pile jutting darkly against the dark sky.

Wade's arm draped around me as we walked up Key Street to my house, passing beneath the half-bare branches of the maples, spectral under the streetlights.

"You okay?" he asked.

"Yeah," I said, but I wasn't. Not really.

At the corner, Victor's lovely old Greek Revival house stood proudly, gleaming with fresh paint, new windows, and tall rebuilt red-brick chimneys. He had at first meant to put a medical office in it, but lately he'd made these other plans.

"I wonder what Reuben meant about talking to Victor again," I said. "What would Victor have to talk to Reuben about?"

The worry went on nudging me as we passed more antique houses—Federals, Victorians, old Queen Anne cottages with their gables looking out every which way. The moon rose, backing the rooflines with silver.

Wade shrugged. "You know Reuben. Or anyway you've heard about him, enough to figure it out. He likes to say threatening things, even when they don't mean much."

"I suppose," I said, not believing it. "He picked on Victor because he was there, probably. And because Victor's so different from most everyone else in town."

Different, I meant, from the fishermen, dock-workers, boat handlers, and rough-hewn but determined entrepreneurs of various stripes that made Eastport a vibrant place. There was another group beginning to grow in town, too, of scholars, artisans, and craftspeople. As we climbed the hill I noted the lights in Ron Cumberland's potting studio, in the old stone house now occupied by a museum curator, and in the neatly kept cottages of a small but increasing bunch of painters, writers, and musicians.

But even among these, Victor with his meticulous appearance and deliberate city airs was a curiosity. Not all the attention he attracted around town was entirely benevolent, though he was working to change this.

"It probably," I said, "just makes him a natural target for a guy like Reuben." I was trying to convince myself, but in fact it wasn't Reuben Tate's behavior that troubled me; it was Victor's. And the reason was simple:

Victor didn't suffer fools gladly, especially with a few martinis in him. And when your line of work involves cutting holes in other people's heads and repairing what you find inside there, you either develop a lot of confidence or you find a way to fake it, somehow.

Which Victor had. He should have stood up to Reuben Tate and blustered at him until it was Victor's ear that Reuben decided to take a bite out of. It was the only reaction consistent with Victor's character.

Instead he had looked frightened. And knowing him as I did, I couldn't help suspecting that I understood why.

"Hey. Going to invite me in?"

We had come to my own house on Key Street: an enormous 1823 white-clapboard Federal with dark green shutters, forty-eight tall, double-hung original wooden windows, and the original stone foundation, much patched but still as fundamentally solid as it had been two centuries earlier when the oxcarts hauled the granite blocks there, and the men laid them into the cellar hole.

It's the rest of the house that is gradually falling down, but that is the natural condition of very old houses. As long as I kept working on it, I could stay ahead of it.

I hoped.

"Oh, I guess you can come in," I told Wade. "Seeing as your shaving kit's upstairs, and your clothes, and your work stuff for tomorrow. We should try practicing some restraint once in a while, though, don't you think?"

He drew me nearer. Much nearer. "I'm practicing it right this minute."

"Oh. Well, in that case, let us not delay," I managed, and his answering chuckle implied absolutely no restraint whatsoever.

Going in the back door, we met Monday, my black Labrador retriever, who greeted us with her own canine version of the old buck-and-wing, toenails clicking on the hardwood kitchen floor.

"Hey, mush-head," Wade told the dog affectionately, opening the refrigerator and the freezer at the same time, and I really knew better than to accept the chilled, cut-crystal flute of ice-cold, perfectly delicious champagne he offered to me then.

But I did accept it, and the next one, too, so that one way and another—

—and what with keeping the dog not only off the bed but actually out of the whole bedroom—

—I forgot what Reuben Tate had said to my ex-husband, Victor, that night at La Sardina.

And I shouldn't have.

2

My name is Jacobia Tiptree, and when I first came to Maine with my son, Sam, I had ideas about how our lives would be, here.

For one thing, I thought I would go back to Manhattan a lot. I was well fixed financially, still reasonably young, and decent-looking; not gorgeous, but my face didn't stop clocks. And I'd lived in the city since I'd gotten off a Greyhound there at age sixteen, alone, penniless, and without an idea of how to do anything useful.

But nobody in the world is so interested in money as a poor girl, and I'd pursued my fascination with a vengeance, first at night school, eventually via grants and graduate work. Soon I was managing large amounts of other people's money along with my own, and I'd become skilled at life in Manhattan:

I could get a cab in the rain, a good table at Four Seasons, or a bagel so fresh that just by eating it, you could learn whole phrases of vernacular Yiddish. In short, I'd grown up in the city, and I thought I might miss it. On the other hand, I was also miserable:

Victor's idea of an amicable divorce had turned out to be one in which the parties stopped short of using automatic assault weapons. No woman, *no* woman, had ever dumped him before, and my doing so had deeply affronted him; his idea of monogamy was serial monogamy—he was faithful to the girlfriends, anyway, although not to me—and the number in the series had climbed to the triple digits by the time I bailed out. But he still felt I was being unreasonable.

Then there was Sam, whose new attitude toward me lay in the no-man's land between carelessness and contempt. Since achieving puberty, a condition he apparently equated with immortality, he'd been running with a posse of computer-literate young outlaws with nicknames like Pillz, Wanker, and Doctor Destructo 357—

—this latter *nom* I had seen painted artistically in bright, poisonous Day-Glo yellow on subway overpasses, up there with the wrist-thick high-tension cables, the sight of which did not reassure me in the slightest—

—whose collective mission in life was, I gathered, to hack into a top-secret military database and start World War III.

At anything else—anything lawful—they were hopeless, which was a part of what made them all so angry. Sam could barely read, a problem that at the time I attributed to his behavioral difficulties, and the others had ditched school entirely. But their illiteracy and general ineptitude overall was, to me, no particular comfort; at World War III I thought this bunch might succeed. For one thing, their personalities fitted their goals: dark. Suicidally apocalyptic and brilliant.

Sam, I discovered during my bouts of shameless, terrified eavesdropping, was especially useful to the project, since while he could barely decipher the label on a cereal box, he could fix absolutely anything. Even while stoned on marijuana, which often he was without even bothering to hide it anymore, he was a real mechanical genius, unfortunately for civilization as we know it.

As for the notion of discipline or a heart-to-heart talk: oh, please. For all that boy listened to me, I might as well have been speaking Urdu. I tried everything, including a psychologist who believed in back-to-the-womb regression. When she turned on the sloshing sound of the amniotic fluid and the *lub-dub* of what was supposed to be his mother's heartbeat, Sam bolted from her office and didn't come home for two days.

Toward the end, I found myself standing before a

Santeria shop window in a neighborhood up above 125th Street, desperately examining a display of magic candles and some vials of powdered sheep entrails, wondering if maybe . . .

Well, I bought a candle—you can always use candles—and a week later I discovered Eastport and fell in love with it at once, in the same sudden, irreversible way that a person might be struck by lightening or run over by a bus.

The town was on Moose Island, as far up the Maine coast as you can get, and reachable only by a narrow causeway. There was no reeking smog, no hostile gangs of drug-addled, dysfunctional little teenaged computer terrorists. Also, there was no Victor, and to get away from Victor at that point I'd have signed up for a colony on Mars.

Still, even as I sold my Manhattan penthouse, complete with twenty-four-hour uniformed doorman, private elevator, and panoramic view of Central Park—

—and even as I signed the papers that meant I owned the shambling, dilapidated but utterly charming antique house on Key Street, stepping into it afterward filled with the shimmering knowledge that something momentous had happened.

Even then, I had no intention of giving up my status as a streetwise, dyed-in-the-wool New Yorker. I would go back to the city often, I thought: on weekends, and during Sam's school vacations.

All of which strikes me as fairly hilarious now, because after a week in Eastport I forgot whether Park Avenue runs uptown or downtown, and didn't care. Soon whole chunks of my past life began dropping away from me like pieces of a plaster body cast, leaving me feeling liberated and exposed, my skin unaccustomed to the air moving freely on it.

Meanwhile Sam's expression took on an odd listening quality, as if he were hearing music. I held my breath, waiting for the other shoe to drop; when he got bored, I thought, he would start agitating to go back to New York.

Instead he took up walking, from one end of the island to the other. He scoured the shore for periwinkles and beach glass, examined obsessively every boat he could wheedle his way aboard, and returned in the evenings with his face glowing pink from all the exercise and fresh air. When he was home he ate like a horse, slept like the dead, and said very little, but when he did speak, he spoke politely.

And there was another thing, which he only confided to me later: in those first days, he really had been hearing music. The tune—he could hum it straight through, and a local Historical Society member eventually heard him, and identified it—was an old one, written by a man who had once lived in our house. Town legend hinted that he had died there, too, and under mysterious circumstances.

But when I learned all this, I was busy and preoccupied; at the time, Victor had just begun threatening to move to Eastport. Probably the tune had survived in downeast Maine lore, I decided, and Sam had picked it up somewhere, possibly from one of the men on the boats.

So I paid little attention to the old town legend.

At the time.

3

Early on the Saturday morning after our dinner at La Sardina, Ellie White and I found Reuben Tate with his throat slit, hanging upside down by a rope knotted hard around his ankles from one of the iron gates in Hillside Cemetery.

His eyes were open, strafing the stones of the old graveyard with undimmed malice. A crow swooped down, attracted by the glint of his upturned boot cleats, and flapped off with a cheated caw. The puddle below the body, dully glistening in the pale sunshine, resembled fresh tar.

"Reuben," Ellie said softly, her face disbelieving.

I said nothing. We'd started our walk as we always did, down Key Street to the bay which was just then brightening to silver. On Water Street, cars and pickups crowded around the Waco Diner, town men having their eggs and coffee before heading out to work.

At the freight dock the *Star Hoisin* loomed massively, cargo bays open. Guys in coveralls and rubber boots went down the metal gangways to the finger piers and onto the fishing boats, the grumble of diesel engines mingling with the slopping of small waves against the breakwater and the cries of seagulls. A bell-buoy clanked as tinges of deep pink rose behind the Canadian islands, dark blue blotches against the lightening sky.

As we walked, I'd been giving Ellie a few stock tips. It was advice I had lagged away from following for myself since I'd been in Eastport, but someone might as well get the good of it. Ellie had been half-listening as she always did, or so I'd thought.

Now in the cemetery all thoughts of money flew from my mind; instead I was busy trying to hold on to my breakfast, breathing the way they'd told me to do while Sam was being born. It hadn't worked very well then, either.

Ellie reached out and touched a finger to Reuben's leather jacket, as if to confirm what she was seeing. The *whoop-whoop* of a squad car sounded somewhere down on the waterfront.

"Be careful," Ellie murmured as if reminding herself, "what you wish for."

I sat down hard, leaning against one of the old gravestones with my head between my knees. The face was bad, shrouded in red, and his hair was no longer the pale whitish color of sun-bleached straw, but it was the hands that really got to me. Stiffened into caked, curved claws, they had obviously been at his throat.

"Nobody," I managed, "wishes for that."

Ellie turned slowly, expressionless. "No. Not anymore."

Then the sirens started again. I got up and called Monday and snapped her onto her lead. The squad cars were coming fast. Somebody must have seen the body before we found it and gone to find Bob Arnold, Eastport's police chief, to let him know.

The thought troubled me; there wasn't much traffic on the cemetery road at this hour of the morning. Moments later, Arnold's squad car appeared, speeding between the maples and the larch trees that made a bright avenue of the road in autumn. But behind him were a couple of state squads, and that wasn't right, either. All three cars pulled to the curb, cherry beacons whirling.

Bob Arnold emerged from his squad and stalked over to us furiously. "Jesus H. Christ," he grated. "One's not enough?"

"One what?" I asked puzzledly, and then I knew: the siren, and the state cops already in town. Another body.

"He was alive when he went up there," I said, gesturing at Reuben. "Somebody tied him and lifted him, hung him upside down."

I was babbling. "And then . . ."

"I get the picture, Jacobia." Arnold pronounced it the Maine way: *pictchah*.

By now it was full morning and a pickup truck was pulling in behind the squad cars. George Valentine got out and walked over to Ellie, while Arnold and the state guys conferred by the gate.

"The guy Victor sewed up last night," George said.

"In the bar? They found him down on the seawall a couple hours ago, cold as a flounder."

A town truck with a bunch of orange traffic cones in its bed parked behind George's vehicle, and some fellows from the highway department began using the cones to block off the road where it entered Hillside Cemetery.

"Couldn't figure what happened," George went on. "Bruises on him. And something blue sticking out of his mouth."

"Blood all over his shirt," Arnold added, approaching. "But that was from the events of earlier, in the bar."

He looked at me. "No mystery there. We've got a complete and fully detailed report of that. Fully," he emphasized, "detailed."

Uh-oh. Suddenly one those details came back to me: blue. But of course what I was thinking wasn't possible.

Behind Arnold, the state men began marking off a perimeter, using yellow tape weighed down with small stones to form a circle about twenty feet in diameter.

"Tell me it wasn't," I said to George, who had been at the restaurant with us. Who had seen . . .

Victor, tossing back that final martini. And afterwards . . .

George nodded, looking unhappy. "Pried open the guy's mouth, see what was in there, that's when we found it."

One of the state officers went back to his car and got on the radio, while the other began marking off a second perimeter a few yards out from the first. At the center of it all, Reuben hung there like some ghastly flag.

"And to judge by how far down his windpipe it was," Arnold went on, "I doubt that fellow just happened to mistake it for a cheeseburger. I don't care," he finished, "how rip-roaring drunk he'd got, couple–three hours earlier."

My mind's eye showed Victor readying himself for impromptu surgery, in the course of which there might be blood. So that Victor, always a poster boy for the compulsively fastidious . . .

"Mistook what?" Ellie demanded.

Monday stopped nosing around and sat down beside me, wanting to go home. Me, too.

"Victor's tie," George said. "What the guy strangled on."

He must have taken it off. Tucked it into his shirtfront, first, but that hadn't been enough for him; it might get dirty. So he'd taken it off.

"Part in his mouth, and the rest," Arnold supplied, "damned near down into his lung. Have to wait for the medical examiner, of course. And the way his dance card's filling up already today, it could take a while. But I'd agree the guy suffocated on it."

Somebody touched my shoulder and I jumped: Sam.

"Mom? I think you better come. Dad's at the house, and he's pretty upset." Sam kept his eyes averted from Reuben.

"Oh, brother. He knows about the tie?" I asked Arnold.

"Yeah. Teddy Armstrong remembered who he'd seen wearing it. I talked to your ex-husband about it a little while ago. Told him I'd see him at your house, and I was on my way over there. But then," he gestured in disgust at Reuben, "I got diverted."

I got up. To Victor, everything was always about him. But this was going to put the frosting on it.

"Did Reuben have relatives?" Bob Arnold asked, squinting at the body. Thinking, I supposed, about a funeral.

Ellie shook her head. "His parents were from away. Both gone now. Buried away, too, I've forgotten quite where. They both had," she added, "that same white-blond hair. And those white eyelashes—to look at them, you'd think they must be brother and sister. But," she came back to the practical present, "he didn't have any brothers or sisters, himself."

Trust her to know; Ellie's memory contained a veritable orchard of Eastport family trees. "Come on, kiddo," I told Sam. "Let's go settle your father down. I guess he must have left that tie in the bar last night. He'd forget his head, you know, you feed him enough martinis."

"Uh-huh," Sam agreed, not sounding convinced, but I just laid it to general upset. When Victor gets going, he can generate emotional shock waves that would shatter the Rock of Gibraltar.

Ellie came too, looking grimly gratified now that the first surprise of our discovery had worn off. She is ordinarily the mildest of souls but her gentleness conceals some icy attitudes, partly I think because her ancestors were cold-water pirates, men who cut their eyeteeth on barbecues of long pig and rum until a hurricane blew them out of the Caribbean, eventually to downeast Maine, back in the 1700s.

Since then her family had flourished in Eastport and the surrounding towns, as tenacious as barnacles and when necessary as coldly pragmatic. I got the impression she felt some rough justice had been served there in the cemetery.

George stayed behind with Arnold, calling on Arnold's radio for sawhorses to hold more perimeter tape and for a second body bag from the small stock of them kept over at the medical clinic.

Which made two more body bags than our little town tended to use in a year. When we have bodies in Eastport they are generally the result of elderly people—and by that I mean very elderly; in Maine, if you should pass before the age of one hundred, your obituary will call it unexpected—signing off more or less on schedule.

So I still felt reasonably sure that the sudden run on body bags was a statistical anomaly, not the beginning of a trend.

Wrong.

4

Before Wade went out on the water that morning, he'd brought all forty-eight of my old wooden storm windows up out of the cellar and lined them against the picnic table in the side yard. I'd bet him I could remove the upstairs window sashes and weatherstrip them before snow fell, and he'd said that if I did he would repair and hang the storm windows for me.

But when Victor is in trouble, he thinks he is a swallow and my house is Capistrano, so I wasn't going to get to the weatherstripping anytime soon.

"Sam," I said as we approached the back porch. "Why don't you go on over and hang out with Tommy Daigle awhile? Let your dad and me have a conversation."

"You sure? He's pretty, um . . . you know." Sam waved his hands in a pantomime of something flying to pieces.

"I'm sure," I replied as reassuringly as I could, and to my relief he headed off. Tommy Daigle was a sensible, good-hearted boy, and his company would be an antidote to Sam's distress.

Now all I needed was an antidote to my own, but I wasn't going to get that, either. Mounting the back steps with Ellie, I could hear Victor in there muttering to himself.

"Well, it took you long enough," he snapped as he saw us.

Scrubbed and freshly shaved as usual, he looked pink as a shrimp. But his eyes were narrowly anxious. I looked at the coffeepot, nearly full when I'd left—Sam had made the coffee, and since he believed it should compete with battery acid, I'd hardly drunk any—and empty now.

Then Ellie and I swung into action: I filled the coffeepot and started it again while she got cups and saucers and sliced bread for toast. I cracked eggs into a bowl, adding milk and waiting for the butter in the pan to sizzle before I dumped them in; she washed the bowl, dried it, and put it away before the eggs had time to need stirring.

Victor looked helpless and puzzled, as he always does when anything useful is happening that does not involve surgery.

"Doesn't anybody want to know why I'm so upset?" he finally demanded.

Ellie put a glass of orange juice on the oilcloth-covered table in front of him. She had not wanted him to move to Eastport any more than I had, but there hadn't been much she could do about it, either. When he wants something, he is as relentless as the hurricane that had resettled her ancestors.

"Maybe you're upset because you have high blood pressure?" she inquired. "That always puts you in a bad mood. Drink your juice. Here's some aspirin to go with it."

She dropped tablets onto the table. "I don't suppose you've thought to take any, yet." Now that he was here, she'd adopted my standard procedure for dealing with him:

First, get him out of his immediate physical discomfort. We would have skipped this, except that it so much simplified stage two: getting him out of my house and back into his own as swiftly and efficiently as possible.

Which was the hard part. I could have just banished him as a general rule, I suppose, but that would have been hard on Sam. And this morning, something serious was up; how serious, I didn't know yet.

"Well, no," he admitted about the aspirin and swallowed them grudgingly. He ate the eggs and toast we fixed for him, too, and drank more coffee.

Ellie glanced meaningfully at me: Now he can *vamoose.*

Not so fast, I signaled back at her, because I was watching Victor carefully and something about him was different:

We'd bolstered his blood sugar, dosed him with aspirin, and loaded him with caffeine until his eyes should have looked like spinning pinwheels. It was not the most politically correct way of dealing with a tiresome ex-husband, I will grant you. But it worked, which most of the time was all I cared about.

Now, though, Victor's mood was emphatically not brightening. Meanwhile, the amount of money I had invested in him at the moment meant that if he was in trouble, I was, too.

"You did leave the tie in the bar, didn't you?" I asked. "I mean, Ted Armstrong will be able to say so."

"N-not exactly." All he needed was a cartoon cloudburst over his head. "I stuffed it in my pocket. But it wasn't there when I got home. Maybe it fell out, when I pulled out some hand wipes. I was on Water Street."

Even that wasn't enough to make him look as unhappy as he did. "So," I pursued, "what's the rest of the problem?"

He looked distractedly at me, which was when I really began feeling nervous; over the years I have come to understand that if Victor doesn't have a malicious gleam in his eye, something worse than Sam's coffee is brewing.

"Tate," he replied. "After you left the restaurant. He came in again, said he wanted to have our conversation."

Uh-oh. "And did you?"

He nodded morosely. "Classic textbook case. I'd never met a real sociopath before."

"But you had met *him* before," Ellie pointed out. "He said he wanted to talk with you *again*. Meaning, I assume, that you and he had spoken earlier."

He bridled instantly. "Well, yes, but—look, I don't want to tell you about it at all, if all you're going to do is try to confuse me."

That's Victor: elbow-deep in somebody else's cranium, he's a model of serenity. Anywhere else he's a basket case, which was why I'd wanted him thoroughly involved in a medical enterprise: it was the only way to make him tolerable.

"Calm down," I told him. "What's the worst that can happen?"

"That they're going to think I did it," he blurted.

Which was not what I wanted to hear. I stared at him, not quite believing that I had. "Victor, what are you talking about?"

"Maybe not the guy with the ear," he went on, "although that's bad enough, and after all, it was my tie they found in his throat. But with him, I didn't have any motive."

And with Tate he did, he seemed to be implying. Oh, this was just fabulous. He pressed his hands to his head. "The police are probably on their way here right now, and—"

"Victor," I cut in. "Just tell us what he said to you after we left. What did he want to talk with you about?"

Then Victor uttered the word that froze my heart.

"Blackmail," he whispered. I sat down.

"Tate was blackmailing me," he confessed, "or anyway he was about to. And everybody in the bar last night knew it."

Worse and worse. "How did they know?"

He shrugged miserably. "He said I was going to hire him: big salary, unspecified duties. Said he'd been digging into what he called my dark past, and that I'd have to pay him money for it."

"He was just bluffing," I said flatly. "I hope you told him to walk east till his hat floated."

Another dark thought struck me. "You didn't, though, did you? Tell him to get lost."

"Not exactly," Victor replied very unhappily. "He knew . . ."

"About the malpractice lawsuit," I finished for him.

Of course; nothing else could take the wind out of Victor's sails so thoroughly.

Victor nodded. "Yeah, that," he uttered defeatedly.

It was what I'd been fearing, telling myself it couldn't be. Because for one thing, how could Tate know? There hadn't been much publicity around here, although it had been in the papers briefly in the city. It had been a fiasco, but only for Victor, and of course for the patient whose death started it all in the first place, in New York.

"I didn't do anything wrong," Victor protested for perhaps the millionth time. "It was emergency surgery. His prospects for surviving were minuscule. And," he finished simply, "he didn't."

Which was all true, but afterward the patient's family had raised a ruckus. And Victor, while apparently blameless in the event, was staggeringly vulnerable. Insurance investigators began looking into his personal idiosyncrasies, many of whom were young and female, some of whom had interesting habits of their own.

It wasn't pertinent, but it could be made to look

absolutely awful. Eventually, the hospital's counsel advised the institution to settle the lawsuit: to admit, tacitly, that Victor had indeed done something improper during the surgery. Whereupon, rather than agree to any such thing, Victor had quit.

"What did you say to him?" I asked, crossing to the window.

With Victor at the surgical helm, a trauma-care center for Eastport had seemed like a good idea. It would keep him busy at the one thing he was very good at, and benefit the whole region. Furthermore, emergency care has two fine attributes, financially speaking:

First, people need it. And second, insurance companies tend to pay for it. Slow going at first, maybe, but the Mayo Clinic was out in the boondocks when it got started, too. Down the line, the thing could be a gold mine.

Only, maybe not anymore. "When he threatened to blackmail you," I went on, "and you let him know he could get away with it by not laughing in his face the way any sane person would have done, what did you say?"

I didn't want to think yet about what I might have to do to replace the money I'd put into in Victor's trauma center start-up, much of it already spent, if it turned out my investment was irretrievable. But that I would need to replace it was a flat-out certainty.

I was financially well fixed, all right. But not *that* well fixed. And now there was that awful word: *motive*.

Victor frowned down at his hands, which were scrubbed clean as always. It struck me then that, at eight o'clock on a Saturday morning, he'd already showered, shaved, and put on fresh clothes: white shirt, navy slacks. Even his prissy little oxblood loafers with the tassels on them looked professionally polished.

All normal for Victor. But . . .

"Well," he admitted, "I'd had a few drinks. And the look on his face, like he was daring me to do something. Like he thought I wouldn't be able to. It . . . well, it got to me, that's all."

Bootsteps sounded on the porch, and Bob Arnold came in. But the words were already coming out of Victor's mouth.

"Reuben's mistake," he rushed on, "was letting himself get backed into a corner, at the end of the bar. So when I walked up to him, he had nowhere to go."

"Victor," I said warningly, but he didn't hear me.

"I reached for him." Victor held up his hands, to show how he'd done it. They were surprisingly large, capable-looking hands with long, muscular fingers.

"I put," Victor went on, "both of them on his throat, and I located his carotid arteries. And I pressed them, so he'd know I could find them again if I needed to."

I waited hopefully for Arnold to cut in and ask what had happened next. But he didn't, confirming my suspicion that he already had more on Victor than even Victor's big mouth had given him.

Just then Sam burst in. "Mom, you won't believe—"

He stopped. "Or maybe you will. You okay, Dad?"

"I'm fine, Sam," Victor said. "I think Arnold has something to say to me, though. Don't you?"

"Yeah." Arnold opened the small paper sack he was carrying. Inside was a zip-lock plastic bag. "Recognize this?"

Victor peered studiously at it. "Yes, I do. It's my scalpel. From my collection of historical items. How do you happen to have it?"

You had to hand it to the guy. He'd known Arnold was coming, and he'd been home to clean up and change clothes, so he must have known the scalpel was missing; that collection was his most prized possession. At that point, I'd have been falling apart.

"Found it at the murder of a guy named Reuben Tate," Arnold said. "Who I understand you had a few words with at the Mexican place last night."

"That's right. This," Victor went on, indicating the blood-caked object in the plastic bag, "is the most valuable of my items. Dr. Cushing, the pioneer neurosurgeon, used it himself."

Suddenly it all seemed to come over him, all he had been saying, and what Arnold was doing here. But even then he didn't panic.

"It would be," he finished, "a pity to lose this instrument. Do try to see that it's well taken care of, won't you?" he asked Arnold respectfully.

That's the other thing about Victor: he is capable of these small instances of grace, during which you just can't figure out how he manages to be such a jerk the rest of the time.

Arnold sighed heavily. "Dr. Tiptree, I'm placing you under arrest. You have the right to remain silent . . ."

And so on. When Arnold finished, Victor got up and pushed his chair in carefully. "I'll be calling an attorney, Jacobia. I'll put the house up if it comes to a question of bail."

He didn't know that in Maine there is, for all practical purposes, no bail on a murder charge. But I nodded; it didn't seem like a useful thing to tell him, just at the moment.

"I'll watch your place till you get home, Dad," Sam said, his face full of shock, and Victor smiled encouragingly at him.

"Good boy. I'll be back soon, though. Don't worry about me."

Then without further ado he went out ahead of

Arnold, who even after informing Victor of his rights hadn't asked where he'd been the night before, once he'd departed the Mexican restaurant.

So I believed that Arnold must already know.

And unfortunately, I was correct.

5

After which everything got worse.

A lot worse. "Dad didn't come home at all last night," Sam said.

It was a couple of hours after Victor had gone, and we were crouched in the back hall, applying steel wool to the old cast-iron radiator that has lurked there since the house got central heating, nearly a hundred years ago. Sam had gone all over the scabrous, red-enameled surface—what *had* someone been thinking?—with a paint scraper; afterward we would vacuum and wipe it thoroughly, preparatory to painting it.

"I got in, and he wasn't there," Sam went on. "So I thought he might be out looking for me. You know how he gets sometimes, like he can't think straight and he goes off half-cocked."

Oh, did I ever. I rubbed a patch of red enamel from one of the delicate fern patterns cast into the antique radiator iron.

This, by the way, is not the method the old-house manuals tell you to follow when you are repainting antique radiators. Their method consists of:

1. Removing the radiators; I mean, actually physically taking them out of the house.

2. Hiring a professional to sandblast them down to the bare metal.

3. Spray painting the radiators, keeping in mind that silver or gold paint inhibits heat radiation, and

4. Hooking the radiators back up to your heating system, again with professional assistance.

This advice has the marvelous advantage of requiring other people to do most of the heavy work for you. But it ignores several crucial real-world facts about old radiators, such as their weight, fragility, and rusted-solid connections to your household plumbing. Following the old-house manual's advice on the topic, in other words, can be a quick route to radiator hell.

On the other hand, stripping one slowly is a fine way to let your emotional engines idle while you are trying to figure out what to do next.

"So then what happened?" Ellie prompted Sam gently.

She'd been going around with the vacuum cleaner, trying to get the little chips of red enamel up off the floor before Monday decided that they were edible.

Sam sighed, moving the steel-wool pad. "So I went looking for him. By then it was way after midnight."

Coming in to find Bob Arnold in the process of arresting his father, Sam had been carrying some things he and Tommy had spent the previous afternoon fooling around with. Now they lay on the kitchen table, forgotten: a pocket-sized, U.S. Coast Guard–issue Morse code instruction book bound in blue imitation leather, and a flat, 1950s-era cardboard box, its brightly illustrated cover proclaiming that it contained a genuine Ouija.

"Because you know Dad," Sam continued. "He wouldn't've tried going to Tommy's, if he wanted me, or called there. It would have been, like, too obvious."

The Ouija board gave me an uneasy feeling. But I

figured that with all that was going on now, Sam might forget about the dratted thing.

"Anyway, I got my bike, rode downtown, out to South End, and back again on County Road. But no Dad. So then I started getting worried about him. I went back and sat around awhile waiting for him."

"Nothing on his answering machine, or anything like that?"

He shook his head, working his way along the side of the old radiator a final time with the pad of steel wool.

"Nope. I thought of that. You know, that maybe he went out for some other reason, somebody'd called him. Then I went through the house to see whether I could figure out what he'd been doing before he left."

"And?" I ran my hand over the now-smooth antique heating fixture. Before there were furnaces, my old house had been heated with stoves, and originally with open fireplaces; the chimneys remain, and when the wind blows hard they howl like a chorus of demented banshees, one in each room.

"And it turned out that while I'd been out hunting for him, he must have been back. Because when I first came home—"

Sam glanced at me; there had been, since Victor's arrival in town, a problem in the definition of just what constituted Sam's home: my house, or Victor's? In the end, Sam had decided on both, but he tried not to rub my nose in it.

"When I first went in," he rephrased smoothly, "I looked in his study. Everything in there was neat and normal like always."

A few feet away, Ellie had been gazing out the kitchen window while she listened, watching the purple grackles moving en masse across the lawn, a glossy regiment. Now she looked over alertly.

"And the second time?"

"He'd been there, in a hurry," Sam said. "Or I

thought he had. His desk drawer was open, and the cabinet where he keeps the old instruments, the antique things from his history collection. That was open, too, and it didn't look so perfect to me, lined up all careful the way he always keeps his stuff."

Victor had bone saws, trephines, gadgets that looked like nutpicks, all of it once the absolute height of high-tech medical equipment; he had collected such things since he was a medical student, buying them at auctions or from private estate sales.

"Like somebody," Sam finished, "had been in there, looking for something. But I just assumed it must have been Dad. Because who else?"

Deliberately, Ellie took a mixing bowl out of the cabinet and got out the ingredients she needed for baking cream scones. She thinks best, she always says, when she is cooking.

"Were the doors locked? Of his house, I mean?" She knew Sam had keys.

"Nah." Sam shook his head. "He does it like everybody else around here does now, locks when he goes to bed. Otherwise—"

He made a frittering gesture with his hands, indicating the general daytime attitude to locking up in Eastport. People walk in and leave things on hall tables all the time: baked goods, jars of homemade marmalade, borrowed Tupperware.

"It's mostly," Sam summed up, "wide open."

Which, with a valuable historical collection in the place, I thought was pretty silly. Victor didn't even lend Tupperware, because he didn't own any; too hard to sterilize properly. But he had probably enjoyed the idea of not locking and had gone overboard with it.

Ellie put on my green plaid apron with the moose-pattern trimmings and the moose heads chain-stitched in green embroidery floss. In it, I always resembled the animal depicted upon it, but she looked fetching.

"So you never did find out where your father was, or what he was doing?" she asked.

Sam finished wiping the radiator, went into the kitchen, and sat at the kitchen table. "Well, not what he was doing," he said reluctantly. He began turning the Morse book around and around on the table.

"But you know where he was?" I put in worriedly.

Because if he did know and hadn't said so, it must have been somewhere—

"In the cemetery," Sam said miserably.

—bad.

He sighed again. "I went out on my bike twice, see. And the second time, I rode through Hillside Cemetery. Dad was on one of the benches."

"Are you sure it was your father? It was dark."

Ellie cracked two eggs expertly, reserving a little white for the glaze and beating the rest into the bowl with some milk. In the bowl already were the flour, sugar, and butter, and the Bakewell Cream powder, which as a substitute for ordinary baking powder is like using rocket fuel instead of gasoline.

"Yeah," Sam said, "I'm sure. He didn't speak, though, so I guessed he wanted to be let alone. So," he shrugged, "I did."

"Move over," Ellie said, shooing him to the side. Sam pushed the Ouija board in its box and the Morse book out of her way, as she deftly floured her hands and kneaded the scone batter twenty times, then flattened it into a pancake shape on the table.

"So you went home," she said. "Back to Victor's, I mean."

He nodded, watching her cut the pancake into a dozen wedges, then transfer the wedges to a baking sheet. Finally she spread them with beaten egg white and drizzled granulated sugar between her fingers until the sugar stopped soaking into the egg white.

"Was Reuben's body already there, by any chance?" Popping the baking sheet into the oven, she dusted her hands together briskly and competently. I took her point: Although the blood had indeed seemed reasonably fresh when we found him, he could have been there a while.

"I don't know. I wasn't looking for it," Sam said.

Absently, he opened the Ouija board box, slid the planchette dejectedly over the varnished surface of the board. It was elaborately painted in crisp, glossy black, the standard numerals and letters spread out across it. The words *Yes* and *No* were displayed in the upper left-and-right-hand corners.

"I was wishing Dad would call me over," he said, fiddling with the planchette. "But he didn't, and then I was past him. I never looked at the gate."

The planchette slipped off the edge of the table and fell to the floor; Monday came over and sniffed suspiciously at it.

Sam picked it up again. "It felt lousy, you know? Not being able to help him. But he never does. Let me help him, I mean. And now if I have to say where he was when I saw him last night . . ."

"No one has asked you," Ellie said. "And I hope you're not thinking of volunteering any information before it's requested."

We sat in glum silence until the oven timer's *brrring!* interrupted my musing: Victor had bathed that morning, so thoroughly that to anyone who didn't know him it would look as if he'd been trying to wash something off.

Even more, I mean, than usual. Ellie took the cream scones from the oven. "So the next time you knew where your father was, he was here? This morning?"

But Sam shook his head again. "After I went to bed, I heard him. It was getting light out, so it must have been around five. I heard the shower run, and after that he did a load of laundry."

Oh, for heaven's sake. Most of the time, Victor's

idea of doing laundry was bundling it up for the maid to take. He'd hired a cleaning person from town three days a week, and a high-school kid to do his yard work, the minute he'd arrived in Eastport.

And now suddenly he was Holly Homemaker.

"What about the jacket he was wearing, and the slacks he had on?" Ellie inquired acutely. "Have you seen those?"

"Uh-uh," Sam replied. "But . . ."

His face fell further. "But he took the trash out. I saw a fresh bag in the bin this morning. He'd put the top back on the bin but he hadn't tied it down, which was why I noticed."

A grin lit his face briefly. "Dad still thinks skunks won't eat his trash if he just *disapproves* of them hard enough."

Then the seriousness of the situation overtook him again.

"Anyway, I had to shove the bag farther down in the bin, so I could get the top shut. And it was soft," he finished in a tone of terminal glumness. "Like maybe there were clothes inside it."

He thought for a minute. "I could call Charlie Martin. Ask him to pick up the trash now instead of waiting for our regular day."

Ellie split a scone, buttered it, and put it in front of him.

"He will, you know," Sam finished earnestly to me. "He will, if I call and ask him."

But as Sam said this, a rumbling sound came from the street. I knew it well: it was the sound I heard each Thursday morning, when once again I had forgotten to put out my own trash and had to scramble to get the cans lugged out to the sidewalk, and the wastebaskets emptied too, if I was lucky.

Opening the back door, I watched the garbage truck roll by: red cab, big bull moose painted in green on the white compactor.

And today wasn't Thursday. "Looks like some helpful person already has. Called him, I mean."

Charlie swung out and started up the driveway to the trash bin, a low, lean-to structure built onto the shed out back of Victor's house. He was halfway there when the Maine State Police squad car rolled to the curb. Two officers got out and waved him over.

I saw Charlie glance at my house as he listened to the officers. Then I closed the door so I wouldn't have to see any more.

"Look," I told Sam. "Whatever trouble your dad's in, the way to help him is not by lying or trying to cover anything up."

He listened disconsolately. Meanwhile in my head an awful refrain was repeating itself: motive, method, opportunity. I was pretty sure the state cops knew that old song, too.

And from what I could tell, Victor had just spent the night putting together a new arrangement for it.

"So," I told Sam, "you say nothing unless you're questioned by somebody who has the authority to do it. And even then, say you have to ask your mother before you can answer. Got it so far?"

Sam nodded gratefully. Ordinarily, he doesn't like asking my permission to do anything, regarding it as an outworn, childhood habit that ought to be put behind him, like a snake's skin. But this time he looked relieved.

"Tell the truth," I continued. "But no more than you've been asked."

He nodded some more, so woebegone I almost wished for a hint of the bad old days: teenaged anger and open defiance.

But not quite. "Got it?" I emphasized.

"Uh-huh," Sam said. "I know," he went on earnestly, "about Dad's trouble with Tate. Dad didn't want Tate telling that he'd gotten sued in New York. He told me he knew people here would find out eventually. But he wanted them to know him better, kind of get used to him, you know. Before they heard about it. He was real worried about it."

His shoulders slumped. "I won't say that to anyone but you two, though. Unless," he added sorrowfully, "the police ask."

Typical Victor: knee-jerk secretiveness, bunker mentality. He'd have kept his New York troubles under wraps forever if he could, and never mind what he'd told Sam he was going to do about it; worrying about looking bad was one of Victor's main ways of *not* worrying about *being* bad.

Typical Reuben Tate, too, from what I'd been hearing: playing into Victor's psychology that way. Sam got up, closed the Ouija box, and took it and the blue-covered Morse code book with him.

"Mom, how could they have arrested him? He's not guilty. He couldn't have done it. He's not . . ."

Sam paused, swallowed hard. "He's not violent. Anymore."

"Right," I said, knowing that we were remembering the same incident. But that was from the really bad old days, and it was over. I put my hand on his arm, made my voice sound confident.

"His talk about threatening Reuben, even if he did say that stuff, it was just talk. Don't worry about it too much. Things are going to be a little rough for a while, but I'm certain that this will all get straightened out just fine."

Sam met my gaze, comforted for a moment. But then his face changed, as he realized that I was lying.

That Victor was innocent of Tate's murder I was certain; I knew Victor too well. It was the getting things straightened out part I wasn't sure of, because what I couldn't come up with was the answer to one simple question:

Neither Ellie nor I had said anything about Reuben

Tate when we'd arrived home from the cemetery to find Victor sitting in my kitchen.

Arnold hadn't mentioned Tate either when he'd called Victor earlier, because at that point he hadn't heard.

So how had Victor known that Reuben was dead?

6

The question of hauntedness was a recurring one in our old house: cold spots on the stairs, strange noises in the attic, doors that opened or closed with odd, mischievous regularity. Once I came down in the morning to find a set of steak knives, their blades all bent and twisted, inside the washing machine.

So having a Ouija board around the place just seemed to me like begging for trouble, but Sam was enthralled with the thing. He took it into the dining room and sat brooding over it, as if it might reveal some hidden secret to him.

"Sam," I said. "It's supposed to take at least two people to get any action out it."

Live people, I meant, and not that I wanted any action; the reverse, in fact, unless the dratted thing decided to levitate itself into the trash. The astral plane had been pretty quiet on our part of Key Street in recent months, and I wished it would stay that way.

"I know," he replied. "I'm just playing around with it."

He'd finished stripping the radiator, put a coat of primer on it, and cleaned up, then spent some time on the phone and afterward just picked at his lunch. Behind him, early-afternoon sunlight slanted brilliantly through the dining-room windows.

"Are you worried about your dad?"

Sam frowned, moving the planchette a fraction toward the Yes corner of the board. "Daigle says lots of people wanted to kill Reuben Tate. He says there are, like, other possible suspects."

Which wouldn't stop a prosecutor from doing his best to pin the deed on Victor. And until recently I'd have been happy to see Victor impaled on a pin the size of a railroad spike. But now that he was in trouble I had to admit that, over the months since he'd moved here, Victor had done the one thing I'd never expected of him: he had *behaved*.

Oh, he was still about as easy to have around as a sprained ankle, and all the emotional baggage I had with him could have filled a boxcar. Still, he hadn't engaged in any scandalous dalliances with Eastport girls, or gotten into feuds with any of the town's leading citizens. He hadn't, as I had been so much fearing, made a public spectacle of himself.

And then there was Sam, whose personal transformation over the past couple of years had been nearly miraculous. Now all he wanted was some semblance of a normal home life, or at any rate one that didn't feature a father confined to prison.

What we needed, I decided, was one of those other suspects Tommy Daigle talked about, preferably one who was (a) not in any sense a member of my family, and (b) the real perpetrator.

"How come you're not down at the boatyard?" I asked Sam.

He shrugged. "Day off. I got twenty hours in, Harpwell says that's enough for this week."

And Sam did, too, his expression telegraphed with perfect clarity. Work on the local guys' boats was all right, as far as it went. Sam enjoyed it, but it didn't offer him much variety.

"Well, it won't be forever. You'll be at school next year."

I hoped. He'd been accepted at Yale, into a special

program, then had discovered Yale wasn't among the top training grounds for marine architects, which was what he planned on being. In the end he'd turned them down, deciding to put off college altogether for a year, which I personally thought was a fine idea.

But now . . . "I don't know, Mom. I'm just not sure that stuff is for me."

I stifled impatience. Dan Harpwell, owner of Eastport Boat Yard, was holding out a promise of a partnership for Sam: better money, more interesting work. Without advanced schooling, though, in computer-aided design, modern methods and materials, even some business accounting, Sam's future at the boat establishment—and in his chosen career—was limited.

"Did you hear," he asked wryly, "about the dyslexic devil worshiper who sold his soul to Santa?"

Well, at least he could joke about it. We'd found out about his dyslexia a few years earlier; it had turned out to be an odd, refractory form of the disability. He'd gotten through high school by dint of taped texts, special therapy, and tutoring. But now with a year off from school he was getting a taste of not having to struggle so hard all the time, and was—temporarily, I hoped—shying at the gate of any further education at all.

"Sam," I began gently, but his shoulders stiffened. Time for a change of subject.

"I think," I offered carefully, for Sam could be touchy if you tried cheering him up too blatantly, "George Valentine knows Morse code. He's a ham-radio enthusiast."

He brightened a little. "Yeah? Hey, maybe I'll ask him about it. You think spirits could learn to send messages in Morse?"

"I don't know," I said, again feeling obscurely troubled. On the other hand, none of the odd events we'd experienced in the house had been malicious. And just at that moment I'd have rented a room to the headless horseman, if it made Sam feel better.

"I think," he said in a wan attempt to make a little joke, "it would depend on whether a spirit knew any Morse code *before*."

He took his hands off the Ouija board and looked up sideways at me, his grin the pale ghost of the one he usually wore.

Whereupon I swear that dratted planchette *twitched*.

7

That afternoon, Arnold drove Victor to the courthouse in Machias, thirty miles to our south. The prisoner's behavior was calm and cooperative, Arnold reported; Victor allowed himself to be fingerprinted, photographed, and placed in a cell; he was given a phone call, which, as promised, he had made to an attorney in Manhattan.

"And that," Arnold finished, "is that." Victor would remain in jail to await arraignment, hearings, and trial.

I gripped the telephone, not yet quite able to believe that it was all so cut-and-dried, or in fact that any of it was real. But of course it was.

"State guys'll be around," Arnold went on, "talk to you and Ellie about finding the body. About what you saw and heard at La Sardina, too. And," he added reluctantly, "they'll want to have a word with Sam."

Which was the part that I was most emphatically not looking forward to. But it was coming; the state's mobile crime lab was in town and the bodies were on their way to the police forensic unit in Augusta; the physical-evidence-gathering part of the program, Arnold felt, would be completed by nightfall.

"Cops're saving your interviews until last," he said. "They know none of you are going anywhere. That'll wrap it up."

"But," I protested, "won't there be further investigation? Isn't there anyone who thinks someone besides Victor is guilty?"

I took a deep breath. "I mean, Arnold, if Victor ever wanted to kill somebody, he'd come up with some goofy plan full of clever, unworkable details. Full," I went on, "of self-glorifying intellectual flourishes and literary-thriller stuff he'd read somewhere and wanted to imitate. A victim," I was practically pleading now, "would die of *natural* causes, before Victor ever even got around to *doing* the actual murder."

Arnold harrumphed unhappily. "Well, if you say so. But Jacobia, that's beside the point. State guys heard what they heard, they got orders of their own, and the orders said go get Victor. I had to twist some arms, even to talk them into letting me do it."

His tone softened. "And listen, Victor threatened the guy. A lot of people heard him. Now it turns out Reuben was threatening Victor, he had information that Victor didn't want getting around."

A vehicle pulled into the driveway; Monday got up and padded to the hall vigilantly, in case it contained any burglars she could lick or nuzzle to death.

"Later," Arnold went on, "the guy gets found with his throat cut and the weapon is Victor's. And Victor's got no alibi for his whereabouts at the time of the crime. And you've got to admit he's done some guilty-looking activities: washing up, getting rid of clothes, and so on. So I ask you," Arnold finished reasonably, "what's left, besides a confession?"

It did look awful. "But what about all the others who wanted Reuben out of their hair? Sounds to me like he had a grab bag full of mortal enemies."

"Yeah, but Reuben, he wasn't blackmailing them."

In the back hall, Monday's wag-o-meter shot up to

redline as Wade came in, home from the harbor. But his face didn't look right to me; it was even more troubled than I'd expected.

Also, he wasn't carrying his soft canvas gun bag. When he is not on a boat, Wade restores and repairs firearms in a workshop he has built into the storeroom ell of my house. Thus, in addition to a fragrance of camellias that tends to appear for no reason like a calling card from a time gone by, the house often smells of gun oil, hot soldering compound, and the bright, sharp reek of metal being machined to produce close tolerances in the working parts of deadly weapons.

But this time no weapons were in evidence. Puzzled, I turned back to the phone. "Thanks, Arnold, for keeping me posted. How's Clarissa?"

In answer, I heard the latest details of Arnold's impending fatherhood. Arnold's wife, a criminal attorney who would have been defending Victor if she hadn't been about to deliver a baby practically that minute, was enormous, elated, and, according to Arnold, so impatient to get it all over with that he "dassn't even look cross-eyed at her."

Which reminded me that somewhere in the world, someone was happy, an assurance I sorely needed. I told Arnold to give her all our love and he promised to, and we hung up.

Out in the kitchen, Wade sat at the table looking thoughtful, a bottle of Sea Dog ale in front of him. He'd gotten the news on our crime wave, I could see from his expression, from the guys at dockside. I sat down with him and told him the rest of it, still wondering what else was eating at him.

"That's a lot of money," he said mildly when I had explained what could happen if Victor remained in custody.

He'd known of my investment in the trauma-center project; just not how much.

"You know that whatever you do about money, it's all right with me. Don't you?" Wade added.

"Yes." It was part of our ongoing success in being together, that neither of us meddled in the other's finances. We just knew we'd have given each other the world, no strings attached.

"Still," he went on, "I'll bet it galls you. Having it a lot more at risk than you planned."

"Right. And that's an understatement."

Wade understood that I was a little crazy about my financial security. Well, maybe a lot crazy: even aside from Sam's feelings and Victor's innocence, if there was anything I could do to avoid losing that money, I was going to.

"And the only way for me *not* to lose it," I said, "is for Victor to get back to his project. Otherwise the whole idea goes off the rails and my investment goes with it, because without a surgeon a trauma center is pretty pointless, wouldn't you say?"

Wade took another meditative sip of his ale. "You can't just find another surgeon, maybe advertise in the city papers? Hire on someone else to fill in for Victor?"

It was a good thought, but not practical. "Downeast Maine is too remote. Victor *wants* to be up here; the rest follows from that. To anyone else this area would look like a career dead end, but he's willing to let it develop."

With Victor heading it, a local trauma center could attract whatever it needed, given time and patience: more money, a rising reputation, other staff.

But without him, its chances were zippo.

"Uh-huh," Wade said quietly when I'd finished, which for him was unusual; ordinarily, his energy could charge a truck battery.

"Sam all right?"

I peered at him. "Hanging in there. What about you?"

"Oh, fine." He frowned at the ale bottle. "I guess.

But this just makes me realize again that I shouldn't have left Victor in the bar last night. I knew Reuben was after him but I walked away. So in a way this is—"

All my fault, he was about to say, and I just stared at him. Self-flagellation was not exactly his usual habit.

"Wade, there was nothing you could have—"

He got up, his face severe. "Done? Yes, there was. A long time ago. But I didn't do it."

He rubbed a big hand over his wiry hair. "I could have, but I didn't. Just like last night. And now . . . look, one thing I know from working on the water is, no one's going to do it for you. If you want something a certain way, you've got to make it that way. And when push came to shove last night, I did nothing."

Looking around the kitchen, he shook his head angrily. "Ah, hell. Got a nice old Remington shotgun in the truck, a guy wants me to work on for him. But in the mood I'm in, if I put a hand to it I'll just screw it up. I'll see you later."

With a grimace of self-disgust he pulled his jacket back on and went out, not even stopping to pat Monday, who watched him go with a look of hurt puzzlement in her eyes.

I felt the same. Like many Maine men, Wade guards a core of privacy; he tells his secrets in his own time, when he is ready. And mostly, that worked fine for both of us.

But at the moment I wasn't in favor of secrets.

Not at all.

8

My lovely old white clapboard Federal was charming and historical, but its state of repair lent new meaning to the term *fixer-upper*. Calling it drafty, for instance, would have been putting it mildly. The way the wind blew through that old place in winter, I might as well have told the oil man to pump heating oil into the street, and burned it there without bothering to run it through the furnace.

And winter, despite the brilliant autumn afternoon, was not far off. So, after Wade had gone, I trudged upstairs to start the weatherstripping project. With me I brought the clawhammer and the pry bar from my cellar workbench, a tack hammer and nails, the enormous heavy roll of copper weatherstripping I'd lugged uphill from Wadsworth's Hardware, and a tape measure.

Hauling them all into the big, bright front room overlooking the street, I began removing sashes from the room's four tall double-hung windows, prying the exterior stops off the frames and lifting the heavy sashes—they are the things that actually have the glass panes in them—out of their channels.

The trick is to avoid cracking the wooden pieces while prying them up, because you will need to use them again when you put the sashes back in; that, or pay a lot to have all new ones custom-made for you. So I proceeded carefully with a type of pry bar called a cat's-paw, its blade wide and thin so as to slide deeply in and distribute the prying pressure.

And it worked beautifully. Easing off the wooden strips, I lined the old square-cut nails up on the windowsill as I removed them. Nowadays, nails are manufactured from miles-long lengths of wire, thousands per minute, but these had been made one at a time by hand and I wanted to save them, though I wouldn't be reusing them. They belonged to the house.

From the window I could see all the way down Key Street to the harbor. Cars had already begun flooding into town, a whole week before the official beginning of the Salmon Festival, which Ellie said was going to go on come hell or high water and never mind the little matter of a couple of murders.

In the park behind the old red-brick Peavey Library, men were busy setting up the striped awnings under which we would eat the salmon supper: steamed new potatoes and boiled corn and blueberry pie, and of course the grilled salmon. A group of town women were slapping a fresh coat of white paint onto the bandshell, where there would be live music. Ellie was among them, her coppery hair shining in the sun, and all over town I could see bright posters, placards, and banners announcing the upcoming festivities.

A nail pierced the tip of my thumb. Staring at the droplet of blood, I heard Ellie's words suddenly in my mind:

Why did Reuben have to come back *now*?

The idea niggled at me as I brushed out the channels where the window sashes had been: dust and old paint chips, bits of the past undisturbed for years, much like the recollections of people returning to Eastport for the festival. Many had grown up here, and now they were coming back to dust off old friendships, regale themselves with old memories, and generally indulge in a little harmless nostalgia for the good old days.

Maybe Reuben had come back for the festival, also. From what I'd heard of him, he hadn't had many friends. But I gathered he'd had victims. So maybe that was why he'd come back now: to prey upon them again.

Thinking this, I unrolled some copper weatherstripping and clipped a length of it. One thing an old house teaches you right away is the value of a good tool; instead of tin snips, I had a cuts-all gadget that was sharp enough to amputate fingers. Using it and the tack hammer, I fastened the copper strip to the top of one of the upper sashes and trimmed it neatly to fit.

Killing Reuben was one thing; having victims led logically to having enemies. But displaying his body, hanging it up like some bloody flag: that was something else. There was also the question of the other victim, the one with Victor's dratted tie in his throat. How had he hooked into all this bad business—if he had? And then there was a final problem, one my mind kept skittering away from.

I clipped another piece of weatherstripping, nailed it into the groove of the window channel. As I did so, a breeze moved stealthily, lifting the hairs on my neck. But it was only a cold draft coming in through the open window.

Replacing the sash in the channel, I checked its fit to make sure it was tight but also free to slide easily up and down. Then I got out the real prize from my window-restoration toolkit: the gimlet. This is a device like a small, needle-sharp-tipped wood screw, but in place of the screwhead it has a wire-loop handle.

Because the thing is this: once the exterior stop was lined up against the sash, there wasn't room to use a power drill. But hammering a nail in was almost certain to split the old wood, and the old nail holes were too chewed up to use a second time.

So, placing the window in its channel and snugging the exterior stop up in front of it, I pressed the sharp tip of the gimlet into the wooden strip, grasped the gimlet handle between my thumb and forefinger, and gave it a twist.

Presto: a new hole, called a pilot hole, just smaller than the nail I intended to drive, so the nail would hold snug. And the hole was already made for it so the old wood could not become damaged. Pleased, I surveyed the bright window again, the wavery old glass turning the view to an impressionistic smear.

Without warning, the remembered sight of Reuben rose in it like a nightmare, his flaxen hair bloodstained, his eyes gazing from behind a red shroud. His hands had been scrabbling in his last moments, but in death they dangled, his unkempt nails maroon crescents.

In other words, they hadn't been tied. Yet he had been alive when somebody hung him on the cemetery gate. Alive and kicking . . .

I blinked the memory away, gazing determinedly at the boats in the harbor, the white clapboard houses etched sharp as ink sketches in the sunshine. But I couldn't so easily get rid of the questions lining up one after another, like the old nails on the windowsill.

Reuben was a fighter. Even Teddy Armstrong, who tossed guys out of La Sardina with monotonous regularity, had hesitated to eject Eastport's bad boy. And though he was a very small man, Reuben still must have weighed 130 pounds or so.

Which would have made getting him up on that gate alive an interesting project. Almost, perhaps, as interesting as finding out who'd done it and why.

But first, I had a decision to make.

Well, two decisions, actually.

9

Wade Sorenson is not a protective man in the usual sense. His idea of looking out for a woman, for instance, is to take her to the firing range and teach her to put six shots into a two-inch target circle at fifty yards. As he'd done with me, and when he was finished I could handle a wide variety of weapons.

And then I'd killed a man with one of them. That the fellow had been trying to kill Sam at the time was some consolation, as was my own nonlethal intention; the bullet was a dummy and the guy's death was a freak occurrence. I'd meant to stop him, not end his life. But none of that changed the fact that the guy had not survived the episode. Since then, the weapons I owned—

—a .25-caliber semiautomatic and an Uberti-made Bisley .45-caliber 6-shot revolver, the sort of gun you might see the good guys blasting at the bad guys, in the old Western shoot-'em-ups—

—had remained securely stored with their trigger locks, cartridges, and ammunition clips in the lockbox in my cellar.

On the other hand, if someone was going around slitting throats I did not want mine to be one of them. So I descended to the cellar, opened the lockbox with the only key, which I wore on a chain around my neck, and removed the handguns.

The semiauto was metallic gray, only a little larger than my hand, and very light. The Bisley, by contrast, was a whopper with a blued-steel barrel, checkered grip, and weight enough to make you think twice about carrying it around; also, it's got stopping power enough to drop an elk.

Experimentally, I slid a clip into the semiauto. Then I just sat there on the cellar steps, holding it for a while. It was the Bisley I'd killed the man with, not the pistol. But that didn't matter. What mattered was that in the same situation, I knew that I would do the same again. And, after months of silently thinking it over, I knew that I could.

It's an interesting thing to learn about yourself. When I was sure of it, I put the handguns back in the lockbox and turned the key, snapped the light switch, and went upstairs. It was not yet time to start adding deadly weapons to my toolkit. And maybe it wouldn't ever be.

But they would be there, if I needed them.

Next step: The drive to Machias took a bit under an hour and felt like five minutes. I had a question, and I needed an answer in order to make my second decision.

The jail is located in the old red-brick county courthouse building, on a pretty side street that as I pulled onto it was quiet; most offices were closed on Saturday. But there were still official deeds to be done, apparently; inside, the lobby bustled with low-key but purposeful activity.

I waited while the desk clerk consulted with somebody about my request. The verdict: yes, but with conditions.

Okay by me. I followed the young police officer who was to be my chaperon down a dingy hall, past offices, a file library, and a coffee room. The uniform for female attorneys, caseworkers, and others who had business here today was longish rayon dresses, jackets, and flat shoes; for the men, jackets and ties.

The inmates, by contrast, were all dressed alike: bright orange jumpsuits that would make them easy to spot in the woods, which is where you would head to if you wanted to escape around here. Victor looked ghastly in his, though under the circumstances I doubted that crisp tailoring would have made him look any better.

The young officer sat on a plastic chair in the corner of the conference room. When Victor came in, I didn't mince words.

"Do not, I repeat do *not* make any incriminating statements to me."

I didn't know what he might have said to Bob Arnold, on the trip down. All I knew was that perjury was not among the crimes I planned to commit for Victor.

Which limited pretty severely the questions I could ask him. But there was one, and as I sat there looking at him across the table in that hideous little conference room, I understood that I already knew the answer.

I'd just needed to see him, so it would be clear to me. And I needed to hear him say it.

He understood; even on his worst days, of which this had to be a real standout, he was no fool.

"Jacobia," he said, and for an instant all his idiocies and posturings evaporated. He was just a man in an orange jumpsuit, tired and frightened.

I'd loved him, once.

"Jacobia," he said, "please help me."

10

"I don't see how all this affects your own situation," Paddy Farrell sniffed, regarding me with a narrow look of unwelcome.

Inside the old sardine cannery overlooking the boat basin, Paddy's fabric-design studio was aggressively white: the pristine walls, recently painted woodwork, and high airy ceilings. On the polished tile floor a half-dozen wooden layout tables were covered with colored drawings and sketches, under track lights as bright as little suns.

"Or why you want to go digging up old misery, on account of it," Paddy added, his salt-and-pepper head tilted suspiciously at me.

In one corner of the big work area, a chemistry-lab bench had been built in, complete with gas jets and oversized, brushed stainless-steel double-basined sinks. Another area was a display module with swatches of bright cloth in jewel-like hues spread on low tables, gleaming like a sultan's riches.

"My *situation,*" I snapped back at him, "is this: Victor's in jail and if it comes to a trial, Sam may have to testify against him. Even if he doesn't, he's very upset over his father being in trouble. Also the money I personally have in jeopardy over the matter would pay off the national debt of Peru. So does that adequately sum up the reasons behind my interest for you?"

At the far end of the studio, cubicles were sectioned off for computer stuff—workstations with candy-colored Macintosh hardware set up on them—and dye testing: the object, I supposed, of the chemistry equipment. Paddy didn't only design fabrics; he tried out his ideas on actual pieces of cloth, to see what effects he could achieve before the work went into larger-scale trials.

"Also," I said, "jerk that he is, Victor didn't kill Reuben. And I'd say an unjust murder conviction is going a little far." In the personal revenge department, I meant; Paddy knew that my history with Victor wasn't exactly silk-lined.

He glowered, still deciding whether to talk to me at all. Meanwhile I thought again how much of a Renaissance man it was still possible to be, here in Eastport. Basic design, dye experiments, fabric tests: with no one around to tell him that he couldn't do it all, Paddy just went ahead and did.

It was, I'd gathered, an unconventional way of working. But stubborn, pugnacious Paddy had made a success of it; from his small Maine island studio here at the back of beyond, he did business with clients in Europe, South America, and Japan, as well as in the United States.

In one corner of the studio hung the big weight bag and the punching bag that Terence worked out on when he wasn't jogging or bicycling. His ten-speed leaned against the wall nearby.

"And Wade," I finished, "has got a mad-on at himself about something. I don't know what, but I know it's to do with Reuben."

I faced Paddy. "So are you going to help me or not?"

He still looked unhappy, pained and put-upon in the extreme, but no longer so flatly rejecting. "You were awfully useful, solving that little tax problem I had earlier this year," he conceded reluctantly.

Paddy was good at earning money hand over fist, not so good at spending it on anything other than his beloved studio. Sending any of it to the government, for instance, was anathema to him. Thus his tax problems had ended up being soluble only by dint of my brushing off my tax-preparer credentials and going to Augusta, and falling on my very own personal knees in front of the revenue officials.

"If I could just cast doubt on the theory," I said. "Show that somebody else is at least as good a suspect as Victor."

Paddy eyed me over another stack of colored sketches. The patterns were for watered silk in shades of salmon and turquoise, the effect a pearly shimmer.

"A suspect," he suggested thinly, "such as myself?"

"No," I denied, although the thought had of course occurred to me. Paddy had been pretty vocal about his feelings, the night before. "Just . . ."

Terence Oscard looked up from a table where he was writing something in a spiral notebook. Lined up nearby with his writing things was a collection of potions, pills, lotions, ointments, and herbal remedies, all of which he used regularly to ward off real or imaginary ailments.

"Paddy was with me all evening," he said firmly. "All," he emphasized, "evening."

The big man waved at the open staircase leading to the top floor, where Paddy had put the living area.

Mounted on each of the pillars under the stairs, and on other pillars dividing the whole area of the workspace, were bright red fire extinguishers.

The effect was of little drops of blood sprinkled evenly on a background of snow. But the cylinders were also reassuring; if a fire got started here it could take the whole downtown with it, not to mention all of Paddy's investment.

"I'm very glad to hear it," I told Terence. His left hand, I noticed, was wrapped in an Ace bandage he hadn't been wearing at La Sardina. But I paid little attention; probably it covered some minor wound that might, to a normal person, be worth a Band-Aid, or no treatment at all.

"It means," I went on, "Paddy can tell me all he knows about Tate and anyone who might have wanted to kill him, without worry about incriminating himself."

Which was not strictly true. If it came to these two having to alibi each other, I wouldn't've put much faith in it. But it hadn't come to that—at the time, I had no particular sense that it would—and in any case there was no sense saying so to Paddy.

"Starting right now," I told him. "Or next spring, I'll let you sort out your taxes all by yourself *and* go to Augusta to try defending the hash you've made of them."

I spoke to both of them; Terence was Paddy's business partner as well as his domestic companion but even he wouldn't go anywhere near Paddy's IRS filings. So my threat carried weight.

Paddy sighed irritably. "All right. I guess it can't do any harm talking about Tate now." His face still said different, though, and I couldn't help wondering why.

"But you'll have to come along with me," he went on. "I'm going over to Deer Island to get some more sketch work from one of my freelancers, and I'm picking up my car there."

He grabbed a portfolio case, a sweater, and his wallet. "And Terence is coming, too. Aren't you, Terence?"

A look of surprise crossed Terence's jutting features, but he put away his papers and got up obediently. Publicly, Paddy was the up-front, bossy one of the pair, but I got the sense that in his quiet way, Terence was the strength of the duo.

"Oh, do hurry up, Terence," Paddy called as I went out onto Water Street. Glancing back, I stepped straight into the path of someone who obviously hadn't seen me coming, either. The resulting full-body collision slammed me against the brick building; for an instant I saw stars.

"I'm so sorry. Are you all right?" The woman I'd run into reached out to steady me, concern on her face.

"Fine." I laughed, a little shakily. She was my size, with pale curly hair and wide violet eyes, wearing navy slacks, a knit shirt, and running shoes. But she'd been hitting the gym regularly, to judge by the punch she packed; there was a lot of muscle mass hidden in that petite-looking body.

She assessed me closely as if to make sure she really hadn't injured me, then flashed an apologetic grin and went on her way. By then, Paddy was on his way out the door, still frowning over his shoulder, and I wondered if maybe this trip to Deer Island with him was a mistake.

But by the time we got to the ferry dock, his mood had lifted, buoyed as always by his unquenchable enthusiasm for Eastport. He was a New York refugee like me, veteran of SoHo and Greenwich Village, but unlike me he'd been born in Eastport, gone away to school and to get his career started, then had come back.

"When I was a kid," he recalled nostalgically as we strolled down the tree-lined lane to the dock where the ferry was just now approaching, "you could stand at the end of the pier there and catch your dinner of codfish. Or sell them. I had a little red wagon. I'd go around to the housewives. Of course," he added, a bit less enthusiastically, "they'd want me to clean them, first."

"Nowadays," Terence put in dryly, "Paddy likes his fish to be broiled with butter and garlic, preferably by someone else. Whatever happened to the little red wagon, though?" he asked Paddy affectionately, dropping his arm over the other man's shoulder.

"Never mind," Paddy retorted, letting Terence's arm linger a moment. But then he stepped away. "The boat's coming in; let's go."

Terence looked crestfallen, covered it smoothly, but not before I caught the look of deep hurt on his face. The ferry slid aground with a scrape of its metal ramp on the beach gravel. Then we were boarding, climbing the metal ramp while cars and sports utility vehicles—most with out-of-state license plates, filled with tourists—went alongside us onto the bargelike vessel.

The grumble of diesel engines propelled the ferry back out onto the water, and we were away, the island town receding behind us and an onshore breeze gusting freshly.

"Great day," Terence called over the engine noise, putting his face into the wind. The tide was running hard, so the ferry pilot skirted the edge of Old Sow, the largest whirlpool in the Western Hemisphere and a navigation hazard even to bigger boats. At the moment its turbulence was like water in a washing machine when the agitator is churning, the difference being that this was *millions* of gallons of water.

Below us, it hammered like fists through narrow channels and slammed against granite ledges, assaulted the tall, precipitous cliffs of underwater islands and gouted up in unseen geysers, in a maelstrom that was mostly not visible from the swirling surface. If you happened to fall into it, though, it would suck you down in a frigid heartbeat and deposit your body miles away.

"It might not," Terence said startlingly, seeming to read my thought, "be a bad way to go. Quick. Decisive."

Paddy was busy paying our fares. "You don't really mean that," I told Terence. "It wouldn't seem fast while you were doing it. Drowning, in that cold water."

He shrugged, glancing at me. "I suppose it depends on your alternatives."

Which was another very odd remark from the usually cheerful Terence; he suffered from hypochondria but in an interested way, not a glum one. Then Paddy approached and Terence's warning glance made me change the subject.

"What happened to your hand?" I gestured at the Ace bandage. "Looks like you gave your first-aid talents a real workout."

Terence frowned uncomfortably. "Took a fall. It's nothing."

But the remark brought to mind again his unsteady episode in La Sardina. And the look on his face was guarded; an unhappy idea struck me. "Terence, are you all right?"

"Never better," he replied shortly, turning away.

Clearly, he didn't want to talk about it. His business; I decided to concentrate on Paddy.

"Why were you so upset that Reuben had come back?" I asked. "I mean, I wouldn't think you and he would have much to do with each other, in the normal course of things."

Paddy's brow furrowed as he leaned on the ferry rail, gazing down into the now-serene water; we'd rounded the whirlpool margin and were on course for the little harbor at Deer Island.

"First of all, there was nothing normal about him.

See, that's what most people don't understand: Reuben was pathological, and he was smart. Too smart. If he wanted you, he found you. And . . ."

He hesitated, considering. "Well, it'll be common knowledge. In Eastport, everything is. Reuben came to see me the other night. Jittering around, hopped up on tequila. Said he wanted my help on something, offered me a deal he said was surefire."

Listening in silence, Terence chuckled bitterly as if the term were an unpleasant private joke, but said nothing.

"What did Reuben mean?" I asked. "What kind of a deal?"

Paddy shook his head. "It doesn't matter. What matters is, I didn't go for it. Told him to get out. When he left, he had that grin on his face, and he was laughing. You know the laugh?"

The high, strangled whinny, like a cross between a cough and a man's last breath; I knew.

"Scared me pretty badly, I'll admit," Paddy went on. "That Reuben could freeze your heart up."

The impatience I'd been restraining since the night before overcame me. "Oh, for Pete's sake. He was just one guy. I don't care how bad he was—how'd he get a whole town so petrified?"

Paddy turned slowly to me. "Right. That's what anyone would think. Anyone who didn't know him. But let me tell you a story."

He lifted his eyes, letting his gaze wander past the high promontory of Deer Island to the passage beyond: blue water all the way to Nova Scotia, which lay like a strip of autumn gold on the far horizon.

"Reuben wasn't just a bully," Paddy said. "He was a criminal: burglaries, arson. If he wanted money, or he just wanted to hurt you, he would do something. And once he had done it, he would get away with it, too; Reuben always did."

"Which," I came back at him, "is what I don't understand. Why was he walking around? Seems to me Bob Arnold could put a guy like that in jail, double-quick."

"That," Paddy replied, "is what I'm telling you about."

We were crossing the international boundary between the United States and Canada, an invisible line down the middle of Passamaquoddy Bay. To our left rose Deer Island, sloping to pebble beaches and finally to sand. On our right lay the island of Campobello, long and low, its little towns toylike along the shoreline. The ferry adjusted course for the final approach to the Deer Island dock.

"Once upon a time, a man from town complained—it's not important about what. A charge was brought against Reuben, and the man promised to testify against him."

Paddy recited tonelessly. "A week later, the fellow who brought the charge was found in his cellar. Slipped and hit his head on a foundation stone, everybody said."

He looked at me. "But they all knew." The ferry slid against the wooden dock pilings, her ramp scraping bottom.

People and cars began moving toward the shore as the deck hand lowered the chain at the bow of the ferry, but I hung back. "They thought Reuben killed him, to stop him from testifying?"

"Not thought," Paddy corrected. "Knew. Reuben would kill your house pets or poison your well. He would terrify your wife and menace your children. He would terrify *anyone*. Which is why," he finished, "nobody ever told on Reuben. As for testifying against him, well, that was a joke. You might as well kill yourself."

We got off the ferry. Uphill stood a small log-cabin

snack bar and souvenir shop, a drinking fountain, and some rough frame buildings containing sanitary facilities. Paddy's old green Peugeot was parked beside the snack bar where his mechanic—the only Peugeot man in five hundred miles—had apparently left it for him.

"But not you," I said as we drove down the narrow, paved two-lane leading out from the dock area. It curved immediately into scrubby, second-growth evergreen forest dotted here and there with modest homesteads: cottages and trailers. A mountain of sand loomed beside a public-works barn, ready for winter.

"Not me," Paddy agreed grimly. "I stood up to him. Me and a few others. That was the key to it, see. Standing up to him. Then he'd back off."

We passed through a crossroads: church, general store with a post office, a diner, and a cluster of dwellings. At a low wharf a battered dragger was tied, its deck piled with lobster traps. Then we were in the country again, finally at the entrance to a warren of lanes lined with cottages.

"So, what was the surefire deal?" I asked again.

He turned right, left, at last down an unmarked rut. "Bottom line was, Reuben said he going to reenact history. You know the big Eastport fire in the late 1800s, took down most of Water Street? He said he could make it all happen again, starting with my place."

The thought made me cringe. His big old building with its antique brick exterior, so gorgeously refurbished inside and with its glorious view, wasn't only a showpiece of old-time Eastport architecture. It was Paddy's baby, so precious to him I sometimes thought the design business was only an excuse for using it in a legitimately tax-deductible way.

Meanwhile, I'd seen pictures of the Eastport fire. They looked as if a bomb had gone off in the middle of Water Street. It had burned right up one side and down the other, leaving only blocks of charred devastation.

"Unless, of course, I wanted to help him with his big plan," Paddy added grimly.

"Help him *what*?" At the end of the lane he pulled to a halt and we got out. Across a short stretch of pasture the water lay flat and motionless, at slack tide.

The silence was stunning. We walked on a grassy path between evergreens smelling of pine sap. A dalmation romped out of the trees at us, grinning, its pink tongue lolling. Terence bent and fondled its ears.

"I was supposed to help blackmail your ex-husband. Scare him into thinking I knew whatever it was that Reuben had on him—not that Reuben would really tell me, you understand, he was too smart to give away his game—and warn him that he ought to pay."

Overhead, a bald eagle circled lazily, just riding the thermals and sailing so low I could see his white helmet, shaggy-feathered white legs, and thick, curving talons: hunting.

"Not that I would have," Paddy added. "It just goes to show how nuts Reuben was, that he would ask me."

We were approaching a house with a rail-fenced garden and some mulched rose beds. "He'd tried that, tried to bully you, back in the old days? When you were growing up together in Eastport?"

Paddy nodded, as the dalmation loped over to me, a frisky creature with coltlike legs. No leash, only a fabric collar from which hung a stamped metal ID tag. Talk about a dog's life.

"What did you tell him?" I asked. "When he came to see you the other night?"

I was still trying to imagine Reuben with his black leather jacket, pegged pants, and cleated boots, in that pristine studio of Paddy's: clicking on the tiles, making demands, and breathing tequila fumes.

Paddy would have hated it. It would have made him angry.

Very angry. And only a few nights later, Reuben was dead.

"I told him go to hell," Paddy replied. "He wasn't going to burn my building. Because he knew if he did I would find him. And then," Paddy finished flatly, "I would kill him."

I was about to ask him if he knew the other victim, the one found suffocated on Water Street. Reuben, it seemed more and more to me, was a such a larger-than-life kind of a person, his death pushed the other one to the background. And no one had yet said anything about any connection between the victims. But I couldn't believe there had been two unrelated murders in Eastport on a single night.

I didn't get to ask Paddy anything, though, because he pushed aside the evergreen branches abruptly, striding away from us down the sun-dappled path toward the house, leaving his final words hanging in the silence.

"Not that he did, of course," Terence said mildly. He drew aside the pine boughs, inviting me to go first.

"Kill Reuben, I mean," he added, following behind.

Paddy's sketch artist lived in a small, ranch-style cottage a hundred feet from an inlet studded with dozens of tiny islands, granite boulders thrusting up through the water's surface.

I wandered to the water's edge. The dog came, too, picking his way delicately on the small stones. The small waves reflected the sunshine glassily, as if lit from below. A scuffling splash, followed by the swoop of the eagle back up into his own bright element, signaled the doom of some poor fish struggling at the ends of those sharp talons.

"Quiet," Terence said suddenly, startling me.

He tossed a pebble into the water. "Not like back in town. All the people, visiting from away."

Another pebble. "Paddy won't talk to me about Reuben."

That troubled me. Just looking at those two, you knew they talked about everything under the sun. Or they had, but something had changed; not for the better.

"The murder . . . he won't discuss it at all," Terence said. "I'm surprised he is with you. Taxes," he twinkled briefly, "or no taxes."

There was the Terence I remembered, funny and kind. Almost at once, though, some deep worry returned to his features.

"So I haven't said this to him, but . . ."

He gestured out at the marine setting. It seemed to go on forever, and for all practical purposes it did. "All that water. So deep and cold. A cove somewhere, weigh a body down with enough stones, or just let the current take it. And bingo, it's gone."

"I've been wondering about that, too. No one ever needed to know Tate was dead," I agreed. "But instead someone took a lot of trouble displaying him. Like," I added, "an art object."

The tide turned and larger waves began slapping on the beach pebbles. Terence's face was thinner than I remembered seeing it over the summer.

"Cemetery fences are supposed to keep spirits in," I added. "You don't suppose that was it?" Wanting to keep him talking, I tried for a tone of casual lightness. "Maybe someone thought Tate was demon enough that his spirit needed to be kept imprisoned."

"Someone should have tried it when he was alive," Terence blurted angrily. But in the next moment he was composed again.

"Anyway, he was tied to the outside of the gate. People with family buried inside are glad of that much. That's what I've heard. So if confining him was what someone wanted they got it wrong. He's no more confined in the spirit world than he was here on earth."

Terence picked up a stick of driftwood and threw it; the dog raced after it, flinging himself into the water and racing back, shaking off bright droplets.

"Why do you think he was hung there, Terence?" I asked.

He threw the stick again. "Messages," he said cryptically.

But I got it; it was what I'd been thinking also, although until that moment I hadn't known it.

"Hanging him up there, showing him off . . ."

Terence nodded. The dog trotted away, tired of the game or perhaps just having had enough of the icy water.

"I don't know why Reuben Tate was killed," Terence went on, dropping the stick on the beach stones. "Although," he added, "I am still not convinced that you believe it."

The eyes in his homely face were insightful, intelligent, and wary. "But," he said, "it occurs to me that having all the Salmon Festival visitors in town enlarges the suspect pool. Some of them grew up alongside Reuben, too."

"And might have had a grudge against him," I agreed. "An old score to settle, something to do with the past."

"If someone was here in Eastport for only a week," he added reasonably, "and managed to escape suspicion that long, once they went home the odds would go up that they would never be caught."

His tone was mild, his expression serene, the view of water and islands so idyllic it seemed that nothing could go amiss in it. But when I turned to reply, I saw that he'd begun putting small, wet beach stones into his mouth, stuffing them in one after another.

Alarm pierced me. There was something really wrong with him. "Terence," I said sharply, and my tone seemed to bring him back to himself.

But not all the way. He spat the stones out slowly, looking at me as if he could not quite remember what he'd been doing.

Just then, Paddy's face showed at the window of the artist's studio. "It's about time he remembered that we're here," Terence remarked as if nothing had happened, and turned back to the car.

His walk wasn't right. He was dragging one leg. "Terence," I insisted as I hurried after him, "wait."

But he wouldn't, or couldn't. As I followed I could hear him breathing in harsh laboring gusts as if he were in sudden pain.

"If you've got that far," he advised, grating the words out, "think about something else. Ask yourself . . ." He stopped, stiffening with anguish, ". . . whether Reuben Tate's body up on that cemetery gate, displayed there like some bloody, appalling human banner—"

He reached the cottage's rail fence, fell against it. "Maybe Reuben's death, and the way he died, wasn't the whole message."

Paddy rushed out, his face full of concern. Twenty minutes later we were back on the ferry as the sun began setting, filling the sky with red. When I asked Terence again what the trouble was, he muttered indistinctly something about an old back injury.

But back injuries don't make you put little stones into your mouth. And Paddy still looked distraught, in contrast to his cool manner to Terence earlier.

Later, when he had Terence settled on a bench alongside the pilot house, Paddy stood with me at the rail of the ferry as it plunged through the chop, spewing salt spray. A breeze had come up suddenly, the weather feeling changeable and the clouds still hanging on the western horizon; they had been there for days.

Paddy spoke regretfully, but not about Terence,

and at the private, fiercely protective look in his eyes I decided not to ask. Instead, he talked about the past.

"I've often wondered why we let it go on," he mused. "All of us guys who went around together back then. We knew, but somehow we didn't believe. How bad Reuben could be. How *evil.*"

I felt that he was trying to direct me away from the topic of his most recent meeting with Tate. For now, I let him.

"Did Wade know? Or George Valentine? Were they also in the group that hung around together?"

Paddy nodded, his eyes fixed on the bright points of light that were Eastport, gleaming in the dusk.

"Yes. But Reuben wouldn't bother them, Wade especially, and George, I think, because he was Wade's friend. Something happened between those two, Wade and Reuben. I'm not sure what."

He turned suddenly to me. "It wasn't the first time, you know. That necktie thing. It was Reuben's doing, I'm sure of it. He'd done it that way before. Or anyway," he added, "everyone in town said he did. It wasn't," he gave the words a bitter twist, "anything that could be proved."

Of course not. This was Reuben Tate we were talking about. From the sound of it, he could have gotten away with kidnaping the Lindbergh baby.

It was nearly full dark but in the deck lamps of the ferry Paddy's eyes shone unhappily. "What bothers me," he said, "is why we tolerated him, even after we knew the things he'd done. It was as if . . ." He broke off, sounding mystified.

"That's the trouble with evil," Terence said suddenly from behind us. His voice was tired but it had regained the amused, faintly ironic tone it usually carried; at the sound of it I saw Paddy's shoulders sag with relief.

"The banality of evil," Terence said. "After a while, it comes to seem so . . . normal. You get used to it. Like," he finished mildly with a glance at Paddy, "almost everything."

Paddy flinched; something, I thought again, going on between them. The ferry nosed in toward the dock.

Once ashore Paddy offered to drive me home, but I refused in favor of the privacy of my thoughts, riding along only as far as the design studio. Terence didn't speak again at all, except to say goodbye with his usual politeness. But by then he didn't have to say any more, or Paddy either:

They'd told me—not meaning to, but it was in their faces and voices—that more had gone on between Paddy and Reuben than Reuben's threat and Paddy's rejection of it.

The mood between them remained uncomfortable too, despite Paddy's newfound solicitude; whatever was happening to them in their personal lives, it wasn't a pleasant development.

And something else: Terence had articulated an intuition I hadn't known I had.

A message: if I could find out what it meant and whom it was intended for—

—or so Terence seemed to believe, and at the moment I was taking his opinion seriously; he had fought through a lot of pain in order to finish telling it to me—

—I might have a line that led to the killer, or at any rate to enough reasonable doubt to begin taking the heat off Victor.

It was Terence's idea about the message having more parts, though, that bothered me the most. There had, after all, been two murders: one with a tie, the other with Victor's antique scalpel.

Maybe Reuben had done the first one, as Paddy thought.

But maybe not. Maybe Paddy was lying, or simply wrong, and someone else had committed both crimes.

And if they were linked, and intended to mean

something, if they'd been done to *communicate* something, somehow . . .

Then it seemed to me that a clear, unambiguous translation was needed.

Soon.

Before the next bloody syllable got transmitted.

11

It was past dinnertime, and I was thinking tiredly of just ordering pizza. But by the time I got home, Ellie had taken over my kitchen and prepared a feast of local delicacies: bay scallops *en casserole* with buttered bread crumbs, fresh tomatoes drizzled in basil vinaigrette, tiny potatoes steamed in their crisp, dark-red jackets, and blueberry cobbler.

"Oh, thank you," I said, taking in the air of calm, domestic competence that had descended on my household like a blessing, as she handed me a glass of wine. "How did you know I would be . . ."

So late, I was about to say, but of course she had known; no doubt somebody downtown had seen me boarding the ferry. The wine was very cold, scouring away the bad taste the afternoon had left in my mouth. And fresh whipped cream, I noted happily, had been made for the cobbler. All I had to do was sit down at the table and eat it, which is the part of Maine cuisine I am best at.

"I don't understand half what I saw and heard today," I said when we were all gathered in the dining room. Ellie had lit candles, and the tin ceilings, pressed with the pattern of acorns and oak leaves, glowed warmly with the flickering light. "But I'm sure Paddy Farrell wasn't being straight with me."

I didn't mention Terence's illness or that his relationship with Paddy seemed to have hit a snag; it didn't seem pertinent.

"Paddy said Reuben wanted him to help blackmail Victor," I went on, "but that doesn't strike me as particularly likely. Why would Reuben think Paddy would help him with anything?"

"You've got that right. He hated Tate like poison. But Paddy Farrell," George Valentine said, applying himself to his meal, "can be cagey when he wants to be. He isn't what you'd call the gold standard for information about Tate."

"You mean he lies? But why?"

Wade shook his head. "Wouldn't go that far, necessarily. But Paddy will leave things out of most anything, when it suits him. Which," he added, "plenty often it does. Might go further, if he thought a fib might make him look better."

It was true enough about his taxes, certainly. He'd tried deducting Terence's vitamins and herbal potions, for heaven's sake, under the heading of "miscellaneous chemicals."

"And for a while there," Wade continued, "Paddy was real scared of Reuben."

I remembered Paddy's angry defiance, which in retrospect did seem like protesting too much. "The way he went on," I said, "you would think Reuben was the one afraid of *him*."

In the dining-room windows, the candles' reflections flared like signal lights. "I hope the weather holds," Ellie fretted, glancing up at them, "at least until after the Salmon Festival."

"Ellie, you've been doing all you can about the festival," George assured her. "Besides, the weekend is still six days off. Not even you can control the weather from that distance."

His tone turned serious. "You might," he said to me, "want to talk to a few more people. Get a more balanced view of things. If," he added, "you really want to go on with this at all."

"Like who? Besides Paddy," it was dawning unwelcomely on me as I said it, "I don't even know where to start."

Wade met my gaze. "You could try Mike Carpentier," he offered slowly. "Knows just about everyone. And he was hooked up with Reuben somehow, seems like I heard."

Ellie frowned. "I never knew that. Mike's years younger. What would he have been doing with Reuben?"

Wade shrugged. "What I heard. Not saying it's gospel. I'll bet he's got some stories, though, even if that one isn't true."

"But they'll be stories of . . ." I began, and then it hit me, as Wade nodded.

"Long ago," I finished. "Like Paddy's but maybe not so many lies. Not embroidered or with things left out. And you think . . ."

"Reuben had only been back in town a few days," Ellie agreed.

"And the way he got killed, seems like somebody was madder at him than even he could make somebody, in that short amount of time," George said, following her thought.

"But," Sam objected, "if it was revenge for something that happened a while ago, why wait so long?"

"Right," Tommy Daigle chimed in; Sam had spent the evening helping him haul the engine out of his jalopy. I hadn't thought they could do it, but Sam had rigged up a pulley device that he said lessened immensely the amount of work required.

"Tate was back to town other times, my mom said," Tommy informed us. "Raised a lot of—"

Hell, Tommy had meant to say, but caught himself. His mother was an old-fashioned disciplinarian, and it showed.

"Ruckus," he finished carefully. "So why now?"

Wade looked thoughtful. "Maybe revenge wasn't all of it. You can put bad things in the past, if they happened then and they're over and done with. But if you thought that same thing was about to happen again . . ."

"Once burnt, twice shy," Ellie agreed, as one of the candles began smoking and George pinched it out.

Their remarks made me think again about the past and the present somehow coming together, connecting the victims in some way I didn't yet understand. I took a sip of the wine Ellie had refilled for me, and chose my words carefully.

"Are any of you"—I didn't include the boys, of course—"going to be sorry if I start really digging into this? Because you're all part of this town's past, too, you know."

I let the rest go unspoken: that Reuben Tate's venom seemed to have touched almost everyone in Eastport. That when you went poking into old secrets, sometimes you also opened old wounds, ones you hadn't even known were there. And sometimes those old wounds belonged to your friends.

I wasn't asking permission, exactly. But I needed to know.

"Least said, soonest mended, in my view," George commented. "Bury him and be done with it, my best advice ordinarily. Mess with Reuben or anything to do with him, get messed up yourself."

He spoke easily. "But then there's Victor. Don't guess you can just let him keep swinging in the breeze."

Ellie tapped her wineglass thoughtfully. "Ordinarily, I'd agree: We're well rid of Reuben and the less said about him the better. But this is different. And he never hung any skeletons in my closet, I'm glad to say."

Wade nodded, but not as decisively as George or

Ellie. "You just do what you have to," he allowed, "let the chips fall."

Not an especially reassuring reply on his part, but at the moment it was all I would get; Wade wasn't the type to unburden himself at the dinner table.

Later, I looked wordlessly at him, and he nodded.

Afterward in the kitchen, helping to dry the dishes, Tommy Daigle informed me that he and Sam were combining the mystery of otherworldly spirit communications with the technological genius of Samuel Morse, by asking the Ouija board to spell its messages out to them in Morse code.

Tommy had a round, freckled face that reminded me of Howdy Doody's, topped with a thick shock of hair so red it made Ellie's look strawberry blond. He'd stuck with Sam pretty much all day, except when he was at home doing the Saturday chores arranged for him by his mother, and I felt grateful to him for it.

"Why do you want messages from spirits, anyway?" I asked, resisting the impulse to brush Tommy's hair out of his eyes. In the city, Sam hadn't had friends like this: simple, steadfast.

"Maybe," Sam said, putting away silverware, "it'll say who killed Reuben."

Tommy brushed his hair back for himself, revealing the dent in his forehead, over his right eye. It was deep and square, a white brand mark without any freckles in it, as if somebody had hit him with a tack hammer a long time ago. I didn't know how he'd really gotten it.

"And who killed the other guy, too," he enthused to Sam. "I mean, hey, it ought to know."

Which I supposed was logical but would be unhelpful even in the (I hoped) very unlikely event that it happened; Ouija-board testimony, I felt sure, cut no ice with district attorneys. What we needed was some shred of actual proof.

But I didn't say this, not wanting to quash their

optimism; Sam had eaten all of his dinner and no longer looked so depressed. When they'd finished in the kitchen, they hurried off to tune in the pregame show and question George about his knowledge of Morse code; I heard him tapping dot-and-dash patterns for them on the living room coffee table, while I wiped off the counters a final time and Ellie hung the dish towels on their hooks.

"Terence thinks one of the visitors for the Salmon Festival may have had it in for Reuben," I said.

"That's possible." Wearing yellow rubber gloves, she rinsed the dish sponge with scalding water, which is what the plumbing in my old house delivers when it is not delivering ice-cold. "But the problem with Reuben is, there are so *many* likely candidates for his murder."

"So I gather. Too bad none of them were in possession of the weapon. But I was hoping you could narrow the field for me. You knowing just about everyone, I mean."

She squeezed the sponge out and stripped off the gloves. "We can't focus on all his enemies, that's a given."

Like everyone, she seemed to assume that Reuben's death was the important one, the other just a sort of tag-along. Probably it hadn't seemed that way to the guy with the tie in his throat; still, in terms of starting to sort this whole mess out, it was very likely true.

She said as much. "Reuben was the one who would have inspired the big-time motive, enough to commit murder about. I really haven't heard anything about the other guy, and I would have if he was in the habit of doing anything even mildly interesting. So it does make some sense to focus on Reuben."

She snapped off the kitchen light. "The trouble is, there are hundreds of people in town now, not counting the ones who live here, who knew Reuben and didn't like him. To put it," she added, "mildly."

She spread her hands in a this-is-obvious gesture. "We can't question them all about their history with him, learn what they were doing before—and during—the time he was being murdered."

"Right." I was getting impatient.

"But," she pointed out acutely, "there was only one, thank goodness, of Reuben. We could focus on *him*."

I noted that she'd begun using the first-person plural. "We? Are you sure you want to be involved in this? You don't even like Victor, and he's the one who's really in trouble."

Besides, she already had a big project on her plate, getting ready for the festival. And I hadn't missed her visceral little shiver of distaste whenever the subject of Reuben came up.

What I kept forgetting, though, were her bloodlines full of seagoing rogues and rascals. Unlike their tropical brethren, the old cold-water outlaws of the downeast Maine coast were notorious not so much for their savagery to outsiders as for their loyalty to one another. Cross ways with them and they might only relieve you of your valuables; injure one, and the rest would grind your bones to make their bread.

"What else," she inquired, "are friends for?"

12

Later that evening Wade and I went over to check on Victor's house; the state police, Bob Arnold had let Wade know, were done with it for now, so we could lock it up.

The black arrowhead daggers of the old, ornate cast-iron fence around the front yard seemed to bristle at us as we opened the creaking gate. Six tall white pillars formed a long, graceful colonnade along the house front, dropping bars of deeper shadow onto the porch. We passed the green-shuttered windows of the front parlor to a side door that led into a small sitting room.

Inside, the air was still and faintly stale-smelling, even though Victor's cleaning help kept the house sparkling enough to do surgery in. It certainly did not have the air of inhabitedness that mine did, the sense of welcome. Without Victor in it, I felt immediately the dark vacancy of the rooms.

Quickly, I went around turning on lights. The investigators had not made a mess of things, or at least not the awful one I had expected. There were smudges of what I supposed must be fingerprint powder. Papers had been riffled through, not left in the order that Victor would have. Drawers had been emptied, their contents scattered, and manila folders lay out on the desk.

But there was no sign of the callous ransacking that I had feared. Victor's fastidiousness was elemental to him, and even after all that had happened between us, I did not, I realized as I noted my own relief, want him utterly destroyed even by proxy.

"There's too much I don't understand," I complained as Wade pulled the drapes and checked the lock on the back door. "All of you seem to think that what happened to Reuben Tate was justice. As if he, or anyone, could have deserved that . . . that atrocity."

On a low table, the day's heap of letters and journals lay where the detectives had left them, after bringing them in and going through them. Wade squared up the pile and set it on a bookcase in which Victor's medical books were grouped by category.

"But I just don't believe in that kind of justice," I said. "Maybe there are exceptions to the rules we've come up with to deal with renegades, but I wouldn't know how to pick them. And it worries me," I finished, "to find out that maybe you do."

I could see him thinking about how to reply as we went into the rest of the downstairs rooms, then to the cellar. Wade checked the pilot light on the furnace, rattled the cellar door, peered into the fuse box. Everything seemed shipshape.

But it was like going through a house after somebody in it had died. Back on the main floor in the front hall stood Victor's antique instrument case, its glass doors open, its contents taken away. Evidence, I supposed, though I didn't see of what.

"That collection was the only thing he brought with him from New York," I said, hoping someone had at least made a list of it. "That and his clothes. Back in the city, he kept souvenirs of his girlfriends: photographs, letters. He had a little black book the size of the Manhattan telephone directory."

Or so it had seemed to me when I'd come upon it one day when I was still married to Victor, while I was cleaning closets.

"But Sam says he got rid of it all," I said. "Took the black book and tore the pages out of it, tore those up, and flushed them down the toilet. Sold his little sports car, stereo, all that kind of thing. All his city toys."

We went up to check the second floor, and Wade climbed the third-floor stairs to make sure the attic door was closed.

"Don't want squirrels moving from there into the house," he explained, coming back down again. "So Victor was really turning over a new leaf."

"Right," I said. A bitter little laugh bubbled up in me at the idea of Victor having squirrels in his attic.

Real squirrels, I mean. "He was never going to be what you might call personally well adjusted," I went on. "But he was trying. For once, he was trying hard. Which is another reason why what's happening to him now isn't . . ."

We went back downstairs. The investigators had

left a light on in the display case. Wade reached in and switched it off, its fluorescent hum leaving a louder silence where it had been.

"Justice," he finished my sentence for me. "You're right, it isn't. I don't think Victor killed Reuben any more than you do. And you're wondering if I think what happened to Reuben out there at Hillside Cemetery—if I think that *was* justice."

"Something like that," I agreed. "That's part of it. And if you do, why?"

It struck me that there were a hundred other things Wade could have been doing, and that I could have closed up Victor's house myself. He just hadn't wanted me to have to do it alone.

"Let's go home," he said, "have a drink, just the two of us in peace and quiet at the kitchen table."

"That sounds wonderful." But Wade's face was stony.

"And I'll tell you," he finished, "a story about justice."

13

When Sam was a little boy, he peered curiously at the pages of the storybooks I read constantly to him. But no matter how often or patiently I pointed at the words and pronounced them, or sounded them out for him, he couldn't learn to read.

What he liked were jumble puzzles. Every morning starting when he was seven or so, he seized the comic pages, located the anagram puzzle and solved it speedily and triumphantly. Some of the words in the puzzles were really rather difficult, but not for Sam. Yet he couldn't decode the simplest printed sentence, a trouble that frustrated us both.

Later I learned that the wiring in his brain was a tiny bit scrambled. His perception problem was such that if the letters of a word were presented to him separately, or in jumbled fashion, he could sort them, but if they came at him all at once or in proper order, he couldn't.

Now, sitting alone at the kitchen table in my old house in Maine, I thought about another little boy with the improbable name of Boxy Thorogood. He'd had a reading problem, too, Wade had told me; Wade himself had been a teenager at the time, but he'd heard his mother and Mrs. Thorogood discussing it.

Boxy's real problem, though, had been more serious. A lot more serious.

On the table before me lay that dratted Ouija board, which Sam and Tommy kept moving in and out of the dining room. Idly, I fingered the planchette.

Wade hadn't remembered why Reuben Tate had taken such a harsh view of Boxy. A foolish reason, he said, or no reason at all. It didn't matter. What mattered was that Reuben would do something to Boxy, to hurt him. All the boys knew it; Boxy did, too. They just didn't know what or when.

An only child, fatherless, skinny and small for his age, the boy spent weeks trying to avoid his nemesis. But each night after supper, Boxy's mother—a good woman, but she had her habits—sent him for a pack of Pall Malls and a half-pint of Seagram's, brooking no argument if Boxy tried getting out of the errand.

So poor Boxy rode his bicycle down Washington Street fast, night after night, knowing that sooner or later Reuben Tate was going to be there to pounce on him. He could run, but he couldn't hide; it wouldn't end until Reuben got whatever cruel pleasure he wanted. Reuben always did.

Then one day Reuben took Wade aside, and some of the other boys, too. "Boxy," he said, a weird grin spreading on his face. He took a roll of high-test fishing line from his pocket, showed it around.

"Boxy," he repeated, and giggled. He was sixteen, then. Wade was seventeen, and the other boys were around that age, too.

Boxy Thorogood was maybe eleven, the same age Sam was when I found him one afternoon in his bedroom, sobbing. The teacher, he said, had called him stupid. Anyway:

None of the boys who heard Reuben threaten Boxy said anything to their parents, or to any adult. They didn't tell Boxy, either. It was hard to explain, Wade said, but somehow they didn't think Reuben would really do it. It didn't seem . . . real.

It got real, though, the next night as Boxy flew down the hill on his bike. Someone had stretched a length of high-test fishing line from one side of the street to the other.

At the speed Boxy was traveling, the fishing line was almost a guillotine.

"He flew off the bike," Wade reported, "hit the big brick building at the far side of Water Street, bounced off, landed on the sidewalk."

The building that Paddy had turned into a design studio years later. Wade didn't see the attack, he had added, but plenty of people did: not who'd done it, but the result. Wade hadn't found out until the next morning. When he got up, his parents were over at Boxy's house already, trying to take care of Boxy's mother.

"It happened," Wade finished, "because I didn't tell what Reuben was planning."

He looked at me. "So when you talk about justice, keep Boxy in mind. It's why some people think the only thing wrong with what happened to Reuben is, it didn't take long enough."

He got up and put his hand on my hair. I reached up and held it tightly, understanding now precisely the depth of Reuben Tate's evil, what it had done to Wade and would go on doing as long as he lived.

"You weren't drinking at La Sardina because you knew he was around," I said. "You didn't want to be . . ."

"Yep. Don't want a buzz on, I see Reuben. Clear head, plenty of self-control." He sighed deeply. "It's the only way."

He spoke as if Reuben were still alive. "And you didn't tell, afterwards? About Reuben and Boxy?"

His hand slipped away. "I did. The others, too. But Reuben denied it, said we were all liars who had it in for him, and the fact was, no one had seen him do it. There was no proof. In the end, nothing happened to Reuben."

The refrain was getting familiar. "Well, something's happened to him now. Thanks for telling me why you're not sorry. I wouldn't be, either."

It was very late. Wade hesitated. "I never told that story before," he said finally, looking a little startled and perhaps a shade sorry at the realization that, irrevocably, now he had.

I thought about how I might feel, as opposed to the idea of how I ought to. "And you'd like to be alone a little while?" I asked. "Get used to the idea?"

His face cleared, and the look he gave me was warmer than any embrace. "Go on," I said, "try to get some sleep. I'll be up in a while."

Moments later I'd heard him going upstairs. I don't know how long I sat there at the table after that, thinking about justice and wondering what was in Reuben's heart, at the end. And about what Terence Oscard had said about evil: that in time it begins to seem normal.

"Mom?"

Sam's voice startled me; coming to myself, I saw that my hand was moving the planchette on the surface of the Ouija board, sliding it in short arcs.

Sam stood in the kitchen doorway in his pajamas, milk glass in his hand.

"Need a refill?" AEDAAA, my hand spelled out meaninglessly; EEDDDAAADDD. An idle motion, like worrying a cuticle or twisting a lock of hair.

"Yeah. Didn't know you were here. What'cha doing with that?" He opened the refrigerator.

"Nothing. Just fidgeting. Sitting here thinking."

"Uh-huh." He frowned at me, pouring the milk. "That thing only works with two people, I thought. Or more. Isn't that what you told me?"

"That's what I've heard." The board's surface was smooth and somehow relaxing under my hand. The sliding helped me to think.

"So why," Sam asked quietly, "does it keep on saying that?"

"Saying what?" I asked innocently, and then I saw it. But of course Sam had spotted it first, the anagram over and over:

DEAD DEAD DEAD.

14

The next morning Ellie and I drove past the lot where the Eastport railway depot once stood. In the nineteenth century the town had been a hub of shipbuilding and commerce: its society as stratified as Boston's, its culture refined, its fads as intense and frivolous. Spiritualism—seances, mediums, and so on—had enjoyed a heyday here, for example, in the 1890s.

"I have no idea," I confessed, "what to think of it." The Ouija board, I meant. The moment I'd seen what it was spelling, it had gone motionless.

In the vacant lot, bindweed and wildflowers had taken over the place where whalebone-corseted ladies had stood on the rail platform, supervising imperiously their trunks being transferred from wagon to baggage car, while the great steam engine took on water and its firebox expelled glowing cinders. When Franklin D. Roosevelt was felled by polio at his summer place on Campobello, it was from Eastport that he began the sad journey home: to war, and into a pair of leg braces.

"I don't see," Ellie replied, "why you should think anything of it at all."

Now the once-massive roundhouse foundation was a circular patch of cracked concrete, grown through by asters. At its edges you could still find clinkers from the locomotives' fireboxes.

"After all," she continued reasonably, "just because a thing produces words doesn't mean it's got anything to say."

Which I thought was a little beside the point. But her brisk commonsense tone eased my mind somewhat, and it was a brilliant day: the sun shining, white popcorn clouds scudding across the blue sky, waving fields of Queen Anne's lace and goldenrod so lovely you forgot all about hay fever.

Ellie turned onto County Road, heading south toward Sodom's Head and the water. Just before the road slanted down to the old salt works, she made a sharp right; moments later we were driving along the coveside, past a few small dwellings interspersed with unkempt pastures and abandoned cellar holes.

"I hope Mike Carpentier's got something to say." I braced myself against the dashboard as Ellie stopped suddenly for a pair of eiderducks waddling across the road. When they had passed she shoved the Jeep grindingly into gear again and trod on the gas.

"He's a place to start," Ellie replied as the road surface roughened, heaved by freeze and thaw and the attentions of winter snowplows. She swerved for a pothole, hit another. My teeth only loosened a little bit.

When I got control of them again, I told her more about my trip with Paddy and Terence.

She listened without comment. As I finished, we were nearing the end of the Cove Road. To our left lay the quiet inlet, calm as a wading pool. Straight ahead: Cobscook Bay and a sharp, two-foot chop, whiffs of sea foam blowing off the whitecaps.

"If they were having a fight, Paddy might give him the cold shoulder. To show him," Ellie went on, "what it would be like if they really separated."

"But when Terence collapsed in pain, Paddy dropped the act and showed his real feelings."

"Something like that, I'll bet. Paddy *adores* Terence," she said. "As who wouldn't? Terence is a sweetie. I hope there isn't anything serious wrong with him. Or between them, either." She swung the Jeep off the pavement, to the grassy side of the road.

A chill, bracing wind blew steadily across the water. In the distance, little boats hustled back and forth from the shore to the salmon pens: feeding, medicating, and tending the thousands of fish being raised in net enclosures under the water.

I got out. "Where's the house?"

She pointed. "Up there."

I followed her gesture past an old Ford Escort nosed into the grass, saw a hill the approximate size of Mount Everest plus plenty of burdock. It was an especially prickly species of the weedy vegetation, too: the kind that, defying common sense and all the descriptions in the botany books, can leap six inches to get its hooks into you.

Fortunately there was a path, but halfway up it the score was already me nothing, burdocks a million. Eventually I called a halt to pull some of the clinging, maddeningly prickly spheres of dark brown plant matter out of my socks.

"Who is this guy?" I gasped. "And why does he

live behind the vegetable-kingdom equivalent of a moat?"

"He wants to discourage casual visits, that much is clear."

Which didn't quite explain it. This uphill trip on a narrow burdock-lined path, by turns stony, slippery with damp grass, and infested with red ants, would have discouraged the Mongol hordes.

"And," Ellie went on, climbing another twenty yards with the ease of a mountain goat, then turning to smile encouragingly down at me, "Mike is an unusual person."

"Yeah. He's got wings. He doesn't walk up, he just flies up. Like a vampire bat." I already had a mental picture of Mike, based on his having had any sort of relationship with Reuben Tate.

Hard, cold, and an incurable fan of heavy metal music, the louder the better. Plenty of marijuana . . . probably he had tattoos. But as I scrambled the last few yards up that damned mountain, I began hearing . . .

Wind chimes. The bamboo ones that sound like a small stream peacefully gurgling. And chickens: a bright-eyed head poked out of the underbrush at us, clucking inquisitively.

Then I smelled smoked fish mingled with the perfume of slow-burning applewood. Someone was smoking salmon, which in Eastport is sweet, pink fleshed, and tender, straight out of the icy-cold waters of Passamaquoddy Bay and directly—whenever I can arrange it—onto my bagel. With cream cheese, preferably, and coffee.

Suddenly the hill didn't quite seem so steep anymore. My ant bites weren't stinging like the devil, either. One of his lesser minions, maybe; Eastport ants are fierce. But as I pushed through a screen of old lilacs toward the picture-book cottage that stood before me in the suddenly open clearing, I didn't care.

Whoever he was, and whatever he'd done in the past, Mike Carpentier had made himself a paradise. The view from the hilltop was sweepingly of blue bay and sky, Campobello spreading low in the middle distance. Beyond loomed the island of Grand Manan, its pale cliffs vaulting improbably, miragelike, on the horizon.

"Wow," I managed inadequately. The breeze shifted, smelling of open ocean tinged with chamomile. Beyond a split-rail fence, a dappled pony placidly munched clover; a couple of goats grazed on the hillside, and there was a rabbit hutch.

No wonder the place was so far uphill, I realized. It had to be, to be this close to heaven.

Then I heard the child sobbing.

She was nine or so, with long golden curls and huge violet eyes streaming tears, crouched over—

Good heavens. A dead cat. She'd dug a small grave for it and was in the act of laying it in there when she caught sight of me and jumped guiltily.

"Hello," I said. "I'm sorry about your cat. Are you having a funeral for it?"

I took a step, stopped short as her eyes flashed hostility, and then, unmistakably, fear.

"Who are you?" She pushed some dirt over the animal's body, but not before Ellie stepped up and got a pretty good look at it.

"My name's Jacobia. This is my friend Ellie."

"I know her," the child said, pushing blond hair out of her tear-streaked face. She wore a red flannel shirt, dungarees, and old sneakers. On her wrist was a thin beaded friendship bracelet.

No other children were in sight. A fast guess: This little girl had made the beaded friendship bracelet for herself. Before I could follow the thought, a man appeared at the cottage door.

"Molly?" he called sharply, then spotted us.

The child turned and ran for the house without a

backward look. We followed under the man's unsmiling gaze. A small cloud pulled over the sun and I shivered, suddenly uncertain.

"Mike Carpentier," Ellie said under her breath as we made our way toward the dwelling, "in the flesh."

"So I gathered." Hollyhocks and black-eyed susans bloomed in the dooryard, mingled with clumps of herbs. A woodpile out back featured an old-fashioned bucksaw, a mallet, and a hand ax. There was a wellhouse with a bucket fixed to a pulley, near a stone birdbath. A vegetable garden spread on the hillside to the west, as high as possible to catch every last fleeting ray of sun.

No satellite dish. No power pole. No phone line, even. Mike wasn't what I had expected, either: big boned and plain faced, wearing thick horn-rims, bib overalls, sandals with socks. His graying hair was chopped short in an uneven hack job he'd probably done himself.

Also, he wasn't friendly. Not for the first time I was glad that Ellie was around to introduce me. But he asked us into the house and it was wonderful in there, the fragrance of gingerbread wafting deliciously from the woodstove hulking at the center of the kitchen. Around it a bewildering variety of craft items lay in various stages of completion:

Stenciled birdhouses. Punched-tin lanterns. Doilies knitted, crocheted, and woven in a rainbow of bright colors. Tea steeped in a stoneware pot set on a cast-iron trivet. There were bentwood chairs with plump homemade cushions, and bright braided rugs on the wide-plank, neatly swept wooden floor.

"I know your husband," Mike said to me. His handshake was firm, his look not as suspicious after Ellie's introduction. "I took Molly," he nodded at the girl, "in to see him a week ago. Headaches. Took her to the clinic, they said it was nothing. But I wanted to be sure."

Victor hadn't officially been seeing any patients. But when word of his presence got around town, people took notice, not paying much attention to his actual specialty. And he didn't like to turn them down if they came and asked for his help; he could practice basic medicine, and it was touching how much he wanted to be accepted.

"Nothing serious, I hope?" The little girl looked healthy if a bit listless and red-eyed, hanging back now behind her father.

"No," Mike said. "Guess the clinic doctor was right. Maybe nerves, your husband said. His place was so clean, and so was he. It gave me a lot of confidence in what he said. What he really thought, he told me, was that the headaches were nothing and would probably go away by themselves. And mostly, they have."

At this the two of us smiled in the time-honored way that a couple of experienced parents will when the children have turned out not to be sick, and the ice was broken.

"I suppose now you want to talk about Reuben," he went on resignedly. "He'd turned into such a booze hound, I'm surprised he didn't die sooner. But that was Reuben, make as much trouble as he could, even dying. And now you want to hash it over."

"Well, yes," I admitted. "I've heard he was your friend, and I'm sorry for your loss, but—"

His harsh burst of laughter cut me off. "Loss?" He waved us to chairs, set out mugs. "Oh, that's rich."

The tea was strong and welcome after the climb. "When Reuben left town the last time I went to church and lit a candle," Mike said tiredly. "But nobody believes it. That's the trouble with a small town, you can never escape your past." He set gingerbread on a plate.

"My husband—my ex-husband," I clarified, and he glanced comprehendingly at me—"is in some trouble over Reuben's death."

On a sideboard stood a framed photograph of a

happy family group: Mike, Molly, and the woman I'd run into outside Paddy Farrell's studio. So that, I realized, was Molly's mother. I hadn't mentioned the collision to Ellie, had in fact almost forgotten about it.

Until now. "But how did you know we would want to talk about Reuben?" I finished.

He shrugged. "Bob Arnold," he replied in a tone that let me know he was no fan of Eastport's police chief.

Or of any official persons, I guessed; Mike was off the grid in more ways than just no power or telephone. His place was like one of those survivalist homesteads you read about, in Utah or Wyoming, where they are preparing for nuclear winter. The pantry was loaded with labeled glass canning jars, a clean quarter inch of wax showing at the top of each: jams, jellies, and preserves. On a shelf over the soapstone sink, next to a neatly organized array of veterinary supplies for the animals, I spotted a CB radio set hooked up to run on a battery.

"He came up to tell me Reuben was . . . gone," Mike said. "See what kind of reaction he got from me, too, I'll bet."

"Why would he do that?"

His laugh was mirthless. "In case I killed him, I guess. As if I'd waste my time on that little—"

"Until just recently I had no idea that you even knew Reuben," Ellie said.

Mike got up, put the kettle back onto the woodstove's cook top. "Well, I did. Twenty years ago, I was his . . ."

Not his friend, surely. Mike was in his mid thirties or so, no older. Which would have made him—

"Mascot, I guess you'd call it. Sidekick. Or pet. He was a lot older than me, in his late teens." He glanced fondly at Molly as the child, who had vanished somewhere, came back in again.

"Sit down, honey," he said. "Eat some gingerbread, and work on your plant hanger. We're going," he added, "to a crafts fair, and Molly's bringing some of her things to sell."

Molly ignored the snack, seating herself at the table and concentrating on one of her projects. Her deft fingers spun long strands of string swiftly and cleverly, knotting them to form an intricate pattern in macramé, threaded with wooden beads.

"She knows all the macramé knots, don't you, honey?" Mike said proudly.

"That's very nice," I told her sincerely, and her smile was lovely. She was the spitting image of her mother.

Ellie was explaining to Mike more about why we were asking about Reuben Tate. "Would you rather discuss it somewhere else?" I put in, indicating Molly.

He considered. "Honey, if you're not going to eat, take that stuff upstairs." Silently, the little girl obeyed, grabbing the cleverly knotted string plant hanger.

Then: "Reuben was a sickness," he said when his daughter was out of earshot. "It was like he somehow put a spell on me. I was fascinated by him at first. His wild ways."

"Later," Ellie drew him out for my benefit, "you married . . ." With a nod at the photo, he mentioned a name I didn't recognize. A good mother when she could be, Mike said. A cook in the merchant marine, so she wasn't around a lot. They were divorced.

"I got custody," Mike said. "She agreed to it. I'd been in a little trouble in the past, but not anymore. No time for getting stoned when you've got a kid to take care of."

Molly's mother had been in town, in fact, on the ship that had come into port the previous Friday evening, the *Star Hoisin,* Mike said. She had come to the cottage, taken Molly on a couple of outings.

Which explained a bit more about why the child seemed a little withdrawn and weepy now. He didn't elaborate on the reason for their divorce and I didn't ask. It was Reuben I wanted to know about.

"So you hung around with him as a kid. He liked you. He never bullied you or hurt you? That wasn't exactly his usual behavior, from what I've heard of the way he operated back then."

A look of regret passed over Mike's plain face. "I wouldn't say he never bullied me. Like I said, I was a little kid he could . . . I don't know. Own, almost. He wasn't abusive sexually if that's what you mean," he finished.

It was. I still didn't understand the attraction, on either side. "How did you end your relationship with him?"

He looked sharply at me. "I didn't end it. He left town. I grew up. Life went on. And that was that."

"He came back," I pointed out. "Several times, according to what I've heard. He didn't try to get in touch with you then?"

"Well," he temporized, "he did, the first few times. But I was married, and then we were pregnant with Molly. I didn't give him any encouragement, so he lost interest. Went on," he added, "to bigger and better things."

His laugh didn't sound convincing. "So how come Bob Arnold wanted to talk with you," I asked, "after Reuben got killed?"

He poured more tea. "Not many people remembered about me and Reuben. You know, it was just one of those little-kid phases. But I guess Arnold recalled, and you know him. God forbid he shouldn't cover all the bases. And something about the way he talked to me about it, I had a feeling he wouldn't be the last one dredging up old stories."

Resentment tinged his voice briefly, went away again. Wade had remembered it too, I recalled, so probably Mike was right.

"But for me, what's past is past and that's the end

of it. This was twenty years ago, remember. Like I told Arnold, in my book Reuben Tate was ancient history."

Not pleasant history, from his expression. But he didn't seem to mind talking about it. "Can you think of anyone who might have wanted to hurt him?" I asked.

Ellie had wandered outside, carrying her tea. Now she came back in and went to the window, where a profusion of houseplants flourished like an indoor jungle. Peering through the glass, she gazed out at the domestic animals and the gardens.

Mike looked rueful. "Oh, there were plenty of those. Open the phone book and point. Reuben was mean . . . and he was smart."

Everyone said so. "In what way? Knowing how to hurt people? Their weaknesses?"

He nodded emphatically. "And how to get some advantage out of them. Just for instance, the only jail time he ever served, it was six months for breaking and entering. Before," he added, his tone even, "he stopped getting sent to jail, because no one would testify against him, here." That matched what Paddy had said.

"Most guys," Mike said, "when they get out of jail, they have nothing more than they went in. It's just empty time. But not Reuben. When *he* got out he had a list of homosexual professional men in Maine. Dentists, lawyers . . . anybody he could blackmail."

Ellie glanced over from the window, peered back out again. Something in the yard seemed to have fascinated her.

"But I don't understand," I said, shocked and revolted at the idea. "How would such a list even get compiled?"

He shook his head. "I'm not sure. All I know is, someone in jail had a list and Reuben somehow got hold of it."

"And you knew about it because . . ."

Matter-of-factly: "He made me type the blackmail letters."

The notion was chilling; just the thought, for instance, of Paddy or Terence getting such a letter made me feel sick. And two decades earlier, even right now in a lot of places, it would have been devastating.

"I had an old typewriter in my room," Mike explained. "And he told me what to write. I didn't even really understand what those letters were saying. Later, though, of course I figured it out."

However improbable—I still didn't see quite how it could have happened—it sounded absolutely like the kind of scheme Reuben would have tried: cruel. Terrifying in the extreme.

In short, right up Reuben Tate's alley. "My ex-husband says that Reuben knew some things about him," I said. "Things that happened in the past, in New York. Can you think of how Reuben might have found out about them?"

It just seemed so unlikely. But Mike answered quickly and surely. "Oh, he'd have no problem with that. He told me about it, in fact, bragging. Went to your ex-husband's house when he wasn't there, snooped through the mail in the mailbox, found out where he'd come from. Then he went to the library, got on the computer, and looked on the Internet in back issues of newspapers. Searched them for your ex-husband's name. Just a fishing expedition, but after he hit paydirt it was easy."

So Reuben had been bragging his plan around, not only to Paddy Farrell. As Ellie had said, underestimating Reuben would be a mistake. "This last time he came back, did he come here to the cottage? Did he ask for anything? Maybe threaten you, too?"

"Actually, he did," Mike replied. "Heard where I lived, climbed the hill. Can't keep a bad man down, I guess. And he was a real bastard."

"What did he want?" Ellie asked casually.

Too casually, and her glance at me as she came to the table was pointed. I got up and went to the window where she had been.

"Oh, the usual," Mike replied. "Had a bottle with him; he'd heard I was divorced. Maybe he thought we'd get to be drinking buddies." He snorted. "As if."

Drawing back a gingham curtain, I scanned the yard with its compost heap and neatly kept animal pens, then stopped when I saw the big chopping block made of a squat, upended log.

It was covered with blood.

15

Those chickens, I thought, my heart hammering foolishly. He butchered a chicken, that's all. I had an abrupt, unwelcome vision of one of the creatures running around headless; a vision, I gathered, that had been reality not long ago. Feathers littered the area around the chopping block. I let the curtain drop.

"So when you knew him back then, you were eleven or twelve, and Reuben was . . . nineteen or twenty?"

Mike nodded. "Something like that. My parents didn't know about it, of course. And the attraction was, he liked to be the power in any situation."

Reuben Tate was just rising like hell in my estimation. Blackmail, murder, pedophilia or one of its cousins—what would be next among his habits: cannibalism?

"And he liked that I would do what he said," Mike went on. "Typing, for instance: I could do that. Not fast, but I could. I was a bookwormish kid. So he made me do it if he wanted something typed. I was scared of him, to tell you the truth."

"But you still spent time with him. How did that happen? I mean, where, for instance?"

"Oh, around," Mike said vaguely. Then he looked straight at me. "See, I was a child. We weren't friends in the way any normal person would use the word. He just had a weird thing about me; I don't know. Like a pet," he repeated.

"Mike," Ellie said, "are you sure you weren't among Reuben's present-day enemies?"

I'd have asked him about the other victim, too, if I'd been the one putting the question, though I might not have asked at all. It flat-out implied that Mike might be a murder suspect. But he seemed not to take any offense.

"Oh, no," he said serenely, looking almost amused. "That's what you still don't understand. That was then, and this is now. What's past is past."

He got up from the table. His hands were red and work-roughened, and there was an ugly-looking recent burn on the back of the right one.

"That looks painful," I said, but he shrugged off the injury easily.

"Can't be too careful with a woodstove. One slip, and the next thing you know, *hssst*! But it's healing okay."

Molly returned as he filled the kettle again, from a big metal carboy of water on the sink. "I probably wouldn't have told you about me and Reuben at all. It isn't something I like talking about. Too," he made a little grimace of distaste, "weird. But I hear Willow Prettymore is back in town for the festival and she's sure to gossip a mile a minute. So—"

He lifted his hands in a what-can-you-do gesture. "I just go on," he said, dismissing the subject. "Would you like to take some gingerbread? Molly, wrap it up for these ladies."

The child scurried wordlessly to obey.

"Mike," I asked, "did Bob Arnold happen to mention anyone else Reuben might have been giving trouble to lately?"

"More than the usual, you mean? No, he didn't really seem to have a clue about that. And I didn't," he went on, "offer any."

Molly returned, handing me the parcel. She was very self-possessed for a young girl, her manner gravely polite. Yet she had an odd, repressed air of babyishness, too; at her age, many girls in the city had already become mall rats.

Mike hesitated as if wondering whether to elaborate on his last remark. Then:

"I hear the Sondergards are playing on the bandstand for the Salmon Sunday supper," he said to Ellie.

"Dad," the little girl interrupted insistently, tugging at her father's sleeve.

As Mike lay a soothing hand on the girl's shoulder, it struck me that Molly might be a wee tad overprotected, especially way out here with no other children of her age to play with. Given a choice, though, I'd take that over a whole mall full of preadolescent girls in spandex halter tops and eye makeup. In Eastport, a child could still be a child long after the city kids were getting rushed willy-nilly into the adulthood.

"Dad, I need you to help me with this," Molly persisted. "I need you *now*."

So the kid wasn't perfect, and if you dropped her in a mall she'd probably go hysterical from sensory overload. But if Mike Carpentier had chosen to stick to a strict parenting route, lots of his own input and not much from anyone else, I couldn't blame him. If I'd done it earlier, maybe Sam wouldn't have had so much trouble.

When we left, the two of them were standing in the doorway, waving serenely, Molly with her macramé project in her hands. The downhill trip was easier and faster than the climb up; in a few minutes we were back at the Jeep.

I opened the gingerbread package; the fragrance of cloves filled the air. "How does he manage up there? No power, no running water. Not even a telephone—what happens if there's an emergency? Can you really raise somebody on a CB radio? And what about winter?"

I ate a morsel of gingerbread. "Or does he hole up in the cottage until spring? Home-school Molly, eat what they've canned from the garden and butcher a few chickens till the snow melts? Pray," I added, "that neither one of them needs an ambulance, or that the cottage needs a fire truck."

Ellie glanced wryly at me. "First of all, Mike is prepared for any emergency short of being at ground zero. I looked around a bit while you two were talking—there's a water tank up the hill in case of fire, a first-aid kit that makes Terence's look like a toy doctor bag, enough canned goods to stock a supermarket out in the shed. There's the radio for emergencies. I doubt there's a whole lot of people Mike chats to on a regular basis, so he doesn't need a phone. And he drives Molly to school every morning, picks her up in the afternoon."

"Drives? But . . . Oh." That Ford Escort, I realized, pulled to the side of the cove road. "So he isn't the hermit he appears?"

"Nope. Just when he wants to be." Ellie pulled the Jeep into my driveway, beside which stood all those storm windows. A pang of urgency stabbed me at the sight of them, because September in Maine is like the condemned man's last meal: fun while it lasts, but it won't put off what is coming.

"Not that the self-sufficiency routine does too much," Ellie added, "for Molly's social life. From what people say around town, I guess Mike doesn't think Molly's peers are fit companions."

She swung out of the Jeep and walked with me to the house. "I wanted you to meet him," she went on, "before I told you much about him, so you could form your own impression. But to tell you the truth I wasn't surprised that Bob Arnold had gone to see him. Mike's a good father but otherwise he's pretty strange."

"Oh, I don't know. I kind of enjoyed him. Just because he's independent, likes to do things his own way. I don't see why it should make a person feel suspicious of him."

I held out the remaining gingerbread. "Want a piece?"

Ellie stopped by the porch steps. "No, thanks. Interesting he should bring up the Sondergards, too. Maybe we ought to talk to them. I think his mentioning them was no accident; he isn't a fool. And the same with Willow Prettymore . . ."

Her voice trailed off thoughtfully.

Checking the mailbox, I found it empty, then remembered it was Sunday. "Come on, Ellie. Aren't you making him out to be more subtle than he is?"

I opened the back door. "Mike's a plain-looking, plain-speaking guy who does what he wants and says what he thinks, from what I can see. I admire that."

Inside, Monday galloped to meet us. "It was weird, his story about Reuben. And I'll admit I had a bad moment with the blood on the chopping block. But all he'd done was kill a chicken for his Sunday dinner. Whacked," I finished, "its head off."

"Huh," Ellie said skeptically, ruffling the dog's ears. "I'm surprised he bothered."

I turned on the coffeemaker. "What do you mean by that?"

She eyed me levelly. "The cat Molly was burying? Did you get a look at it? A good," she emphasized, "look?"

"No, why?" I picked up the gingerbread again, meaning to put it in an airtight container, since Ellie didn't want it.

"Because," Ellie said, patting Monday's head and

making more kind noises at her, "somebody had wrung that cat's neck."

I dropped the gingerbread in the trash.

"Oh, and one other thing," she added. "The man Paddy said was going to testify against Reuben? But instead got found with a bump on his head," she finished, "down in his own cellar?"

"You know about that?"

The coffeemaker burbled. I turned from the refrigerator where I was getting out the cream. I had not mentioned that part of my trip with Paddy and Terence.

"Uh-huh." Ellie reached up into the cabinet, came down with cups and saucers. "Paddy always likes to tell that story when the topic of Reuben comes up, so I figured he'd told it to you. But for some reason there's always one aspect of it he leaves out."

If he thinks leaving something out'll make him look better, Wade had said of Paddy, *he'll do it.* "What part is that?"

Sunshine from the tall kitchen window fell slantwise on the cup Ellie was holding, filling it with milky light.

"The man in the cellar was Paddy's father," she said.

The telephone rang.

16

"Jacobia. Good to talk to you. Wish it were under different circumstances."

"Hello, Ben." It was a voice from the bad old days. Bennet Berman had handled Victor's side of the divorce. "Since when are you doing criminal cases?"

"Since never. Just getting the ducks in a row for

your ex. He'll have a criminal defense attorney, of course. I'm not even licensed to practice in Maine."

Right; divorce as a metaphor for all-out nuclear war hadn't yet gotten fashionable up here in moose country, so there wasn't much real call for Bennet's area of expertise.

"But Victor wants me on the team," Bennet went on. "He seems to feel there are ways I can be effective."

I banished memories of just how effective he'd been against me; as Mike Carpentier had said, that was then and this was now.

And Victor needed all the help he could get. "So what kind of quacking are you hearing, Ben? From the ducks in the row."

His laugh turned mirthless. "Well. It's still the weekend, so things aren't high gear yet. But I've got a faxed preliminary medical report on the victim. Victor said"—Bennet's tone was puzzled—"that you would want to hear it."

"You're kidding." Back in the old days when I was a money manager, Victor seemed to feel my job was the equivalent of being a bank teller. Instead of listening to my financial advice, he preferred to have his stock accounts churned by a sweaty-palmed guy in a cubicle somewhere out in East Omaha.

But Ellie and I had nosed rather thoroughly into Eastport troubles, before—with, I might add, good results—and although Victor had never indicated approval, apparently he had noticed.

"Here goes." Bennet began reading, paraphrasing as he went: "Death due to major hemorrhage, ligature marks on the ankles, at least one sedative plus alcohol in the blood. Details aren't in yet, so we don't know what kind of drug it was."

So that was how someone had gotten Reuben up on that gate: he'd been alive, all right. But maybe not kicking. Which meant it would have been taken less physical power than I'd envisioned.

"No blood on Victor," Bennet went on, "which isn't so good. Seeing as he'd spent the previous evening treating an injury from a bar brawl."

"Well, but that's reasonable. He would wash. Victor washes if anybody looks at him cross-eyed, and that wound he'd stitched up was pretty bloody."

"That's not how you'd play it if you were the prosecutor, though. Could be the injured guy's blood Victor washed off. Or . . ."

Right. Or it could have been Reuben's. "What about his clothes? Had he thrown them out, or washed them?" Sam had said Victor ran the washing machine and put out a bag of garbage, and the truck had come, though it wasn't the regular day for pickup.

"Neither. Burned 'em in the burn barrel behind his house. They think they're going to find blood evidence on the remains of them, which he'd disposed of afterwards in the trash."

Oh, criminy. "So the laundry was . . ."

"Towels and whatnot from the shower he took. Won't be able to type the blood, though, most likely. Same with the blood in the traps," Bennet continued, "under the sink and so on. Seems that according to Victor, he regularly ran enough hot water and bleach down there to sterilize the whole sewer system." Even burning the clothes wasn't so far-fetched, for Victor; once they were contaminated he'd have treated them like any other medical waste.

"Sure," Bennet said resignedly when I explained this to him. "I can see it. I couldn't say this to you when we were on opposite sides, Jacobia. But Victor's a strange little duck, in the hygiene department especially."

"Yeah, tell me about it. You only had him on your agenda for thirteen months. I had him for a dozen years."

"But," he went on, "try floating that Mr. Clean stuff past a jury. They'll laugh in your face. Because there's still the small problem of the weapon. How'd somebody else get hold of it?"

Let's see, now: After explaining to the jury that Victor was so fastidious that he actually carried antiseptic hand wipes in his pocket in case he had to talk on a strange telephone, we could go on to say that he lived in a town where people didn't always lock their doors when they went out, because for one thing they didn't need to, and for another, they never knew when someone else might need to get in. Thus, anyone could have taken the scalpel.

Sure. And if pigs had wings, then smoky links could fly. "So what's the plan?" I asked dejectedly.

"Tomorrow morning I'll be lining up my Maine colleagues, see if we can try for bail. It won't work, of course. And we'll try for a decent alibi. But I doubt that'll happen, either. Sam say anything to you about seeing Victor that night?"

My heart sank. "Uh-huh. Listen, Bennet, I don't care what he saw. I don't want Sam testifying against Victor."

A brief pause. "Well, we're not there, yet. Let's just see how things develop, all right?"

I already knew how things would develop: like one of the tumors Victor was so good at taking out. But occasionally one of them was so fast and malignant, no one could stop it.

"Bennet, did Victor say how he knew Reuben Tate had been murdered?" It was the part that still bothered me the most, that he'd known before he should have. I could explain all the rest, but even I couldn't explain that one.

Bennet's deep, unhappy sigh was the echo of my own. "He says he got two phone calls early that morning, the second from your town cop, Bob Arnold. Arnold wanted to talk to Victor about the other guy who died, with the tie in his throat. So they agreed to meet at your place."

Which jibed with what Arnold had told me in the cemetery. "And the first call?"

"Well. This is the difficult part. Victor says he got a call from someone he didn't recognize. That the voice was disguised; he couldn't even tell if it was a man or a woman. A high whisper was the way he described it."

"Telling him Reuben Tate was dead."

"Right. Told him Tate wouldn't be bothering him anymore, and enough more about what happened—Victor says he doesn't remember the exact words—so Victor knew how Tate had died. Then hung up."

"This was after Victor had done all his washing and so on."

"Uh-huh," Bennet agreed unhappily. "And Victor says he can't explain why the garbage guy came. Says he didn't call him. What the garbage guy says, he doesn't know who it was. His kid took a message, kid's like five years old. So you see the problems."

My turn to sigh. "You bet."

"Jacobia," his tone was hesitant, "among your complaints in the divorce was that Victor is a rather skilled and habitual . . ."

"Liar. Sure, there was that. But, Bennet, it was about women. This is different. This is . . ."

A set-up, I wanted to say, still trying to get used to the notion myself. A deliberate plan to get Victor blamed . . . But I thought I'd better examine this idea before talking about it.

Bennet, I noticed, wasn't mentioning it either. Your honor, my client has been framed—

Right. And before that, he was abducted by aliens. "Bennet, is there anything I can do right now to help?"

He cleared his throat delicately. "Well, Jacobia, you can explain how I'm going to get paid. Sorry to have to mention it, but Victor was vague on that point."

Victor had put every cent he owned into his trauma project: plans, a site workup, architects, regulatory research. Getting a start-up medical thing going was very expensive.

"Oh, I'll bet he was vague. Send me the bills, Bennet, and I'll work it out with him when this is all over."

"Will do. And I'll keep you posted with any developments."

Hanging up, I found myself alone in the house. Ellie had signed up to help make costumes for the children's parade, part of the upcoming festival; she'd gone off while I was on the phone with Bennet, and Sam and Wade were out, too.

So I thought I might work on the windows; heaven knew they still needed it. But the big old house felt echoingly empty all around me, which was unusual for it, and even from upstairs I could feel the presence of that dratted Ouija board.

As a result I hit my thumb twice with the hammer, then took a nick out of my palm with the cuts-all tool. The weatherstripping would not lie flat, curling this way and that like some bright copper snake, wriggly with malicious willfulness.

So after half an hour of doing things wrong, then making them worse by trying to fix them or do them over, I called Bob Arnold and asked him to meet me at Bay Books.

17

The bookstore on Water Street had been an old-style pharmacy with a soda fountain, in its previous incarnation. Bailey James had kept the red leather stools and booths, the beveled mirror behind the fountain's marble-topped counter, the fizzy-water dispenser and the bottles of syrups and flavorings. Then she'd brought in bestsellers, the latest mystery novels, a magazine rack that carried *WIRED* and *The Drood Review,* and a pay-by-the-half-hour Internet connection.

The result combined the charm of old Eastport with a modern hit of Y2K-and-beyond snazziness; in one visit, you could satisfy your addictions to caffeine, whodunnits, the World Wide Web, and of course that most necessary Eastport commodity, local gossip.

Bob Arnold wasn't there yet. I slid onto a stool at the counter as Bailey began making my regular drink, a coffee frappe.

"So tell me," I said as she squirted whipped cream on the concoction of coffee, ice cream, vanilla, and a sprinkling of cinnamon, "about these musicians in town for the festival, the Sondergards."

In one of the booths, Darcy Morrell from the Women's Guild was explaining to Heather Banks how to piece a log-cabin quilt; her canvas workbag was open and bright fabric swatches were laid out on the table between them.

"Heywood and Marcus," Darcy said, looking up from her quilt pieces.

"Father's a minister. Son too, I think," Heather added.

In the booth just behind them, Chuck Wilkes broke off from insisting that Passamaquoddy Bay harbored lobsters the size of Volkswagens but you never saw them; they never came up from where they had been spawning for a hundred years.

"Sing-along revivalists," he said. "Call themselves Bible Belters, go around Maine in a big Winnebago, singing for Christ."

"Snake-handling," Chuck's companion contributed, peering over his coffee. He wore denim coveralls, rubber boots, and a cap that said MOOSE ISLAND MARINE. "Speaking in tongues and so on. Falling down in religious fits. That's their specialty."

"It is not. They're nice men," Bailey said admonishingly. "I declare, that's the way foolish stories get started."

She handed me my change from the old-fashioned register. "They're up at the Heddlepenny House, staying all week. Heywood has a piano-type contraption and a guitar. And Marcus I believe plays the banjo."

I thought Bailey might as well unhook the Internet link; all the information anyone could ever need was already there in the store.

"They go to early services at First Baptist when they're in town," Heather said. "So they're probably home by now."

Just then Bob came in, got a coffee, and walked with me to the booth in the back of the shop, the look on his round, pink face one of abiding disgust.

"This murder business," he said, sliding in across from me, "is not the kind of tourist attraction the chamber of commerce had in mind when they started advertising us as a big downeast Maine travel destination, tryin' to get publicity."

He took a swallow of coffee. "City manager's office is in a tizzy gettin' calls from reporters who want to know does Eastport have a serial killer? 'Cause if we do, we can all get on *Hard Copy,* but if it's just us folks killin' one another, that ain't as newsworthy."

Oh, he was on a tear. I tried edging him in a new direction.

"Well, but you know what the flip side is, don't you? It's that most of the time, the great big world out there leaves us alone, way up here at the edge of the continent. To do things the way we want to, take care of things that way, too."

He nodded reluctantly. Bailey came over with the cream and sugar, caught my expression, and didn't stick around to chat.

"Which," I went on, getting to the point, "I think somebody did when they finished off Reuben Tate. Took care of things their own way, I mean. And I'll tell you another thing, Arnold: I think somebody set Victor up for it on purpose."

I didn't feel so nervous about floating this theory with Bob as I had with Bennet. As a small-town police chief, Bob had seen a lot of odd things, and their oddness hadn't prevented them from being true. His gaze sharpened as I told him about the call Victor said he'd gotten, and the mysterious coming of the trash truck.

"People in town knew Reuben was giving Victor trouble," I said. "And I know of people who'd been in his house, probably seen his collection of surgical instruments. You can't walk down the hall without passing it."

Well, Mike Carpentier had been in Victor's house recently, anyway, and likely there were more. "I don't suppose you've heard about any fingerprints, by any chance? On, say, the weapon?"

"Nuh-uh. Glove marks on his skin, maybe. Burn 'em, or toss 'em in the bay, they're gone forever, probably."

"Darn. But my point is, if you hung back and watched for your chance, you could steal a scalpel from Victor's collection and kill Reuben with it, on a night when Victor had no alibi for his time. That Victor had threatened Reuben, and that he had a reason to clean up so thoroughly—"

"Him bein' a few fish short of a bucketful, in the rub-a-dub department," Arnold put in accurately.

"Right. That would be, from your angle if you were a sneaky murderer, just dumb luck. Whenever you find out about it, you use it, even work it into your plan. Take advantage," I finished, "of happenstance."

"Nothing dumb about the rest of it, though," Arnold said shrewdly. "And the call would seal it. He'd know Reuben was dead when he couldn't have yet, and he couldn't prove how he found out. Same with that garbage truck."

"Seems Reuben was talking up his plan to blackmail Victor, too," I said, "so more than one person might have thought to take advantage of that. And sometimes when people get away with things, it's because other things just happened to go their way," I finished. "Like the bar fight, and Victor's hygiene fixation. You couldn't plan that, it would be a couple of lucky breaks you would use, just because they came along."

Arnold nodded. "Maybe," he allowed. "But what about the drugs in Tate's system? I hear he was loaded with sedatives. The state boys," he added sarcastically, "let me in on a few things."

"I don't know. I didn't say I had it all figured out. But I doubt Victor's the only one on the island with a bottle of Valium or whatever. For all I know, Reuben had them himself."

Arnold shook his head. "Reuben liked uppers more, though I guess if somebody offered to fix him up with something he'd take it, no matter what it was. I had his head, I'd want to be out of it a lot too. What we've got left is someone who's smart, angry, and in the right weight class to lift him up there."

"And there's another thing." The worry that had seized me the previous evening came over me again. The thing about shooting someone is, you do the deed from a distance.

But this had been close-up work. "Whoever did it is really dangerous, Arnold. To be able to—"

The sight of Reuben hanging there came back to me again full force and I shuddered, unable to help myself. Even a little blood can look like a lot.

And this was a lot. "Yeah," Arnold said reluctantly. "That, too. Like whoever done it had a whole lot more in mind than just killing him."

"Like the method itself was supposed to . . ."

He nodded again. "Say something. I thought about it. And . . . look, I'm not supposed to talk about this. But the patronizing attitude on those sons of bitches . . ."

The state guys, he meant. From their point of view, Arnold was about as credible a law enforcement officer as Deputy Dawg.

And it hurt his feelings. "Guy on the breakwater, tie in his throat," he said.

"Right. That's another thing I'm curious about."

Arnold eyed me acutely. "I'm guessing your interest isn't on account of your still having a soft spot for your ex-husband."

"No. I've got serious financial reasons for not wanting him to stay in trouble. And Sam . . ."

"Yeah. His old man. Hard on a kid. On top of which, the worse pain in the tail a fellow is, the more you feel you've got to go the extra mile for him, sometimes. Prove to yourself you are not bein' a jerk yourself."

"Yes." I exhaled gratefully. That part was just so hard to explain, but Arnold had put his finger on it. "But look, it's not just me. I've got—"

"A funny feeling that maybe all this isn't over with?"

I blinked at him, surprised.

"Me too," he mused. "You say somebody called Victor, told him about the body in the cemetery? Said it was Reuben dead, but Victor didn't know who it was calling?"

"That's right." A suspicion struck me. "Arnold . . ."

"Because," he said gravely, "I didn't think so much of it at the time. Figured it was just somebody who didn't want to get all involved in a bad business."

He looked up at me. "But yesterday morning right after we found our first victim, I went across the street from the seawall, into my office. Got an answering machine in there, it's not set up to go through the dispatcher, 'case Clarissa wants to call me on any personal matter, and I'm not in the car."

To tell him, maybe, that the baby was coming. "And that," he finished, "was how I found out about Reuben. Course, by now that machine's number is common knowledge. But I didn't recognize the voice. Hung up 'fore I could ask, too."

"No caller ID, I suppose?"

"Nope. Line's just for me, didn't want to pay more on it."

"The other guy," I said, "the one who was strangled. Is he from here? Does he have a family?"

The victim's name, Arnold said, was Wesley Bodine. "Weasel for short. And by inclination. That fellow was pure no-account: beat on his wife, wouldn't support his kids, rowdy and mean when he wasn't so drunk he could barely navigate. Worst guy in town, in fact, or anyway he was, up till Reuben came back. Not many people knew about him 'cept the guys he drank with 'cause he kept himself to himself and so did his wife, till she took the kids and went back home to her folks in New Hampshire. But I knew."

Arnold glanced around to check that we weren't being eavesdropped on. "And the tie wasn't the only thing," he said, keeping his voice low. "In his mouth. Weasel didn't have many teeth left but he had a few. And the medical examiner says there was a chunk of what looked like skin stuck on one of 'em."

It took me a moment to make sense of the implication. "Not Reuben's."

Arnold nodded soberly. "That's right. Hell of a lot of bad things were done to Reuben in his last hours. But no one bit him."

"So unless you think there were two *other* killers—besides Reuben, I mean—running around Eastport on Friday night . . ."

"And I don't," he said firmly. "Tiny town, middle

of nowhere, and two unrelated murders on one night? It's just too damned much coincidence. No, I think whoever did Reuben also did the Weasel. Two victims, one villain."

"But the state cops don't agree. They're thinking two killers. So it doesn't matter that Victor doesn't have a cut hand, either."

Arnold's tone was even. "That's right. Like I say, they never wanted Victor for Weasel in the first place, so this won't change things in that regard."

So much for a stroke of luck. Another odd thing struck me. "So how do you know about this skin shred, anyway? Arnold, you wouldn't happen to be related to the medical examiner? Or . . ."

In downeast Maine, everyone was related to almost everybody else. Arnold looked wise.

"Ice fishing. He comes up winters, we go out and swap ourselves a few tall stories, drink beers. Kind of activity the college-boy investigators think is beneath 'em. You keep the information to yourself, though," he warned. "He gets in trouble, leakin' things to me, he won't be telling me no more. Or comin' up fishing no more, either."

"I'll keep my lip zipped," I promised.

"And don't go thinkin' it gets your ex off the hook, either," he repeated brusquely. "Way this'll all happen, they'll prosecute Victor for Reuben's murder, you can bet on it."

"But . . ."

"They can put a case together any way they want to, and the way they'll do it is the way they think'll get 'em a conviction. They're not going drop a bird they already got in the hand, to go off hog wild lookin' for somebody else. No sir."

"But common *sense* . . ." I began. Suggested, I meant, that the deaths were connected somehow.

"Paddy Farrell says Reuben killed somebody that

way before," I told Arnold. "With a tie, I mean. That right there makes a link of some kind, doesn't it?"

Arnold shook his head firmly.

"Heard the tie story myself, but be realistic. First of all, no one knows for sure it's true, however much everyone in town is so convinced that it is. Top of which, that's a lawyer's job, try to get Victor out a' this pickle with sense, common or otherwise. And it'll happen at trial. If," he added roughly, "it happens at all."

He raised a stubby finger. "And it ain't guaranteed to work then, either. Common sense—the idea that one person killed both Weasel and Reuben, and that one person couldn't be Victor 'cause his hand ain't bit—that's one thing, but evidence is another. And they've got good evidence against Victor for Reuben's murder."

He paused, and when he spoke again his tone softened. "To them, old Weasel's tooth is neither here nor there. But you might manage to make something of it, nosy and bone stubborn as I know you are. And something else."

I looked up, puzzled. "I watch, you know," he said. "Town doings, it's my job to know all about them. And when your ex came here, I know it put a hitch in your git-along."

I nodded, smiling at the phrase. It was pure Arnold. "I'd thought I was free of him. And then . . ."

"And then," Arnold agreed. "But you didn't badmouth him all around town, set him up so that people here wouldn't accept him. You didn't take your pound of flesh."

But I'd wanted to. Oh, I had wanted to. And that, I suddenly realized, was why Arnold was telling me all this: a good town cop, he'd been paying attention to my behavior just as much as to anyone else's. Based on it, he had made a decision to help me.

As much as he could. At this point, it was really all

out of his hands. He got up. "Guess I better go check on Clarissa. Doctor says she could have that baby any damned second, which I sure do wish she would."

Then he grinned. "Know what they're startin' to call you and Ellie, hereabouts? On account of all your interest in murder and mayhem and whatnot?"

As I've mentioned, it wasn't the first time Ellie and I had nosed around into intriguing local doings. Just the first time someone in my family was intimately connected to them.

"No, what?" Embarrassed, I swiped moisture from my face. Funny how you can take bad news and stay composed, but one kind word and the waterworks start running like the fountains of Rome.

"The Snoop Sisters," he said, and I burst out laughing, as he had intended. Then he went out, paying for his coffee at the register like any other citizen, leaving me to think.

Which wasn't exactly easy; at the moment my ideas felt more knotted-up than Molly Carpentier's macramé. But from what I could see so far, the situation boiled down to a pair of possibilities:

1. Two killers, one (in a prosecutor's eyes) being Victor.

Or more likely:

2. One murderer and two victims with no link between them, except that their deaths seemed part of someone's attempt to send a message.

I carried my glass back to the fountain.

"I'm so sorry for the difficulty you've been having," Bailey James said kindly. "I hope it all ends up okay."

"Thanks," I replied. "I do too."

But not just for me, I added silently as I went out. And not just for Victor, because the feeling I kept having wouldn't stop:

The feeling that the message was meant for all of us.

18

Heddlepenny House, a private home set up as a bed-and-breakfast, was a tall Victorian structure replete with gables, porches, bay windows, and lots of elaborate carved trimmings. Turning the knob on the hand-operated bell set into the ornate front door, I gazed down Washington Street past the massive granite-block post-office building on the corner, to the water beyond.

A little red-and-black-painted dragger bobbed jauntily on the light chop riffling the bay. Farther out, the ferry churned faithfully along its route, sun glinting off the windshields of the cars lined up on the deck, the passengers bright splotches.

A man opened the door: handsome, fortyish, with dark hair, a deeply cleft chin, and an attractive baritone voice. "Come in," Marcus Sondergard invited when I had introduced myself.

Guests had the run of the place at Heddlepenny House so it was not unusual that Marcus himself had opened the door. He led me to the parlor where an older man stood gazing out the window, onto Washington Street. Heywood Sondergard, Marcus's father, was a tall burly fellow whose grooved, good-humored face said he was in his late sixties, wearing a blue chambray shirt with pearl buttons, faded jeans, and a leather belt with a small but elaborate silver buckle. He had a luxuriously thick head of silver-white hair, pale blue eyes with bushy white eyebrows flourishing above them, and a gaze that while sympathetic was also very knowing.

"God is merciful," he intoned, his blue eyes darkening at the mention of Reuben. I'd explained who I was, the trouble Victor was in, and that I hoped they might help me understand it.

"But He is also just," he went on. "I have no doubt that young Mr. Tate is where he belongs. He chose to reap the wind," Heywood said, "and he is sowing the whirlwind."

The tongue of the belt buckle was shaped like a cross with a rose vine twining up it: the rose of Sharon. "Now, Dad," Marcus contradicted indulgently. "We don't know that. The Lord works in mysterious ways."

"Hmmph," Heywood uttered skeptically, but subsided for now.

"Dad," Marcus explained, "leans more toward an Old Testament interpretation than I do. An eye for an eye and all that."

His tone grew nostalgic. "Gosh, I grew up hearing Reuben stories." He looked around fondly. "This was our house, once, did you know that?"

I hadn't. Marcus went on. "When we lived here, Reuben was the kid your parents always warned you about. Dad was a minister here, so I suppose I got a little more guidance than most local kids."

He glanced affectionately at the older man. "Dad was very popular," Marcus added proudly. "Big attendance at his services on Sundays, and he was wonderful with the youngsters."

Marcus wasn't only big and handsome, I noticed suddenly. He was powerfully built: thick neck, muscular shoulders, broad chest tapering to a flat, narrow middle. His forearms, under the rolled-up sleeves of his white shirt, looked as solid as mutton roasts.

"Now, Marcus," the older man cautioned. "You know what pride goeth before. I ran a youth group, that's all. The boys and girls liked it because I made sure it had plenty of music. Nothing so remarkable about that."

"Dad's too modest," Marcus said. "But if he wants to hide his light under a bushel, so be it. Anyway, after Mother died the two of us were left on our own. Rattling around this house like a couple of marbles, weren't we, Dad?"

Heywood's deep voice rumbled agreement. "Decided to take our ministry on the road," he said. "So the Lord," he added, "sent us a Winnebago, and off we went."

This back-and-forth explanatory banter was an act they'd honed perfectly, I realized, though to be fair I supposed that if I had to explain myself in a new town every week, I'd get pretty good at it, too. A flyer on a low table, exhorting me to hear the heavenly melodies of the Bible Belters, said they'd done a dozen shows over the past three weekends, in places ranging from a tiny logging camp in the Allagash region to an art museum in South Portland.

"We're looking forward to performing for the home folks," Marcus said affably. "Would you like to see our setup? It's all out in the Winnebago, but maybe you'd like to see that, too. Dad did all the interior on it. I'll show you if you'd like."

"Marcus, you brag about me too much," Heywood grumbled as we got up. But it was clear that he was pleased.

For my own part, I thought Marcus wanted to talk to me alone, so I followed his lead. The Winnebago stood on a blacktop apron at the back of the house. Along a picket fence making a border between the lane and the yard, the season's last zinnias tangled in bright profusion.

I stood at the end of the back walk, breathing fresh air; the Sondergards were pleasant enough, but something about their mutual admiration society felt a little smothering.

Not false, exactly. Only as if the two of them were old hands at circling the wagons and did it as a sort of knee-jerk reflex. The feeling went on bothering me, as Marcus welcomed me into the Winnebago.

"Goodness," I said inadequately, gazing around. "You think of these things as being sort of claustrophobic. But . . ."

He led me through. The bunks were pods equipped with reading lamps, TVs, stereo headphone sets, and telephones, each snug and secret-feeling, wonderfully private. The bath was the same: all you could want tucked in so cleverly that you didn't perceive how small the cubicle really was.

That left space for three compact but well-furnished common areas, one set up as a sort of meeting-and-dining room. Adjacent was a galley kitchen, featuring the usual appliances as well as a calendar with the Bible Belters' upcoming appearances marked on it, an oiled maple chopping block, and a rack holding a set of good French steel knives. "Dad fancies himself a gourmet cook," Marcus said jovially.

The other area, at the rear of the big vehicle, was more casual, with books, reclining chairs, a compact weight machine and an exercise bicycle—that, I realized, must be how Marcus stayed in such good shape—and the duo's musical instruments.

"Have to keep the vessel of the spirit in order," Marcus remarked, seeing me notice the workout devices. "And these are the tools of our trade."

He waved at the keyboard synthesizer; I recognized it only because Sam wanted one. I did know what a guitar looked like, of course. And there was a banjo.

At the sight of it, my fingers tingled; all the modern and bluegrass stuff they played at La Sardina had made me begin coveting one, though I hadn't gone any further with the idea.

"Go ahead," Marcus invited. "I'm no Earl Scruggs,

but I can play a little. Go on, pick it up, it won't bite you."

He waved me to one of two practice chairs with a music stand in front of them and sat beside me.

"Hold it like this, put your fingers there, and strum," he instructed, so I did. "Now like this . . ."

Ten minutes later he had taught me three chords, my fingertips felt as if they'd gone through a meat grinder, and I'd seen the dermatological makeup on the back of his right hand.

"The Lord," he opined, "has blessed you with a little bit of musical talent."

"A very little," I laughed, putting down the instrument.

I couldn't tell what the makeup covered; it had been applied carefully. An unusual birthmark, perhaps, slightly rough. Or a gash closed with Dermabond or some similar surgical adhesive.

Even Krazy Glue will close a wound in a pinch, I'd learned from Victor, and the makeup could be bought in the drugstore. I didn't want to stare; if talking with Arnold hadn't primed me to notice it, I never would have.

But now I had. "Is this what your dad did with the kids in his youth group?" I asked. "Get them hooked on music, then slip the religion part in on the side?"

"Something like that," he agreed cheerfully. "But," he added, his tone turning serious, "you didn't come here for music lessons. Or a history of Dad's old church-related activities."

"No," I admitted, "I didn't. I'm looking for more facts on Reuben Tate. Information that might help me find out who really killed him. Because my ex-husband didn't."

His expression flickered cautiously; for all his practiced manners, the topic of Reuben made him uncomfortable. "Dad and I only got into town a few nights before Reuben died," he said. "But I'll help if I can."

"Did he harass you in any way, after you arrived? Ask you for money, threaten you, try to start arguments with you—did he get in your face? Or in your father's? Did you see him at all?"

Marcus looked thoughtful. "I didn't see him. My father did. Reuben came here while I was out having the Winnebago serviced. Dad wouldn't say what they talked about. I'm glad," he went on, "you're asking me these things and not him. Reuben upset him very badly. Dad stayed up half the night, praying over it."

Marcus rose, parted the venetian blinds at one of the big vehicle's windows, and looked out. "He's a vigorous guy, but he is getting older. I wouldn't want him," Marcus finished meaningfully, "upset any further."

Those wagons circling again. I thought of asking Marcus what his dad had been praying about, then decided to cut to the chase, instead.

"Did Reuben have anything to do with your mother's death?"

It was a guess based on nothing but a wild intuition. A funny kind of resonance had invaded the room just when they'd mentioned her, something unspoken between them. But at my query, Marcus's frank gaze retracted as emphatically as a welcome mat being rolled up.

"He didn't murder my mother," he said after a moment. "Not in the way that most people mean the term. But I'm sure that he was responsible for her death."

"In what way?"

Marcus turned from the window. "He scared her to death. Oh, I know, it sounds melodramatic, but she was vulnerable to that. Her heart was bad; everyone knew it. But if you're wondering if my dad would ever really act out that eye-for-an-eye stuff . . ."

Or get his big, strong son to do it, I thought clearly, and Marcus read my thought.

"Or get me to do it," he finished, "all I can say is that Dad and I have hardly been out of each other's sight since we arrived in Eastport."

Oh, terrific, another we-can-alibi-each-other scenario. A new thought struck me, and I had nothing else so I went with it:

"Have you by any chance met my ex-husband around town," I asked, "since you've arrived?"

I followed Marcus out into the bright Sunday afternoon. He shut the door of the Winnebago, turned. "This is the one you're trying to help out? Who's been arrested?"

"That's the one." I made my voice sound regretfully amused, as if Victor were a teenager who'd been picked up for some bit of harmless mischief.

"I'm afraid he has rather a penchant for getting himself in trouble," I went on, as we strolled into the garden. The tall white chrysanthemums bobbed in the breeze, flanked by the bright red masses of fruit on the thorned barberry bushes.

"Dark curly hair, intense expression, abrupt manner," I went on, describing Victor. "He's a very clean sort of man. Fastidious to a fault, actually, enough so that you might remember him."

I picked a chrysanthemum. "You see, anyone who could help pinpoint his whereabouts in the few days before the murder might end up being of assistance."

Marcus nodded, enlightened. "Oh, sure. Now I remember him. Smells like soap?"

That was Victor, all right: special antibacterial soap with hexachlorophene in it, which you could get only by prescription.

"We met him in the Baywatch restaurant where we were having lunch, the day after we got in," Marcus said. "He even gave us a little tour of his place. Lovely old Greek revival, isn't it?"

"Yes, it is." Victor's friendliness to strangers was a

new development, part of his program to be accepted in town.

Meanwhile, Marcus couldn't very well not mention this little meeting; anyone might have seen him and Heywood entering Victor's house. "And Victor is such a hospitable fellow, it's true."

When it suited him. "But our talk was very general," Marcus said. "I wish I could think of something useful, but . . ."

"That's all right. I appreciate your telling me about this. And thank your dad for me, too."

"Will do." He raised his big right hand unselfconsciously in a sort of salute as I went away down the sidewalk. When I glanced back he still stood there, watching me go, his face unreadable at that distance.

19

"They've all three of them been in there," I said to Wade an hour later. We were up in the front bedroom taking apart a whole window frame, at Wade's insistence.

"Mike Carpentier, Marcus Sondergard, and Heywood Sondergard, Marcus's father," I went on. "What'll you bet that Terence and Paddy've also been in Victor's place recently?"

"And could have seen that instrument collection," Wade said. "I don't know, though, how much that's going to help you. It's a pretty big net you're casting."

"Right," I agreed glumly. "Because who knows who else was in the house? At this rate, it could've been half the town. Did Marcus have any birthmark or a scar on his right hand, back when you knew him?" Mike Carpentier, I recalled, had a burn on his.

"Not one I remember. But not that I necessarily would recall something like that, either."

Wade had brought a six-foot piece of one-by-eight pine board along with his circular saw, two sawhorses, the clawhammer, and a bag of nails, plus the electric drill. I'd brought a tape measure and a detailed, exploded-view diagram of a modern window frame, which if it couldn't be jury-rigged to work in an antique house I was in deep trouble.

Wade's eyebrows went up as he got a good look at the window I had been working on earlier. "Exactly how did you manage to destroy this, again?"

Embarrassment swept over me. "Nailed the weatherstripping in backwards," I confessed. "Which," I added, "anyone could make that mistake, and I was preoccupied. Then of course I had to pull it out again. Which was when the old framing piece split."

"Uh-huh." Wade looked at me hard, then relented. "At least you're trying. This old house hasn't had so many repairs going on inside it since it was built, I'll bet."

He eyed the frame again, then hefted the pry bar and tore what I thought was a hideously large and important piece off of it. Plaster bits clattered to the floor. "Hey, look at this."

He fished around with his fingers in the crevice between the inner and outer walls. "I stand corrected. Someone has worked on this window before."

He drew out some tightly folded, yellowing newspaper, mostly intact. "Somebody packed this in here, trying to block a draft," he said, tossing aside the paper.

I picked it up. It was torn down the center, obliterating the date. But the quaint typography put it in its era: fresh news, 150 years ago. Others much like it had been in the walls of the downstairs ell, stuffed in there apparently as makeshift insulation.

The brittle pages were filled with ads for patent remedies, notices of public meetings, and reports of local events from a time when ladies wore elaborate hats with ostrich feathers in them, men raced horses hell-for-leather along the Shore Road, and they all gathered formally to attend. . . .

Concerts, including one at the Eastport Hotel on the Friday night previous to the newspaper's ancient issue. The fragile old sheet detailed a fine performance, well attended and marvelously entertaining, by a local musician: one Jared Hayes, resident of 20 Key Street.

As I read, a faint thread of the old music Sam had hummed to me played in my head: a goblin tune, haunting and sweet.

Wade looked up puzzledly. "Did you hear something?"

"No." I put aside the newspaper. "No, I don't think so." My mouth felt dry. The house seemed filled with an expectant silence.

And then nothing, as if a mist off the water had gathered up suddenly and evaporated.

"Kids all liked Sondergard," Wade said, turning back to the window. "Ones of us who were in his church youth group. Pastor Sondergard, that is. What we called him then."

"You didn't like Marcus?" I tried to recapture the sense I'd had a moment ago, as of someone about to whisper urgently to me.

But it was gone. Wade held up the tape measure. "Oh, he was kind of a geek. Filled out some, I'll say that much for him."

He laid the one-by-eight across the sawhorses, marked it, and picked up the circular saw. Since his unburdening of the night before, he seemed easier in his skin: talkative, not so worried. After he cut the board, he marked it once more and cut it again.

Had I been doing it, I'd have used a handsaw and taken half an hour. "Can I see that?"

The circular saw was heavy. "Like this?" I laid a piece of waste board on the sawhorses.

Wade nodded, steadied the wood. "Press the trigger and cut."

Brrr-anngg! It was done. Two pieces clattered to the floor.

"Good," he said, and picked up the clawhammer again.

Cheered—I have never been much good with power tools, but when you are trying to do things swiftly there is nothing like an electric motor—I resolved to get some scrap boards and practice with that circular saw again, sometime. This was, however, the only cheery thing about the task at hand, because it turned out there was a lot more wrong with the window frame than the damage I had done to it.

"Rot back here," Wade muttered, pulling crumbling wood out of the crevice. "Can't leave that."

Well, I could have, but he couldn't. Half an hour later, the bedroom wall looked as if a small missile had blasted through it.

"Sometime soon, better find out where the leak is," he said, dampening—no pun intended—my spirits further. If there was rot, there was water coming in somewhere, and I dreaded finding out more about it.

The repairs, though, went pretty swiftly: measuring, fitting, and nailing. And this time I set the weather-stripping pieces in their places the right way, so the sashes slid snugly and easily on them.

"Marcus's mother was a great big formidable woman," Wade said after a while. "She had some heart trouble, but you sure couldn't tell it by looking at her. Hilda, I think her name was."

"Marcus said she was vulnerable to fright."

Wade nodded, fit a sash back into its channel. "Yep. Marcus played piano back then. Fancied himself a little prodigy."

He set a molding strip back on, gave the gimlet a twist, put a nail in. "And anybody who thought they were good at anything, naturally that attracted old Reuben's attention. So what happened, one day Hilda caught Reuben trying to break Marcus's ring finger, get his allowance money out of him."

"Uh-oh." I was starting to see what was coming.

"Yeah. And heart condition or not, she wasn't the type to take a lot of backchat out of a kid, even Reuben. She grabbed him, dragged him into Washington Street, and shook him till he got away and ran home, her shouting after him, waving a big stick."

"Yikes. But she didn't catch him? Sounds like Reuben got off easy."

Wade tipped his head ambivalently. "Depends. No, she didn't catch him, but a week later they found Hilda Sondergard out in her garden. She'd had a heart attack. No one noticed for a couple of hours. Gone."

I slid the sash up and down, enjoying its new, draft-free condition and the absence of sticking or wobbling. Only forty-six more to go . . . "But what'd Reuben have to do with that? How would anyone know he'd done anything to her? If he did."

"Like I say, everyone knew she had heart trouble." Wade put the nails in the bag, unplugged the circular saw. "The theory is, Reuben hid out there. Jumped out at her. Scared her to death."

"I don't see," I began, "how you could prove—"

"You couldn't," Wade said flatly. "But when they rolled her over, they found money beneath her. Nickels and dimes. The exact amount of Marcus's allowance."

I took the sawhorses apart, put the pieces under my arms, and started downstairs with them, Wade following with the other tools.

"It was the big story in town for a while," he said. "Then Reuben took off, turned into a drifter. Ran different scams here and there. Came back sometimes, left again. Mostly he moved from town to town. Kept his forwarding address current with the post office here, though, to get those checks from that trust his mom had set up for him."

He reached past me to open the cellar door. "Then the two Sondergards left. And I've often wondered," he added, flipping the light switch in the cellar landing, "if it was coincidence."

"If what was?" I set the sawhorse parts on the floor.

"That every time Reuben moved on to greener pastures," Wade replied, putting the circular saw on its shelf in the corner, "a certain pair of itinerant musical ministers showed up there too?"

I turned to face him. "Come on. How would you know that?"

He spread his hands. "Jacobia. I couldn't forget him. Boxy. Or Reuben either. It's always preyed on me, just kind of eaten at me. So," he confessed, "I kept track of him. Where he showed up. Kind of hoping, you know."

"That you would hear about something else? Hear about it—"

"And be able to stop it." He frowned. "And then there's that flyer the Sondergards put out, about their musical dates."

I'd seen one in the parlor of Heddlepenny House. "They've been sending it for years, and I'm on their mailing list because I was in the youth group, I guess," Waded added.

"So you knew where they were, too."

"Yeah. And like I say, I suppose it could be a coincidence," Wade said, coming out of the cellar stairwell behind me.

Tommy and Sam were at the kitchen table, drilling each other in Morse code and high-fiving each other when they translated the patterns correctly.

"Reuben and the Sondergards," Wade said, getting himself a beer out of the refrigerator. "Same towns, same time, so often. It could be," he finished, "meaningless."

But I could tell from his voice that he didn't think so.

Me, either.

20

Later that afternoon, Wade went down to the dock to check on his freighter-piloting schedule for the coming week, and I went out into the yard and dragged out the aluminum extension ladder. Encouraged by my triumph with the electric saw, and reminded of leaks in general by the rot Wade had found behind the plaster, I thought I might fix a small leak that I had already located over the kitchen window.

About this leak, I thought, there was no mystery whatsoever: Every time it rained, water poured into the space between the sash and the aluminum storm window with which—for what reason, I had no idea—that one window had at some time been fitted.

This, by the way, is a constant feature of old-house fix-up: wondering why someone has done something idiotic that you have to undo, redo, or otherwise somehow finagle. Probably someday, a thoroughly annoyed person will wonder the same thing about many of my amateur repairs; in an old house, necessity is often the mother of some pretty funny-looking inventions.

Fortunately, however, this particular fix looked relatively straightforward. So I took Monday, the ladder, and the caulking gun filled with polyurethane caulking material—

—silicone caulk is indeed indestructible, as advertised, but it has a bad habit of letting go of porous old wood, which is of course what my old house was mostly made of—

—and prepared to do minor battle.

While I worked, I thought about Reuben Tate following the Sondergards, or vice versa. Surely the state police investigators would be interested in that idea.

The trouble was, in order to tell them about it I would have to get Wade involved, and I didn't want to. The less interest the better if it was focused on my family, I decided, at least for now. And since Ellie was still busy stitching children's costumes for the festival, I decided to wait before trying to interview Willow Prettymore, too; I'd been lucky with the Sondergards, but history suggested that a familiar face like Ellie's might ease my way considerably, in the snoopy-questions department.

In the backyard, I put up the ladder, cursing mildly as I struggled to find a level place for it. Meanwhile, Monday ran circles around herself, rejoicing in the fresh air and in the fact that she was not on a leash; Sam had actually managed to teach her to stay in the yard, which for a Labrador retriever is like teaching it to do algebra.

But finally I got up there, and as I'd suspected, a strip of old wood on the framing above the window was loose. My plan was to nail it, slather it with caulk, and pray that my fix stopped water from pouring through it: handy-dandy, I thought, reaching confidently for the strip of window trim.

Which came away in my hand a good deal more swiftly than I had anticipated. Flailing, I did manage not to fall off that blasted ladder. But obviously the wood around the window had been exposed to water longer than I'd thought. Instead of being solid with one loose place in the middle, the whole strip was the consistency of damp papier-mâché, from one side of the window top to the other.

And down both sides, I realized with dawning horror as I tapped the wood experimentally. The siding gave off the punky, hollow-log sound that meant it was holding together mostly via some dim, vegetable memory of being solid, at some time in the distant past such as for instance when it used to be a tree.

While I frowned at it, Monday plunged into a pile of fallen leaves and rolled joyously, then began snuffling along the edge of the perennial garden, where I'd heaped more leaves in hopes of discouraging my best crop: weeds.

Cautiously, I tugged on a piece of siding. It came away as if I were tearing off wet newspaper; underneath, a colony of dark beetles swarmed in the sudden sunlight.

All thoughts of handy-dandy, one-afternoon home fix-it work flew out of my head; this wasn't a job I could do myself. This would take carpentry of the kind done by people who ordered their lumber and nails by the hideously expensive truckload.

Probably it explained the rot Wade had found upstairs, too; this water wasn't only coming in around the aluminum window. It was from above, as I could tell by pulling on siding higher than the window frame. A sick sensation started somewhere in the pit of my stomach; possibly the leak was in the roof.

The idea made me think I might break out in hives, because the roof of my old house is three full stories above the ground, not counting the peak above the attic. Working on it myself was out of the question, and hiring somebody to climb up there meant finding someone who was:

1. drunk enough to consent to do it, and
2. sober enough to be able to.

Also, the person had to know how to perform roof work. And although that combination is not as rare as you may think—

—men in Eastport climb cheerfully up steeples, ship masts, and shaky, slapdashedly assembled scaffoldings, and walk along roof lines to reflash chimneys and install lightning rods without even dropping the pint bottles of fiery brown liquid with which they are, in order to go up there at all, necessarily equipped—

—there is a final requirement: When it comes time for the job, you also have to find a place in your house where you cannot see out any windows, in case the person you have sent up there should fall past one suddenly, waving that pint bottle.

So it's a big project even aside from what it costs. Slowly, I replaced the cap on the caulking gun, turning to see where the dog might have wandered off to. But she was still in the yard; as I spotted her she readied herself to pounce, and plunged her nose curiously into another pile of dry leaves.

And let out a shriek.

21

"The dog is fine," Ellie kept saying two hours later as she drove us home from the animal clinic on the mainland. Even though it was Sunday evening, the vet had agreed to meet us there when I told her what had happened.

Crazed with sudden pain, Monday had run without knowing it straight into my arms, or I might never have caught her. I'd grabbed the rat trap she was trying to shake off and muscled it open, praying for only a bruise. But the horrid thing—like a mouse trap only bigger, much bigger—had cut a gash on the side of her nose.

Now she was stitched up, medicated for pain and infection, and sedated, her glossy black head cradled quietly in my lap. The vet hadn't said anything about owner's tears being therapeutic.

But I shed them anyway. "Sam raked those leaves three days ago," I managed. "That *thing* must've been put out there since then. If I'd stuck my hand in it, it could have broken my wrist. We're lucky it didn't fracture Monday's nose."

Ellie nodded grimly, saying nothing. The look on her face as she glanced in the rearview said it all. Monday sighed, grieved and puzzled by the whole ordeal, and burrowed her head tighter against me, wincing when her nose brushed my sweater.

"Has this happened to anyone else around town lately? Mean pranks, meant to hurt someone?"

"Not that I've heard." Ellie hesitated. "This is the kind of thing that Reuben would do, not a normal person. And I'm not sure it was a prank."

I'd filled her in on the Sondergards' travels, the way they had mirrored the drifting of Reuben Tate from town to town.

"I don't mean to upset you any more than you are, but you've been asking a lot of questions about him," she went on. "Word's spread."

She was right. Pranks in Eastport were pretty exclusively of the ring-your-doorbell-and-run variety, not the snap-your-hand-off kind. And by now almost everybody in town knew that Victor was in trouble and I was trying to get him out of it.

"I called Willow Prettymore," Ellie added. "Explained your situation. And never mind what Mike Carpentier might think, I didn't get a feeling that Willow's exactly dying to talk to us."

The woman Mike had been so sure would blab to us about him and Reuben.

"Too bad for Willow," I retorted angrily. "She's going to."

Then the import of Ellie's first comment sank in; I wondered abruptly what other surprises someone might have prepared for me.

Ellie met my gaze in the rearview again. "That trap might have sat there until spring, you know, without you or anyone else finding it."

So if the rat trap had been intended to discourage me from asking any more questions, she meant, then there might be other things intended to accomplish that goal, too: attacks that didn't depend as much on blind chance, but were equally anonymous—

—assuming, of course, that Ellie and I weren't jumping to conclusions.

"If somebody told me to stop digging into this," I began. "Threatened me right up front . . ."

"Then it would be obvious there was something to dig into," she agreed. "And Victor would stop looking so guilty, maybe even to the police."

"But this way . . ."

I let the rest go unspoken. This way, someone could go on being subtle about suggesting that I mind my own damned business, without raising anyone else's suspicions about the status quo.

Subtle for now. The thought made me angrier. "You've set it up with her?" I asked. "With Willow, to meet with us?"

"Uh-uh. She hung up on me. Willow's a tough one."

"We'll see about that," I said as I smoothed Monday's ears. The vet said it was lucky that the thing had caught her sideways, not full on. "We'll just see."

We were nearly at my house. "At this point," I went on as Ellie turned into the drive—I averted my eyes from the storm windows—"I'm so mad that to get rid of me, Willow Prettymore's probably going to have to break my jaw."

Ellie stopped the Jeep, her eyes meeting mine

again. "Yes, but be a little careful, too, will you, Jacobia? Whoever's doing this . . ."

"I know." The awful scarecrow sight of him rose again, as if Reuben himself were behind today's mean deed. Which of course in a way he was. . .

That night we all pampered the dog to a fare-thee-well, and I explained to Wade and Sam about the rat trap: that my chronic nosiness might just possibly have annoyed someone.

Wade raised his eyebrows, saying nothing but meaning plenty, and I knew we were going to have a very interesting discussion later. Sam nodded gravely, filing the information away to think over in private before he commented on it.

Then he went back to nursing Monday: sitting by her dog bed on his sleeping bag, where he meant to spend the night, speaking very quietly to her without ever stopping—I listened once: he was telling her knock-knock jokes—and rinsing her nose with warm water at frequent, regular intervals.

If I had tried this she would have run up three flights of stairs, to the back of a closet in the attic, and stayed there until I gave up. But Sam is a repairing type of boy; not only did she tolerate his method of canine wound care, but it worked:

The next morning, Monday ate the soft food I prepared for her and drank some water. The gash looked clean, if still very swollen; her eyes were clear, her mood subdued but cheerful. She even frisked a little when I put down her breakfast—Sam, after a careful inspection of her condition, had consented to go to work—and she licked my hand as I got her settled back onto her dog bed, preparatory to my leaving the house.

The .25 semiauto was in my sweater pocket. Setting out into a morning of thin clouds and watery sun, I could feel it there: a lump of misery like the one in my heart.

Despite what I'd told Sam and Wade, because of

course I'd had to warn them, all night I'd gone on resisting the idea that the rat trap really had been put there on purpose. There were, I kept insisting to myself, other possible explanations.

Only none held much water and at last I'd given in: Someone wasn't kidding.

"Listen," I'd said to Wade, who was just then waking up as he always did at the crack of dawn, "there's another thing. All this is about Victor. And I can't help thinking that you must be feeling . . ."

Annoyed. Even a little jealous. Something.

He'd clicked on the lamp. "Maybe if I'd done what I ought to all those years ago, this might not be happening."

He sat up. "So I'll tell you what. Until I say so, why don't you assume I'm okay about whatever you need to do, all right?"

Which was typical of him. "Yes," I agreed, wondering who I'd been in a past life to deserve him: St. Teresa of Avila, apparently.

"And," he continued, "if Victor bugs me, I'll be the one to take care of it. We all square on this?"

"Perfectly," I'd agreed, "square."

"Okay. C'mere," he'd said sleepily, and held his arms out.

I slid into them. Like I say, Wade is not a particularly verbal guy.

But when he wants to, he gets his message across.

No one answered the door of Heddlepenny House, but I found Marcus out in the Winnebago, on the exercise bicycle.

"Your father," I said, "was on that list."

His eyes narrowed. "What list? I don't know about any list."

But it was the only thing that made sense.

"The list of gay men Reuben Tate got hold of,

somehow. He tried to blackmail them. And that sort of story would have ruined your dad in this town, back then."

He started to reply, but I got in ahead of him. "You made it sound as if you left right away, but you two stayed in town for years after your mother died. A long time, if your motive for leaving was grief over her death. But then Reuben went to jail for six months, and when he came back . . ."

He was staring at me. "When Reuben came back," I finished, "he did something that drove your father out of Eastport."

The flywheel on the exercise bicycle spun down with a low whine. "You're wrong. Without her, my dad couldn't stand it here. He tried for a long time, but everything reminded him; he had to get away finally."

"What did your father and Reuben talk about the other night?"

He picked up a small freeweight from the rack of them near the exercise apparatus and began hefting it up and down nervously.

"I told you, I don't know. Dad took him into the study, in the house. Half an hour later, I heard the door close. When I went in, Reuben was gone."

"Your father didn't say what they'd discussed?"

Marcus shook his head. "Said it was pastoral. He's serious about the confidentiality of that. It was one reason the kids all went to him with their problems, back in the old days. Although I can't imagine what Reuben could talk about that would have to do with solving any of his problems. Or about religion."

"Maybe they talked about how you two and Reuben kept ending up in the same towns, time after time. So which was it, Marcus—was he following you, or were you following him?"

He went to the refrigerator in the galley kitchen, came back with a bottle of water, and drank nervously from it. "I don't know what you are talking about," he repeated.

I felt like punching him. Maybe he was a good musician, maybe not. But he was a lousy liar. "You know, Marcus, I used to be a money manager, back in the city. Investing, tax counseling. That sort of thing."

"How," he remarked uninterestedly, "interesting."

"Some of my clients were crooks," I went on.

He looked sharply at me.

"And liars. Skilled ones, not like you. Sometimes they even lied to me. And since I didn't want my name on anything that could be proven fraudulent—since it was my job to make sure it couldn't be, in fact—I would ask them questions. Know what I found out?"

"What?" he replied resentfully, picking up a towel, wiping it across his face. He was starting to look even more uncomfortable.

"Nobody ever says they don't know what you're talking about when you ask them about what somebody else did. They say it when you ask about what *they* did. Or they don't say it at all."

Marcus frowned thwartedly. "I don't want to talk to you anymore. All you want to do is stir up trouble."

"It's already stirred up. Two men are dead. Where is your dad, anyway? Maybe he can manage to give me a straight answer."

Anger flashed in his eyes. "You're not a police officer. You can't just barge in here and ask me questions like this."

"Sure I can. And you can refuse to answer. Of course, if you do, I'll just go ask somebody else."

I got up, looked between the slats of the venetian blinds. "Do I look like a quitter to you, Marcus?" I asked, and waited.

He sighed defeatedly. "Dad's at the lake. We had a camp out there. Sold now, but he still likes to fool around on the water."

Boyden Lake was a few miles west on the mainland. It was big, and there were quite a few camps on it. "Want to give me a hint? Or should I just go down to Bay Books, ask around, maybe mention why I want to find him, to ask him about that list and what he did to get on it? I'll bet people would be fascinated."

He slammed down the water bottle. "Look, my father is a good man. He did a lot of good for this town, kids especially. He gave them somewhere to go, something to do, he helped them with their problems. And a lot of them, if they care about anything today—if they go to church, or like music, or try to help people—it's because of what they learned from him. And the example he gave."

I could think of at least one kid whose problems Reverend Sondergard hadn't helped with at all. "He doesn't deserve to have his name blackened now," Marcus went on furiously. "To have you digging up old dirt."

Boxy Thorogood would have raced down Washington Street right outside the Sondergards' house, the night Reuben ambushed him. And according to Wade, he'd been a member of that youth group: the youngest member, more helpless than most against a guy like Reuben. But I didn't say this, or anything. I just let Marcus rant, noticing that the mark on his right hand was again covered skillfully with makeup.

And when he had finished, and saw that I still hadn't given up, he scribbled me a little map.

22

Traffic along rural Route 190 was busy, lots of motor homes and vans piling into town for the festival. At the airfield small planes crowded the usually quiet tarmac, and the tourist cabins at Harris Point sported barbecue grills, bicycles leaning against the porch rails, and badminton nets strung up in the side yards.

It all looked like someone's happy dream of an island autumn in Maine, and I can't tell you how uneasy it all made me feel, as if the other shoe were just hanging there waiting to drop. Marcus Sondergard was hiding something, and I had little confidence that his father would tell me what it was.

But I had to try, because something very bad was happening in Eastport and it wasn't over: as if Reuben, for all the sick, purposeful display someone had made of him, wasn't quite dead.

The unusual number of vehicles didn't slow me much, since they were all heading into town; outbound, the only obstacle was a slow eighteen-wheeler, just ahead of me, hauling a massive crane and apparently having some kind of engine trouble. Its WIDE LOAD sign barely described adequately the size of the vehicle, but finally it found a bit of shoulder and pulled to the side.

And then it was smooth sailing. After the causeway came a short jog onto the Golding Road: rolling pastures, dark granite outcroppings, crosshatchings of orchard trees studded with red and yellow apples. Scrub pine closed in on the roadside until a dirt cut opened to the left.

I put the car on the shoulder, its tires in the sand that had accumulated over years of icy winters, and hiked into the brush. Hundred-year-old spruce trees, originally planted as windbreaks, towered in rows. I passed an old well hole, its cover rotted in and its throat choked with stones. There was a cellar hole, too, now a shallow depression edged with arm-thick rose canes. A barn foundation humped under mats of thick grass behind the collapse of a rail fence. A hundred yards ahead, water glittered in a gap between two small structures: the camps.

In Maine your camp is your summer place,

whether primitive or elaborate. These were little old clapboard houses, each situated pleasantly on its ledge in the sunshine overlooking the water. A dirt path between them led down to a short dock.

"Hello?" Marcus Sondergard was sliding a dark-green kayak into the shallows. Two paddles lay on the dock.

"I'd hoped someone might be out here," he said cheerfully, "to take a ride with me. But no such luck."

Until you showed up, his expression communicated hopefully. The kayak was a two-seater. Heywood wore dark canvas slacks with the same leather belt I'd seen before, the cross-and-rose buckle glittering in the sun, plus a gray sweatshirt and old sneakers. His hair, as thick and youthfully luxuriant as his son Marcus's, shone nearly as silver as the belt buckle. "Care for a spin?"

The problem with a kayak, as I understood it, is that it could roll upside down, so your head would poke straight down into the water like the stick on a popsicle. But I did want to talk to him. And the water there was quite shallow. Maybe I would only break my neck on the lake bottom, instead of drowning.

"This isn't a social visit," I temporized.

"I know," Heywood said calmly, his blue eyes perceptive. "I know exactly why you're here. And"—his eyes twinkled—"two-person kayaks don't roll. Come on, we'll talk on the water."

Ten minutes later, with his help I'd maneuvered myself into the kayak's aft cockpit, and I wasn't even completely drenched. "Don't worry," he said, "I'll do all the work. If we do tip, just cross your arms and tuck." He demonstrated.

Sure, I thought; in my dreams. But I took a paddle, held it as he instructed, and did nothing with it, also as Heywood instructed.

And then we *skimmed.*

The water's surface was bright as a pearl and seemed to offer no resistance; under Heywood's power we shot from the dock, then turned, parallel to the shore. His energy struck me as I watched him work the paddle, turning his face into the sunshine and basking in it, moving the craft without any visible effort.

"Now," he invited. "The reason that you are here is . . ."

"Was he blackmailing you? Reuben?"

Heywood kept paddling. "Yes. The accusation was false. But I was frightened. I wish I hadn't been. Still, I was."

"Marcus didn't want to tell me. He seemed quite frantic."

"Marcus is very protective of me."

I could see both of Heywood's hands from where I sat. There was no mark on either of them.

But there wouldn't have to be. As he'd said, Marcus was very protective.

"And the other night? When he came to Heddlepenny House, was Reuben up to his old tricks? Or was it really, as Marcus says, a pastoral visit?"

He tipped his head slightly, in apparent contrition. "I told Marcus that so he wouldn't worry. Tate wanted money."

"Surely that didn't surprise you?"

His shoulders moved in a sigh. "I had hoped that my tactic with Reuben Tate had finally borne fruit. But I was disappointed."

"What tactic?"

A little silence. Then: "I'm an old man. I don't care what people say anymore. Nor did I ever, really. But Marcus—he cares very much."

Not an answer. I began thinking that Heywood Sondergard, for all the simple, beaming goodness of his public persona, might be a slick character.

He dipped the paddle again. "Still, there's little enough love in the world as it is. I won't condemn any variety of it, even by denying a story that isn't true. Not anymore."

"But Marcus might. For your sake or his."

He feathered the paddle expertly, replied with subtle skill. "Marcus is a young man. From my point of view, anyway. He has never had much to do with women at any time in his life. Except, of course, with his mother."

Suggesting, I thought, that Marcus could have been the actual blackmail target instead of Heywood. But not admitting it. Blowing smoke at me was what he was doing. On the shore a deer drank placidly: young male, fuzzy nubs of antlers.

"He has a woman friend now," Heywood went on. "Lovely woman. Lives in Portland. But I fear she may be growing impatient. We all feel time passing as we get older."

"Why don't you tell him to go?"

If you know he's ruining his chances, I meant. Heywood heard the implied criticism, replied easily to it.

"It's not that simple. Marcus has a sense of duty. And what would he do? There aren't," he added gently, "a lot of employment opportunities for a man who has spent his whole adult life as an itinerant Bible thumper, banjo player, and freelance do-gooder."

Correct; I just hadn't thought of it.

"No, if I wanted to send Marcus out into the world without me, I should have started thirty years ago. As it is, he's stuck with me until I die."

The thought hung in the bright air. "And then?"

The kayak shot skimmingly on the water. "I made provision," he admitted, "once I realized how I'd crippled the boy. Without me there's no musical duo, and Marcus is no solo artist, he knows that. Even that small source of income will be closed to him when I'm gone. But . . ."

He turned the kayak back toward shore. "I arranged a sizable life-insurance benefit. He'll land on his feet."

The water was crystalline, minnows flashing as we went over them. "And," he added, "despite the lady's impatience, I believe she thinks half a million—and Marcus, of course—are worth the wait."

"Practical move," I said, considering it with my financial head. A stake like that, properly invested, was just about right. Interesting too the way he'd dangled diversionary bait in front of me, so that suddenly we were talking about Marcus instead of about Reuben. I aimed my next question carefully.

"Do you think he resents it? Marcus, I mean. That you acted in certain ways when he was young, and that's turned out to have influenced his whole life?"

But not carefully enough. His answering laugh was hearty and knowing. "You're asking whether my son is psychologically damaged enough to commit a murder in a particularly hideous fashion?"

That was fair. "Actually, yes."

"Well, he's not. Marcus couldn't kill anyone. Take it from a man who really knows him. But why don't you suspect me? Too old?"

Suddenly I liked the Reverend Sondergard a lot despite the way he was evading me, or maybe even because of it. He was smart, a clever talker, impossible to offend, and no fool. *Because you don't have a wound on your hand,* I wanted to tell him.

But Marcus did have. Or might have; I still didn't know what the mark was.

"I'm just trying to understand it all," I said. "I know Reuben threatened you. It *was* you, not Marcus? Since you raised the question, really; I want to be absolutely clear about it."

A nod. "It was me."

"And that drove you out of town. You don't care anymore, but Marcus still wants it kept quiet. You both think Reuben had to do with the death of your wife, but neither of you can prove it. And you still haven't explained what you meant about the tactic you mentioned, why you and Reuben kept ending up in the same places."

Another silence, longer. "It's true that when I decided to leave back then, he threatened to follow."

Suddenly I understood. "So the hunter became the hunted. I suppose you had a connection here at the post office, to keep you current of his forwarding address."

Wade had done it too, but he had stopped there. Going on with it was a brilliant turnabout, the one thing Tate would never have expected. To be *pursued* . . .

"What I still don't see, though, is the reason."

He dug his paddle in. The kayak tilted startlingly. I leaned the other way from reflex, crossed my arms over my chest.

The craft settled. When he spoke again his tone was harsh. "No, of course you don't. Why would you? I'm an old guy who sings Jesus music. I'm surprised you even noticed."

He pushed us toward the beach. "He'd killed my wife, scared my son, mortified my spirit. But yet I was a man of religion." He said it resignedly, as if it were some chronic, incurable disease.

"So I prayed over it. What could I do when confronted with an evil like that? What was my task that had been set for me? What," he intoned, "was my duty?"

A flock of mallards rose from a cove all at once, the sound of their beating wings huge in the bright noonday silence.

"I wanted his soul," Heywood Sondergard said. "I wanted his immortal soul. And I was determined to have it." He set the kayak parallel to the dock.

"So you and Marcus followed him. What did he think of it?" I tried to imagine. "It must've driven him nuts."

Heywood chuckled. Somewhere an outboard roared, then fell into a low, steady rumble. Across the lake, a kid ran off the end of a pier, landed in the water with a splash, shouted at the cold.

"At first he would try to attack us. Throw things, try to start fires under the Winnebago, that kind of behavior."

Heywood sounded almost indulgent. "Then he began trying to avoid us. To Reuben, we were the conscience he never had."

"So the other night, why did he . . . ?"

"Visit, and threaten? I suppose back on his home territory he felt stronger. He thought he might get the upper hand again. But he didn't. I refused his demand, laughed at his threat, and told him we were going to follow him till the day he died."

At the memory, Heywood sounded pleased. "And you know what? I think Reuben finally believed me. He looked . . . frightened."

"And you figured what, that he'd break down someday? Throw himself on your mercy and beg forgiveness? Embrace salvation?"

Heywood waved a hand as if acknowledging the unlikeliness of any such thing. The kayak slid in against the dock pilings.

"I didn't know. I only knew I had to try what I could, that if he were saved it would have made it all worth it."

He set the paddles on the dock. "That a change of heart was the only thing that could make any of it worth it."

A car was pulling up to the camps. "My ride," Heywood said.

I had a last question but didn't know how to put it. The killer almost surely didn't know about the skin shred in Weasel Bodine's mouth, and if I tipped that domino over I didn't know what might happen. Besides, I'd promised Bob Arnold not to mention it.

I could ask one thing, though: "Was Wesley Bodine ever a member of the youth group you had at the church?"

He didn't have to think about it. "I don't remember anyone by that name. And I would; I knew all the youngsters quite well."

"I see. Well, thanks for talking to me. You cleared up a lot of things I'd worried over. And I don't suspect Marcus anymore," I added, putting just the right touch of shamefaced apology into it. "I'm afraid my imagination must just've kind of gotten away from me."

As I'd told Marcus, I'd met some great liars in the city. What I hadn't said was how much I'd learned: watching, listening. Or how much I'd practiced the art myself.

Heywood had told the truth about not knowing Wesley Bodine. Now he smiled forgivingly, turned to walk toward the car.

"Oh, and by the way," I said casually, "if Marcus ever wants a cosmetic surgeon to check his hand—for that scar or birthmark or whatever it is—my ex-husband can refer him to a great one."

Heywood stopped, turned back again slowly, his blue eyes fixing me in a gaze that was deliberately transparent. The belt buckle winked slyly at me.

"I don't know what you're talking about," he said.

23

Walking back along the rutted dirt track, I found the farm ruins still mouldering in the slanted sunlight, gnarled branches of old apple trees casting crooked shadows. Thick clumps of pale, blue-green iris foliage marked the old perennial garden, ancient roots pushing out of the earth like massive knucklebones.

A scallop dragger puttered in the channel at the end of the old Toll Road as I crossed the causeway back onto the island. In my rearview a line of cars had begun forming; off-islanders, most likely, impatient to reach their destination after a long drive.

There was nowhere for them to pass and I'd been just loafing along. I hit the gas hard and sailed into a long uphill curve, my thoughts still on Heywood's last comment. He'd been lying.

The engine coughed. I glanced at the dash. The gas gauge's needle sat on E. Impossible—but there was no time to worry about the implications of it; I was already into the curve.

The engine died, slowing me suddenly. The power steering went too, and to make matters worse, a car behind me was speeding up, pulling out, trying to pass.

Disastrously worse, actually: An air horn shot my attention forward again. An eighteen-wheeler, coming the other way around the curve . . .

I hauled the steering wheel, struggling to get off the road. The right front tire bit into the soft, sandy shoulder, slowing me further but not, I felt suddenly, slowing me enough. Ahead was a metal guardrail, beyond it thin air followed by a three-hundred-foot drop to the water, and of course I had no power brakes at that point, either.

The truck got bigger, its air horn blasting again. The car that had been trying to pass was now right beside me, aimed head-on at the truck. He couldn't back off; the other cars had pulled up, closing the gap. But the big vehicle didn't have anywhere to go either, because to its right was a vertical granite cliff, the continuation of the ledge that the road had been built into. The only area of shoulder was occupied by the massive, disabled crane-hauling rig I'd seen earlier, on my way out.

Oh, it was fascinating, and happening so fast, yet slowly, too. Gracefully, inevitably. In the next few instants, several of us were going to die, not a thing I could do about it.

Suddenly the car beside me slammed mine, with a thud that snapped my head sideways. It jolted me toward the rail, which was a puny thing, toylike, and then I couldn't see the rail at all because it was underneath my front bumper. Thin air yawned ahead of me and he *jolted* me again, trying to get by; a metallic groan said the rail was giving under the pressure.

Then with a shriek of metal on metal the other car scraped past, skinning the eighteen-wheeler and my front fender by a matter of inches. My front bumper bent the guardrail out another fraction, trying to uproot the rail's support posts, stopped.

And then it was over, the big rig's air horn howling one way, the car speeding away in the other. The ones behind me kept on going too; there was nowhere for them to stop.

I just sat there, looking out over the dashboard to the water. A seagull swooped down, peered curiously at me with a sideways flash of his beady eye, flapped away again.

Finally I picked up the car phone and called Bob Arnold, my hands shaking and my voice an odd, breathless cartoon version of itself. And then I waited by the side of the car, its emergency blinkers on, hoping the vehicles coming up from behind would see the flashers and not give the car a final, over-the-edge bump. It didn't take long before I heard the crunch of a car pulling onto the narrow verge, and I turned expectantly, figuring that Arnold could put his squad's cherry beacon on, stop traffic long enough for me to empty a gas can into my vehicle's tank and get into the driving lane again.

But it wasn't Arnold. It was the blond woman I'd collided with outside Paddy Farrell's and whose photo I'd seen at Mike Carpentier's cottage: Molly Carpentier's mother.

"Hey," she said cheerfully, getting out of her rental sedan. "Problem? I'm Anne Carpentier."

She strode toward me. "Hope you've recovered from that smack I gave you. I get to barreling along on some errand, don't always watch where I'm going."

She stuck her hand out and I shook it, introducing myself. Her grip was firm but not overwhelming in that crushing, I've-got-a-point-to-make way that some very physically fit women affect.

She eyed my car. "It looked like you hit the guardrail," she said. "So I just wondered if you were okay. Guess it's not as bad as I thought, though."

"Yeah, I'm fine," I said, noticing those violet eyes again. Then I explained briefly the fix I was in, not expecting there was much she could do about it but glad, actually, for some company.

"Bummer," she commented succinctly. "Hey, I've got a coffee Thermos in my car. Want some?"

I accepted gratefully and found a Styrofoam cup in my backseat; moments later we were chatting like a couple of old pals.

"I met your daughter," I said as she poured steaming liquid from the Thermos. "She's a beautiful little girl."

Anne Carpentier nodded proudly. "Yeah. She's a peach all right. I've been a little worried about her, now that I'm away so much." She went on to confirm what I already knew about her: merchant marine, lots of travel, not very frequent visits home.

"But Mike's doing a great job with Molly," Anne finished. "I wouldn't be able to keep working if I didn't think so."

I didn't say anything. The idea of leaving Sam for months at a time when he was little would never have occurred to me; doing it would nearly have killed me.

Anne drank some coffee, looked pointedly over the cup at me. "Lots of the guys I go to sea with are fathers. Nobody tells them they're bad fathers, or implies it. People have to make a living, you know."

Her tone was gentle but the meaning of her remarks was not. "I'm sorry. It's none of my business. It's just that . . . Well, you don't think she's a little isolated?" I hazarded.

But at this she only laughed. "You've been listening to too much Eastport small talk. I asked Molly about that, and it seems she has a perfectly satisfactory social life at school. And she does see a few other children outside of school, too. It's just that Mike looks them over pretty carefully, and he's stepped on a few toes doing it."

She looked out over the guardrail at the water. "That's the thing about him, see. I couldn't live with him. I never should have been married at all," she added wryly, "if you want to know the truth. Definitely not to someone as sensitive and complicated as he is."

"Because?" It was an oddly personal admission from someone I'd just met, but it didn't feel that way. I got the sense that Anne Carpentier wasn't much for meaningless small talk, that she made a habit of cutting right to the chase. I liked it.

"He keeps things to himself," she replied. "I don't pick up on them, then his feelings get more hurt. And they stay hurt. I'm more the bull-in-a-china-shop type, wade right in and battle to the death, you know? Take care of things and pick up the pieces later."

Her face as she said this was as calm and sunny as a summer morning, her yellow curls bobbing in the breeze off the water, her remarkable eyes untroubled.

"But Mike would fight wild tigers for Molly," she finished. "And that's what's important, if I'm not there to do it."

She put the top back on the Thermos, caught sight of Arnold in the squad coming around the curve. "Looks like your ride's on its way," she remarked. "I'm going to get moving."

"Thanks for stopping." I was glad she had. I liked the fact that she would pull off the road for a stranger who looked to be in trouble. "Are you going to be in town long?"

She shook her head, getting back into her car. "Going out tonight. Hey, nice meeting you. Maybe see you next time."

She started the engine. Cars on the road were still passing in a steady stream, and I didn't see how she would make it back into the traveling lane without help; I stepped over to stop the traffic so she could get out, but she was already nosing the rental onto the pavement, getting the oncoming cars to make way for her by ignoring them, so they had to let her in or hit her.

Gutsy, I thought. She waved cheerfully and drove off, as Arnold pulled into the space she had vacated.

"This tank was half-full," I answered his admonishing look, "this morning."

"Uh-huh," he said. "Sure Sam didn't drive it? Or Wade?"

I didn't bother to answer that; he knew Sam walked and Wade always took his truck. Instead, I told him about Monday's nose.

"That makes two incidents," I said. "Somebody

siphoned the gas out of that tank, Bob, when I was out at the lake."

He peered under the car. "No leak, or not big enough that I can see."

"Bob, the tank's empty. And don't you think I'd have noticed if I was leaking gasoline all the way home? I'd have smelled it."

"That's true." He squinted out at the water, considering.

"If the engine cut out and I'd lost power brakes and steering on Washington Street, I'd have gone right into the boat basin."

He still didn't quite buy it. "Wouldn't you have seen a gas puddle that size? Out at the lake? Smelled it there, too?"

"Not if somebody came prepared," I said. "Listen, I'm going back."

He lifted the two-gallon gas can he'd brought, began transferring the contents to my tank. "How about I follow you? Be on the safe side."

After what I'd been through, the safe side sounded good to me. He stopped traffic while I backed gingerly onto the pavement. Ten minutes later we were back on the Golding Road, pulled up behind my earlier tire marks on the soft, sandy shoulder.

No huge puddle of gasoline was in evidence, not that I'd expected any. I got down on my knees, peering and sniffing. There wouldn't be much. . . .

"Here." A few round, shallow depressions like raindrops in the sand, smelling of gas.

I got up, waiting while Bob came over, crouched, and got up again looking thoughtful.

"I grew up poor," I said. "I know how to siphon gas."

"You don't," Bob agreed, "want to get it in your mouth. I've dragged a few kids to the hospital on that score. You can breathe it in."

"Clear plastic tube, suck on it till the gas rises,

drop the end low but before you taste it, it keeps running into your gas can. Or whatever."

"Couple of drops," Bob said, "will always get spilled."

He looked down at the raindrop marks, toed the sand by the road. "So how do you want to play this? File a complaint?"

"No. Actually, I'd appreciate it if you kept it quiet."

"Sure you know what you're doing?"

"Nope. I just know I've got a lot more questions to ask, and I don't want to do anything to change what's going on while I'm still trying to figure out what it is. That's all."

Somebody wanted to play it subtle; I could, too. He blew out a breath, settling himself behind the wheel of his squad car.

"Jacobia," he began unhappily.

Suddenly I was glad he didn't have X-ray vision; the little .25 semiauto was in my sweater pocket.

"I won't do anything rash," I told Bob Arnold earnestly.

Hoping it was true.

24

That afternoon, we got the call I hadn't wanted: Sam was to be questioned by representatives of the district attorney's office, but not by the police. The whole thing had simply become a prosecution matter. Also, the meeting was to happen ASAP.

Sam took the news badly, his face mulish, shoulders hunched. He'd just gotten home from work at the boatyard and was grubby and irritable. "Let them put me in jail if they want to. I'm not going to do it."

"Sam, it's not as if you'll tell something new. Your dad has spoken with them, they already know what you'll say."

I could be present, I'd been told, but could not communicate with Sam or assist him while he was giving his statement.

"Are you going to do it?" he demanded. "Talk to them?"

"They haven't asked me." They weren't saying why about that, but for now, they didn't want any of the rest of us.

Only Sam. "Great. I get to be the traitor."

Because he was the one with firsthand knowledge of Victor's being in the cemetery that night. But there was no reason to act as if we had something to hide; I'd called Bennet and he'd agreed with me.

"Look, why don't we just go down there and get it over with. Refusing to cooperate might only make things worse."

He looked up miserably, hands clenched on the kitchen table. His nails were grimy, his fingers battered and banged up as usual from the physical work he did. "How?"

"Sam, if you won't talk to them, they'll think you know more than your father has said. And obviously you wouldn't be trying to keep quiet about something good, would you? Doesn't that make sense?"

"I guess so." He got up reluctantly. "So, did they say they want me now?"

"Now." I traded my sweater for a jacket and ran downstairs to put the .25 into the lockbox, feeling that carrying a weapon into Bob Arnold's office went a little far. Sam went as he was: boots, sweatshirt, and beat-up jeans full of paint smears and oil stains.

"Tommy's got something for you," he said as we drove down to Water Street.

"Yeah?" I glanced at him. His face was set in the look it wore when he was going to the dentist. "Some papers. His mother found them at the library, said you might want 'em. You're sure this isn't going to hurt Dad?"

"I'm sure," I told him, though I wasn't really. I just knew what Bennet and I had decided: that the alternative could be worse. And since Victor had already spilled his guts, as Bennet had put it, there seemed little to lose.

The Eastport Police Station was a two-story frame storefront furnished with metal desks and office chairs. Inside, the state ADA was a civil, serious-looking young man in suit and tie.

Bob Arnold wasn't there. The young man looked spiffy, and a bit taken aback at Sam's appearance. But he stepped manfully up to the task of conversing with someone so clearly of a lower economic stratum than himself, and of course I did not swat the patronizing smile off his peach-fuzzy face.

So it all went reasonably well, at first. After the introductions, Sam told the same story he'd told before. But then they got to the part about Victor in the cemetery.

The young man frowned. "I'm not sure I understand. You rode right by, even though you knew your father was sitting there?"

Probably his own father was one of those nurturing types you see on the network TV dramas. Wise expression, steadying hand on the shoulder, stern but fair. Hey, somebody's got to have one.

"That's what I said." Sam's face was stoic.

"You didn't stop. Ask him what he was doing there. See if he was all right."

"No. I didn't."

"Why not?"

"He saw me. If he'd wanted to talk, he'd have spoken."

"Did you think then that something might be wrong?"

A fair question, but I could see where he was going.

"I thought . . . I thought there might be," Sam conceded. "My father was sitting in a cemetery in the middle of the night."

"He wasn't in the habit of doing that," the young man said. "So you thought it might indicate something unusual."

"That's right." Sam's voice was a monotone.

Still, that Victor's actions might indicate an unusual state of mind was no great revelation. And Victor's mind was frequently unusual, as many could testify.

Then came the curveball. "One last question: Have you ever seen your father strike anyone in anger?"

Sam hesitated. Then, in a low voice: "Yes."

"Whom did he strike?

"My—" He swallowed hard. "My mother. But that was . . ."

A long time ago. I sat horrified. How had they learned that? No one even knew about it except . . .

And then I realized: Somehow they'd gotten Victor to admit the incident, and now they were using it: This is what we'll make your son say in public if you don't play ball with us.

This and more: all the dirt from the divorce. They wanted a confession and were using Sam to try to get one.

"The interview," I announced, "is over."

The civil young man in the neat suit and tie didn't bat an eyelash. "So your dad's capable of physical violence."

"He only got angry that one time," Sam protested.

"Sam. Stop talking right now." I crossed the room and got in front of him. "Go out to the car."

The young man looked up at me as if I were a housefly and my buzzing annoyed him. "I'm nearly finished."

His tone of strained patience was what did me in. I reached down, wrapped my fingers around his Windsor knot, and yanked hard on it.

"My son's a minor. The interview is over when I say it is. Got it?"

I let go. His eyes were big as pie plates. "I'm going to take into account the fact that you are upset," he spluttered as I turned away from him.

"Do that. And from now on if you want to talk to my family, bring a court order." I seized Sam's arm, propelled him out ahead of me, letting the door slam.

"Sam, I apologize." I got into the car beside him. "I had no idea he would know enough to try to discuss that."

Bennet either, apparently, and so much for following any more of his advice.

"It really sucked," Sam said, slouched beside me. He looked shell-shocked.

He'd been ten when the incident happened: Victor and I so hideously angry at each other, we hadn't even known he was in the room. Victor said later he'd have sat there and let me beat him bloody, if only he could have wiped the look of fright off Sam's face.

It was the closest to an apology I ever got from Victor. But nothing like that had ever occurred again, and I hadn't brought it up in the divorce.

"You were pretty good in there, though," he said at last.

I glanced cautiously at him. "Thanks. I hope when that punk thinks it over, he won't decide to have me charged with battery. Sam, about your dad and me . . ."

His shoulders moved impatiently. "I guess somebody must've scared Dad, or he wouldn't have mentioned it."

It was what I thought, too, that the prosecutors had taken a sworn statement, asked him about violence in his past. And Victor couldn't very well not tell the truth about the incident, because I might.

"Sam," I tried again, "if you could just explain to me . . ."

Why this bothered him so much. After all, he had gotten over other things, ones that hurt me worse than a single, never-to-be-repeated face slap.

He blew out a breath. "Okay, look. After the divorce was over you forgave him, or whatever you did, so that I could have a dad. And that meant I had to step up to the plate, and be a son."

"I never meant to obligate you to . . ."

"That's okay," he went on impatiently, "it worked out okay. Only once in a while I'd be getting along with him all right, and suddenly it would pop into my head that I ought to be punching his lights out. For what he did."

He turned to me. "I mean, that smack he gave you, that was just the cherry on the cake. There was so much more, but I was a little kid, it was what I could understand."

So it represented something to him. "Okay. And now?"

Sam sighed heavily. "Now we've . . . I don't know. Built around it, or something. And I guess it's not such a huge deal, to talk about him in court. Like you said, he's already told them stuff. But, Mom, he's so weird. And with the school thing going on, too, like maybe not wanting to go . . . I'm afraid he'll decide I'm doing it all to punish him. School, court, everything."

He gazed at me in youthful appeal. "Like, that I've been saving it, like it was my big guns, you know? And now I'm taking my chance to hit back at him any way I can."

Which for Victor was not only possible, it was likely. "Not because it makes any logical sense, but . . ."

Sam nodded energetically. "He thinks he deserves it. I know he does. That trauma-center thing means a lot to him 'cause it's a way to make something decent work out with you. Mom, I think he'd marry you again if he could. I bet that's what he was sitting out there thinking about, in the cemetery."

Now there was an idea right out of my absolute worst nightmare. "You do know it's not going to happen," I said evenly.

"Yeah, yeah. Don't worry, Mom, if that ever started looking possible I'd tie you up and smuggle you out of here on one of the fishing boats. Or Wade would."

He managed a laugh, sobered instantly. "It's like he's been on this shaky little raft, though. And now it's sinking, and he might think I'm, like, secretly glad, like I think it serves him right. And you know Dad: if *he* feels bad . . ."

Right. He would find a way to make you feel bad too. He was, as Sam said, so weird.

"And then it'll all get messed up again," Sam finished. "The whole Dad thing. Like a boat you've been working so hard building and then it gets smashed."

"Sam, I'm going to do my very best to try to prevent that," I told him as we pulled into our driveway. "Really."

"Yeah. I know you are."

He smiled weakly at me. But he didn't sound at all convinced that I would be successful, and at the moment neither was I.

Inside, Sam went upstairs and stayed there while I checked on Monday, whose nose was healing nicely. I gave her a liver biscuit, which she took delicately, carrying it under the dining-room table to gloat over it before she ate it.

Then I called Bennet. "Listen, Mr. Hot-Shot Attorney," I began when his secretary put him on. "I don't know what you were thinking when you said it was okay to—"

"I know," Bennet cut in tiredly. "Jacobia, I'm sorry. I just found out myself. This is what happens when you're in one state and your client is in jail in another."

"Right, a state of confusion, and by that I mean both of you. What happened to the criminal lawyer you were supposed to be lining up? Where's the skilled, on-top-of-it-all defense he's supposed to be getting, preferably from someone who has seen an actual copy of the criminal codes *and* is in the same area code as Victor?"

Bennet let me rant on this way a little longer, until I ran out of breath. Then:

"Jacobia, he's demanding to interview them." Bennet sounded very discouraged. "Wants to make sure he feels they're competent, he says."

"Competent? Bennet, he's the one who needs . . ."

A competency hearing, I was about to say. Then I realized that Bennet's glum tone wasn't only the result of my being angry with him; during the divorce, he had absorbed the equivalent of white-hot lava and had never lost his chipper, we'll-get-through-this professional attitude.

"Bad news," I guessed aloud, and he sighed heavily.

"Victor took advantage of the attorney-client privilege a little while ago," he said quietly, "on the phone to me. Right after he told me that the war of words you two had for a marriage escalated to more than words. And he'd told the cops about it."

"He slapped me on one occasion. One only, Bennet, and that was . . ."

"Drugs they found in Reuben's system," Bennet said, ignoring me. "Sedative drugs. Ever wonder where he got them?"

"Well, it could be anywhere," I said, nonplussed. It was, I'd thought, the hardest part about it all to nail down. "How would I know where . . . Oh. Oh, Bennet, you don't mean . . ."

Thanks for that other thing, Reuben had said to Victor on his way out of La Sardina.

"Victor prescribed them for him," Bennet confirmed. "Tate was pushing him around and one of the things he demanded was drugs. A pick-me-up, Victor says Tate called it."

"But these were—"

"Yeah. Victor got the bright idea that what this guy really needed was a tranquilizer. So he wrote him a 'scrip, but not with a brand name that Tate would have recognized. He used the drug's generic name, the chemical name. And he knows Tate filled it from the local pharmacy, 'cause the druggist called him, checking to make sure it really was a legitimate prescription. Tate being the kind of guy, I guess, who everyone knew would steal prescription pads if he got a chance. But this time he hadn't."

"Oh, hell," I said, sinking onto the chair in the telephone alcove. "He didn't look sedated in the bar."

"Just got the 'scrip that afternoon. Took some after you saw him, maybe. Victor says on top of alcohol, the stuff would really knock you for a loop."

"So it could look like Victor was setting him up to kill him. Has Victor told anyone else about this, Bennet?"

The attorney let out an exasperated breath. "No. This is the thing he's really worried about. I can't seem to make him see it, that it's nothing compared to his real troubles. That he wrote a prescription that wasn't warranted . . ."

But it was precisely the kind of thing that Victor would get his britches in a twist over: his precious medical integrity.

". . . And it's what he was doing out there in the graveyard," Bennet finished. "Agonizing about it."

"And now he's sitting down there in a cell without any legal counsel. What did you tell him?"

"To stop being a damned idiot. That he's as able to judge the competence of attorneys as I am to judge brain surgeons. To get off the dime, pick a lawyer from the list I faxed up, and do what the lawyer tells him. Think it'll work?" He laughed.

The advantage of dealing with the attorney who handled your bitter, go-for-the jugular divorce is a shared appreciation for black humor; the chances of Victor's putting his trust in a lawyer he'd picked from a list was about the same as his dialing 1-800-SHYSTER and throwing himself on the mercy of whoever answered.

"Okay, Bennet," I said. "Keep on keeping on, please. I know you're doing your best. And hey, it could be worse."

I told him what Sam had said about Victor sitting out there maybe thinking about remarrying me.

Bennet laughed again. "You two ever tried that, I'd come up there and murder you both myself. It'd be a mercy killing."

Soon after, we hung up, Bennet because his day had made him thirsty for a vodka gimlet, and me because the kitchen had that bright, clean-as-a-whistle look that meant it must be time to start dirtying it up again, by cooking dinner.

I thought it might cheer Sam up, too, but he didn't appear downstairs. I'd made fish and potatoes, a hearty, strengthening meal, but Sam's portion had gotten all shriveled and dried in the warming oven by the time Tommy Daigle came over at around eight o'clock, went upstairs, and stayed for a couple of hours.

Later, when I saw him coming down again, his freckled face looked troubled.

"So, what have the two of you been up to?" I asked lightly.

But Tommy wasn't fooled; he had a mother himself, and knew all the information-getting tricks. "Oh, nothin'. Doing the Morse thing, gettin' decent at that. And fooling around with the Ouija board. Man, but isn't that thing some wicked strange, though."

It was downeast Maine phrasing; as far as I knew, Tommy had never been farther from Eastport than Bangor, three hours away. He pulled his jacket on, remembered something in the pocket.

"Hey, my mom found this at the library, said I ought to give it to you."

He pulled out a folder. I couldn't think what Tommy's mother might have found for me at the library; some recipes maybe, or curtain patterns. She was ferociously domestic. As he handed it to me, I noticed the red, inflamed mark on the back of his hand.

Seeing me blink at it, he shrugged embarrassedly. "Reached for the salt instead of asking to have it passed. Ma smacked me with a serving spoon."

"I see," I replied carefully. "You get smacked often?"

"Oh, no, Mrs. Tiptree. Don't you go thinkin' that. Jeez, that kind of story got around, Ma would kill me for sure."

Tommy grinned earnestly at me as he said this, to show he was only joking. "Paddled my behind some when I was a kid. Guess I earned it. My uncle, he was a one, though."

He winced, as if remembering. "Gave me this here." Pointing to the dent over his eyebrow, shaped like a . . .

"He wore a big ring," Tommy explained. "Hit me backhanded with it one time, I bothered him about something."

The deep scar was shaped like a square-cut gemstone. "He's changed, though. He's okay now. Don't worry about me, Mrs. Tiptree," he finished solicitously.

"Okay, Tommy. Tell your mom I said thanks for the library stuff." A foolproof biscuit method, I expected, or a new way of basting a turkey.

But when he was gone I found no recipes inside the folder. Instead it held copies of old newspaper articles about my house. Or rather, about one of its previous occupants: Jared Hayes.

The first clipping was an untorn copy of the same paper Wade and I had found stuffed into the woodwork, detailing facts about the local composer and fiddler and his latest tune: "The Pirate's Revenge." It had debuted to much enthusiasm in the ballroom of the Eastport Hotel, September 27, 1831.

All present had agreed that it was much the finest dance tune Hayes had produced, the *Eastport Sentinel* reported; they hoped he would supply many more as pleasant to the ear and as persuasive to all those who might otherwise be tempted to remain "wallflowers."

But he didn't. Carrying the folder into the dining room, I turned to the next photocopy, which reported that on the night of the dance, Jared Hayes had gone missing from his residence at 20 Key Street. The *Sentinel* ran his likeness, dark eyed, bearded, and intense, with a headline that read HAVE YOU SEEN HIM?

No one had. From the remaining articles in the folder, it seemed Jared Hayes was never seen or heard from again.

25

And then four whole days went by in which nothing happened, and I thought I would lose my mind.

Willow Prettymore refused to speak with me. It got so she hung up the telephone hard, banging it down, as soon as she heard my voice. When I wasn't calling her, I talked to a lot of other people, but none of them had anything useful to say.

Meanwhile, Mike Carpentier and Molly stayed on the hilltop; Paddy Farrell, Terence Oscard, and the Sondergards were seen around town as usual. I weatherstripped twenty windows, leaving twenty-six remaining to do, and practiced until I got pretty good with that circular saw; I called the carpenters about the rot in the wall, and Monday's nose healed. But nothing more, and in particular no more pranks.

Or attacks, depending on how you looked at them. Gradually the topic of Reuben Tate's murder faded too, replaced by anxious questions about the weather: Would the rain drown out the Salmon Festival or hold off? A low over the Midwest was threatening to combine with another, more threatening one over the Carolinas and roar up the East Coast.

Finally, the wheels of justice turned with excruciating slowness; Victor's bail was denied, as was a pretrial motion to dismiss, both hearings attended by an attorney Bennet had bullied Victor into accepting, and the case was transferred to superior court. Victor himself had begun calling me on the telephone, alternately worrying and complaining; Sam lost weight and took on more hours at the boatyard to distract himself.

"The hell of it is, I actually miss the damned fool,"

George Valentine grumbled, meaning Victor. "How's he doing?"

It was the Saturday night before the Salmon Festival, and we were eating boiled lobsters at a picnic table by Wilson's dock.

"Victor's okay," I told George. "As well as you can expect."

I hadn't felt like cooking, and we couldn't get into any of the other restaurants, the town was so jammed with visitors. Past more tables crowded with folks who'd gotten the same idea we had, Campobello Island shone in the sunset like a long bar of gold.

"Says hello," I added. "Says he wants you to keep holding a good thought for him."

The truth was, Victor wasn't doing well at all. His bravado was determined but behind it I detected the truth—he was scared. But Sam was listening, so I spoke carefully.

"Sam can visit him," I said, "next week. Unless he's out."

Which was unlikely. A wisp of smoke from the outdoor brick fireplace where they boiled the lobsters tinged the salt air, making it smell like autumn.

"Huh," Wade said. "Sam, do you think that's a good idea?"

"Sam will be fine," I put in firmly; Wade caught on and bent to his dinner. Actually, I thought it was a terrible idea. But at my objections Sam had turned so stonily mutinous that I gave in.

"Sorry I've been scarce," Ellie said, changing the subject as best she could.

"That's okay." I poured wine, spilling some, sopping it with a napkin. "I know you've been busy with the festival."

I'd hoped the outing might lift my mood; instead I seemed to be infecting everyone else with my glumness. It was awful, like the supper after a funeral for someone that no one had liked. Sam picked listlessly at his food, excused himself, and wandered off; the men finished and got up too, to chat with Tim Poole, the fish-market owner.

Tim at least looked cheery at the sight of all the customers eating his lobsters. People had brought candles, silverware, and tablecloths, even tape players; it was becoming a party.

"I guess you think I've left you in the lurch," Ellie said.

The thought had occurred to me. Every time I finished the weatherstripping on another storm window, I got a different view of the town. And Ellie always seemed to be in it: hanging bright streamers, stringing paper lanterns, or finishing the bandstand paint job.

"Maybe a little," I admitted. "But it's not as if anything's been going on. I'm stonewalled."

A payment was due on the option-to-buy for Victor's medical-building property, a great big whacking payment. If I didn't ante up, the option would expire.

"Nothing more about the house?"

The old clippings, she meant. In the evenings to busy myself I'd been poking around the library. But the dusty tomes in the historical collection gave no clue as to what had happened to my old house's tenant. Nor did the microfilms of antique newspapers supply any hint; brief follow-ups said he continued missing, but nothing more. And then there was nothing at all, as if the violinist and composer Jared Hayes had vanished not only from Eastport but from the face of the earth.

"Nothing about anything. I swear, Ellie, this week has been one long fizzle from beginning to end."

"Don't be so sure of that," Ellie said. "It might seem like I've bailed out on you, but I've been working behind the scenes. You know what we do while we're foil-wrapping a thousand potatoes for baking or mixing up another thousand blueberry biscuits?"

"Talk," I said, feeling a sudden dart of hope pierce me. She sounded confident. "About . . . ?"

"Willow Prettymore, for one. That's her over there, by the way."

I turned sharply. "Where? You mean that . . . that bombshell?"

It was the only word for the woman at the nearby picnic table: tall, blond, built like a swimsuit model only more so.

A lot more so. Willow Prettymore was encased in a sheath of some shimmery white material, dripping in gold jewelry, and shod in the kind of spiky-heeled pumps that make your legs look like stilettos, an honest-to-gosh mink stole draped over her arm.

"She's staying up there," Ellie said, pointing to one of the Motel East's balconies overlooking the water. "The best room, of course." Trust Ellie to know.

"Wow," I said inadequately.

She was having an argument with a man who looked like an ape dressed in a suit: long, thick arms and bunchy-muscled shoulders, hunched posture, and dark, glowering eyes set too close together under a low forehead.

A few words reached us as the conversation grew agitated. Willow wanted the man in the suit to locate a waitress, pronto. But Poole's was self-serve; you went inside to choose a victim, waited for it to be boiled over the fire before dismantling it with your own lobster equipment, and cleaned up after yourself.

I got up. "I've been trying to corner her for days. Now I'm going over there and . . ."

"Wait." Willow and her companion figured out the routine, began moving toward the Quonset to peruse the big lobster tanks.

"I already asked her," Ellie said, "and it's no go. Willow isn't going to say a word to us about the murders, at least not without a good reason to get involved. And right now she hasn't got one."

"What are you talking about? She can't just . . ."

"Actually, she can. Free country and all that. But," Ellie raised an index finger wisely, "I have a plan."

She gazed out over the water. "Willow," she said, "used to look a lot different from the way she does now. Her teeth were all rotten, and if that's her natural hair color I will eat this lobster shell. Also, Willow's reputation was as dirty as ditchwater—rude, crude, and if it wore pants she would sleep with it. But she had a kind of natural cunning, I'll say that for her. And eventually she decided she wanted more."

"So she got out of town," I guessed. "Slicked up, found that guy, maybe he's the source of all that glitz she's dolled up in. Married him, now she's reinvented herself and come back to . . ."

"Right. Show the home folks how well she's done for herself, maybe even rub their noses in it a little. Which Willow has and wants to go on doing for a few more days."

They stood by the lobster pots, Willow drawing the mink closely around her in the harbor breeze. The loutish fellow hulked beside her, hands dangling at his sides. You could see he didn't know what to do with them when he wasn't making fists.

"What I hear in town," Ellie went on, "he's some sort of behind-the-scenes mover and shaker in Portland, maybe not such a nice guy."

Of course there would be talk about him, plenty of it right on the money, too.

"But no matter what *he* is, the last thing *she* wants is to mess up her shiny new image with an ugly old story, dredge it all up again," Ellie finished.

"What old story?" I tried to go on sounding interested, but when I heard this last part, my heart sank discouragedly. All I'd been doing was listening to tales of the old days, and none of them had helped.

"The story," Ellie said, "about the night Reuben Tate burned down Uncle Deckie Cobb's shack."

She turned to me, her green eyes luminous in the last fading glow of an autumn evening thickening steadily to night.

"With," she added, "Uncle Deckie still in it."

I felt my jaw drop.

"Willow was there," Ellie said. "But she doesn't want the memory refreshed around town. Bad for her new identity as a woman of means and importance. She cares about that a lot."

I was still busy absorbing Ellie's earlier statement. "So Reuben was a firebug, too."

Her forehead furrowed. "Yes. You couldn't tell what he might do." She got up and began clearing the table.

"Anyway, the word is Willow's going to be around a few more days. Make sure she sees everybody, and more to the point, that everyone sees her. So tomorrow at the salmon supper maybe you can corner her and explain a couple of things."

"Such as, she talks to me or I talk to everyone else? Spruce up their memories of her old, unimproved situation? Sounds like a plan."

Just then Tommy Daigle's jalopy appeared around the corner, horn blaring and headlights flashing, the big raccoon tails Tommy thought so much of flying like banners. The jalopy pulled over, Sam got in, and the cherry-red glow of the taillights moved away up Water Street.

Ellie and I gathered our paper trash and put it in one of the barrels Tim Poole had stationed around the area, wrapped up our lobster tools and butter and so on to take home. In the near darkness, the fire in the brick stove under the lobster pots leaped orange and yellow.

"So tomorrow you confront her and question her," Ellie said, meaning Willow.

"Right," I said doubtfully. "But I still can't say I'm confident it's going to do any real good. I've been chasing her because I don't have much else. But what can she tell me that I don't already know?"

Ellie turned, her hair like flowing copper under the yard lights Tim Poole was turning on. The dock he'd built shone yellow with new, raw wood, looming over the glinting wave tops and scenting the damp breeze with the pine-sap smell of fresh logs.

"Jacobia. When I say Willow cares what people think, I mean she *really* cares. And who do you suppose she despised finding out had gotten here ahead of her when she got back to Eastport? Who could wreck her reputation just by existing?"

"Reuben Tate," I replied slowly. "Her partner in teenaged crime." Suddenly I got what Ellie was implying. "But, Ellie, that doesn't mean she could or would . . ."

Kill him, I was about to say. Because how would she get the weapon, or know about Victor, or . . .

"Just meet her," Ellie interrupted. "Then come and tell me what you think Willow might or might not do. Because the image is impressive, and it probably cost a mint," she finished with a glance at the glamorous woman seated a few tables from us. "But it's fake, and what it's covering . . . well, Willow would do almost anything to keep people from remembering it."

26

Later that evening, sitting up in bed with Wade:

"I'm not going to lose the house. I might have to go back to work. But if I do, big deal. People in Eastport work harder than I've ever worked in my life, and think nothing of it."

I put my chin on my clasped hands. "It's not," I finished, "the end of the world. Tell you what, though,

I sure wish I had been paying more attention to my own investing instead of giving all those stock tips to Ellie. If I had, I'd be sitting on a big fortune by now." Aside, I meant, from the one I was losing.

He chuckled. "Don't know she hasn't, do you? Done something about them herself, I mean. Ellie's pure Maine, you know, keeps money matters pretty close to the vest."

"Be that as it may." I turned to him. "I'm not kidding, Wade, I've got to do something about this."

"Will you," he asked soberly, "be able to stay on here? To work, or would you have to go away?"

Trust him to find the crux of the matter. I'd been avoiding thinking about it too hard, but push was coming to shove. Very soon I would have to decide about that land-option payment. And from that, everything else would fall like a row of dominoes.

The operative word being *fall*. "I don't know," I admitted. "The kind of thing I'm good at, individual client work, takes face time. I probably could come home on weekends."

I'd gotten past the stage where I'd had to be at clients' beck and call, back in the city. But they all still needed to be sweet-talked, scolded, or simply educated. They had to be protected from a variety of scams, flimflams, and rackets. And they'd all needed heavy-duty advice before doing deeds more complicated than brushing their teeth. In the rarefied world of rich people, structure is everything; they plan their activities with an eye to the tax implications, down to the penny.

In other words, they hire somebody like me: cool head and keen eye. Or so I'd thought.

"I'm sorry, Wade. I've told people a million times not to let their emotions affect sensible financial decisions. And now look how awful my own decision has turned out."

"Oh, hey, wait a minute. First of all, it hasn't

turned out any way, yet. And second, it wasn't your emotions that got you to this point."

He looked at me, shrugged in concession. "Okay, so it wasn't all your emotions, anyway. But the area needs the trauma center, Victor's a good fit for it, and having this thing happen was like getting hit by lightning. You couldn't have seen it coming."

"Thanks. That makes me feel better." I settled against him. "Once, it was all I wanted to do, you know. Wheeling and dealing was exciting. But I'm not sure I have the energy for the money business anymore. Part of why I'd just talk about it to Ellie, I guess. Instead of acting on stocks I heard about, or read about."

"I haven't noticed any lack of energy. And I still think you are exciting, even if you're flat broke."

I smiled against his shoulder. "That's because you're not one of those boring nitwits who think money's an aphrodisiac."

Which clearly he didn't. At the moment, for instance, I didn't have a dime on me. Or anything else, which was turning out to be awfully convenient.

"Aw. You mean it's not? Another myth bites the dust."

"Don't worry," I told him, shifting slightly. "There are plenty of soft, pliable young girls out there, ready and willing to keep that particular myth propped up. As it were."

"Oh." He paused. Monday woke up, looked around, and jumped off the bed.

"You know," he said in a different voice, "you'd better stop doing that or I might start mistaking you for one of those girls. The soft, pliable ones."

He turned toward me, smelling of soap and fresh air. Sam wasn't home; he had left a message to say he was staying the night with Tommy Daigle.

"That," I managed from the tiny part of my brain that could still form a coherent thought, "was pretty much the whole idea."

27

The next day was Salmon Sunday, so long awaited and now so absolutely upon us. Clouds loomed on the western horizon, heaped up dark and ominous like clenched fists, but moved no closer as the sun rose red over the Canadian islands.

"It can rain all it wants, but *later,*" Ellie said worriedly around noon, peering out my kitchen window.

The town was packed with people and more were arriving by the minute: parked along the curbs, pulled onto lawns, crowding along the sidewalks pushing strollers and lugging backpacks, and gazing enviously at the lovely old white clapboard houses they passed.

Personally, I felt there was a big patch of clapboard that somebody was more than welcome to; the carpenters had come and dropped off the estimate for replacing all that siding and some framing beneath it. They would go over the unhappy news with me later, they said, after the festival was over. Now, the backyard was littered with the siding they'd torn off, to peer underneath it, and the envelope they'd left lay on the kitchen table like an unexploded bomb. I didn't even want to open it.

By contrast, Ellie was a sight for sore eyes in a pale yellow T-shirt, a turquoise jumper, white sandals, and a necklace of tiny turquoise lumps. Her red hair was tied back with a white grosgrain ribbon, and she was wearing the small emerald earrings George had given her when they got married.

"You look," I told her sincerely, "absolutely stunning."

She turned hopefully to me. "Do you think so? I wanted to make a good impression on the visitors."

"The only way you could make a better impression would be by handing out hundred-dollar bills," I said.

Outside, Tommy's jalopy rumbled into the driveway. The boys thundered in, grabbed oatmeal cookies and glasses of milk, and galumphed upstairs. Wade and George had already gone down to the park to set up the barbecues and start marinating the salmon.

Ellie checked her clipboard. "Plates, cups, napkins, ice," she recited. "Lemons. Oh, gosh, I forgot about tartar sauce."

"Who's going to glop up that salmon with tartar sauce?" I asked, but only rhetorically; as the mother of a teenaged boy, I know there's no accounting for tastes. "Never mind, I'll go get a gallon of mayonnaise and a jar of pickle relish. Will that do?"

"Yes," she said, looking around a little wildly. "It's like putting on," she said, "a military campaign."

"Napoleon would be proud of you. Now get out of here. Just the sight of you is making me nervous, and if I get distracted I'm likely to mix that relish into sour cream by mistake."

She looked anxious, then laughed, sounding a little short of breath. It was touching, really, to see her get nervous; she was so calm ordinarily, you felt like checking to make certain that she actually had a blood pressure.

Watching her go, I was pierced again by the thought of how much I really didn't want to leave Eastport. But then I had to start doing something about that tartar sauce. So I sent the boys to the IGA, but when they got back—

—dashing in, depositing the enormous jars of pickles since the store had run out of relish, and hurrying away again as it had suddenly occurred to them that there would be girls at the festival, actual out-of-town girls whom they did not already know, so Tommy wanted to wash and wax the jalopy—

—it turned out that running the pickles through

the blender reduced them to green goo. I had to chop them individually and mix them into the mayonnaise with a spoon. By the time I was done, my hands smelling infernally of pickle juice, it was time to leave.

The carnival atmosphere on Water Street was palpable: craft booths, cotton candy, strolling musicians, kids on skateboards. In the park behind the library the barbecue grills were fired up and the scent of woodsmoke mingled with the tang of the marinade simmering. The striped tents over the long lunch tables from the grade school looked festive, people were unloading trays of food from the backs of pickup trucks, and everyone seemed happy.

The sky was still bright, though it was now getting on for three o'clock; the supper began at four. So even though a sly little breeze had sprung up, riffling in the napkins and setting the scalloped edges of the tent canvases fluttering, I was happy too. Eyeing the storm clouds still keeping their distance like animals who are not sure whether to attack, I thought we might yet squeak by in the weather department.

I set the tartar sauce with the rest of the condiments on the front table near the coffee urns. Mike Carpentier lugged over yet another jug of lemonade and one of iced tea. Sneaking a glass of tea, I tasted fresh mint, and enough sugar and caffeine to power a jet engine, as Mike and Molly began setting the plastic jugs into an ice-filled barrel. They must have been preparing for this for half a year, I realized, saving the jugs for this occasion.

A couple of men were pitching horseshoes behind the freshly painted bandstand where the two Sondergards, Heywood and Marcus, were setting up their instruments. Then somebody rang the big brass bell that used to be the Eastport fire alarm, and the crowd *surged*:

Local politicians donned aprons and took their places in the serving line, smiling determinedly even as a strengthening breeze sent barbecue smoke swirling into their faces. The Sondergards broke into a rousing version of "I'll Fly Away" while the food workers began serving salmon fillets as fast as they could spatula them off the hot grates; next came baked potatoes, boiled sweet corn, and blueberry biscuits.

It was going just like clockwork despite a couple of rain spatters: threatening at first but then slackening as if taking pity on us. "So far, so fine," Ellie said, appearing behind me.

I'd been watching Sam and Tommy exchange Morse-code messages with a pair of penlights. They seemed to be commenting covertly on a group of young women from out of town.

"You've done beautifully," I told her, waving at the crowded tables under the tents. "They're all having a high old time."

Bob Arnold strolled the lawn casually, a smile on his face and professional watchfulness in his eyes. I went up to him.

"Where's Clarissa?"

At the sound of her name he smiled helplessly as he always did when she was mentioned; petite and darkly pretty, Clarissa as a lawyer was hard as nails—she'd been a big-time criminal prosecutor before she came to Eastport—but she had a soft spot the size of Montana for Arnold, and he adored her.

"At home, with her feet up. Says she feels like the Goodyear blimp. Week late, now, but the doctor says just be patient. . . . I hope she's gonna be all right."

I put my hand on his arm. "First babies are late sometimes." Across the lawn, people who'd grown up in the area and then moved away were signing the Old Timers' book, leaving addresses and phone numbers: a bright idea of Ellie's for next year's fund-raising.

Bob brightened. "Yeah, huh?" He glanced at his squad car, pulled up onto the lawn behind the bandstand. "I think I'll go call her."

"You do that," I laughed, hoping Clarissa had the portable phone by her side; Bob would be calling her every fifteen minutes for the rest of the afternoon, I could tell.

Then I saw Willow Prettymore in one of the food tents, her hair piled today in a gleaming chignon. With her were the apelike man I'd seen the night before and a pair of young teenaged children: identical blond twins, one boy, one girl.

Together they looked like a political poster extolling the virtues of the good old-fashioned nuclear family, except that when the father of the family walked, his knuckles practically brushed the ground. Willow caught me eyeing her, got up, and stalked from the table coldly.

Just then the Sondergards flew into an old Dillard tune called "Biggest Whatever," the subject of which was—

". . . forty feet high, had a gleam in its eye, and a big purple patch on its craw . . ."

It was, naturally, the biggest whatever that anybody ever saw; Marcus sang the story of the creature in his fine, accurate baritone, managing not to break into laughter. And Heywood . . .

Well, Heywood Sondergard *rocked*. White hair flying, blue eyes flashing, in the chambray shirt with the pearl buttons and the belt with the silver rose-of-Sharon buckle on it, he played that old guitar as if he had been born to do it.

Which, I realized belatedly, he had. Heywood was a natural showman. "Oh," I said faintly, and Ellie nodded.

"None of us kids in his youth group cared much about the Bible stories," she said reminiscently. "But we liked the music. He had that same belt back then, with the rose-and-cross buckle. Funny the things you remember."

I looked around. "Where'd Willow go?"

Leaving Ellie to dish out seconds of the potatoes and sweet corn, I scanned the crowd as I moved away from the tent toward the bandstand. Marcus left Heywood to take a solo, came down from the platform, and headed for the drinks, wiping his forehead.

I kept looking: no Willow. Nearby, I heard one of the girls Sam and Tommy had been scoping out—close-up, they were older than I had thought—telling Sam about a boat-design job that she wanted at a firm in Newport, Rhode Island.

She was very pretty, with dark eyes and glossy chestnut hair. And she wore the kind of clothes Sam likes to see on girls: tailored jeans, navy cableknit sweater with a small red collar peeping out at the top like a little danger flag, plain leather shoes on her small feet.

"Of course," she was saying loftily to him as I approached, "I'll have to finish college first. You can't get anywhere good in the boat-design business without a degree, and maybe even a master's degree. I'm also majoring in engineering."

Sam's face fell. Then I saw his brain kick in. His shoulders squared, and he tipped his head seriously at her.

They hadn't noticed my approach. "Where," he asked the girl, "are you getting these degrees? In nautical design, and fine art, *and* engineering? And how much does it cost?"

Hey, you can listen to your parents all you want. But if you really want the scoop on something, ask some kid your own age.

On the other hand, I'd have sent him to canine obedience school if I'd thought it would make him happy. Another spatter of rain fell chillingly, pattering on the tent roofs. I left Sam to plan his future on the advice of a perfect stranger, squinted around for Willow again, spotted her blond hair for an instant, then lost her once more as someone else came up behind me.

It was Terence Oscard, dressed in a white knit polo shirt, tan slacks, and deck shoes. A white cardigan was tied by its sleeves around his shoulders. He wore the clothes well, but the look on his face didn't match the casual outfit. Also, he was carrying a parcel wrapped in brown paper and addressed in Magic Marker, which struck me as odd: it was prepared for mailing but there were no post-office hours on Sunday.

"Jacobia, can we talk for a minute?" He paused, then rushed on urgently. "I don't care what Paddy thinks of this, or how mad he gets. There's something I've got to tell you."

We sat on the library steps, looking out over the street. There was a clown juggling oranges, a magician producing quarters from behind children's ears. Mike Carpentier went by with Molly, the child looking coltishly pre-teen in shorts and a T-shirt but still carrying a rag doll. Then Terence was speaking, and what he said sent all other thoughts out of my head.

"Reuben didn't just threaten Paddy the other night. He tried to kill him. Put his hands right around his throat, Paddy had to fight him off. And I know how stupid this sounds, but it seems to me that Reuben's still trying."

I looked hard at him. He was pale, and even thinner than I'd last seen him. The Ace bandage he'd worn a few days earlier was gone, replaced by a smaller, less dramatic-looking wrap of gauze.

"Terence. Believe me, if someone's trying to hurt Paddy, it isn't Reuben. I saw him in that cemetery and I can guarantee it."

He shook his head impatiently. "I know he's dead. But don't you feel that he's still around, somehow? I mean, we talk about him. Telling old stories. Recalling things he did. Being glad he's gone. And it's *unhealthy*. It's like the old saying, do you remember? Speak of the devil . . ."

"And," I finished, "the devil appears." A chill

prickled foolishly across the back of my neck. "But that wouldn't account for any actual physical attempts on Paddy."

Terence sighed. "You know that open circular stairway he insisted on, when he designed the loft?"

I knew it. I'd been in the upstairs living space: parties and so on. The stairs were an invitation to vertigo or worse.

Terence went on. "How I fell was, someone had left a bunch of thread tangled across the top riser. This," he lifted his taped left hand, "is nothing. I could have broken my neck."

"There's fabric all over the studio," I objected. "Couldn't it have blown there, or gotten dragged there, somehow?"

He frowned. "I don't think so. He's neat as a pin when he's working. But that's not all. The other night I went out for a walk. When I came in, all the gas burners on the stove had been turned on. It's not an electronic model, either, you have to light it with a match. The place was reeking with gas."

"Well. That is more straightforward. You can turn on one by accident, or absent-mindedly. But not all four. Or not normally, anyway."

Delicately, I did not suggest that Terence might be a little absent-minded lately, himself. But he got the drift.

"Any health problems that I may be having do not bear upon the problem we are discussing," he said, his arm tightening on the parcel he had tucked under it.

I might have believed him, but he slurred a couple of words as he said this, and didn't seem to notice. There was beer, and probably some hip flasks, too, among the festival attendees. But Terence wouldn't have touched any.

I wanted to ask him to unwrap that bandage, let me see the hand. Then I could be certain he wasn't just shining me on, or at least not in that department; that he hadn't wounded himself on one of Weasel Bodine's few remaining teeth, for instance, perhaps in an effort to protect Paddy. Because it had occurred to me that one reason for killing the hapless Weasel might be that he had seen Reuben's murder. And if Paddy was involved . . .

But the medical examiner's report on Weasel still wasn't out. And as a result, the promise I'd made to Bob Arnold to keep mum when it came to any information about that skin shred was still in force.

"Anything more?" I asked. "Other attempts on either of you, suspicious events? And . . ."

A new possibility occurred to me. "Where's Paddy now?"

If Paddy and Terence really were on the outs, and Paddy wanted to get rid of Terence, not just break up with him . . .

"He's eating his salmon and having an argument with Clinch Brockway," Terence replied. "Paddy thinks he ought to be able to put a balcony on the back of his building, and Clinch says it'll be an eyesore on that historical structure."

Terence managed a laugh. "Actually, I don't think Paddy really even wants a balcony. But he loves an argument. More than he likes grilled salmon, even. He'll be there awhile."

Across the street, some little girls had gotten a box of sparklers from somewhere and were trying to light them. I kept an eye on the girls, none of whom could have been more than seven or so, as they enjoyed the forbidden activity.

"Have you," I asked Terence, "told Bob Arnold about this?"

He shook his head emphatically. "Paddy would have a fit. He says—can you believe this?—he says none of it happened. He's convinced it was all my imagination . . . or so he says."

Great. Now I could worry about that. Was it live,

or was it Memorex, as recorded by Terence's perhaps unreliable mental processes? But who would want to kill Paddy or Terence?

"I don't know," Terence admitted slowly when I asked him. "But I've been thinking. Two fellows got murdered. I've been thinking of how it could have happened. I mean, exactly how."

Me too. If someone killed the Weasel first, for instance, that ruled out the Weasel's possibly having witnessed Reuben Tate's death. Which meant there would have to be another motive for . . .

Across the street, the girls looked up guiltily as a woman's voice called from the tent area. Still carrying the sparklers, they scampered across the library lawn, up the hill, and out of sight.

". . . Play with those things, you do it where I can see you," the woman's voice scolded. "Go right over there by that fence and stay there, where there's nothing to catch fire."

Terence frowned, distracted. "What kind of a name is that, anyway? Weasel . . . sounds like a cartoon character."

I looked at him sharply. His face had slackened.

Then he snapped back, just as a small commotion came from behind the library. Puzzled, I got up, then identified the sound: the little girls. They were screaming, but not just to hear the sound of their own voices. Kids will do that. But these little girls meant it. I ran, Terence behind me.

The tables were still crowded, the folks who'd been last in line just starting on their dinners, others finishing desserts or coffee. The girls gathered by a low fence dividing the park from a private yard. Around them lay a few burned sparklers, powdery with gray chemical ash.

Lashed to the fence, its cloth belly slashed and its button eyes torn off, a paring knife protruding from its cloth body, was Molly Carpentier's rag doll. One of its little black cloth shoes lay in the grass beneath it.

Molly stood staring. "I put her down," the child said softly, her eyes huge. "Just for a minute . . ."

Mike Carpentier seized his daughter's shoulders, turned the child, and gave her a little shove toward the tents. "Go and sit down. I'll get her. Go on, now." Slowly, the child obeyed.

"This is what happens." Mike said angrily. "Little savages. This is why," he yanked the rag doll from its bindings, "I have to keep her away from them. Or she'll end up just like them."

The other girls had moved away, sniffling, herded by their mothers. I thought their first shock had been real; the doll was an awful sight. But once they'd gotten going, each shriek had made the next come more easily, till they were frightening one another even more than the doll had frightened them.

Terence had gone to sit with Paddy. From the looks on their faces, it seemed they were arguing, Paddy clenching his fist and slamming it onto the long table. Terence said something, got up, and strode back in my direction, passing the drinks table with the brown paper parcel still under his arm. Paddy followed, but stopped by the iced tea and lemonade glasses, grabbed one of the few remaining filled ones, and swallowed some of it angrily.

Marcus came down from the bandstand, grabbed a lemonade also, and ran back up again. Willow Prettymore appeared suddenly, took another from the two that were left; the pitcher was empty.

Gotcha, I thought, starting toward her. And I wanted to refill that lemonade pitcher, too; the latestayers were enjoying the music, and the cleanup crew was bound to be thirsty as well.

Heywood came down from the bandstand as Marcus went into a reprise of the "Biggest Whatever" song. Mike Carpentier passed the drinks table just as Willow did, still propelling Molly, who stopped to reach for a glass, looked imploring at her father, then moved along fretfully without a fresh drink.

On the lawn, the little girls looked up and began laughing, their fright forgotten at the funny song that Marcus was singing. Heywood laughed with the children, then continued across the lawn toward the drinks table, stopping to accept congratulations on the performance. Finally he picked up the last remaining glass of lemonade and took a swig from it.

The unpleasantness, it seemed, was over. But something still felt rotten in Denmark. For one thing, I did not at all like the expression that appeared suddenly on Heywood's face.

Wincing, he looked down at his glass and frowned, putting his hand to his throat. From across the lawn I heard him cough, then try to say something. Willow put down her glass and took a step toward him, her face creasing abruptly with concern.

A rumble of thunder broke the sudden silence as Marcus cut off in the middle of a rousing second chorus and ran to his father. Suddenly it was pouring, the skies opening drenchingly, tent tops flapping and poles rattling as the squall hit us.

"What's happening?" Ellie cried, rushing from the grill area where she had been wrapping salmon fillets and putting them into a cooler. George and Wade turned together from the desserts table.

Terence reached me, shoved the brown paper parcel at me, and ran to help. Marcus reached his father's side at the same time. Bending convulsively, Heywood staggered and fell, his glass of lemonade flying from his hand in an arc of pale yellow.

Willow stopped, watching the liquid splash, and Marcus knelt helplessly by Heywood while Terence peered over his shoulder. "Get an ambulance, somebody!" Terence shouted.

Turning, Willow considered her own glass there on

the drinks table. She hadn't yet tasted it, apparently; now she picked it up again and sniffed cautiously at it.

The scream she let out then made the little girls sound like amateurs.

"Poisoned . . . My God, we've been poisoned!"

28

"We don't know what was in the glasses," Arnold said. "Let's not be jumping to conclusions."

His face, though, said otherwise. Reuben Tate's death or even Weasel's was one thing; spiking a preacher's lemonade with a dose of poison at the town picnic was something else again.

"Bob, we should try to get Victor's attorneys informed. If this is all part of a pattern, it's obvious that Victor couldn't have—"

"Nothing's obvious," he replied flatly. "Except maybe that getting lawyers to call back on a Sunday night is impossible. And even if you did, getting the state people to call them back, even later on a Sunday night, is about as likely as walking on water."

"Well, I'm going to try. Who knows, maybe a miracle actually will happen and they'll be in the office."

But of course they weren't. In the telephone alcove, I ran the gauntlet of the attorneys' voice-mail while sheets of rain cascaded against the darkened dining-room windows. Finally I got a human being, the answering-service operator.

Five minutes later I hung up, having been (1) assured by her words that one of the partners would call me back very soon, and (2) informed by her tone that I shouldn't hold my breath. Urgent calls from the ex-wives of imprisoned murder suspects, she seemed to feel, were not exactly tops on her list of items needing the full, focused attention of her employers right that very minute.

Another huge gust of wind rattled the windowpanes, which now looked as if someone were out there hurling big buckets of water against them. That siding, I thought dismally, imagining the rain positively gushing in through the rotten clapboards.

"Whatever it was," Arnold was saying when I got back to the kitchen, "it was in Willow's glass, too."

"Arnold," I said, "you know what it was, just as well as I do. It smelled just exactly like the bait Howard Waldrop put out last summer when the rabid skunk showed up."

It had been a real scare. Other than red ants, skunks were the most numerous pests on the island; bold and half-tame, they would saunter insolently right up to you before turning to spray you with dead-on accuracy. We'd had to keep our dogs and cats in, and children were supervised scrupulously, after a skunk staggered down Water Street snapping and foaming.

"Yeah," Arnold admitted. "I know. Smelled like varmint bait. You can buy forty kinds of stuff smells like that, any hardware store. But I'm not saying it's anything till after the tests."

In the living room, Sam and Tommy were watching a ball game; George and Wade were still at the park, loading the tables into a truck and taking down the tents.

Arnold frowned. "I got all the names, who was there. Which doesn't mean someone couldn't have put it in the glasses earlier, then took off. Christ, what a mess."

The coffeemaker finished burbling so I got out the cups and the cream and some sandwiches I'd put onto a plate. Outside, the storm battered and hammered.

"At least with all this rain, I doubt many people will be leaving the island tonight," I said as we sat down. "You can talk to them while they're still here, instead of having to find them at wherever they've gone home to."

Bob nodded, biting into a chicken salad sandwich. One of the drawbacks to working at any Eastport food event is that you're unlikely to get any of the food yourself.

"Unless some idiot tries driving over a flooded causeway," he agreed darkly. "Which I have no doubt some idiot is going to do. But we've got barriers set up at our end, police at Pleasant Point've got barriers at theirs, flashing lights and so on. High tide, all this wind, decent storm surge—going over that causeway, next couple hours, you better have pontoons."

A muffled pounding came from the back door; Monday leaped and began barking. A moment later, Marcus Sondergard came in, drenched to the skin.

"I . . . I'm sorry," he managed, looking around wildly. "I have to . . ."

Monday stopped barking and started wagging; once an intruder is actually inside the house, she feels, the whole guard-dog act is pretty much beside the point. Marcus's dark hair clung in sodden ringlets to his head, his white shirt plastered to his skin, and he was shivering hard.

"Come in here," I ordered. "We'll get you into some dry clothes and get some hot coffee into you, before you catch—"

Your death, I'd been about to say, noting that the rain had washed the makeup stuff off his hand. But I couldn't see the mark on it without making too big a point of it. Just then Sam stuck his head in from the living room.

"Sam," I said, "take Marcus upstairs and find him some of Wade's dry clothes to get into, please. And a towel for his hair, and so on, all right?"

"C'mon," Sam said agreeably, and Marcus allowed himself to be led away. When he returned, his hair was not dripping, and he was wearing dry socks and a gray sweatsuit, and not shivering quite so violently. His hand was covered smoothly with surgical makeup again. So he carries the stuff with him, I thought.

But he still looked as if he had been run over by a truck. "It didn't hit me," he said, wrapping his hands gratefully around a mug of coffee, "until I was about to leave the hospital."

He gazed around at us, his eyes huge and dark with emotion. "The fellow from the ambulance service told me he would drive me home. And I realized: Dad wasn't with me."

Marcus made a helpless little sound like a laugh, only it wasn't. "Knowing it was coming for as long as I have, I wouldn't have thought it'd hit me so hard. But . . ."

"Wait a minute. You knew this was going to happen?" Arnold looked astonished.

Marcus nodded, staring at his mug, not realizing what Arnold meant. "Five years I've known. We both did. Doctors told him he could live a long time or go any second. A stretched place in a big artery like a weak spot in a tire, was how they explained it to me. If they operated on it he probably wouldn't survive, they said. So they didn't."

He glanced up, caught Arnold's expression. "Oh, you thought I meant . . . No. Not that someone would try to hurt him. I meant my being prepared for his going . . . naturally. Not this way. Who would want to hurt Dad?"

That was my big question, too. Marcus hadn't had time to do a perfect job with the cosmetic; the edges of the mark showed long and slender, with some odd-shaped crescents at the center of it, like the edges of petals. "What are your plans now?"

I put it generally, but the answer I wanted was specific: Had he known about the life insurance?

Because if he had, I couldn't help thinking that a

grown man with an impatient woman waiting in the wings might tend to get a little impatient himself, waiting for dear old Dad to pop off as he was predicted to. Add to that a big life-insurance payoff, so his son didn't have to worry about money, and . . .

Well, the comfort of a clear conscience can compete very effectively with the lure of cold cash, in my experience.

"I'm going to move to Portland, sell the Winnebago, and open a music store," he said, "with the proceeds of Dad's insurance."

So much for the idea that he might not have known about his coming windfall, or that his thought processes might be unhinged by grief. Still, he looked stung by my narrow-eyed glance at him.

"I've known for a long time that Dad wouldn't live forever. And he told me he'd taken out a policy for me. Is it so terrible that I tried to think about the rest of my life?"

Okay, so maybe it wasn't. I apologized to Marcus, and if he knew I still had mental reservations, he didn't show it.

"Anyway, I just felt . . . well, lost, when I got back home. All his things . . . it didn't seem real that he was gone. So I went out. I didn't realize how bad it was, the storm. But once I was out, I got disoriented, and when I saw your lights . . . Well. I'm grateful for the dry things, and the coffee. I'll be okay now."

"You're sure?" I followed him to the door. Arnold was on his way out too and offered Marcus a ride back to Heddlepenny House.

"Yep." He nodded decisively. Like his father, he was either for real or one of the more accomplished liars I'd ever met.

"Come on, Sondergard," Arnold growled, tugging on his yellow slicker and pulling his black sou'wester onto his head.

When they were gone I shoved the door shut

against a rain-filled gust of wind. In the darkness the branches of the trees in the side yard lashed wildly, yellow leaves showering from them.

"What do you make of that?" Ellie asked.

"Not sure. But if I were going to knock somebody off, I'd do it when a couple of other people had already been knocked off, wouldn't you?"

"You think Marcus might have poisoned his dad? But they were so close."

"Right. Peas in a pod. Maybe," I said as I took my rain slicker off the hook, "it got a little snug in there. Maybe . . ."

On the hall shelf lay the package Terence Oscard had shoved into my hands as he rushed to help Heywood.

"Maybe helping Heywood along with a swig of poison was just hastening the inevitable, in Marcus's mind. Ending," I finished, "the suspense." Leaving Terence's package where it was, I grabbed a pair of flashlights and my car keys.

"Meanwhile," I said, "when Marcus left the bandstand this afternoon, there were three glasses of lemonade on that table. I know because I was looking at them, thinking about putting out some more."

I dropped the car keys into my slicker pocket. "When he got back onto the bandstand, there were only two." I pulled a pair of rubber boots onto my feet.

"One of them Willow picked up," Ellie said, following my thought. I'd described this to her. "And the other one, Heywood got." She pulled her own rain gear on and took an umbrella from one of the other hooks.

"Marcus had a one-in-three chance of choosing the one that was harmless. So," she concluded, "maybe Marcus was just lucky or something."

"Right," I said, pulling on my rain hat. "Or something."

Tomorrow morning, the weekend would be over.

Ordinarily, the town's visitors might stay longer, but lousy weather combined with the news that Eastport harbored a murderer would make the causeway look like the Long Island Expressway.

And somehow I had no doubt that one of the first cars onto the mainland would contain a tall, statuesque blonde, heading for the hills.

"Let's," I said grimly, "go find Willow Prettymore."

29

The Motel East was a low, well-kept structure of dark wood with a blacktopped parking lot and manicured landscaping. The lot was full of cars, most with out-of-state plates, the blacktop awash and the shrubberies bent in the driving wind. We made our way among them and headed for Willow's door, which was around back facing the water.

The wind howled as we struggled to keep on our feet; the tide was so high that the bay itself surged nearly onto Sea Street, below the granite ledge the motel was built on.

Then the door opened, and whatever Ellie said got us in.

"I don't know what you're doing here," Willow began, "but I am very upset, and I wish you'd just—"

"Shut up," I gasped, still busy catching my breath after the maelstrom outside. Her jaw dropped, and she fell silent.

The room was huge, equipped with two queen-sized beds, three armchairs, bureaus, and a big TV. A kitchenette held a small sink, a microwave, and a coffeemaker. Pulled up in front of the television were the two young blond kids I'd seen earlier, now in thrall to the screen.

A bottle of Cutty Sark and an ice bucket stood on the sink. "You can't . . ." Willow tried again. Ellie walked over to the sink, poured a stiff slug of Cutty, and handed it to Willow.

"This is my friend Jacobia. You're going to talk to her, or tomorrow we're going to start reminding people why your nickname used to be 'Willow the Pillow.' I believe it had something to do with lying down," she finished sweetly. "Isn't that right?"

Willow took a slow, furious swallow of her Cutty Sark. "You always were a holier-than-thou little bitch," she grated in low tones. "I knew I shouldn't have come back here."

So much for the image. I glanced at the kids but they were watching a wrestling match with the sound turned up loud. No husband was in evidence. "Have the police been here?" I asked.

"Just Bob Arnold," Willow replied resentfully. "He thinks we'll have to stay an extra day, for the state police. I told him it was inconvenient and he got extremely huffy with me."

She took another gulp. "As if it's any concern of mine what goes on among the locals."

She gave the final word a scornful twist, and suddenly I realized how hard it would be, trying to figure out who might've wanted to poison Willow Prettymore. I, for instance, had only known her about three minutes, and I wanted to put a couple of cyanide-laced ice cubes in her Cutty, just for the fun of it.

"Be that as it may," I began. She was wearing Joy perfume, full makeup, and enough gold jewelry to sink a battleship.

"I'd still like to know what puts you in the same category as Heywood Sondergard, Weasel Bodine, Mike Carpentier, and Reuben Tate. I mean, in the sense that I think someone wants to kill you all, and so far has succeeded three times out of four."

That widened her eyes, all right. If she wasn't acting. I was lying a little bit myself. But only a little bit. I went on:

"Someone dosed the last two glasses of lemonade very fast, as they were passing by the drinks table. And as you and Heywood were already nearly in the act of reaching for the glasses."

I'd been thinking hard on the way down to the motel. "To be sure," I finished, "that the right people got them."

"But . . . how?" She stared at me in shock.

"Have you any idea how little rat poison it takes to kill a person?"

Or whatever it was, and I didn't know how much it took, either; all I knew was that it smelled like the stuff. But maybe Willow did know; she'd been standing by that drinks table, too.

"Palm two doses," I theorized, "preferably folded in slips of paper so it doesn't get on your skin. Then . . . just walk along, dropping the stuff in. Toss the paper slips in the trash."

I sat down at the Formica-topped table in the kitchen area. "The killer would have come prepared, hoping for a good moment. Maybe even mutilated Molly Carpentier's doll, to get attention focused elsewhere. The timing didn't quite work out, maybe, but it worked well enough. And when the moment arrived, bingo."

I smiled at her. "Neat, sweet, and complete. Only you didn't happen to drink from your glass. How," I finished, "convenient."

"Oh, now wait a minute! You don't think I had anything to do with—"

"I don't know. I'm trying to find out. And until now I must say you haven't been very helpful. I'm wondering why not. And don't," I added, "give me any nonsense about your reputation. I'd think helping to solve a murder would do wonders for it, but you haven't bothered."

"Mike Carpentier hasn't been attacked," Willow retorted waspishly. She refilled her glass, sat across from me at the table. She hadn't invited me to sit, but I had decided to anyway; for all her glossy image she was a little short in the manners department.

"Maybe he's behind it all," Willow added, her voice filled with venom. "He's nuts enough."

"Oh, but he has. The doll mutilation was pretty graphic. I'd say it went beyond distraction. If I were Mike, I'd be wondering if it was meant as some kind of a preview."

I was cold, damp, and not feeling like standing on much ceremony. Someone should have taught Willow that the high-class society ladies she was apparently trying to imitate were generally more hospitable, and less jewel encrusted, than she imagined. I got up, found the coffee and equipment, and started the coffeemaker while Willow regarded her whiskey glass sullenly.

"I'm not saying you've all been attacked at the same time, you see," I went on. "Or even to the same degree, so far."

On the television, large men in spandex grappled with each other. Ellie had joined the children and was watching the wrestling match with the air of one raptly learning about social customs on Mars. She glanced up absently, intent on the sight of one very large man pretending to stomp hard on another very large man's throat.

"Is this," she wanted to know, "real? Or faked?"

"Neither," I said. "It's Greek theater. You know, struggle and climax and catharsis, and all that."

"Oh," she replied comprehendingly, and returned to studying the spectacle as if she were an anthropologist.

"The police are going to question you very comprehensively," I told Willow. "Along with your husband. Where is he?"

She shook her blond head impatiently; probably he was out somewhere trying to buy a case of bananas, maybe some peanuts. Willow's perfect pale hair had escaped its chignon, and her pink lipstick was thick on the plastic whiskey glass.

"We had an argument," she admitted.

Darn, and I had missed it: all that jungle chest-beating. At the supper he'd sat apart from the rest, glowering like something out of a traveling circus.

"He didn't want to come in the first place. I wanted to show off, he said. I just wanted people to see that I'd . . . that I'd . . ."

A sob escaped her. I poured her some coffee. She sipped it, made a face, drank more. "I'm sorry," she muttered. "I'm not usually so disgusting. But Ellie was right," she went on a little drunkenly, and I thought the Cutty bottle was turning out to be a stroke of luck. "When I grew up here, I was the town slut."

She looked up miserably. "I just wanted them to know I'm not Willow the Pillow anymore. Is that so awful?"

"No," I said, pitying her suddenly. "It isn't." Just then it occurred to me what I didn't see anywhere in the room.

"Um, Willow, may I use the bathroom?"

She nodded, and I found my way to the facilities. Closing the door, I locked it as quietly as I could, the sound from the TV covering me. As I'd hoped, Willow's purse hung on the hook behind the door.

A quick rummage was all I had time for: keys, wallet, usual credit cards, and a driver's license. A couple of hundred in cash. No handy tin of Acme rat killer. But at the bottom of the bag was an interesting discovery: a small orange plastic bottle of Valium tablets. Three or four of them rattled lonesomely around in the bottom of the bottle.

Which made me wonder: Victor had written Reuben Tate a prescription for sedatives. But was that the sedative Tate had in his system when he died? The definitive toxicology tests, Bennet Berman had informed me, wouldn't be back for a couple of weeks.

Tucking the bottle away swiftly, I flushed, ran the water, and went back out to the kitchenette. Either the Cutty had begun making Willow feel even more talkative or she'd decided it was time to blow some smoke at me; I couldn't tell which.

"My husband is in business with all the right people," she sniffled.

Visions of organ-grinders danced in my head; with difficulty I kept a straight face as she went on.

"We belong to the country club. And he's decided to go into politics." She looked up blearily. "All of it is very important to him. You see, he came from a very poor family, and . . ."

Oh, please; not another old story. For a minute there I was tempted just to bonk her over the head with the Cutty bottle.

Instead I sat down again. "So I guess a scandal, even an old one, could hurt him in a lot of ways. Financially too, maybe."

She snorted, not prettily. "Especially an old one. God, his opponents could go to town on me. Old dirt's the hardest to clean up. As for money, well, you know what they say: it's who you know that counts. And if people don't want to know you anymore . . ."

She trailed off, then rallied with an effort. "One thing about Eastport, it doesn't matter how much money you have. It's how you act that people judge you on, here. But boy, do they ever."

A hideous gust of wind shook the building; the lights dimmed and the draperies shivered as the windows thought about breaking, decided against it. Thick, water-resistant pelt or not, I hoped Willow's creature-feature husband was tucked snugly into the Waco Diner or at La Sardina having a beer.

"What about Reuben?" I asked. "I heard you were with him the night he set fire to Uncle Deckie Cobb's shack."

She looked up, her mascara-smeared eyes surprised. It didn't seem like an act. "No. I was *following* him. I was *not* with . . . that was Mike Carpentier. I was following *them*."

Another rush of wind roared. The lights flickered. We held our breaths until the power came on steadily again. The kids clicked the remote control through the channels.

"Why were you following them?" I glanced at Ellie, whose gaze remained studiously fixed on the television screen. But I could tell she was listening.

Willow looked impatient. "We—Mike, Paddy Farrell, and I—all lived within sight of one another, you see. On Beech Street. And Reuben used to climb the trellis into Mike's bedroom window at night. Stay there, sometimes for hours."

I'd heard of Beech Street, didn't think I'd been on it. It was in a ramshackle part of town, I knew that much. But twenty years ago, probably it hadn't been run-down. "When Mike was about twelve, and Reuben was—"

"Right. Nineteen or so. God, it was weird." She grimaced, remembering. "He used to get these little animals and bring them to Mike. Mikey, we called him back then. A bird in a cage one time, and another time I think a puppy. How Mike explained those to his folks, I don't know." She sat up straighter, shook off the recollection.

"But you were supposed to be his girlfriend, right? I mean, sort of, anyway? So did you ask him about that? Or ask Mike?"

Willow nodded reluctantly. "Sort of his girlfriend. He was the bad boy, I was the bad girl: perfect fit, right? And sure, I thought I would ask him about it. Sometime when I really wanted a split lip, or a black eye."

She frowned impatiently. "I wouldn't have asked Mikey anything like that, though. He was just a little kid."

Willow finished her coffee, looked around for more. When I didn't get up immediately, she went and got it herself, putting the pot and a bowl of creamers and sugar packets on the table.

Not for the first time, I thought about money and manners: that sometimes when people forget they've got it, they remember how to behave. But it's a hard thing to forget for some people, especially ones like Willow who've had to try so hard to get it.

And like you, a small voice whispered unpleasantly in my head. I banished it, concentrating on what Willow was saying.

"He would do that, though," she went on. "Take a liking to one of the kids, make a pet of them. Or a dislike, and . . ."

Make a mess of them, I wanted to say, thinking about Boxy Thorogood. But she was going on pretty steadily and I didn't want to interrupt her.

"Anyway, that night they *both* climbed out of Mikey's window again, and that was different. I was curious so I followed them."

She paused, her forehead furrowing. "Uncle Deckie had a shack at the edge of town. Boards, tar paper. They went inside. Then they came out, Reuben kind of giggling the way he did and Mikey looking . . . I don't know. Strange. Like maybe he was in shock or something."

Willow looked over to make sure her kids weren't listening. Ellie's head tipped bemusedly at the TV; the kids' faces were blankly avid.

Willow sighed. "And then the place just sort of . . . erupted. A ball of flames. Deckie, screaming inside. He screamed for a long time. And Reuben just stood there. Giggling."

"Did you try to get help? Or tell anyone, afterwards?"

Her face closed abruptly. "Someone must have seen, because the fire sirens went off almost right away. After that I ran. But not," she added, "until after Mike Carpentier saw me."

She shivered, as if trying to shake off the memory. "He got home afterwards somehow, so hardly anyone else ever knew he was there but me. But if looks could kill, when he saw that I knew he was there that night, I'd have been dead on the spot."

"And neither one of you ever told anyone officially that Reuben did it."

Her laugh was scornful. "You still don't really believe it, do you? How bad he was. But that's because you weren't a part of it. You didn't tell on Reuben Tate, see. You just . . . didn't."

The kids were getting restless, saying there was nothing to watch on TV. I thought if the wind kept up they'd be watching a dark screen soon; the lights flickered again, warningly.

I got up. "So that put the nail in your coffin, reputation-wise," I guessed. "Who was it put the story around that you were there with him? Implying you were in on it, instead of Mike?"

She nodded, began clearing up the coffee things. "I don't know. But I couldn't really prove otherwise, could I? So I didn't bother denying it. I just got out of town as soon as I graduated, swore I'd never come back. And do I ever wish I hadn't."

Another gust, more ferocious than any before, hit the motel and made the structure shudder. The windows thrummed as we all waited to find out whether they were going to burst in at us, Willow in the act of rinsing the coffeemaker's basket at the kitchenette sink.

"What did Weasel Bodine have to do with any of it?" I asked.

Willow looked surprised. "Nothing," she said. "Who's he?"

The lights went out.

30

The power was off for only a few pitch-black instants, but when it came on again Willow's face had firmed up determinedly; she began making the subtle, ushering movements of the practiced hostess, informing us that the party was over.

"Did you see Reuben before he died?" I asked as she handed me my rain slicker. "Did he come around, making a pest of himself?"

"Oh, sure. Wanted money. And he'd done his homework. Reuben always did. Always knew," she finished, "how he could hurt you."

She gave me my rain hat. Ellie got up from in front of the television and said goodbye to the kids.

"Said he'd rake up all the old gossip," Willow went on. "I gave him," she added a little shamefacedly, "fifty dollars to go away. Do you think the police will keep us here for very long?"

"I don't know," I began, and then the door flung open, wind-driven rain sheeting past the big man himself: Willow's husband. He wore a bomber jacket, wide-wale corduroys, and running shoes, all drenched; shoving the door closed, he frowned in displeasure, and not only at being wet.

Willow hastened to introduce us as two old Eastport chums, a story he accepted scowlingly but without questions; it was just possible, I thought, that his development level was preverbal.

Although that of course would have ruled out aspirations to politics, so probably he was able to pronounce words, if not necessarily to understand all of them. Also it seemed to me that Willow was a little afraid of him, or why not tell him the truth about why we'd come?

"Good t'meet 'cha," he managed finally, not offering a hand or the pretense of a smile.

"Likewise," I replied, noting again the big, square head and blocky neck, the meaty, plug-ugly cast of his face.

Businessman, my aunt Fanny. This guy was a thug. It was the pinkie ring on his right hand that finally nailed it for me: a thick, vulgar object of gleaming gold, dripping with diamonds, about as subtle and tasteful as a set of brass knuckles.

I didn't get a look at the left hand, to see if there was any mark on it. He kept it stuffed in his jacket pocket, probably to keep it from bumping along on the ground when he shambled.

Meanwhile, there was one final thing I wanted to make sure of, while I still had the chance.

"Willow," I said, "you must meet Victor, my husband, sometime. Even though we're divorced we're on such good terms and I know you'd enjoy hearing about . . ."

This, you see, is the trouble with very fast improv: you run out of logic long before you run out of breath. All I really wanted was to confirm that she'd never been in Victor's house. Which I felt fairly sure she could not have been, but . . .

"Actually," she said, "I have. Met him, that is. Jeremy," she waved at the blond boy in front of the TV, "fell off a bike the first day we were here. Hit his head hard, and someone said go see Dr. Tiptree. So we went, and he was so kind and reassuring to us. Wasn't he, dear?" she added to her husband.

"Mmmph," he agreed, pouring himself a Cutty.

Which was when I finished pulling on my rain stuff fast and got out of there. Because suddenly I felt I needed a Cutty, too.

Maybe even a double.

31

The lights started flickering again as we made our way back to the parking lot and went out decisively as we got into the Jeep. They stayed out as Ellie's car key found its way to the ignition and the dashboard lights began glowing like a handful of sparks in the streaming darkness.

"Are you thinking what I'm thinking?" Ellie asked as we made our way down Water Street. Store signs swung wildly, rain hammered the Jeep's roof and fought against the sweep of its wipers, its headlights bars of yellow, probing ahead. "And are you still carrying that little gun?"

"I'm thinking that Willow might be too light to have lifted Reuben; she's built, all right, but not that way," I replied. "The husband could have, though. Or the two of them together. There's Valium in her bag, and nobody's told me that the drugs in Reuben's system weren't Valium, yet."

I took a breath. "Maybe Willow told her husband about Reuben, and they decided then how they would get rid of him if he started looking like a real threat to their—his—plans. Setting Victor up to take the blame could have come from Reuben's own bragging; he might have said more to her than she's letting on."

"They'd have had time to work up a real scheme for getting rid of him," Ellie agreed. "And if Reuben went back to the motel to ask Willow for more money, they could have given him a dosed drink there."

"All of which is an awful lot of blue sky," I admitted, "but it could have worked. I didn't get a look at the husband's hand, but the two of them had been in Victor's house and could have seen the surgical-instrument collection." A pair of killers would've made all the tasks that needed to be done a much easier proposition.

"So if that's it, why would Willow tell us how bad Reuben could have made it for them, maybe ruining her husband's election prospects and so on? Why give us what amounts to a motive?"

We looked at each other. "To make it seem," we said in one voice, "not like a motive."

"But what about him being in business and in country clubs and all? And . . . politics?" Ellie questioned. "He just doesn't seem the type."

"Hey, people have elected real TV wrestlers to political office. This guy only looks like one. Well," I amended, "he would look like one, with another million years or so of evolution. As for business and clubs, well, people like people who can get the job done, you know? There are plenty of movers and shakers in high places who wouldn't be there except that they've got money. And if a fellow has been careful not to get any convictions . . ."

As opposed, I meant, to everybody knowing that he'd done bad things. That part some people actually were attracted to, because it meant he could do bad things for them.

"I guess," Ellie conceded. "Sure blows my fantasy of what fancy-pantsy social life is like, though."

I had to laugh; once upon a time it had blown mine, too. "But Willow was right," I said. "An ugly story about her would be a find for her husband's political opponents, especially if he's managed to stay officially clean, himself. It could be the only thing they'd have to use against him. Subtly, but effectively."

A trash can rolled across the street in front of us, driven by the wind; Ellie swerved around it. Foamy whitecaps slammed the breakwater, then fell back for another run at it.

"So," I went on, "maybe Reuben finally threatened the wrong guy. But if Willow and Mr. Personality got rid of Reuben to shut him up, and faked Willow's near-poisoning to draw suspicion away from themselves, why do it so dramatically? And why kill Weasel and Heywood?"

Ellie glanced at me, waiting.

"Maybe to make it," I answered my own question, "look as if the three deaths are related. And yes, I do know that's overkill, two murders to cover one, but that doesn't mean it's not true. And to answer your other question, no, I'm not carrying the gun."

"Jacobia, I thought we agreed that caution ought to be the watchword, until . . ."

"I know. But I put it away. It started feeling foolish, day after day and no action. I'll carry it if I go somewhere alone."

"All right," she agreed reluctantly, sounding as glum as I felt. "This is getting to be—"

"A crowd scene," I finished for her. "Mike Carpentier's been in Victor's place with Molly. Willow and the goon-guy have been there with their kids. Marcus has been there, for heaven's sake, touring the place. And I suppose any minute now I'll find out Terence and Paddy were regular visitors. Tea and crumpets, or something, with Weasel serving all of them as the butler."

We drove slowly past Wadsworth's Hardware, its sign dangling by one chain length, the other snapped off. Lines of raindrops drummed across the street, sheets of water flinging themselves at the storefronts.

"Drat," Ellie muttered. "I'm pulling over. I could

drive off the fish pier in this and not know it till we hit bottom."

Cautiously she turned into the tiny parking lot above the boat basin. The dock lights had gone off, so the gleams of white paint on the boats tossing and lurching against their mooring lines were barely visible. Corralled up inside the dock pilings, they made me think of a lot of horses panicking in a barn. To our right loomed Paddy Farrell's building, also pitch dark.

"Next thing you know," I said, "we'll find out Reuben had been in Victor's office, getting treated for an ingrown toenail. Maybe Reuben took the scalpel and slit his own throat with it."

The sheltered spot by Paddy's building kept the wind and rain from battering us so badly. I settled down to wait for the power to come back on or the storm to back off, preferably both.

"Just wait," I fumed in exasperation. "They'll all turn out to be suicides. Weasel will turn out to have stuffed the tie down *his* own throat. We'll find a note from Heywood, too: sayonara."

"Suicide," Ellie objected distractedly, "is a sin." Then: "What's that up there?"

"Molly's *doll,*" I ranted on—the heater in the Jeep was not powerful and I hate wet feet—"will turn out to be possessed by a horror-movie demon, self-animated and self-destructive."

"I don't think so. Jake, will you look a minute?"

The rain let up a little as if gathering itself for another deluge. "What *is* that? And do you hear something?"

I peered where she was pointing: glimmers of light moving intermittently behind Paddy's windows. "It looks like they turned on flashlights. Or lit some candles."

"I don't think Paddy would use candles up there," Ellie said. "He's paranoid about fire in that old building. Even with all the fire extinguishers he has, I don't think he would . . ."

Light shone once more at the loft windows, then careened away. The wind screamed again; it was nuts of us even to be out there. "I don't hear anything except a gale blowing," I said.

But then I did. Light bounced off the inside of the window again: not a candle. A flashlight or battery lantern, swinging. And the sound I heard was not the wind, although very like it.

Somebody screaming.

32

The power went back on as we reached the stairs inside the old building, tracklights and torchières blazing on blindingly to reveal the shape of Terence Oscard crumpled by the bottom step.

"Jesus, oh Jesus," Paddy moaned, clutching his head. He'd stopped shouting at the sight of us, but he was still frantic.

"Sit," Ellie told him. "I'll call the ambulance. Jake, look at him, will you? See if there's anything . . ."

To be done for him, she meant, and at first I didn't think there was. The back of his head was a pulpy-looking mess, and he wasn't breathing until I turned him.

"Don't move him, you'll paralyze him!" Paddy shouted. "Oh, my God . . . Terence always said you never *move* somebody, you could damage their spinal cord."

"Paddy, if he's not breathing, it won't do him much good to have an intact spinal cord, will it?"

That much first aid even I knew, but suddenly I wished I'd taken Terence up on the loan of that Red

Cross book. Still, once he was shifted so that his jaw wasn't blocking his windpipe, he took a shuddery breath, then another. "We really, *really* need a medical person here right now," I called to Ellie.

"They're coming," she reported, returning from the phone. "Paddy, what happened?"

"I . . . I don't know." Paddy looked dazed. "I thought he was down here reading, but when the lights went out and he didn't say anything I went looking for him with the flashlight. And I found him here . . . like this."

He knelt by Terence's body, reaching out to touch the unconscious man's face. His palm cradled Terence's rough cheek.

"Terry, please don't die. Please, Terry—" He looked up desperately. "Are they coming? Did they say they were coming?"

"Yeah, they're coming," I told him. A siren approached. "Go out and wave them down so they know where we are."

He gathered himself and went. "Here, over here!" I heard him shout, out in the street.

Ellie came back from the rear of the work area where Paddy kept cardboard, bags of fabric scraps, anything he was going to put out in the bin as trash. Being Paddy, he'd installed a small, very visible red-lit Exit sign back there.

"Go look at that door," she suggested mildly, and when I did I found the wooden frame around it splintered, the broken wood fresh and gleaming under the chipped-out white paint. The area around the heavy lock set and deadbolt were especially chewed up. Someone had jimmied it, using a pry bar or something like one.

Even that wouldn't have worked, though, I saw as I examined it more closely, except for one thing. The pry-bar attack had been done energetically, but the lock was designed precisely for that sort of criminal assault. Paddy was no slouch at any security; he didn't confine himself only to fire precautions.

His locks would have held. I didn't touch them but I didn't need to. The door stood ajar, so the bolts of both the cylinder lock and the deadbolt were clearly visible.

Unless someone had unlocked it after it was jimmied, the door hadn't been locked in the first place.

33

"Jesus H. Christ," Bob Arnold exhaled angrily. "Is there some kind of drug has gotten into the water around here? Making people crazy?"

It was late, but Teddy kept the bar at La Sardina open for us; we were all too wired up to go home. The tail end of the storm had snapped around with a last vicious twist, splattering the windows with bursts of rain; huge swells rolled into the boat basin, the small craft bobbing and straining uneasily at their mooring lines.

"Did Paddy have anything to say?" Ellie asked.

Bob shrugged. "Thinks maybe Terence heard someone breaking in, went to the stairs, yelled to Paddy, someone caught him there."

"Weapon?" I inquired.

"Nah. Run outside, toss it over the seawall, end of story. Time anyone finds it, it's all washed off. If anyone does."

"Good trick, readin' with the lights out," George Valentine observed neutrally. He'd heard the ambulance siren and come down to see what might be the matter.

"Yeah," Bob Arnold agreed. "Asked Paddy. Changed his story a little. Now he says the two of 'em'd had a set-to, earlier. When that happened, sometimes Terence'd just sleep downstairs."

He sighed, ate a pretzel from the bowl of them on the shiny wooden bar surface. "But then he started feelin' bad about it. Paddy did, I mean. Called downstairs, no answer, got a flashlight and went down lookin' for his buddy."

Wade's big arm rested on my shoulder and I was glad to have it there; even with all that had happened recently, the sight of Terence lying there helpless had really thrown me.

"It could have been," Ellie said, "that someone mistook him for Paddy, in the dark."

Wade and George glanced at each other. "Paddy," George said, and Wade nodded at him.

"What?" Bob Arnold demanded.

"We were all in what was left of Heywood Sondergard's youth group," Wade said uncomfortably, "at the end of it, just before Marcus and Heywood left town. Mike, Willow, Paddy, and us." His hand took in George and Ellie. "Little Boxy Thorogood hung around too, for a while. Junior member. Till," Wade added, "Boxy died."

"Yeah, so what?" Arnold said. "I know that." He spied a pot of hours-old coffee on the hot plate, got up, and poured a mug of it. He held the pot out to us, noted our refusals, sampled some, and shuddered.

"You trying to tell me someone's knockin' off old members of a church club? What, maybe they didn't like any of the hymns you guys sang?"

He hoisted himself back onto the barstool. "Besides, what about the other members? Why single you out? For that matter, it ain't even all of you—unless you three have been suffering from problems you haven't reported."

They shook their heads. "And," he finished, taking another handful of pretzels, "why now?"

George examined his fingernails. "Point is, Terence

wasn't part of it. He wasn't hooked up to Reuben in any way."

Wesley Bodine wasn't, either, I thought, but Paddy was. I kept quiet, though, so George would talk more.

"And I've been thinking," he went on. "We all gab about how if you stood up to him, Reuben would back off. Even Paddy, though he really didn't. But that wasn't the whole story, only half."

He looked up. "The other half was, if you showed you were scared of him, he would never quit. And even after you stood up to him once, he would try again. Just one more time."

"That's right," Ellie recalled. "He cornered me in the back of Leighton's store after I'd beat him up."

George frowned. "You never told me that. What did you do?"

Her smile was beatific. "I kneed him in the groin just as hard as ever I could. Then I paid for my Popsicle, stood outside eating it until he came out limping. He didn't even look at me."

"Great," Arnold said flatly. "I'm impressed. You three faced him down, he don't bother you anymore. But Reuben, you might just want to remember, is dead. He is not running around bothering *anybody*, anymore, so what's going on now, this ain't Reuben's one more time. Even though," he conceded reluctantly, "it sure as hell does feel as if it is, doesn't it?"

He drank more terrible coffee, grimaced. "Just like the bad old days."

It was an unpleasant echo of what Paddy Farrell had said in La Sardina. "Who else was in the group?" I asked. "In that last year, when all the worst things happened? Paddy's dad, Boxy Thorogood and Deckie Cobb, Mrs. Sondergard . . ."

Silence. I waited for them to remember. But after a moment I realized: the silence was my answer.

"No one," Ellie said finally. "The other kids just kind of dropped away. We would have too, eventually.

And then Marcus and Heywood left town, of course. But even before that, it wasn't fun anymore."

She looked into the mirror behind the bar. "In a way, Reuben killed that, too. And there wasn't even anything to bury."

George got up decisively. "Come on, kiddo. Long day. I want to be shut of it."

Wade left some money on the bar, called to Ted in the kitchen as we went out, to let him know he could lock up. "Paddy going to be all right, up in Calais?" he asked Bob Arnold.

At the hospital, he meant. Paddy had gone in the ambulance with Terence.

"Yeah," Arnold said, heading across the street to where his squad car was parked. The rain had stopped, and puddles stood gleamingly under the yellow streetlights. A few stars had shown up, poking tentatively between the streaming clouds.

Bob straightened tiredly. "They didn't know, Terence, if he is going to make it or not. I think they're going to LifeStar him out of there. Said they'd keep me posted. Paddy wouldn't leave."

A thump of regret hit me: If Victor's trauma center were operating now, they wouldn't have to LifeStar Terence anywhere. Whoever was doing all this wasn't only killing people right this minute; next year some little kid would fall off a skateboard, or a logger would get creamed by a shifting load, or the boom would swing suddenly on a sailboat.

And instead of prompt surgery within the first hour—the golden hour, as Victor always called it—the victim would get a helicopter ride to Portland or wherever. Better than nothing, of course.

But a long way from ideal. That was the gap my goofball ex-husband had wanted to close. And crazy as he was in every other way but that one, he could have done it.

George and Ellie got into the Jeep together; I rode home in the pickup with Wade. "Arnold asks good questions," I said as he downshifted for the Key Street hill.

"Yeah. How come others from the group, and not the three of us. And why now? Although the answer to that last one's pretty clear," he added, turning into the driveway. "It's someone from away who's doing it, someone who's in town for the festival."

"Or," I suggested, "someone who wants it to look that way."

His shoulders slumped. "Huh. Yeah, that too, maybe."

Half a block away, Victor's house looked dark and forlorn. A branch had blown down onto the porch roof, crumpling a section of gutter, and wet leaves were plastered to the pristine white siding like dirty handprints.

"And that door was open," I said. "It couldn't have been broken in, those locks were good ones, *and* there was no need for it to be. Unless someone already inside wanted *it* to look that way too."

"In that case, why not lock it after you broke it?" Wade inquired reasonably.

I put my hands to my head. "I don't know."

"My question doesn't have anything to do with any of that, though," Wade went on, shutting off the engine. Sometime during the day, he'd found time to haul in all those storm windows.

"What I want to know," he demanded of the dripping darkness, "is why? What Reuben started should have died with him. But it's not." We got out, crossed the sodden grass to the back porch. In the hallway, Monday's toenails clicked welcomingly.

"Because," Wade went on, "whoever did for Reuben, that's one thing. I'm not condoning it, but I understand it."

He unlocked the back door, and I realized with a

sad little thump of startlement that he must have locked it, even though Sam was home: another evidence of Reuben's legacy of fear.

"So?" In the kitchen, a wave of tiredness washed over me and I sank into a chair.

"So you'd think if someone wanted to go on doing bad deeds, they'd do them to other bad guys like Reuben. If," he added, "you could find any. Instead, someone's targeting his victims. Almost as if they are finishing the business he can't finish himself."

I looked at him. "You're brilliant."

"But not brilliant enough." He peered into the refrigerator, closed it again. "What's the good of that?"

I got up. "It's the link. What they all have in common—not only that they were in Sondergard's group. They were *victims* in the group—even Heywood, if you think being blackmailed and having your wife murdered makes you a victim, which I do. Maybe even Weasel, if he's connected to the group in some way we just haven't figured out yet. And you know, I'll bet someone thinks that also makes them villains."

He thought about that. "Like if a woman goes to a bar, she ends up having to fight off some drunk, people say she shouldn't have been there in the first place."

"Right. Or a guy ends up living in his car and eating out of a soup kitchen. Nobody ever says, Hey, that could be me. They say the guy's a loser, he should try harder. He gets blamed, and so does she. The victim gets turned into the villain 'cause it makes somebody feel, Hey, that *couldn't* be me. Or something," I trailed off unhappily.

"Huh." I could see him turning it over in his head. But then he frowned.

"Close, but no cigar. For one thing, you'd have to kill off the whole darn town. Everybody got victimized by Reuben, or almost everybody, at one time or another. And," he put the nail in the coffin of my theory, "it still doesn't account for Weasel. If he had been hooked up to our group in any way, Jacobia, I'd remember it."

"Oh." The energy went out of me again. He was right.

"Sorry." He shrugged helplessly.

"That's okay." But it was *something* about being a victim, I was sure, combined with some threat or actual behavior of Reuben's that had gotten it all going again.

And something more, a third thing I kept almost realizing. But every time I tried to get my mind around it, it fluttered away, as wispy and elusive as gossamer.

The lights were on in the dining room but there wasn't a sound from in there. I got up to look, found Sam hunched over the dratted Ouija board.

I wished he weren't. I'd managed to rationalize my creepy experience with it; just my subconscious, I'd decided, spitting out the gist of my current preoccupation again and again.

But I couldn't get over my uneasiness about it. Around me, the old house was as silent as a held breath. A pair of earphones were on Sam's head; he glanced up and saw me.

"Hey," he said, pulling the earphones off.

"Hi. What are you doing?"

He shrugged. "Just fooling with this. The radio gets shortwave. If I listen enough, maybe I'll be able to translate Morse in my head. You know, like if you live in France pretty soon you can speak French?"

From the earphones came the distant, tinny sound of dots and dashes. Something about Morse code had always sounded urgent to me, even when it probably wasn't.

"Dad called earlier, kind of upset," Sam went on. "He says the diet in jail is not nutritionally balanced, it's a violation of his rights. Also the reading material is inadequate."

I could imagine. "You settle him down?"

"Yeah." Sam managed a grin: his game face. I was glad to see it, didn't like thinking about how long he might have to wear it.

Now I needed my own. "Did he ask about the interview? With the DA, I mean?"

On the table, the Ouija board lay silent and motionless, its black letters and numerals sharp against its polished surface.

"Yeah. He told me again," Sam recited, imitating Victor uncannily, "that it's out of my hands, I had no choice, and if I beat myself up about it anymore, he's going to kick my butt."

It's one of the very most annoying things about Victor, that once in a while he will blindside you with bighearted behavior. It would be so much easier just to hate him up one side and down the other.

"Don't stay up late. Work tomorrow," I reminded Sam, but he had the earphones back on already and couldn't hear me.

In the hall I spotted a fluff of dog hair, like a shadow in the corner. But when I bent to reach for it, there was nothing. As I straightened, my glance fell onto the hall shelf.

The package Terence had shoved into my hands that afternoon was still there, wrapped in brown paper, marked PRIVATE & CONFIDENTIAL. It was addressed to a firm of attorneys in Bangor, Maine.

Hefting it, I discovered that it felt like spiral notebooks stacked one on top of another; you could feel the wire bindings along the side of the parcel. Half a dozen of them, maybe.

No stamps on it, though, and the string was starting to come undone. Tape, actually, would be better for it. I could rewrap it, and perhaps just glance at the contents as I did so.

"Guess I'll go on up to bed," Sam said. He snapped the radio off, interrupting a sputter of dot-and-dash. Then he paused, squinting at the Ouija board in puzzlement.

"Something funny about that thing," he said.

34

I feel that falling out of the sky can be prevented by not going up into it. Ellie, however, does not share this opinion, as I was reminded very early the next morning when she showed up at a ghastly hour, full of what I regarded as a ghastly plan.

"Ellie, these notebooks," I said, waving at them spread out on the kitchen table. "They're . . ."

"We'll be back by lunchtime," she interrupted firmly in the tone her pirate ancestors might have used while persuading people to walk the plank. "Or probably before. Grand Manan's only half an hour, as the crow flies."

I did not point out that crows fly with wings that are attached by muscles and tendons, and that if God had meant me to do it too, He'd have attached some to me.

"But," I protested uselessly, "the notebooks are . . ."

"I got a phone call while I was out last night. Message from George's cousin, on the machine."

Which didn't help much. Half of downeast Maine consists of George Valentine's cousins, the other half his aunts and uncles.

"So?"

"So Harriet Thorogood wants to talk to us."

I stared. "Harriet . . . *Boxy's* mother? I thought she was . . ."

"Dead, I know. But she isn't. She's in a nursing home."

"Lovely. Why didn't you mention this to me? Anyway, I'm very happy for her, that she's alive. Still, I fail to see how flying over to see her there will advance our understanding of anything. In fact, after flying at all I will be in no shape to . . ."

But Ellie had already turned off the coffeemaker, filled up Monday's water bowl, checked the stove knobs to make sure they were off, and scribbled a note.

"I'll explain on the way," she promised, hustling me out.

But she didn't, or at least not immediately, because Ellie had been up and going strong since her usual rising time of five in the morning—in Maine, late sleeping is seen as a sure sign of deficient moral character—and had been to the Waco Diner with George for breakfast. So she had plenty of news:

Terence had indeed been transferred to Portland and Paddy Farrell had driven down there to be with him. Paddy would come back this evening, Ellie went on, to close up the studio; after that he would return to the medical center in Portland for the duration of Terence's stay there.

"No word on Terence's actual condition," she added, "other than that he's still unconscious and in intensive care."

So he wouldn't be letting on who had clobbered him anytime soon. I'd brought along the notebooks, which now lay in my lap. They were Terence's diaries, and what they contained was still spinning in my head like the glass bits in a kaleidoscope.

"Ellie," I began, picking up a notebook, "we need . . ."

Instead of listening, she set the parking brake on the Jeep in the visitor's lot at the airfield and got out.

Set in a pasture overlooking blue water, the airstrip looked too short to land more than a helicopter but was actually long enough to accommodate a good-sized Gulfstream, a fact that was of little comfort to me since I didn't want to go up in any of those either.

Reluctantly, I got out of the Jeep. The air was crisp and washed clean by the storm of the night before, smelling of sea salt and evergreens, and the light had the fragile clarity of a Maine island in the early morning, unspoiled and full of bright innocent promise.

On the other hand, waiting on the tarmac was an aircraft that looked as if it had been glued together out of balsa wood and construction paper. Eyeing it, I opened my mouth to object.

But that was useless too. "We," said Ellie, "are going. In that. Now." She marched toward the plane.

The low metal Quonset building of Quoddy Air, Inc., looked like something that leather-helmeted cropdusters flew biplanes out of, back in the 1930s. The whole idea of my going up into the sky was ridiculous anyway, I thought wildly.

And then I *was* going up in it. Strapped in, shaking, and in imminent danger of supplying my breakfast for examination by my flying companions, I saw the end of the runway vanish under the nose of the toy plane. Another moment and Passamaquoddy Bay fell abruptly away beneath us; under the circumstances, I guessed it was better than seeing it rise abruptly toward us, but not much better.

The plane banked right. The pilot was cheerful. I took this as a good sign. Until he turned off the engine.

"You know," I said faintly, in what I imagined was a nice, conversational tone, "I believe that when the airplane is actually in the air, hundreds and hundreds of feet off the ground or in this case, actually, the *ice-cold water* . . . "

"You don't have to scream," Ellie said. "I can hear you."

"Beautiful, isn't it?" the pilot asked. "Nothing but wind noise. Hey, look down there—it's a whale."

It was a big, dark shape moving along very slowly in the indigo bay, and I had no doubt that I would be getting much more closely acquainted with it in the immediate future.

"Better fire it up again," Ellie suggested kindly. "Jake's getting pale."

With a grin, the pilot started the engine. Have I mentioned that he was approximately fourteen years old? Anyway, it only coughed two or three times before catching and running evenly, which meant only about ten seconds when I was so terrified that I had no discernible vital functions whatsoever, if you didn't count all the ones I thought I might lose control of any minute.

The plane was a three-seater: me and the pilot up front, Ellie strapped in the rear. Her expression was glowingly radiant, the look of a little kid with an all-day pass to the carnival.

Seeing her face, I realized suddenly that if the plane did crash, there was little that I could do about it. Possibly this thought was the result of all the neurochemicals pouring into my system, like the ones that supposedly make you feel cool as a cucumber while you're about to be devoured by a tiger, although I don't see how anyone could really know that.

Slowly my fists unclenched. The waves looked like crumpled aluminum foil. A boat bobbed, the size of my little fingernail. Far to the west, over Nova Scotia, the remnants of last night's storm loomed darkly like an evil kingdom towering into the sky.

"So," I said, "tell me again why we are going here. What's she want to talk to us about?"

"I don't know," Ellie replied. "Harriet wouldn't say. We'll find out when we get there."

Strapped in or not, I was about to pop her one, but then we were landing, a process whose details—especially the part about dropping to earth way more rapidly than I thought could possibly be normal—captured me utterly until it was over.

Ten minutes later we were climbing the steps to Olde Bayview Nursing Home, a short walk from the airfield.

"So this is Boxy's mother, who lives here, and she's seventy years old," I said, trying to get straight in my head what Ellie had been saying to me while the runway pavement was coming up at us so damned fast.

"Seventy isn't old enough for a nursing home," I added.

"It is for Harriet. She started failing when Boxy died. Not long after that," Ellie went on, "she gave up her house and came here to live. Since then she's been going downhill. Her mental functions. Sleeps most of the time, doesn't speak at all, that sort of thing."

She pressed the doorbell on the low, white-painted concrete block structure. What the place lacked in snazziness it more than made up for in regular maintenance: clipped hedges, a lawn like a putting green, riotous flower beds. A very old man with a very humped back was scattering bonemeal lovingly around the feet of some perfect rosebushes.

Someone inside buzzed us in. "I knew she lived here," Ellie went on, "but she's been completely uncommunicative for so long, I never even thought of mentioning her to you. What I *didn't* know was that she's not out of it anymore. She's woken up, George's cousin says."

In the foyer, a golden retriever got up and greeted us with wags and tongue lolling. From behind the reception desk, a woman smiled and offered the visitors' book. The place smelled of soap and fresh floor wax. Ellie signed the book, and we were directed down a hardwood-floored hallway so shiny that I could see the soles of my shoes in it, yet somehow it wasn't slippery.

I made a mental note to ask someone there how they managed the trick, since my floors could certainly use an application of the miracle substance. I knew of only two possible conditions for old wood floors: gritty or *whoops!*

"It should be one of these rooms," Ellie murmured. The cleanliness here was stunning: windows glittering like diamonds, woodwork so unsmudged that it seemed to have been painted—glossy enamel, in a fresh, springlike shade of mint green—that very morning. A faint hint of something medicinally camphorated hung in the air, mingled with the smell of a cake baking.

"George's cousin works here," Ellie added, "did I mention that? The one," she added, "who called last night. And Harriet's doctor says her mental trouble started with a stroke."

At which I finally got it: so *that* was how the cousin hooked into it. In Eastport, the maze of social, work, and family connections was mind-boggling, and it was mostly Greek to me.

Only not to Ellie. "But if you ask me," she went on, "Harriet's breakdown was on account of a broken heart." We came to the door of a large common room: braided rugs, crocheted afghans, a large yellow cat ensconced in a sunny window.

"Then the other day someone told her Reuben was dead," Ellie finished. "She's been bright as a new penny, since."

"I still don't see, though," I objected, "why she wants to talk to us."

"I don't," said a shaky old voice at my elbow. "I want you to talk to me."

Harriet Thorogood was a small, fragile woman with thin white hair, tiny bones, and the dark, sharp eyes of a bird. Wearing a flowered dress with a white lace collar, rolled stockings, and orthopedic shoes, she sat alertly in an upholstered armchair that seemed big enough to swallow her up.

"Someone said you found him after someone cut

him, hung him to bleed. I want," she demanded avidly, "to know how he looked."

Ellie and I glanced at each other. Neither of us wanted to relive finding Reuben or to report the gory details. But she was Boxy's mother.

So we sat down together and told her.

Rather, Ellie did. While she talked, I kept seeing Harriet Thorogood as she'd been twenty years earlier: not fragile, still vigorous, with a ten-year-old son.

I saw her come to the door with a cigarette in her hand. A drink, maybe, poured on the kitchen counter while she finished the dishes. There was a radio playing show tunes behind her, and when they told her what had happened I felt her eyes going wildly from one to another of their faces.

Searching for the one that would tell her it was not true.

But none of them had.

When Ellie had finished, Harriet sighed and looked away, satisfied.

"Mrs. Thorogood," I said, "didn't Boxy ever ask anyone for help about Reuben? You, or any adult? He was in the church group, for example. Didn't he ask for help from Reverend Sondergard?"

Slowly she dragged her gaze back. Some of the brightness had already gone from her expression, as if now with this last thing finished, she had little reason for remaining alert.

"No," she quavered regretfully. "He never. I wished he had of, I'd o' skinned that Tate bastard"—*bahstid*— "alive. And he mustn't have asked the reverend for any help, or the reverend would've helped him. Wouldn't he?" she demanded.

Her cloudy eyes were full of a last appeal: surely her son hadn't asked for help against Reuben Tate, only to be refused.

"Of course he would have," I told her, with more

confidence than I felt. "I'm sure he'd have done anything he could, if he had known."

"Well, then," she muttered. "There's an end to it. I thank both you girls very kindly." With this her head drooped, her tiny fingers plucking unaware at the cotton fabric of her dress.

So: no new, revelatory information, nothing illuminating to add to another sad old story. Just an old woman who wanted some punctuation for the end of her tragedy.

And one other thing.

Back at the airfield, I climbed into the aircraft with no assistance, settling in the front cockpit seat and strapping the safety harness over my chest. Swinging around, we hurtled down the narrow runway and, it felt like, straight off a cliff.

Air punched up under the plane, lifting it, and we climbed suddenly, bouncing a little in the crossways air currents around the island. I didn't care.

"You're gung-ho all of a sudden," Ellie said, watching me carefully. "I'm sorry nothing useful came of this."

But it had. "I understand," I said. My voice flew away on the engine noise. "The part of it that I hadn't been getting."

We banked hard right, arrowing toward Moose Island, on it the town of Eastport, the causeway ribboning east across more blue water, and finally the forested coastal plain, a vast swath of autumn reds, yellows, and evergreens rising to the mountains.

"What I didn't get was the physical act," I said. "Putting the blade to his throat and cutting it. Because . . . well, how? I mean, how could *anyone* do it? How could any human being actually do a thing like that?"

History, of course, suggested that lots of them could. Were, probably, right this very minute. And yet . . .

The nightmare memory of Reuben hanging in the graveyard still came to me at odd, awful moments. But this time, what I had imagined of Boxy's mother came, also:

How she had felt. My mind tried to put Sam in Boxy's place, but I wouldn't let it. That far I couldn't—wouldn't—go.

And didn't need to. Sunlight glinted suddenly on the plane's front window, turning it into a mirror.

35

There was another crucial task to accomplish that morning, and by the time I got home it was the hour when normal people might actually be in their offices. So, although it was not what I wanted to be doing—

—Ellie was sitting at the table reading Terence's diaries, and the faces she was making as she did so made me want to start hashing them over with her immediately—

—I began making phone calls.

When I was finished, it was several hours later, and I'd kept Victor's trauma center from becoming a dead issue for one more day. Bankers, builders, real estate salespeople, medical regulators, prospective investors:

I promised them all that Victor's arrest had been a terrible error, the kind of thing that happened in your worst nightmares. I said that the wheels for releasing him were in the process of turning and he would be out tomorrow.

Well, it was the kind of thing that happened in my worst nightmares, anyway; that much was true. But it was the last time I would get away with saying any of the rest of it. The land-option payment was due in twenty-four hours. So if Victor stayed in jail for more than a day longer, it was all over.

"Have you," Ellie asked quietly, "read these?"

I sat down and put my face in my hands. "Yes. Pretty low tactic, I guess, snooping in them when he's not even around to object. But what Bob Arnold said about him really struck me."

"That Terence might have done it himself. Hurt himself, I mean, by throwing himself down the stairs. The bottom step was messy, maybe from his landing there after someone hit him. But maybe just from his landing there . . . hard."

"Yeah. He'd fallen once before, or so he said. His behavior on the ferry and at the festival was odd, too. It made me think he might be ill."

The diaries, though, opened a whole new can of worms. They were dated on the covers; Ellie opened the most recent one again.

"Paddy owed Terence a lot of money. Apparently he'd lent it to him to put into the design studio. *And* they were breaking up."

She looked at me, disbelieving. "But I can't imagine them without each other. It would be like dividing Siamese twins."

"Meanwhile, Terence was looking to get his money back," I recited. "And Paddy couldn't pay. So Terence was about to sue."

Glumly, Ellie looked at the pages again. "Which is something else I absolutely can't believe, under normal circumstances. And it looks as if, even if that never paid off, Terence would be okay financially. I never realized it, but I guess he's wealthy. Or so it says here."

"Right. Not the show-off type." I examined once more the pages with their well-organized paragraphs and crisply set-off things-to-do lists, each task checked off as it was accomplished, interspersed with notes about his and Paddy's imminent breakup.

There were notes about his finances, too: CDs,

money market accounts, a portfolio of blue chips. Like the kind I should have had, except that in the past couple of years I'd let that aspect of my financial life slip, handing Ellie all my juicy stock tips instead of following them myself.

Terence's personal finances were news to me but not a huge surprise. I'd done Paddy's taxes, but knew Terence's situation only as it related to his partnership in Paddy's business. He had done his personal taxes himself, and from the look of these notes he'd done them as well as I could have.

Now I thought about his good, casual clothes, his easy, self-effacing way of approaching most situations. It all spelled money, but so quietly you never would notice it unless you were looking for it.

As Terence—a quiet, civilized man—had intended. "I'll bet he had his other affairs in order too," I said. "Terence is a neat freak." Only at the end of the final book had the diaries' careful system of organization begun deteriorating.

"So I'll bet Terence has a will tucked into a safe-deposit box somewhere," I said, "and a copy in his desk."

"Right," Ellie said. "But why would he—"

"Your next guess, I suppose, is that I am the beneficiary," Paddy Farrell said, appearing suddenly in the hall behind us.

A thump of guilty embarrassment hit me. We hadn't heard him come in, and it was pretty clear what we were doing.

"Paddy, I hope your being back this early doesn't mean—"

"That he's died?" Paddy's expression was haunted. "No, he's hanging on. For now."

He stared at the diaries. "Sorry to startle you. I knocked but you were apparently engrossed in your reading. I came to ask about his package. But I see you've already dealt with it. In," he added bitterly, "your great wisdom." He turned to go.

"Paddy, this isn't the way it looks."

"Oh, I think it is. It'll make great dinner conversation all over town, Terence's poor delusions, like his crazy idea of suing me. Have fun, chewing over our relationship. You're right about his will, by the way; I'd get everything if Terence passed. As if," he finished bitterly, "I would want it, then."

He opened the door; I got up and stopped him. "Okay. As long as you're here, I'll ask: What about it, Paddy? What's all this about Terence wanting to leave, wanting his money and your not wanting to pay it back to him?"

His eyes were hard and glittery. "Oh, it's not enough to read his diary? Pry into his private secrets? You want details?"

I shook my head impatiently. "I want to know if you hit him, Paddy. Maybe you had an argument over his leaving, and over the money. You lost your temper, the way you do sometimes. And then set it up to look like an intruder. That's what I'm asking you."

All the fight went out of him; he sagged against the door.

"No," he whispered, aghast. "We argued, but not over money. It's true I don't have it to give him, but that's not the point. The trouble was that he was talking about leaving again, and he *couldn't* leave. . . ."

"Why not?" Ellie asked.

He looked at her as if the answer must be obvious. "Because he's ill. He can't be alone. Surely you've noticed."

He turned to me, distraught. "Jacobia, I thought you at least understood, since the other day on the ferry. He stumbles, he talks strangely—that's when this whole idea of his going away began, when he started behaving . . . irrationally. And it was getting worse all the time."

He began pacing the kitchen. "It's why I took him to see your ex-husband—once he'd have jumped at the chance of another medical examination, but he'd gotten so strange . . . and now your ex was the only doctor Terence would agree to be examined by."

His face clouded with guilt. "But I still didn't believe he was really sick. He was always saying he was, you know. I tried acting cold to him, to let him see how it would be if we really did part."

A huge sigh escaped him. "But," he finished miserably, "I was wrong. I guess I just didn't want to believe it. When he got so ill on the ferry, that's when I started really thinking—"

"So you've been in Victor's office too," I interrupted.

"Yes." Paddy looked taken aback. "Why shouldn't we have? He scheduled Terence for tests, referred him to a man in Portland, much to Terence's dismay. But now, of course, all that is pretty much beside the point. We know what the trouble is."

Yeah, he'd been bonked with a crowbar or something. "Paddy, what the hell are you talking about?"

He pulled a chair out, sank into it, his face bleak. "I'm saying," he uttered, "that even before what happened last night, Terry was dying."

The words hung there. "I don't understand," I managed after a shocked moment. "Terence is always so . . ."

"Healthy," Paddy finished for me. "So healthy it was a joke. But aside from everything else, he was—well. It's a dangerous world, Jacobia."

Suddenly I knew what was coming. Eastport's not perfect; we probably have as many knuckleheads as anywhere else. But much of the time, we tolerate one another's differences pretty well. And when you've gone without overt hatefulness over your neighbors'—and your own—differences for a while, you can start thinking maybe the rest of the planet's ills won't come around to afflict you either.

So I hadn't considered it. But:

"He's been HIV-positive for nearly thirteen years," Paddy said quietly. "Or technically he has been—there's been no detectable virus for a long time, but they never call you cured."

"So his being a hypochondriac, studying first aid, all the herbal remedies, working out and jogging, and so on," I began.

"Were his ways of coping," Paddy agreed. "Along with his real medications, of course. He'd been one of the lucky ones, always responding well to treatment, even in the early times when the medicines weren't as good as they are now. We thought that might go on forever. It never occurred to me that something else might go wrong."

He took a deep breath. "But *before* he was in treatment, just around the time I met him a dozen years ago, he'd had some headaches. The doctors said then that they were probably from some kind of an infection that had left a scar in his brain. And now, just because he's getting older, or whatever, the scar had begun changing and starting to press on something important."

"But . . . can't it be removed?"

"No." He sounded heartbroken. "If it weren't for this injury, we wouldn't even know about it yet. And now with the skull fracture and all the damage beneath it, Terence would have only about a ten percent likelihood of surviving the surgery, the doctors told me."

"And his mental status? How'd they say the tissue would have affected it? Before the injury?"

"Paranoia, delusions, emotional outbursts, unsteady gait, a slur when he talked. More to come. Any of that sound familiar?"

He straightened with an effort. "He was sending his diaries to his attorney in Bangor for safekeeping.

Another of his crazy ideas. But I'll do it for him now, if you'll let me have them."

Ellie gathered them up and gave them to him unhesitatingly. "Sure, Paddy. We'll be keeping a good thought for him. And you."

"Right," he said, accepting the volumes.

He nodded wanly at Tommy and Sam as they came in, Monday galloping happily behind them, and went away down the street, his step so slow it made me think of a man walking to the gallows.

"You don't suppose he's lying," Ellie said as the boys began raiding the refrigerator. "I know that sounds awful, but . . ."

"You can't fake an actual lesion. If it's on the scans they took at the hospital, it's there. And it fits his behavior."

The boys came back in from the dining room, where they had set up their snack. "Hey, Mom," Sam said, "Tommy got this great idea. We've set up battery lanterns in our windows, so now we can signal in Morse code at night. Secret messages."

"And everyone," Tommy put in, "will be mystified when they see these lamps flashing. Because the thing is, with Morse code you can tell right away that it means *something*."

"From," Sam enthused, "the pattern. But you don't know *what*, so it seems, like, even more secret than it is."

Patterns; there were patterns all over the place, and they were driving me crazy, but . . .

"Sam," Tommy called back from the dining room, where he had gone with a jar of pickled herring, some cheese, a few leftover deviled eggs, a box of Ritz crackers, and a liter of Coca-Cola. "Let's ask the board about those girls at the park yesterday."

"Come on, what's the spirit world know about girls?" Sam retorted, grabbing a bottle of milk. "Dead girls, maybe, but we want live girls."

Maniacal boyish laughter greeted this impeccable teenaged logic, as Sam snagged the Oreos bag. "Tommy," he confided to me as he went out, "is just so not with it about girls."

His face grew serious. "You know," he added, "I think I probably will go to college after all. Bridget"—the girl from the salmon supper—"thinks it's probably a good idea."

Great. Maybe Bridget would be able to come up with some way to pay for it, too, now that I was going to be penniless in about ten minutes.

Then he was gone and I sat down with Ellie, who was looking miserable. "Rotten of us to snoop in those diaries," she said.

"Maybe. But if we hadn't, Paddy wouldn't have told us all he did."

"I guess. It's what he didn't say that's bothering me now."

"Yeah. Somebody bonks your buddy over the head, there in the darkness. Under the circumstances you would be thinking: Maybe that was a mistake; maybe there was a murderous intruder. But he hit the wrong guy—maybe the intended victim was me. And I just don't get it, about that unlocked door. It doesn't fit anything."

"Maybe Paddy's too heartbroken over Terence to worry about it," Ellie said. "Somebody coming back for a second try, I mean."

"Sure. Or—" I hated to say it, "maybe he knows they won't."

Because Paddy's story was neat, but everyone's was. That was the whole trouble. Some truth, lots of poetry; hard to sort out.

The phone rang, and I told the boys to let the machine take it: it was the zoning commissioner wanting to know if Victor would appear at the appeals board meeting, at which the variance for the zoning on the trauma-center property would be considered.

It rang again: it was the loan officer from the bank where Victor needed to borrow a zillion dollars, to buy all the medical equipment he needed just to get started. I'd forgotten those two when I'd been making my calls; there were so many of them.

"Maybe," I offered, "we should ask the dratted Ouija board who killed Reuben."

"No!" She looked shocked. "I don't want that thing getting a whiff of Reuben. It wouldn't," she added frowningly, "be prudent."

My thought exactly. "Only kidding," I assured her. So far, everything had been going just as Reuben would have dreamed: from bad to worse. I didn't want him getting an actual hand in matters even if the hand was only made of ectoplasm, or whatever moves a planchette around a Ouija board.

If it does. "Anyway, the situation is this," Ellie summed up. "Everyone's got a motive, and a story, and everybody—"

"Could be lying," I finished, "about some of it even if they aren't lying about all of it."

The whole truth about the end of the trauma center was just then hitting me: *finis*. Game over.

"Ellie, I've got to start getting past all this."

She ignored me. "So what do you say we just go and talk to everyone again. Just . . . talk to them once more, the ones that we can find, anyway. See if anything they say doesn't fit or isn't what they said the first time."

In the dining room, the boys guffawed at some spirit-world witticism. "And if we don't? Learn something new, I mean. What then? Because we've already *talked* to . . ."

The phone rang. Determinedly, I closed my ears to it. After a few rings, the machine picked up again.

"Ellie. I mean it, I've got to start thinking hard about my options here. I've got to think about . . ."

"Giving up." She watched me carefully as she said it.

"I know," I went on quickly, "you don't like the idea. But I didn't get Victor into this pickle. And it's starting to look as if I might not be able to get him out. This time."

As opposed, I meant, to all the other times: the palimony-demanding girlfriends, the scamsters who regarded Victor as the perfect flimflam target, the obsession he'd had over a famous television attorney, who had responded to his many unappreciated overtures by having him served with two restraining orders, one in New York State and one that barred him from coming within 250 miles of Atlanta, Georgia . . .

Well, suffice it to say that if I had all the hot water I had gotten Victor out of over the years, I wouldn't have had to worry about that weatherstripping; I could have run the radiators for centuries with the windows wide open and stay plenty warm.

Which reminded me: If I didn't get back to work on the house very soon, I'd be running the radiators outdoors, because they would be the only thing left standing when the rest fell down. The weatherstripping itself wasn't completed yet either, and the rain of the night before had left a stain shaped like Africa on the kitchen ceiling, courtesy of those rotten clapboards.

But Ellie was still watching me. "Okay," I gave in. "Once more. We'll make a few visits. And if that doesn't work . . ."

The words tasted like poison in my mouth, but I just didn't see much choice. The phone rang again: it was one of the main prospective outside investors in Victor's project; he'd read the papers, seen Victor in them, and wanted an update.

The machine thweeped, recording the guy's message.

"Then," I finished as the phone rang again and I ignored it, "it's endgame."

36

Marcus was vehement. "I have no idea why my father told you that."

He was packing to leave. They were all leaving, tourists and visitors, getting out of town in a steady stream up Washington Street like ants departing a rained-out picnic.

"Following Reuben Tate," he said scathingly. "Why, that's ridiculous. Our engagements were booked months in advance. We'd have had no idea where Reuben might be. It was impossible."

He flung shirts into a suitcase, in one of the Victorian bedrooms in Heddlepenny House. The oval mirror above the ornate carved dresser reflected his irritation.

"Not to mention pointless," he added. "What reason could we have had?"

"Your father suggested he wanted to convert Reuben," I said. "I got the sense that saving such a doomed, damned soul would've been a feather in his cap. Spiritually speaking."

Marcus made a sound of disgust; his hand was again covered with dermatological makeup. "My father had no idea how bad Tate really was. And didn't take spiritual trophies in the foolish sense that you're implying. Why he said we were pursuing Tate," he repeated, "I simply cannot imagine."

Heywood's funeral was scheduled for Friday, in a tiny town in Florida where, it turned out, he had been born. His body, now at the medical examiner's, would be shipped there; if it did not make it in time, they would have the services anyway and bury him later.

"How could your father not know about death threats, arson, and murder? About the terrors Reuben inflicted on the members of the children's group your father was in charge of? And it's well known that Reuben was supposed to have frightened your own mother to death, after she punished Reuben."

"That's nonsense, too," Marcus retorted swiftly. "My mother had a heart condition; she could have died of it at any time. But that part was forgotten because it wasn't suitable fodder for the gossip mill, that's all. Not sensational enough."

"But you said yourself you thought . . ."

"I admit I said it," he retorted, snapping his case shut. "But I was a victim of the hysteria the town has about Tate."

What about the coins under her body? I wanted to ask, but I wanted more for him to go on talking.

"And the notion that Dad ignored his young parishioners' problems is really a slur on his name. That really," he faced me, "is going too far."

I noticed, however, that Marcus did not precisely deny it.

"Are you sure it's not exactly what Reuben threatened to say about your father? The last time he saw him?"

Willow had said that Reuben did his homework, knew how he could hurt you. So why wouldn't he have updated his arsenal against Heywood, dropped the story about being gay in favor of one that might work better now that times had changed?

Especially if there was a grain of truth in it.

"As I told you," Marcus declared, "I don't know what he said to my father, but I can guess: that he'd keep coming back until one of us gave him money. Anything else is pure fantasy on your part. And for Dad's sake, I'd appreciate your not repeating it."

He swung his case off the white tufted chenille spread that covered the four-poster. "Now, if you'll excuse me, I have a long way to go, and since I'll have to do all the driving myself, I want to get a head start."

It was two in the afternoon, too late to get a head start on anything. He was getting out, was what he was doing. But I let him leave. I couldn't stop him.

Besides, he'd already given me what I wanted.

At the door, he turned to me. "Look, I hated Reuben. But I didn't kill him. And I certainly didn't kill my father, your foolish suspicions notwithstanding."

He sounded so sincere. Everyone did. "Marcus," I asked quietly, "what's on your hand?"

I'd promised Bob Arnold, but I couldn't help it, and since Marcus was leaving, he wouldn't be telling anyone I'd asked.

I hoped. "The spot," I added, "that you always keep covered up with the makeup?"

At this he whitened suddenly, his face tightening as if painfully wounded. Then he turned and stalked out.

"Part of what he told us is true," I said to Ellie when we got to the street. "They weren't following Reuben. Heywood never even said so, not in plain words."

In my mind, I went over the talk I'd had with the older man at the lake. "Heywood Sondergard just went along with whatever I said, let me draw conclusions."

The Winnebago's engine roared to life. "And now," I went on, watching the big vehicle lumber up Washington Street toward the causeway, "Marcus is getting out of here like his hat is on fire and his pants are catching. What's he in such a big hurry about?"

"But they still did," Ellie recalled, meaning Reuben and the Sondergards, "end up in the same towns at the same time. It could hardly have been coincidence. So . . ."

"Right," I said. "Tate was following them. Their concerts were booked well in advance, so it wouldn't be difficult. And the reason he would go on doing that would be . . ."

"Money. One of them—Heywood or Marcus—was paying him."

"Absolutely. My question is, for what?"

"Let's," Ellie said thoughtfully, "go see Mike Carpentier one more time."

37

The house on the hill was as storybook pretty and remote as ever, the bay shining gloriously below it and the sky blue above. Mike was turning the compost heap behind his vegetable garden, his hands encased in leather gardening gloves.

"He was on it," he confirmed. "The list Reuben had; Reverend Sondergard was one of the men I wrote letters to, when Reuben got out of jail."

"And did he? Pay, that is?" Once again I was struck by the assertive neatness of the garden area, and in fact the whole service portion—firewood, food production, and trash burning, composting, or recycling—of the acre of paradise:

Paper went in a barrel, to be reduced to a smaller volume of ashes. The ashes apparently went in the compost heap, as did all vegetable waste. Bins held bottles and cans; a wooden box with a slat top received all meat scraps.

Only this last part of the arrangement seemed to need some tuning; animals had been at the scrap bin, and a couple of gnawed chicken bones lay scattered near it.

He saw me looking at it. "Damned vermin. Sometimes they're smarter than people."

"You could get a cat." The tactless words were out of my mouth before I thought about them. He made a face of distaste.

"Don't care for them. Speaking of vermin, though, yeah, I think Reuben got some money from Heywood. Don't know for sure. I was on the giving end, the giving-trouble part. But not on the receiving end, where the money was. That part was all Reuben's."

He stuck his pitchfork into the compost as Molly's face appeared at an upstairs cottage window, then vanished again.

"Is she all right?" I asked. "After what happened at the supper? It must have been awful for her, seeing all of that. And her doll . . ."

"I made her another one," Mike said shortly. "She's fine."

"Willow says," Ellie told Mike, "that you were at the fire. The night Deckie died."

"Willow," Mike replied, "is a lying fool. All she wants is to cover her own dirt, by making a big show of somebody else's."

Willow was also halfway to Boston by now, according to the proprietors of the Motel East. The police had been there first thing, done their interview, gotten her address and phone number. We wouldn't be seeing her again, or her intriguing husband, either.

"You mean you weren't there?" I said, glancing at the scrap box again. Something had gnawed through the side of it; something small, sharp toothed, and hungry. "Willow lied about that?"

"I said I wasn't," he replied flatly. "And I don't see how you knew Heywood Sondergard was on that list, either. Reuben never told anyone, and he told me not to. And I didn't."

He glanced up sharply. "Molly! I said stay inside."

A glimmer of blond hair vanished around the corner of the house, and the door slammed.

"After all," he went on, plunging the pitchfork into the compost again, "there's no sense blackmailing somebody whose dark secret is common knowledge, is there? So I shut up."

He dug energetically, but stopped suddenly, his shoulders sagging. "It was all a long time ago," he said in less combative tones. "Reuben was in the past."

I looked out over the water. "Sometimes the past lives on. When people do more than hurt us. When the hurt does damage."

I was thinking of Victor: how sometimes you just can't get there from here. It changes you, finding that out. But if you're like Mike you go on, build around it somehow. Or like Sam.

"He wouldn't let me be," Mike said suddenly. "I was afraid to tell anybody. He was always around. Even in my own room . . ."

"It must have been scary," I said. If adults in Eastport were frightened of Reuben Tate, what must it have been like for a child? "I'm surprised it really didn't scar you for life. If," I added gently, "you're sure it didn't?"

Because building around it really isn't the best solution. If you have to, then you do it, allowing for the radiator that can't be removed, the supporting wall that must remain where it is or the rest of the house will fall down.

But it can leave you in a wicked fix. He straightened. "You know, it might have scarred me. For a while I thought it had, he scared me so damn badly. But then we had Molly, and somehow after that I was okay again. You know how a kid can straighten out your priorities whether you like it or not?"

"I do," I said, thinking of life after Sam. "All of a sudden you're a sensible grown-up person, because you have to be. You do things you never dreamed of being able to do."

He smiled at me. "When I first saw her, and I realized this helpless little creature was depending on me . . ."

"Right," I laughed, remembering. "You thought oh my God, the poor thing, it'll starve, or I'll drop it, or something."

"Yeah," he agreed with a grin. "How old is yours?" he asked, leaning on the pitchfork.

"Seventeen. I didn't," I added, "drop him. And he eats as if he's starving, nowadays, but I didn't starve him back then. You and your ex worked it out okay, I guess, about raising Molly. I met Anne, by the way."

Mike nodded. "Better this way for all of us. Anne's a good person. She cares a hell of a lot. She's just not cut out for what people think of as the normal wife and mother thing. That's all."

Which was what I had gathered from her, too. I gazed around the little homestead; Ellie had made herself scarce. There were hollyhocks in the dooryard, and the trellis up the side of the cottage was still full of roses, their perfume wafting lightly on a warm offshore breeze.

"You've done a great job here," I said, meaning it. "The gardens, your ways of taking care of everything, and the trellis. I do love a trellis."

His look sharpened for an instant, then relaxed. "Thank you. All the work is difficult sometimes, but it's worth it. That was one thing the Reverend Sondergard said that was worth something: 'Mikey,' he told me, 'if you want things to be a certain way, you have to make them that way.' "

Wade had said that, too, I remembered. That must have been where he'd gotten the phrase: from Heywood Sondergard. Out on the water a barge puttered steadily toward the salmon pens.

"It was bad for a while," Mike said. "And the divorce itself was hard." He gazed around the small homestead. "But we're all right now, and we're going to be even better."

Hearing him say it made me wish I had some wood to knock for him. "Was there ever really a list?" I asked quietly, gazing out at the bright water. "Of gay men Reuben was blackmailing? Or did he just make that up, about getting hold of one in jail?"

He shook his head regretfully. "I don't know. I've wondered about it myself. He had names, addresses. But—"

"But how would he have gotten them?" I finished for him.

Mike nodded. "I believed him back then, but now I guess it's more likely he just picked those guys out of a bunch of phone books. Yellow Pages listings of doctors, dentists—men he thought would have some money, or had a lot at stake. Maybe some would pay, Reuben would be thinking. And maybe some did."

"What if one had called the cops on him, instead?"

He shrugged. "If they had, he'd just make himself scarce for a while. And none did that."

A deep breath. Then: "You were right about the night at Deckie's. I was there, Reuben made me go along with him. Later I said it was Willow; that was more likely, and it took the heat off me. I was scared my folks would find out I hung out with Reuben, and then he might hurt them. But I don't really know what Sondergard paid him for, or if he paid. Reuben added something to the letter that I didn't see," he confessed. "A note of his own."

Molly's face reappeared at the upstairs window. "Is that her room?" I asked. "With the roses, and the view?"

He smiled. "Yes. At night she can see the stars. She loves her room. She feels so safe there. I know people think I'm too strict with her," he added, walking with me toward the house. "But I want her to have a real childhood, not be smearing on makeup and wearing sexy clothes at eleven or twelve years old. There's plenty of time for her to be a grown-up later."

The little girl emerged cautiously onto the back step of the cottage. "Dad? Can I go play with Barney?" At the sound of his name, the pony in the railed enclosure looked up hopefully.

"All right," Mike allowed. "But stay away from

those feed sacks. Something's got into them again; I'm going to have to clean them up. And don't get too dirty, please. We need to go to town, and we don't want to look like little ragamuffins."

Molly scrambled happily down the porch steps and ran to her pet, an apple for his snack clutched in her small fist. Ellie looked up from where she had perched on a rock overlooking the bay, came to say goodbye.

"Mike, did Reuben say anything else the last time you saw him? Anything at all that might help me?"

He shook his head. "Only that we were all going to remember him. That he was going to make a big splash."

Well, he'd gotten that much right, although not, I guessed, in the way that he intended or could have foreseen. As we were leaving I noticed again the pretty well-house, its stone cistern and peaked roof surrounding a red-painted hand pump.

"It must be a project in winter," I remarked. "Doesn't it freeze up?"

Mike laughed. "Oh, you can keep it running okay if you know how," he replied. "No one had running water in the old days, and they didn't die of thirst."

Yes, but what's past is past, I was about to tease him, then decided not to. Mike Carpentier had taken what he wanted from the past and made a paradise of it.

The rest he'd put firmly behind him, with an effort of will and an amount of hard labor that I could only imagine. It didn't seem right to make fun of it.

So I didn't. Making my way downhill behind Ellie to where the Jeep was parked, I thought that if grit and a willingness to work could be bottled and sold, Mike would be a millionaire by now, except of course that money wasn't what he wanted.

"Peace of mind," I said, breathing in the fresh, salt air at the foot of the path. "If more people went after it, they might find out that *things* aren't important.

Even," I added, glancing back up, "running water and electricity."

"Personally, I like my peace of mind to be equipped with modern plumbing," Ellie retorted, "and central heating. It's lots easier to give up things when you know you can have them back anytime you want them. Like," she added, "Mike Carpentier can."

I glanced in surprise at her as she swung the vehicle around and gunned it toward town. "Molly's mom," she reminded me, "*is* in the merchant marine, after all. They make good money."

Which put a faint new gloss on things: that Mike had income would have been common knowledge to people in Eastport. Maybe including Reuben, who might have wanted a piece of it. That could have been why he had bothered hotfooting it up that hill. But I believed Mike, that he hadn't felt threatened by Reuben anymore.

Still, I felt a little disappointed. "So he's not exactly subsistence-farming that acre," I said. Somehow it tarnished the fantasy. On the other hand, the fantasy had been unrealistic; making a living for yourself and a child off a Maine acre would take more than a hard worker.

More like a miracle worker. Meanwhile, I'd thought we were heading home, but at Route 190 and Washington Street Ellie didn't turn left as I'd expected. Instead she shot straight forward.

I peered at Ellie's gas gauge; she likes to let the Jeep run on fumes periodically, and after my empty-tank episode of a couple of days earlier, I was still gun shy.

"It'll get to Perry and back," she said, and glanced in the rearview. "Huh. Didn't Mike say they were going to Eastport?"

"That's what I thought. Why?"

"He's behind us. Molly with him."

"So he changed his mind. Going to Calais, maybe."

"I guess." She drove in silence awhile.

"So why *are* we going to Perry?" I asked finally. "Is there someone we should talk to there, too?"

Spruce trees, cedar posts, fields, glints of water went by. "No," Ellie said, pulling up to the corner at the end of 190.

She glanced left, scooted onto Route 1, avoiding a big old Chrysler making a signal-free left turn into the Farmer's Union Market and after that a green panel truck backing out of the Perry Post Office. Then she turned into the gravel parking lot of the New Friendly Restaurant.

Mike Carpentier's Ford Escort went on up Route 1 in the direction of Calais, which didn't surprise me; even someone as back-to-basics as Mike needed the Rite-Aid or the Wal-Mart once in a while, not to mention McDonald's or Taco Bell.

The New Friendly was the opposite of all those: a low, red wooden structure with big white-framed windows and no hint of mass-produced anything, backed up against a salt marsh. Cattails waved their chocolate heads over the tide-filled inlets, small waves making zigzags of their reflections on the water.

Inside, the eatery was crowded with groups of men in denims and gimme caps, families ranging from babies to grandmothers. The special, the board behind the counter said, was clam pie.

Ellie slid in across from me at the only vacant booth and opened her menu. "I have to admit it looks a little bleak," she said. "We've talked to everyone who might have anything useful to say to us. We've snooped, and pried, and read diaries that didn't belong to us. You've gone up in an airplane, for heaven's sake."

The waitress came, took our orders, went away again. Ellie resumed: "And now everybody's leaving town except Mike. And his life, never mind what Reuben did twenty years ago, is just ducky."

We sat in discouraged silence until the waitress returned; Ellie bit into her haddock sandwich. My coleslaw was crisp and peppery.

"It's over, Ellie. Somebody's gotten away with it, at least for now."

She nodded without quite agreeing. "And what about your own problems? The money you're losing, I mean."

Misery over the topic made me sigh. "Well, I'm going to take a major hit over the trauma-center project," I admitted. "Seed money, pretty much by definition, is money you don't get back if things go wrong."

"And since you can't get Victor out, it's going to."

"Right. We gave it a last shot, but we've done all we can."

My hands made helpless sawing motions over the table. "I've got to face it, all the practical stuff that needs doing. Instead of running around chasing Reuben Tate's old, evil moonbeams."

"What *are* you going to do about the money?"

I didn't want to tell her. But I would have to, sooner or later. "Well. It might take a little while, but I think I can get things back on track."

Precisely how I would have to do that, though—that was the hard part. "The big project is to get Sam's living and tuition money together, now that he's decided to go to school. If not for that, I guess I could build a portfolio from here, from Eastport, just on my own investing. But . . ."

But that wasn't all of it. What I didn't say was that aside from money for expenses I needed a big cash cushion just to feel decent. Otherwise, I was a poor girl again.

"I can get a cash flow going if I move back to New York, set up in practice again. Investment counseling, financial plans, tax structuring . . . all the stuff I used to do when I lived there."

No more early-morning walks with Monday on

the breakwater, in the salt-fresh dawn. No coffee frappes at Bay Books, with the new best-sellers and the latest gossip. No more knowing and being known by everyone in town; in Manhattan, life had been fast-paced and exciting, and I'd been one of a million busy strangers.

No Wade. Not for a while, anyway. "I can come back here," I managed weakly, "often."

She was looking at me as if I'd just arrived from the planet Mars. "Can I ask you a question?" she inquired seriously.

Without waiting, she went on. "What do you think I've been doing with all the investing tips you've been handing me for two years, wallpapering the bathroom?"

Actually, that was what I had thought, or something like it. She'd never said any more about them. "All those ideas you kept on giving me? You think I *wasted* them?"

She eyed me incredulously. "Is that what you think I think of your ideas, Jacobia? All the knowledge and experience that you worked so hard to get, even though you don't brag on it now?"

She sounded quite affronted, so it took a moment before the import of her words hit me. "Beg pardon? You mean you've been . . ."

Crisply, she reeled off the names of a dozen publicly traded companies, all of which had appreciated smartly over the previous two years, just as I had predicted they would. Then, knocking my socks off, she told me exactly how much each had appreciated, as well as where it had closed at the end of trading on the preceding Friday.

Finally, she confided how much money she'd made, and it was a good thing I didn't happen to be wearing full dentures when she told me, or I'd have been searching the floor for them.

"I put in everything my folks left me when they

passed on," she continued briskly. "And anything else I could salt away when the opportunity arose. So," she concluded, "when Sam needs school money or whatever, you send him to me."

I opened my mouth to protest.

"Shut up," she explained. "You're not leaving. It's a stupid idea. I swear, Jake, you're smart all right, but sometimes your big-city brains don't have enough powder to blow your own bottom out of a bathtub, common-sense-wise."

"Oh," I heard myself say faintly. "But you . . ."

Of course she had. In this whole wide world there is nothing more practical—or closemouthed about it, especially when it comes to money—than a downeast Mainer.

"I will charge you," she said, "enough interest to keep you from feeling too guilty. Assuming you end up really needing it."

The girl on the Greyhound hadn't had a hope of any help. She'd forgotten, even, how to ask for it. Ellie waited to see if I understood how to accept it.

Then it suddenly occurred to me that if you need a big cushion, you must be expecting a hard landing. And I wasn't; not anymore. My friends would help me.

Whatever happened. A weight like a ballast stone lifted off my shoulders. "I'll come to you if I need to," I said gratefully.

"Well, of course you will," Ellie replied. "You're not *that* foolish. As for Victor . . ."

She was about to tell me again that it was too early to quit. But it wasn't. We had pieces of the pattern, but they just kept on whirling and they might go on doing it forever.

So I braced for Ellie's argument and prepared to resist it, an old Wall Street adage echoing in my head: Don't chase your losses.

It was excellent advice. But I did not get the chance to insist that I was going to take it.

She glanced past me, her face changing. "Don't look now, but it appears to me that someone didn't quite manage to make it out through the departure gate."

I let my glance stray casually to the mirror behind the lunch counter, just as the man in the doorway looked into it, meeting my gaze:

Marcus Sondergard.

38

"The Winnebago was giving him trouble," I said, repeating Marcus's grudging explanation for his presence, as we pulled out of the restaurant parking lot. "So what?"

"He must have been nearly to Ellsworth when he noticed it," Ellie retorted. "He's been gone a couple of hours."

She took the left onto Route 190, back toward Eastport. "So why didn't he have it fixed there? He's got engine trouble, that means it's not running well. Why drive it all the way back here?"

"Ellie," I said, seeing where all this was going. "I said I was finished."

She stared stubbornly ahead as I went on: "I've got a roll of weatherstripping the size of a wagon wheel in my house. And if I don't get the carpenters over for the back wall soon, the phrase *winter kitchen* is going to be a literal description. And . . ."

And besides getting my house ready for cold weather—a task that even without carpentry was as lengthy and detailed as the one the NASA people undertook, getting the space shuttle set for lift off—there was now Victor's place to get ready for the winter, too.

Two mints in one, if by that you meant what it was going to cost me: window caulking and insulation rolls do not come cheap, and neither does a tankful of heating oil every other half-hour.

"Furthermore, I still have a money situation to confront," I said. "Your help is a safety net for me but it is not a windfall. And all Sam's school arrangements, paperwork and so on; Victor would have done all of that, but now of course he can't."

In short, compared to all I had to accomplish in the coming weeks, the Augean stables needed only a little light vacuuming and dusting, and I hadn't even thought about the difficulties posed by Victor himself, locked up in the Washington County Jail.

I doubted his noble attitude was going to last long. For Sam's sake, there would have to be a visiting schedule. Care and upkeep: fresh fruit, toiletry items, psychiatry for me so I could tolerate it. That sort of thing.

"So I mean it," I said, then chanced to look out the Jeep window. While I'd been stewing, Ellie had been driving: over the causeway, into town, and . . .

"Ellie, would you mind telling me where we are?"

Tumbledown vacant wooden bungalows, tiny yards overgrown and trash-blown, the fences not much more than heaps of kindling. I'd walked all over Eastport but I'd never been on this dismal, dead-end alley before; somehow I'd missed knowing it even existed.

Which was not, from the looks of it, any great loss: broken windows, toppling chimneys, falling gutters. The house at the end of the short row of broken-roofed structures was so covered with old vines that it was hard to tell there was even a building under there at all.

Ellie pulled over to what had once been a neat, straight sidewalk but was now a broken jumble of concrete scrap. "This is the street Paddy Farrell, Willow Prettymore, and Mike Carpentier all lived on," she said, "back when we were kids."

Old wooden screen doors with hand-turned ornamental corner brackets sagged brokenly onto the remnants of wide front porches. Tall, graceful windows were capped by lintels like bushy eyebrows, now rotted and sagging; cracked front walks where the girls had played hopscotch and boys bounced balls now sprouted with weeds.

"The end one that's falling in under all that rose vine was Mike's house, the middle one was Willow's, and Paddy lived in this one," Ellie said, pointing at the nearest wreckage. "Beyond the field," she waved generally, "was Deckie Cobb's shack."

The whole street looked abandoned. Junk cars lurked under shredded remnants of tarps. Here and there a hopeless little hand-scrawled For Sale By Owner sign peeked from behind a broken windowpane; otherwise, these places had been forgotten.

"Oh," I said faintly. It was really heartbreaking; if you squinted, you could see how lovely it all once had been. And it was as good a demonstration of how lost in history the motive for Reuben's murder might be as anything I could think of, bolstering my decision to quit searching for something I would never find.

Ellie seemed to be getting the idea, finally, too; she gazed a moment longer, her forehead furrowing briefly, at the sprawl of rose cane burying Mike Carpentier's old homestead.

"I just wanted to see it once more," she said. "I thought maybe . . . But I guess not."

We headed back to inhabited territory, riding in silence until we reached Water Street, where I thought I saw a familiar blond glint. "Isn't that . . . ?"

Couldn't be. But Ellie saw it too and pulled over in front of Peavy Library: old red brick, dark and glowering, against an interior of yellow light crosshatched by the leaded panes of the arched windows.

Then I saw clearly the pale gold hair, sleek and shining as she got out of a rental car in the parking lot of the Motel East: Willow Prettymore. She took a key from her bag and entered one of the motel rooms, closing the door behind her.

Ellie made a U-turn and headed down Water Street in the other direction. "Ride with me a little longer?"

I nodded resignedly, feeling the quicksand of another wild-goose chase gathering around my feet: Willow had come back for a pair of earrings she'd forgotten and was searching the room for them. Or some similarly silly and intensely irritating reason. But the room Willow entered wasn't the one they had been in, I realized. Then, parked in front of La Sardina, I saw Paddy Farrell's Peugeot. "But he's in Portland. Unless . . ."

A bad thought hit me. "You don't suppose Terence died, and Paddy heard about it so he didn't go back?"

"No. Wouldn't you go? If nothing else, there would be some arrangements to make. Besides . . ."

At her gesture, I peered out the Jeep's rear window. Paddy was just coming out of La Sardina, pausing to speak with someone on the doorstep just out of sight.

Paddy looked reasonably normal. Grave-faced but not a basket case, as he would be if Terence had passed away.

"Someone called them," Ellie said quietly, "I'll bet. It's just too much of a coincidence otherwise. Willow was in Boston, or nearly. Something must have seemed awfully urgent to get her to face down that thug of a husband, rent a car or whatever, and drive back. Marcus Sondergard has a telephone in that Winnebago?"

"Yes. And the whole town knew Paddy was in Portland, at the medical center. They'd all be reachable if you tried hard enough. Still . . ."

It's an awful leap to assume that, I was about to say, only Ellie wasn't having any.

"But which one of them was the caller and which other ones were the recipients?" she pondered aloud.

Then she swung left onto Clark Street, uphill between small wooden bungalows with shining yellow windows and lace curtains, and left again into Hillside Cemetery. From here it was only a few blocks to Key Street, home sweet home.

A cup of coffee, I thought longingly, and silence; my own thoughts. Later, Ellie and I would make dinner together and the boys would help eat it, then take over doing up the dishes. But for now I needed—

Without warning, Ellie pulled to the side of the road and stopped.

"Ellie," I began, "I understand you're not ready to quit, and I sympathize. Really I do. But I hardly think a graveyard is any place to pull over and have a conversation about it. Which," I went on, "I am prepared to have at some point in the future, seeing as we now have this new, curious information about . . ."

Well, I didn't know what it was about, when you came right down to it. But they were all back in town for something, that much was obvious.

I gazed out the Jeep window. The storm had torn down some of the old wild grapevines that grew on the cemetery gate where Reuben's body had been hanging. They reminded me of the rope he'd hung from.

". . . about whatever it is," I finished uneasily. "So start the Jeep, please. We can think much better in my kitchen than we can in . . ." *A cold, dark graveyard,* I was about to say.

But Ellie didn't let me.

"I can't," she confessed. "We're out of gas."

39

"There's a gas can in my cellar," I said, summoning patience I'd never known I had. "We'll just walk home, and . . ."

Ellie wasn't listening. She rolled down her window, looking at the cemetery gate. The night air was damp, fragrant with cedar and the tannic smell of the wet leaves lying thickly everywhere after the rain.

"Ellie," I began. She turned and gazed at me, then back at the grape foliage now dangling haphazardly.

"All those vines," she said simply, and then it hit me:

Such a small thing, unremarkable. So innocent.

Until you knew. "The trellis," I said numbly.

Ellie nodded. "Willow said Reuben used to climb a trellis to Mike Carpentier's room. Like the trellis on Mike's cottage now."

"Mike's daughter, Molly," I said slowly, "is the age Mike was back then."

"And he's fighting vermin at the cottage. He'd have rat poison, and traps."

"The trouble he was in," I said thoughtfully. Everyone in Eastport would know what it was; they always did. But not me, because I was from away.

"Drugs," Ellie replied. "Marijuana, some heavier stuff. You can bet he's not doing it with Molly around, but it might be he's still got connections."

Right; Mike had mentioned that he didn't get stoned anymore. And I'd already come to the conclusion that the tranquilizer in Reuben's system didn't have to be what Victor had prescribed. Now I tried imagining it.

"So what if Mike's going along as peacefully as always, but then the ex-wife comes home, finds out Reuben's been at the cottage. That he was pestering Molly, that he invaded her room. Hears from Mike, maybe, about the scalpels at Victor's place."

"And she doesn't react the way Mike did," Ellie picked up the theory. "For her it's not enough just to send Reuben packing because, for one thing, she's got to go back out to sea on the merchant vessel, won't be here to help protect Molly."

"Maybe she wants to be certain Reuben won't try

anything like that again," I agreed. Battle to the death, Anne had said. Take care of things; pick up the pieces later. Maybe I should have taken her words a bit more literally. "And Mike could have known that Reuben was blackmailing Victor from Reuben himself, when he was up there."

"She hatches a plan that includes duping Reuben," Ellie said. "Later throws a few curveballs in your direction, thinks maybe she can get you scared."

"Stopped by the side of the road that day to check me out," I agreed, "see if I had any inkling about her, which of course I didn't. And now the boat's back out to sea, which is why we haven't thought of her; she's not around. And why there haven't been any more mean tricks. But . . ." Before Heywood died and Terence was attacked.

I stopped: big problem. "Only she's *not* around, is she?" I finished. "Anne went back out to sea before . . ." Before Heywood died and Terence was attacked.

A hand thrust in through the open window, seizing Ellie's hair. A knife gleamed.

"That's right. But you two have figured out way too much. Why couldn't you let it go? If you had, I wouldn't have to do this."

It was Mike Carpentier, eyes alight with purposeful malice. So much for my thinking that I could tell when people were lying to me. Now I saw Ellie's throat move as she swallowed hard, and an ooze of blood showed at the knife edge.

"The three of us are going to drive downtown," Mike said.

"We can't," I said quickly. "We're out of gas."

Mike sighed in a way that suggested tolerance strained to the breaking point.

"Out," he ordered me, and although I have never been much good at taking orders, I followed that one. At his instruction, I took the gas can from the trunk of his Escort where it sat with some sandbags, a coil of rope, flares, a blanket, the standard set of tire-changing equipment, and a big water jug; as usual, he was prepared for anything.

I emptied the gas can into the Jeep. "I should think," Mike said as I replaced the filler cap, "you'd have learned to be ready for emergency situations like this one. Running," he finished scornfully, "out of gas *twice*. Hand me that rope."

"Yeah, silly me," I said, thinking about the revolver locked safely in the box down in my cellar as I obeyed.

Mike waited, still ready to skewer Ellie, as I got back into the Jeep. Then he ordered Ellie out, slipknotted the rope around her neck, and climbed into the Jeep's rear cargo area very quickly before yanking her back into the driver's seat.

"Now," he said, removing the rope. "Drive, and no tricks."

"Wouldn't dream of it," Ellie whispered. The knife was aimed at the back of her neck.

"You've been following us?" I managed as we pulled away from the curb.

"Yes. I knew when you came to the cottage earlier today that you must've put at least part of it together, or why would you come back? And then when you drove by my old house and sat there looking at it . . . then I was sure."

We hadn't been, of course, at the time. But he hadn't known that. He gave us a lot more credit than we deserved.

Unfortunately.

His conversational tone was more chilling than a shriek. "I never meant to hurt you, Jacobia. I'm sorry it's turned out this way."

Terrific. So maybe he would tranquilize me, too, before he cut my throat.

"I only wanted to distract you, get you busy with

something else," he went on. "Send you off in another direction."

"Right," I snapped back as a burst of anger washed over me. "Somewhere like the hospital. That rat trap could've broken my wrist, you know. Instead it got my dog. Someone's pet cat could have walked right into—"

I stopped, remembering the poor creature Molly had been burying. "It's what he used," I understood aloud. "Reuben brought her that pet to win her over. The way he brought all those animals to you—to try softening you up, I suppose—he brought the cat to Molly."

All at once I figured out how he had kept those long-ago puppies and birds from his parents' notice. Ellie's voice told me in memory: *Somebody wrung its neck.*

"He wanted to repeat history," Mike agreed grimly. "With my daughter." He frowned suddenly. "Turn at the next corner."

But just then the familiar rumble of Tommy Daigle's jalopy came up behind us. Its horn erupted in the loud *ooh-ooh-gah* that Tommy loved so dearly, and that he sounded at the slightest excuse.

"It's the boys," I said. "Just let them go by, Mike. They aren't involved. Put the knife down so they don't see it. Ellie won't do anything, will you, Ellie?"

The jalopy's headlights glared in Ellie's rearview, flashed high and low. The horn *ooh-ooh-gah*ed raucously again.

"Right. Especially since I'm aiming it at the back of the driver's seat," Mike said, "and it's long enough to go all the way through."

As we neared the corner, Ellie touched the brakes, touched them again to slow for the turn. The jalopy kept coming behind us and she tapped the brakes once more.

"I want them to stay back," she explained, but

instead they followed us onto Sullivan Street. Ellie kept touching the brakes all the way down the steep hill, finally signaling for a right turn at the bottom. The boys went the other direction.

The knife returned to Ellie's throat. "When you get to the lot by Paddy Farrell's studio building, pull in and park."

Wade's pickup sat by the Quonset warehouse out on the dock. Beside it was George Valentine's red panel truck. Hope rose in my heart as I spotted the vehicles. But the men were nowhere in sight.

"Reuben victimized you," I said. "Did he hurt you? Touch you?"

Mike laughed bitterly. "He didn't have to. He was toxic at a distance, like poison gas. He just threatened to touch me."

Ellie pulled in beside Paddy Farrell's building. "He liked little boys?"

Mike blew out an impatient breath. "Being a boy had nothing to do with it. It was power he was into; that's a whole different thing. As to gender, Reuben was an equal-opportunity victimizer."

He squinted up and down the street, saw no one. "He didn't touch me. But he told me what he would do to me *someday*," he went on. "And made me listen. Said if I told anyone he was coming into my room at night, he'd kill my parents."

He turned to me. "Night after night. Can you imagine what that's like for a child, not to want *someday* ever to come?"

He took a shaky breath. "He had no reason to be the way he was. He was just . . . broken. Someone should have drowned him at birth," he said. "But nobody did so I cut his throat," his voice grew chillingly ecstatic, "and let his blood run."

There were lights on in the cannery building. "Reuben's blood," he finished wonderingly. "All of that blood."

His tone grew efficient. "Let me out first."

He kept the knife at Ellie's throat, beckoning her from behind the wheel. On the sidewalk he kept the blade hidden by his side, aimed now at Ellie's body.

"Walk with me," he said. "We're going in. You two wanted so badly to understand this. Now you're going to help me finish it."

"Finish . . . sending your message," I said, because it was all coming clear now; too late.

"You didn't tell your parents or the police what Reuben was doing," I went on. "But you told someone: Reverend Sondergard. When it got to be too much, you must have gone to him and asked him to help you."

It was Heywood's only possible link to the whole thing. But it still didn't explain the Weasel. "Why . . . ?"

"Shut up." We were approaching the narrow door at the end of the row of brick buildings, their front windows boarded against mischief so the place looked more like an abandoned tenement than a high-tech design studio.

Which was the way Paddy wanted it. He liked that stark urban contrast between gritty exterior and airy inside. From the street you couldn't tell anything about what was going on in there.

"I begged him," Mike said. "Reverend Sondergard. He told me that I should pray about it. He would pray too, he said. But I guess," he finished as he urged us into Paddy's building, "the old coward just didn't pray hard enough."

Inside, he locked the door behind us and lowered the bar that Paddy used for extra security. And then the thing I'd begun fearing back when he appeared in the cemetery came true:

All of them. The folding chairs that usually resided along Paddy's long conference table were set out separately in the big workroom with the overheard lights glaring down:

Willow Prettymore. Marcus Sondergard. Wade Sorenson, looking furious but unable to do anything about it. And George Valentine, likewise incapacitated. Each had been tied, wrists behind, ankles bound to the legs of the chairs. Neat and complete.

On the table lay a canvas satchel. I didn't like thinking about what might be in it; Mike's penchant for careful planning and preparation made the possibilities unpleasant.

"How the hell did you do that?" I demanded, struck by the sheer unmanageability of it. And yet there they were.

Mike smiled, proud of his accomplishment. "Paddy was here when I arrived. He was easy. Willow got here next, and I hit her with a brick. Tied her."

A runnel of blood on Willow's terrified face confirmed this. Mike gazed around. "Then Marcus arrived."

The enmity in George Valentine's glance at Marcus, combined with the darkening bruise developing on George's temple, told me what must have come next. Marcus had ambushed George, tied him up at Mike's instruction. Otherwise, Mike had threatened, he would use the knife on Willow.

"Wade? Are you all right?" There was an enormous purple lump over his right eye.

He looked disgusted. "He called us separately, asked us to meet him here. Told each one of us he had something to say about the murders, couldn't tell anyone else. Spaced the arrivals five minutes or so apart, give him time to do the necessary. And then Marcus ambushed us one at a time. He didn't," Wade added, "have any choice."

But that still left . . . I peered around, puzzled.

"Told me he knew who killed Reuben," Wade went on, "but he was afraid, needed my help. Fooled me but good," he finished, angry with himself.

A few feet away from him, Paddy sat glowering,

tied like Marcus. "You should," Paddy said, "have been praying for *brains*, you tone-deaf little Jesus freak."

Paddy had never been a great fan of organized religion, but I thought this was no time for them to be sorting out their theological differences. Especially since, if someone didn't come up with a way out of this pretty efficiently, it looked as if we were going to be getting answers to an entire spectrum of deep, important questions about the afterlife, real soon now.

"Sit." Mike waved at the two remaining chairs.

We didn't have a choice, any more than Marcus had had. Ellie looked pale but composed, seating herself. I sat too, readying myself to rocket back up again the very instant Mike took that knife away from Ellie's neck, which he would have to do in order to begin tying one of us.

But then I realized: If Marcus had tied the others to keep Mike from cutting Willow's throat, who'd tied Marcus? Not Mike; he was busy doing his knife-handling act.

Then a small voice came from the shadows under the circular staircase. "Dad?" Molly Carpentier quavered. "Dad, can we go home now?"

"Get over there and do what I told you," Mike snapped, his eyes glittering dangerously.

Reluctantly the child came out. In her hands she held a ball of thick brown twine, the kind all those hanging planters at the cottage were made of. And if it could hold up a heavy earth-filled planter without breaking, it could probably hold us.

Which it did. Molly wrapped the stuff repeatedly around Ellie's wrists and ankles, then around mine. "I'll try not to cut off your circulation," she said, tying the final knot. I didn't have the heart to tell her that pretty soon I wouldn't have any.

"Mike," I said. "I know you want Molly to get the message you never got. That she's not alone, that you will help her if someone gives her trouble. But is *this* what you want her to know? That the answer is violence?"

Suddenly Willow Prettymore broke her silence. "That's a lot of bull. There's no message. Things didn't go little Mikey's way and now he wants revenge, that's all. . . ."

Mike was at her side in an instant; Willow broke off and uttered a thin, breathy little scream as the knife moved fast. A line of bright red ran suddenly down Willow's pale throat, into the collar of her white blouse.

"Shut up," Mike whispered. "Or next time I'll really cut you." Willow stared, whimpering.

"Your time to talk," Mike grated out at her, "was when you *saw* him going in my window at night. But you never told anyone. You were older, I was just a little kid, I needed help."

Mike looked around contemptuously. "But if Reuben was after me, then he wasn't after any of you. Isn't that right? You could forget him for a while. So you did. All of you . . . you just did."

"Why didn't you stand up to him?" Ellie asked sadly.

He spun on her. "Sure. And be another Boxy Thorogood, go down hard. It was different for you guys. You were Reuben's own age. Me and Boxy were eleven years old."

"Dad," Molly began faintly.

"*Quiet.*" The little girl shrank back, frightened.

"But why hurt Terence?" Paddy asked sadly. "He didn't have anything to do with any of this. He wasn't even here."

"He really did fall, that first time," I said to Paddy. "And hurt his hand. And turned those gas burners on, himself."

"Yes." He eyed me helplessly. "But the thread he said he'd tripped on . . . it wasn't there. That was his mind," Paddy mourned heavily, "telling him something bad was about to happen, he was so *intuitive*, Terence was, and then Mike really *attacked* him. . . ."

"Shut up." Mike whirled on him, spitting a reply. "I mistook him for you in the dark, you artsy little *fake*. Always talking about facing Reuben down, always ready to get into a big argument. But he killed your own father and you still didn't do anything because you were afraid. You know it's true, don't you?"

Paddy's face hardened. "What should I have done, Mike? Drop to his level? Sneak around killing people?" *Like you*, his look added clearly, but Mike didn't see it.

"And when he came back," Mike went on, "threatened to burn down your *building*, what did you do?"

He grimaced mockingly. "You *whined* about it. 'Oh, big, bad Reuben's back, somebody *save* me.' I could have told you how well *that* works," he finished scornfully.

Outside it was full dark, and beyond Paddy's studio windows the water was calm, each little fishing vessel in the boat basin seeming to perch upon a mirror image of itself. From Campobello, the lights of shops and houses reflected in straight, bright lines to the water, like bar codes drawn in Day-Glo markers.

"You didn't jimmy those locks to get into the studio," I said, understanding it now. "Terence hadn't even locked them—he wasn't thinking right, so he'd left them open."

I looked at Mike. "You thought you were equipped to break in. You weren't, but then it turned out you didn't need to. You still broke the door frame, though, because . . ."

Cold comprehension washed over me. "Because if things had gone entirely your way, Paddy would be dead by now. And Terence might or might not be here to let you in. Once you saw how big those locks were, you decided to give yourself a head start on getting through that door next time."

Breaking the frame, weakening the structure . . . people think about the locks they install. Too often they don't worry so much about what that expensive hardware is set into: solid wood, or a splintered door frame slammed back together with a couple of good-looking but easily-pulled nails?

On the other hand, it had turned out not to matter, anyway, because once again, dumb luck had favored the prepared mind. Too bad that in Mike's case, the prepared mind had lost a few marbles in the Thou Shalt Not Kill department.

"You've been planning this a long time, haven't you, Mike? Planning on finishing things, tying up loose ends, and doing it here, like this. But I still don't see how you got Victor's tie, or why you had to kill Weasel."

His face showed exasperation; apparently I didn't appreciate his cleverness fully enough to satisfy him. "I watched, and I waited, and I took advantage of every little thing that happened, that's how. I was outside La Sardina, saw Reuben and your ex and the rest of you through the window."

The thoroughness of it was terrifying. "Once you'd decided that night was *the* night, you hurried to his house, waited until Sam left, took the scalpel, and went back downtown," I said. "But what if things went wrong, and it turned out you couldn't use the scalpel after all?"

His face flattened stubbornly. "Then I'd find another way. But mostly, they didn't go wrong. Later the tie was on the street where your ex dropped it. Reuben picked it up, had it with him."

"And then," the last piece dropped into place, "Weasel saw you with Reuben. Weasel was on the seawall that night, wasn't he?"

Memo to self: When you're looking for connections, remember that the absence of a connection might also be meaningful. . . .

"Weasel saw you," I went on, "but you didn't notice it until it was too late. You couldn't afford anyone remembering you were with Reuben on the night Reuben died. So you had to go back and kill Weasel Bodine, and what better way to confuse things than to use the method everyone in town thought Reuben had used, long ago?"

He nodded smugly. "Now you're getting it."

It had been yet another improvisation; he was good at them and had used them skillfully. Because it wasn't enough to have a careful plan; to make a thing like this work, you had to use every happenstance, too, seize it and turn it to your advantage.

Which he had. "You've got guts, I'll give you that much," I said, still hoping to put a new spin on things. "The poison . . ."

"Rat killer," he confirmed. "I tried not to use too much. It wasn't supposed to work so fast."

At this, Ellie got into the act, trying to keep him talking. "That doesn't sound like you, Mike, always ready for anything. I mean, you didn't check on the dose?"

He looked impatient. "You can't just call someone and ask that kind of question. Besides, if it didn't work the first time, I'd get to kill him twice, wouldn't I?"

Keep him talking . . . I thought hard. "Reuben was drunk, and he was probably drugged, too. You invited him to take a ride. In the cemetery you lured him from the car. . . ."

He took over the story eagerly, this being, after all, the last time he would ever be able to tell it. "I was ready to drug him myself. Reached out to one of my old buddies, got something to use on him."

Hideously, he produced a syringe. "I didn't need it, though."

Because Reuben had probably already taken what

Victor had prescribed, on top of alcohol. "And once you had the rope around his ankles, he was helpless. You didn't have to lift him. You tossed the end of the rope over the gate and hauled him, using the pulley action for," Sam's words came back to me, "mechanical advantage."

Wade was quietly working to pull his hands free; I wanted to keep the conversation going, so he could. "The only thing that really went wrong was Weasel biting you while you killed him. So you covered it by burning yourself on your woodstove. Then . . ."

"And then," Mike said dreamily, "I put him in a fix that made the one he'd put me in look like a fairy tale. Now I'm going to wipe out all memory of what he did to me, and show Molly that I can stop it from ever happening to her," he finished.

"How," Marcus ventured, his baritone voice uncertain, "are you going to do that?"

"You know," I began brightly, because this was exactly the part I didn't want Mike getting to anytime in the immediate future, "now that you've taught us all a good lesson, this would be a fine opportunity to follow up on it, by—"

Letting us all go, I was about to say. But he didn't seem to be listening.

"This building," he uttered in a dead voice, "should have burned down years ago."

I could see Marcus's hand now: the mark on it. Once he'd left town, he must have washed off the makeup. He saw me looking at it, flushed angrily.

"That was it, wasn't it?" I asked him. "What you tried so hard to protect your dad from: his own actions."

Tommy Daigle's cheerful face rose in front of me, with the scar on it. "That's the mark of his silver rose-of-Sharon belt buckle," I said, "on the back of your hand. And Reuben knew it."

He added a note, Mike had said about the blackmail letter. *Reuben always knew how to hurt you.*

And if word had got out that one of the Bible Belters used to belt the other one—suddenly I wondered how they'd chosen that name; deliberately or unconsciously?—well, then neither of them would have had a career in musical soul-saving ever again.

Or so they had feared. So they had paid. "Your mother was formidable in public. But in private, your father . . ."

"But he'd *changed,*" Marcus insisted, struggling against his bonds. "He didn't deserve to—"

"Yes, he did," Mike said flatly. "What he got, and more."

"Wise up," George said scathingly. "Everyone's going to know we were here. And they'll figure out that you did it."

"Oh, really?" Mike turned in mock interest to him. "And how are they going to know that? Especially since it's Ellie's car parked outside, not mine. Mine's blocks away, and I was careful to speak to each of you personally. And I'll be far away," he finished smugly, "before the fire even starts."

That reminded me: "You called Victor to tell him Reuben was dead, called Bob Arnold, even called the garbage truck to take Victor's trash. How? You don't have . . ."

But of course he did. Always prepared: he would have a car phone, of course. For emergencies. Still, how had he gotten . . .

"The phone numbers to reach Willow and Marcus were in the Old Timers' book," Ellie said bleakly. "From the Salmon Festival."

"That's right," Mike said. "As for Victor, I kept watching him all that night, after Reuben was finished off. That was the tricky part, what Victor did afterwards. Working with it all and making sure it fit what I wanted to have happen. And now . . ."

Proudly, he opened his satchel: wax cubes like the kind on all those canning jars in the cottage's pantry. Sparklers, from the same bunch of leftovers, I supposed, as the children had been playing with at the Salmon Festival.

And finally—seeing this, I began at last to feel really afraid, because it would work; what Mike had in mind was going to work beautifully—a large can of liquid charcoal starter. Opening it, he began squirting it around with the happy air of a person releasing air freshener into a musty room.

"You know," said George, "I always knew you were nutty as a fruitcake. But this really caps it. You know what, now? I'm glad I never lifted a finger for you."

Ellie shot an admonishing look at him, but he wouldn't stop. "He did stuff to all of us, Mike. He was a bad guy. But you—I think you're worse. 'Cause you can stop yourself. And Reuben—he couldn't. Reuben just couldn't."

In answer, Mike squirted charcoal lighter under George's chair. "Talk all you want. Yakity-yakity. But better make it snappy. You'd better say *all*," he emphasized, "that you have got to say. Because pretty soon—"

He took one of the sparklers, stuck the wire end into one of the blocks of wax. "Pretty soon, your little vocal cords are going to be busy, screaming your lungs out."

He lit the sparkler. "I set the sparkler here," he said in a singsong, explain-it-to-children voice, placing the small wax block in a puddle of the flammable liquid. "Eventually, it will burn down low enough to tip over, or a spark will fall."

"Jesus, Mike, what's wrong with you?" Willow hissed at him, kicking at the sparkler to try to knock it out of the liquid.

Her foot didn't quite reach it, but the sparkler *tee-*

tered, its bright chemical-flare head tipping dangerously low toward the spreading pool.

I held my breath. The sparkler teetered up again but now the wax cube was melting, the burnt sparkler wire sagging dangerously downward. . . . Mike caught it, extinguished it. "Uh-uh. Not yet." Then he finished placing sparklers into the cubes, set them around.

"Outside, Molly," he ordered. "Start walking. I'll catch up to you where we left our car. Get in and wait for me there."

"But, Dad . . ." The child gazed around unhappily, seeming only now to understand fully what was about to happen.

"*Out*," Mike snarled, turning on Molly, whose eyes widened in fear. But she stood her ground bravely. "Dad, I don't want you to hurt them. Now let them *go*, this is *bad*."

Mike's voice went frighteningly flat. "You do what I say or I'll make you wish you had. Understand?"

Molly didn't; not quite. But I did, and the knowledge made my blood run even colder than the sight of those sparklers set up in the puddles.

"It's what he said to you, wasn't it?" I put in quietly. If I could get him, even if only for an instant, to see the pattern that he was repeating—

—to see precisely *how* Reuben Tate was surviving, in *whom* he lived on—

—but Mike wasn't hearing me. All he could hear was Reuben's exact words, long ago as he terrorized Mike.

And all he could do was repeat them.

Molly turned and ran, and I knew from her face that she wouldn't tell anybody. She was too frightened. Suddenly it hit me that she must have been there in that graveyard. She must have seen; that was the point of it all, really. No wonder she was scared. I heard the door open, then slam shut.

Wade quietly worked his wrists and ankles, still trying to loosen the twine. But he wasn't getting anywhere; George either.

Or me; the thin cord had bitten in enough to make my hands swell. I couldn't see whether Paddy or Marcus was even trying.

And Mike was moving fast, squirting more flammable stuff, its fumes thickly choking.

"If you light a match now, there'll be an explosion. You'll go up along with us. Think: There's got to be a way to settle all this without—"

He looked pityingly at me, shaking his head, then went to a panel of switches at the end of the work area and examined them. Finally he flipped one of them, and I heard an electric motor begin turning somewhere, felt cool air moving against my face.

"Ventilation," Paddy said defeatedly. "For working with dye and solvents and so on. With the draft . . ."

He slumped against his bonds. I got it: That fan would suck the fire into an inferno, just like a chimney.

"Mike," Ellie began sternly. "I want you to stop all this nonsense right this—"

He began lighting the sparklers, quickly, one after the other. I thought he might say something more, but he didn't. Not a word. Everything had already been said.

Finally he approached me with the syringe, its wicked tip glittering, stepped behind me, and stabbed me abruptly with it.

"Sorry," he said softly. "I really did like you." I felt the stuff going in, a brilliant shot of anguish and a hot, swelling lump in my shoulder. His hand hovered over a switch by the door.

The lights went out. The door slammed. He was gone.

Instantly, we were shouting, struggling, fighting to escape that damned macramé twine, but without, please God, tipping over one of the sparklers, whose heads fizzed glaringly in the darkness and reflected from the flammable pools around them.

"Damn it, Sondergard, you *wimp,*" Paddy grated out, his voice tight with the pain of pulling against the rough cords that held him. "You should've—"

"What?" Willow demanded, the word a sob. "Let that bastard get his knife into me? Paddy, you always were a heartless . . ."

"Quiet." Wade's deep voice sounded authoritatively in the flame-punctured darkness. "Just work on these ties. Tear your skin off if you have to, there's fire extinguishers all around, on the walls. Just get to one, and—"

The injection hadn't hit me yet. Apparently it had all gone into my shoulder muscle, and not into a vein. But in the next few moments I wondered if that was lucky or not:

A spark fell. Instantly, flame billowed up. In its glow, all the room filled up with shadows, dancing evilly as lines of blue flame skittered horridly from one pool to the next.

A *whump!* of fire exploded to the ceiling, blocking my last view of Ellie, her eyes dark pools of fright. Willow began to scream, a high, wordless shriek of protest.

Blood slicked my wrists. The cords slid, only the tiniest amount. Wade bumped his chair toward me, wanting, I supposed, to help me, but nothing was helping.

And nothing was going to. Through a rising haze of whatever it was he'd shot me up with a puddle of fire crept toward me, pausing nastily for an instant, then coming on with a rush. The air was choking, searing my eyes and throat. Somewhere a bottle exploded, and a worse reek filled my nose stingingly: fabric dyeing chemicals.

With a tearing sound that I realized only distantly

was my own flesh ripping, one of my hands came free. But I couldn't do anything with it, the other and my ankles were still bound, and what I smelled now, hideously, was the stink of burning hair.

Howling from somewhere. Another explosion. Scalding-hot air like a lungful of boiling water ripped down my windpipe.

Suffocation, I realized; hot smoke and burning chemicals. Then it seemed I was being carried away. Something inside me dug its heels in, wouldn't go.

But there was no help for it.

40

People say having a near-death experience is fascinating: the white light, your relatives all beckoning to you, and so on.

Personally, I've seen enough white lights in my life not to be unduly impressed by another one, and if you knew my relatives, you would know why I don't find the notion of them waving to me particularly attractive, either. In my youth, before I got on that Greyhound, when any of my relatives beckoned it was usually to get some fool to pull over so they could hijack his truck.

"Mom," Sam said from his chair in the corner of my bedroom; since what we had taken to calling "the incident," he refused to let me out of his sight for very long.

"What?" I opened my eyes. It had been three days, and I was beginning to get a little concerned about him.

"Are you *sure* a Ouija board takes two people to operate?" He frowned at the card table where he had the dratted thing set up. "Because . . ."

"Sam," I said patiently, as well as I could through

my sore, smoke-rasped vocal cords. My hand was bandaged, and the injected sedative had made me sick as a dog; I didn't remember what the emergency people had done about it, only that it hadn't been pleasant.

"A Ouija board doesn't take any people to operate. A Ouija board doesn't *do* anything."

He frowned stubbornly. "But . . ."

Just then Ellie hurried up the stairs and came in, looking lovely and *au courant* in her new short haircut. Only a few small places on her ear still showed pink where she had been burned.

Thirty seconds more, Bob Arnold had said, and it would have been the ball game. As it was, Mike Carpentier had managed a solid base hit: The building was rubble, everything Paddy owned gone, the space nothing but a blackened crater.

But everyone had made it out alive. "He's here," Ellie said. "Should I send him up?"

"Dad!" Sam rushed to the stairwell. "Hey, Dad—you weren't supposed to get here until . . ."

"Tonight," Victor agreed, coming in without being invited to survey me in all my invalid splendor.

I'd been told to stay down. The lungfuls of vapors I'd gotten had been pretty corrosive, and I was struggling to obey. But what Victor said next made me want to hop up and swat him mightily.

"I convinced them," he intoned loftily, "of my innocence, at last." He glanced at me, caught my expression. "Of course," he added hastily, "your mother did help."

"Uh, yeah," Sam replied dubiously, glancing at me also. "It was a real team effort."

Clearly, Sam was deciding whether he wanted to get into this subject with his father right off the bat. I shook my head—Victor was always at his most impossible, following a narrow escape—and after a moment Sam grinned at me, rolling his eyes.

"Yeah," he said, clapping Victor on the shoulder in mock congratulations. "Good job, Dad."

Victor glanced suspiciously at him, seeming to know he was being made sport of, then let it go.

"So what's this story Chief Arnold told me about a burning building?" he wanted to know.

His tone conveyed clearly that this sort of thing was little more than he expected of me, considering my complete lack of any common sense whatsoever. Which, looking at Victor and realizing that once upon a time I had believed it was a good idea to marry him, I thought was pretty much right on the money.

"It's a long story," I said. "But it was Sam and Tommy Daigle who got us out of it. And Ellie. Without her, we'd have been toast. Although," I added with a sharp glance at Sam, "it sure took you long enough."

"Mom," he defended himself, spreading his hands. "We had to find Bob Arnold. And then we had to *convince* him, which on account of Clarissa was busy having the baby—"

Clarissa, it turned out, had delivered a perfectly lovely and absolutely healthy eight-pound girl, just at the very moment that Ellie was in the act of having her hair burned off. Furthermore, Clarissa had done it at home after a labor of about ten minutes, so Bob Arnold had been understandably distracted.

"But how did you know to go *get* Bob Arnold, is what I don't see," Victor questioned, having apparently already heard some of the story's details but not all of them.

He frowned puzzledly. "You see them in a car and they go one way, you go the other. So how . . . ?"

"That's where Ellie came in," I said. Even for Ellie, it had been amazingly quick thinking.

"The boys were behind us in their car. And on the way down a hill, it would be normal to touch the brakes. Mike wouldn't suspect any mischief. So Ellie did touch them: Morse code. SOS."

The idea still blew me away: Sam and Tommy fooling around with something, and later it saved all our lives.

"Well, isn't that clever, now," Victor congratulated Ellie patronizingly.

Fortunately for him, he didn't reach out and pat her on the head. The gleam in her eye at the moment reminded me that in the old days, Ellie's rascal ancestors used to while away the time between looting square-riggers and swigging rum by filing their teeth into sharp points.

Now she only smiled, a thoughtful, private smile, as Victor turned away. "But why would this Mike have been suspicious?" he queried, and began picking snoopily through the items ranged out across my dresser top.

"From what Arnold told me," he went on, "until he snapped, and began behaving in a somewhat suspicious manner . . ."

He picked up a silver button I had found between two old floorboards in the attic, made a dismissive face, and tossed it down onto the crocheted dresser scarf.

". . . no one suspected *him,*" he finished. Then he began poking into the jewelry box that Wade had built for me, his attitude proprietary, as if he had a perfect, inalienable right to do so.

"*He* shouldn't have been suspicious of *us,*" Ellie answered, seeing that I was speechless with fury. "But he had a guilty conscience. So he thought we understood much more than we did."

She walked over and began restoring my dresser things to order, stepping deliberately in front of Victor to do it, so that he had to move away.

"His plan nearly worked," I added. "He almost did make it seem to be too much trouble, to keep on trying to get you out of jail."

He had the grace to look grateful, but only for an instant. "And the trellis? What did that show?"

"Again, nothing in itself. But Reuben climbed one when Mike was a kid, to terrorize him. He was trying it again on Mike's child, on a similar trellis. And the connections between those things were strong in Mike's mind. He thought we would see them too, much sooner than we actually did."

"Reuben made Mike a killer," Ellie said, "in the sense that he gave Mike what it took to be able to do it, fear and rage. But unlike Reuben, Mike still had some remnant of a conscience, and that, in the end, was what caught him up."

Victor pondered this for about a millisecond. Then:

"Well, that's all very edifying, I'm sure. And it's over. Jacobia, is there anything good to eat in the refrigerator? Jail food is hideous, and I'm starved."

He rubbed his hands together in what he apparently thought was a display of charming eagerness.

At this, I considered telling him of the lovely red berries among the weeds in the garden: nightshade, among the deadliest of the natural poisons. When I was busy getting him out of jail I had somehow missed noticing the obvious alternative to his imprisoned status: that he would be *here*.

Which was when Wade came in, his knapsack over his shoulder. He and Ellie had been putting their heads together earlier, but I didn't know what about. Now he took in the scene:

Me propped up on pillows, Sam at the card table, Ellie in the doorway, and Victor, there in the middle of it all, looking smugly sure of his newly regained position as king of the castle, even if this particular annex of it did happen to be my house.

The phone rang; Sam ran to answer it.

"Hey, Victor," Wade said pleasantly, putting down

his bag. "Welcome back. Glad everything worked out okay for you."

Then, astonishingly, he began taking off his clothes.

It was his bedroom, of course; Wade's and mine, I mean. But somehow I don't think Victor had quite understood that, before.

Slowly, Wade unbuttoned his shirt and hung it on the chair where he always hangs his work clothes until he washes them. He sat, removing his boots and socks as casually as if he were used to stripping down in a room full of people.

Which he was not. To Wade, there is a border between the land of clothing and the land of not wearing any, crossable by invitation only. Now, as Ellie left the room very quietly, Victor cleared his throat and began frowning with extreme discomfort.

Seeming not to notice, Wade pulled his belt off and undid his pants. He looked fetching and entirely unselfconscious; that he did this in front of me often must suddenly have been, to Victor, illusion-smashingly clear.

Until that moment, I do believe Victor thought the idea of my having any sort of romantic life apart from him was just some ridiculous fraud I kept attempting to perpetrate on him, just to annoy him. And the rest of it, of course, was only an extension of that: Victor's belief that somehow I still belonged to him.

Wade stood up, destroying as he did so any possible remnant of this mistaken—not to mention utterly Cro-Magnon—notion.

"Well," Victor croaked, glancing about wildly for somewhere to rest his gaze, not finding any, and backing toward the door.

"Say, isn't that Sam calling me?" he asked flusteredly at last, then turned and fled.

When he was gone, Wade approached, looking I thought rather convincingly Cro-Magnon himself.

In the nicest possible way, of course.

41

That night, Ellie and I went onto the porch for a breath of air. The sky was full of stars as if someone had punched pinholes in it, letting light through from the other side. On the eastern horizon lay the false blue dawn of moonrise.

"You put him up to it," I accused her, meaning Wade.

"I never," she denied innocently, then temporized. "Well, I did say I thought you needed some help setting Victor's head on straight, making him see reality. And anyway, what's wrong with a little help from your friends?"

It wasn't reality. I was no more Wade's property than I was Victor's, and Wade would be the first to say so. But as illusion, it was better than Victor's idea that I was still somehow part of his harem.

More fun, too. "Thank you," I told Ellie sincerely. "What's going to happen to Molly, do you suppose?" The child had seen it all; that, bottom line, had been the reason for Reuben's murder.

"Anne Carpentier's flown home. Pretty shocked, from what I hear. I don't think she had any idea Mike was capable of anything like this."

"No." *Sensitive and complicated*, she'd called him, while she herself was the perfect example of "what you see is what you get." I'd have bet money that she'd never even had an inkling.

"She's a tough cookie, though." Ellie's voice was approving. "She'll get Molly through it, if anyone can."

I thought so too, but it wasn't going to be an easy task. In trying to protect her, Mike Carpentier had done his daughter more damage than he'd prevented. "If anyone can," I echoed.

We stepped off the porch, strolled down Key Street to Water Street. Ahead lay the granite-block post office building, across from the blackened remains of Paddy's studio.

"Victor's project getting back on track?" Ellie asked. Beside us Monday ambled companionably, pausing to snuffle up a piece of apple core before trotting on.

"In a New York minute," I said, still amazed at the speed with which he had done it. "The district attorney decided not to press charges about the prescription he wrote Reuben, under the circumstances." Which wasn't such a complete no-brainer as it sounded, since it was that prescription drug, in part, that Reuben had been incapacitated by. Victor had been lucky.

A bat swooped past, twittering as it gobbled the last of the autumn insects. "This afternoon he was working the phone so fast I thought it was going to melt in his hand. He's got a new idea to add to his plan. And it's such a hot money maker, he's already got folks begging to be in on it. Alternative therapies."

She glanced sideways at me as we headed downhill past the Quoddy Tides building, its little frame structure perched neatly on an outcropping overlooking the boat basin. Beyond, Leighton's Variety was doing brisk business in quarts of milk, packs of cigarettes, all the things people suddenly discover they want in late evening, or they just want a little ride to the store.

"Herbs," I explained. "Acupuncture, massage, hypnosis." People wanted those things, too. And increasingly their insurance would pay for them. The trauma center would be a great resource for Eastport, but with the alternative-therapies clinic he was now planning to add, I thought Victor had actually stumbled onto something brilliant.

"Listen," I said. "I don't want to get your hopes

up. But Victor's planning something else, too. He's going to Portland tomorrow."

Her face lit up. "Terence?" she asked, her voice not daring to sound optimistic.

"Uh-huh. He's stabilized but still comatose. Victor says he won't get any better until somebody removes the blood clots from the injury, and that would be very risky."

I took a deep, lung-cooling breath of the damp, salt-tangy air, more delicious than any champagne.

"Victor wants to do it, though, and he wants to go after the scar tissue at the same time. I don't understand all of it," I confessed. "But Victor's been on the phone with the surgeons in Portland, and he seems to think he can get Terence through it."

What he'd said, actually, was something about one hand tied behind his back. But I was sure he would really use both of them.

She frowned. "What about Terence's illness? And doesn't somebody have to give permission? For the surgery?"

"There's no reason people with HIV can't have this surgery, Victor says. That's not a factor, given Terence's good health otherwise. And Paddy can give permission."

A thump of regret hit me as I thought of this. If I hadn't been so diverted by the diaries, I'd have paid more attention to the letter Terence had written to go with them, to Terence's attorney.

"Terence was confused. But Paddy was right, he had enough sense left to know something bad was happening to him. In his last lucid moments he gave Paddy power of attorney and appointed him his legal guardian. The letter was to tell his lawyer so."

I heard Ellie sigh. "So Terence will get a chance."

Out on the water, the ferry was making its final passage to Deer Island for the night, its deck a puddle of light. The waves of its wake began slopping desultorily on the gravel shore.

"A little chance," I agreed.

Which I guessed was all any of us got. Only for some of us, little miracles happened too.

"Sam's staying around here *and* going to college," I said. This time he seemed really sure of it. "He told us at dinner. He'll work part-time at the boatyard, commute to the University of Maine in Machias. Best of both worlds, it seems to me."

Also, it gave him a way to start that he felt he could handle. Later, Dan Harpwell would help him plan how to go on.

"Wonderful. How did he decide, finally?" Ellie reached down and took an urchin shell out of Monday's mouth.

"Victor. Can you believe it? He told Sam that he, Victor, I mean, really needed Sam around to help him—to assist him in the task of acclimating himself to downeast Maine culture, was the way he put it, and if Sam wanted to go to school could he please find a way to do it *and* stay here in town? Two minutes later, it was decided."

"Huh," Ellie said. "You know, that's the truly annoying part about Victor. Which is he? Blackhearted, or heart of gold?"

We turned back toward home. "Neither," I said as we passed Peavy Library and began climbing Key Street, beneath the bare-branched maples looming spectral under the streetlamps. "Victor's heart, I have decided, is a two-tone model."

At my house, the workshop on the top floor of the storeroom ell was occupied, Wade's shape moving behind the window shades. He was reconditioning the storm windows, as he'd promised; he'd done the rest of the weatherstripping, too, while I recuperated.

A little help from my friends: so hard to ask for.

But it was getting easier to take.

Inside we found there'd been a visitor in our absence: some books lay on the kitchen table, and a note from Paddy. It seemed he'd found them in an old strongbox in the rubble of the studio: sheet music, and ancient leather-bound volumes, all handwritten.

"Thought you might like to see these," the note from Paddy finished. "Off to Portland—fingers crossed."

The first piece of music, written in ink that was faded but still legible, was titled "The Pirate's Revenge," and like the frontispiece of each old diary volume it was signed: Jared Hayes.

The fiddler who had lived in our house all those years ago, and had vanished from it . . .

"Why would these things be at the cannery?" Ellie asked.

"I have no idea," I replied, paging carefully through the fragile old sheets of music.

Sam's voice: "Mom? Can you come and look at this, please?"

"Just a second." I scanned part of a diary: dates and places where Jared Hayes had played. Notes about what he'd eaten, music he was working on, a violin he expected to receive. Very special, he wrote, a wonderful instrument, lovely and fine.

"Jake," Ellie said quietly, peering over my shoulder. "He quit writing."

In the workshop, Wade was listening to his favorite Chet Atkins CD. "Cosmic Square Dance" rang out, ending in its weirdly jubilant, minor-keyed violin solo.

"I know," I said, distracted, still staring at the name on the diary page: *Stradivarius*. "He vanished, remember?"

It would have been a fine instrument, all right. So how had a downeast Maine fiddler ever dreamed of having one? For that matter, how had he managed to live in this house, which at the time had been a luxurious dwelling, on an excellent piece of property? Jared

Hayes had been a musician, not a ship's captain or a prosperous trader.

"No," said Ellie, frowning at the pages. "I mean he stopped in the middle of a sentence. The ink trails off, as if . . . Have you had any more manifestations lately?"

Flickering lights, she meant, or the faint, sad perfume of camellias. Music playing when no one in the house was playing any music.

A cold spot, there on the stairs and gone.

"No," I said, realizing there hadn't been. "It's been quiet as . . ."

As the grave, I'd meant to say, but decided not to. Monday looked up from her dog bed in the corner, listened intently.

"Mom?" Sam's voice, from the dining room. "It did it again."

"What?" I called, distracted.

"Maybe," Ellie said, "we should look into the disappearance of Jared Hayes."

A breeze came in, riffling the pages of the fiddle tunes on the table. I went over, meaning to close the kitchen window. But it was already closed.

Outside, the moon had risen, glazing the pointed fir trees with a rime of silver. High in the sky, Canadian geese arrowed southward and were gone.

"Look at this," Sam said quietly. "Really, I mean it."

Only a single lamp shone dimly in the corner of the dining room, our shadows moving hugely in the wreathed acorns-and-oak-leaves pattern of the high tin ceiling.

The Ouija board lay on the table. "I didn't touch it," Sam insisted. "But it kept pushing against me. Like Tommy was pushing it for a joke. Only, he's not here. So finally I got up to come and get you two. And then, when I wasn't touching it at all . . ."

He waved, mystified, at the smooth wooden board:

the letters and numerals, the black-painted words: Yes and No.

One in the upper left-hand corner.

And one in the right.

"It *moved*," Sam insisted. "When I was nowhere near it. All by itself, it *zoomed* up into the corner there. See it?"

The full moon shone brightly through the dining-room window, painting a silver triangle on the board's surface and lighting the planchette, which just then uncannily resembled a man's hand.

It was pointing to Yes.

ABOUT THE AUTHOR

SARAH GRAVES lives with her husband in Eastport, Maine, where her mystery novels featuring Jacobia Tiptree are set.

MALLETS
AFORETHOUGHT
A
Home Repair Is Homicide
Mystery
SARAH GRAVES
AUTHOR OF UNHINGED

If you enjoyed **Sarah Graves's**
WICKED FIX

you won't want to miss any of the exciting books in her *Home Repair Is Homicide* mystery series.

Look for **THE DEAD CAT BOUNCE, TRIPLE WITCH, REPAIR TO HER GRAVE, WRECK THE HALLS, UNHINGED, MALLETS AFORETHOUGHT,** and **TOOL & DIE** at your favorite bookseller.

And look for the next *Home Repair Is Homicide* mystery,
NAIL BITER,
available in hardcover from Bantam Books.

"LIVELY & CHARMING"—*The Dallas Morning News*

HOME REPAIR IS HOMICIDE mysteries from

SARAH GRAVES

The Dead Cat Bounce	$6.99/$10.99 in Canada
Triple Witch	$6.99/$10.99
Wicked Fix	$6.99/$8.99
Repair to Her Grave	$6.99/$10.99
Wreck the Halls	$6.99/$10.99
Unhinged	$6.99/$10.99
Mallets Aforethought	$6.99/$10.99
Tool & Die	$6.99/$10.99
Nail Biter	$6.99/$9.99
Trap Door	$22.00/$28.00

Please enclose check or money order only, no cash or CODs. Shipping & handling costs: $5.50 U.S. mail, $7.50 UPS. New York and Tennessee residents must remit applicable sales tax. Canadian residents must remit applicable GST and provincial taxes. Please allow 4 - 6 weeks for delivery. All orders are subject to availability. This offer subject to change without notice. Please call 1-800-726-0600 for further information.

Bantam Dell Publishing Group, Inc.
Attn: Customer Service
400 Hahn Road
Westminster, MD 21157

TOTAL AMT $______
SHIPPING & HANDLING $______
SALES TAX (NY, TN) $______

TOTAL ENCLOSED $______

Name ______________________

Address ______________________

City/State/Zip ______________________

Daytime Phone (______) ______________________

www.bantamdell.com

SG MYS 11/06

IT'S NO MYSTERY...

Bantam Dell has the finest collection of sleuths around, from professional P.I.s to unwilling amateurs

RITA LAKIN

GETTING OLD IS MURDER
$6.99/$10.99

GETTING OLD IS THE BEST REVENGE
$6.99/$9.99

LOIS GREIMAN

UNZIPPED $6.99/$10.99
UNPLUGGED $6.99/$9.99

LESLIE CAINE

DEATH BY INFERIOR DESIGN
$6.99/$10.99

FALSE PREMISES
$6.99/$10.99

MANOR OF DEATH
$6.99/$9.99

LINWOOD BARCLAY

BAD MOVE $6.99/$10.99
BAD GUYS $6.99/$9.99
LONE WOLF $6.99/$9.99

CYNTHIA BAXTER

DEAD CANARIES DON'T SING
$6.99/$10.99

PUTTING ON THE DOG
$6.99/$10.99

LEAD A HORSE TO MURDER
$6.99/$10.99

HARE TODAY, DEAD TOMORROW
$6.99/$9.99

BRIAN WIPRUD

PIPSQUEAK $6.99/$10.99
STUFFED $6.99/$10.99
CROOKED $6.99/$9.99
SLEEP WITH THE FISHES
$6.99/$9.99

Ask for these titles wherever books are sold, or visit us online at *www.bantamdell.com* for ordering information.

BD MC1 11/06